Praise for Thomas Fleming

"I don't read Thomas Fleming just to learn about American history. I read Thomas Fleming because I want to smell what the Americans in that time smelt, to see as our ancestors saw, and most important to feel every emotion, every thought, and every moment that the people of our country felt."

—W. E. B Griffin, *New York Times* bestselling author of the Brotherhood of War series

"Thomas Fleming is one of my favorite writers because he combines powerful storytelling with the skills of a superb historian."

—John Jakes, *New York Times* bestselling author of *North and South*

"Fleming's in-depth knowledge of period and culture, his ability to separate the myth from the reality; all help you discover the very essence of what it means to be an American."

—Margaret Truman, *New York Times* bestselling author of the Capital Crimes series

"Thomas Fleming gives us history with the urgency of a great story, story with the force of real history, a combination unbeatable if you thrill to a fast-paced tale and care about your country!"

—David Nevin, *New York Times* bestselling author of *Dream West* and *Treason*

"Fleming re-creates, in precise detail, not only history but atmosphere. His research is so thorough that readers can believe every word."

—Morgan Llywelyn, international bestselling author of *1916*

A PASSIONATE GIRL

THOMAS FLEMING

TOR®

A TOM DOHERTY ASSOCIATES BOOK
NEW YORK

This is a work of fiction. All of the characters, organizations, and events portrayed in this novel are either products of the author's imagination or are used fictitiously.

A PASSIONATE GIRL

A Tor Book
Published by Tom Doherty Associates, LLC
175 Fifth Avenue
New York, NY 10010

www.tor-forge.com

Tor® is a registered trademark of Tom Doherty Associates, LLC.

ISBN-13: 978-0-7653-4560-8
ISBN-10: 0-7653-4560-9

First Edition: March 2004
First Mass Market Edition: January 2009

Printed in the United States of America

0 9 8 7 6 5 4 3 2 1

To my grandparents
David Fleming and Mary Green
Thomas Dolan and Mary Fitzmaurice

Could we live it over again
Were it worth the pain,
Could the passionate past that is fled
Call back its dead!

—Oscar Wilde
"Roses and Rue"

A PASSIONATE GIRL

You Might as Well Let Him Have Me, Mother

I can remember as if it were yesterday the moment when our lives changed forever. We were kneeling in the parlor on the night before May Eve, in 1865, reciting the rosary. Before we began, Mother had asked us to remember the soul of Peter Malloy, our cook's oldest son, who had been killed in a great battle in Virginia, one of the rebel states of America. We had heard the sad news on the same day that we learned that the war between the northern and southern parts of America had finally ended. As Mother was halfway through the third decade of the rosary, my brother, Michael, entered the room. He looked neither right nor left, nor at Mother, nor at me or my sister Mary, nor at the two maids who knelt with us. He walked past us as if we were invisible and took Father's hunting gun from the wall and turned again to vanish into the night. As the door closed, I heard one of the maids whisper, "God be on the road with you."

I looked at Mother and saw death on her face. But I felt not a shred of pity for her, though I can feel it now. I felt only pride, passion, fury. I was a living, breathing contradiction of the soft, sweet words of the rosary. "Hail Mary, full of grace," Mother said, continuing the decade as if nothing had happened. But she knew, as I knew, what it meant. Michael had defied Father and joined the Fenians, the Irish Republican Brotherhood. He had sworn an oath that cut him off from the sacraments of the Church and the forgiveness of God and promised to commit any crime, even murder, to free Ireland from the British. In my heart I had sworn the same oath.

That night, in our bedroom, I rejoiced in Michael's courage. "I wish I were a man. I would have walked out with him," I said. My sister Mary could only think of the pain he was causing Mother and Father and wondered why Michael had had to make his declaration so brutal, almost sacrilegious. "Couldn't he have waited until we finished the rosary?" she said.

"It's that kind of thinking that has made slaves of Irishmen and Ireland for the last six centuries," I replied.

"Oh, Bessie, Bessie," Mary said. "Remember what Father told us only last week, when we were talking about old Ireland?"

"I remember," I said. "I hated him for it."

"Bessie," Mary cried. "That's a sin. Even to say it."

"I love him, too, as much as you do. But not when he talks like a coward."

That was Bess Fitzmaurice to the inch in those days. Loving and hating within the space of a breath and meaning both to the utmost throb of her wayward heart. Mother used to blame it on my Fitzmaurice blood, plus a draught from my paternal grandmother, who was an O'Brien, thus combining two of the wildest families in old Ireland. The Fitzmaurices were royal bastards (signified by the "Fitz"), and the O'Briens, the ancient kings of Thomond, were famous for the way they blinded their enemies when they captured them. Mother's people, the MacNamaras, were the opposite sort, all peace-loving scholars. Which explained my gentle, obedient sister Mary.

Father had told us these bits of lore, along with a lot of other things about old Ireland, at supper one night. He was trying to explain to me and my glowering brother why he would never join the Fenians nor any of the other wild men who thought they could right Ireland's wrongs with a gun. Wrongs there were aplenty, he admitted, but we were one of the families who were exempt from the worst of them. We had one of the finest farms in the county of Limerick, on the shores of shining Lake Fergus. True, we did not own it, we had to rent it from Lord Gort, whose ancestors had no doubt seized it from an Irishman long ago. But the rent was fair, and we had enough money to hire four families to do much of the work and show an honest profit at the year's end.

Would it have been better to have had such a farm in old Ireland? Father asked. The answer was no, he said. If you stopped to think of it, the British had done some good things in Ireland along with the bad. They had made a nation where before there had been three or four hundred petty chiefs, each of them calling himself a king. "Sure the country was a puzzle map," Father said, "never at peace long enough to let an honest man get in a harvest. There was always King This or King That cantering down the road on a rough little pony at the head of his army of barelegged gossoons to fight the king over the river or the king beyond the bog."

"Better to fight and die as free men than farm as slaves," I said.

I was the only one who would dare to talk back to Father, but this time even I went too far. He ordered me away from the table, and the next morning Mother made me apologize to him.

On the morning after Michael took the gun, there was nothing but gloom at the breakfast table. Mother had told the news to Father when he returned from the meeting of his Freemasons lodge in Limerick. Father was a Protestant, which was how he had come to obtain our handsome farm in the first place. His grandfather or his great-grandfather had quit being a Catholic to avoid the laws and prejudices that prevented any man of the old faith from rising in Ireland. But Father put no stock in creeds and articles of religion. What counted with him was an honest and loving heart, he often said, looking at Mother while he spoke. He had no objection to our being raised Catholic, even Michael, his only son, because he was sure the old prejudices were dying away on both sides.

But this new passion swirling through the land, this fury for Ireland's freedom, found him totally unprepared, especially when it confronted him in his own home. Michael had caught the fever at the university in Dublin and had passed it on to me. All Father could do that morning was stare past us at the empty place above the mantel where his gun had hung. Mother had warned me in advance to say nothing, and for once I thought it prudent to obey.

Our maids, Bridget and Peggy, were in a pother because it was the day of May Eve, when the old gods were supposed to come back to earth and the fairies were out in throngs looking for victims. Bridget, the fat one, strewed primroses at the front and back doors to keep the little people out and told us how she had been sure to make the sign of the cross with the froth from the milk pails first thing. No food was given to any beggar on May Eve for fear that he might be one of the little people in disguise come to steal a coal from the fire and weave an evil spell around the house. We believed none of this, of course, but Mother had long since given up trying to change the minds of the maids and other country people who worked for us.

Peggy, the thin maid (the skinny melink, we called her), undid Father by asking him in all seriousness what she should do if a man on the run came to the door. "What in God's name do you mean by that?" Father snapped.

"Sure there's going to be a row, is there not?" Peggy said in her brainless way. "Hasn't Master Michael gone to fight with the Fenians in Limerick city? I heard him telling Miss Bessie here the other day that they had taken a vow to avenge the old treaty or die."

She was talking about the Treaty of Limerick, which the Irish signed in 1691, surrendering their army to England. The treacherous British promptly violated the treaty, creating one law for Protestants and another for the Catholic majority.

Father looked like he might weep at any moment. I had never seen him so undone. "Any man who comes to this door will be given the charity of the road, even though it is May Eve," he said. "We will ask no questions about where he is going or where he has been."

Mother thought this a good time to summon me and Mary to help her with the breakfast dishes. Further contriving methods to get me out of Father's way, she announced that I was to accompany her to Mrs. Malloy's cottage on the lakeshore to see if she was all right. I groaned but acquiesced. To tell the truth, down deep I was a little frightened about what might happen to Michael with that gun in his hand. He was no soldier. At heart he was a poet, a writer. Indeed I may be writing these words now, so many years later, as an attempt to tell, in place of him, the history that engulfed us.

Obedient as my sister Mary for a change, I put on my cloak and seized the basket of meat and vegetables Mother packed for old Mrs. Malloy. The poor thing was a dear person, but she tended to be tiresome, now that I was a grown woman of nineteen. More than anyone, perhaps even more than Mother, Malloy knew I felt cast under by the beauty of my older sisters, Annie and Mary. Not that I was ugly. But they had Mother's pure white skin and calm presence and dark green MacNamara eyes. They were always perfectly composed, every ringlet and ruffle in place, while I was always in disarray, my hair flying, my lip curling. I was out of tune with the times, which treasured women like Annie and Mary, delicate creatures who seemed to breathe poetry, when actually they had scant use for it.

Although Malloy wearied me somewhat now, I was loyal to her forever because of what she had done for me when I was eleven or twelve. My mother's nephew, Barry MacNamara, was visiting us. He saw me with Annie and Mary and called me the Ugly Duckling. I ran crying into the kitchen, where I collided with Malloy. When I sobbed out my woe, she grew vastly indignant. Her round red cheeks inflated like a balloon until I thought she would explode.

"Sure you're never cryin' about the face that God Almighty chose for ye!" she said. "Haven't ye a nice white skin where there's many a one born black as our ould turkey and blacker! Haven't ye soft fair hair and a fine pair of eyes when there's them that's born white-headed with eyes as red as a pet rabbit's? And haven't ye a mouthful of strong teeth when ye might have them black and crumblin' like Casey's youngest, her with the hump and the squinny eyes, God help her?"

She swept me to her ample bosom and dried my eyes. "Cushla mavourneen," she said. "Did I ever tell ye the tale of the duke's son who got sot on a poor lovely young girl? 'I'll marry ye, poor as ye are,' he said to her, 'if ye'll promise me ye'll hold up your head and not care a tinker's curse what anyone says to cheapen ye.'"

"'I will,' says she. 'I will hold up my head.' And what'd she do but go into a little lane and cut a twig of furze and pin it in her dress so that every time she hung down her face the way poor folk do the furze druv it up with its sharp spikes and by the next day she held her head as high as the queen of England."

Mother would never have told me a story like that, because she did not want to make me proud. Her faith taught her that humility and forgiveness were the great virtues. I instinctively disagreed with her, and Malloy's folk wisdom gave me a first glimpse of why. There was something in me, a spirit, a voice, call it what you like, that despised the thought of bowing my head, begging pardon, turning the other cheek, all the habits of meekness that a woman was supposed to cultivate. I imitated Malloy's heroine from that day and cultivated the habit of holding my head high and looking everyone straight in the eye.

I found deeper justification for my ways when Michael came home from the university with his mind aflame with love of the old Irish sagas, the tales of Finn and his warriors, of bold Cuchulain and his exploits. I stayed up a hundred nights reading them, too, wearing out my eyes by a flickering candle in my convent school in Limerick. I found in them not only Michael's pride in ancient Ireland and her fighting heroes but women like Queen Maeve and Emer and Dierdre of the Sorrows, beings who leaped from the pages as creatures of fire and ice, who dealt with men not as meek helpmates but as equals, even superiors. These became my heroines. I secretly worshipped them, not only for their independence but for the free proud way with which they gave themselves to men, with none of the creeping shame and guilt about sexual love that the priests had inflicted on Ireland.

Mother could not understand what had happened to me when I came home and announced that I would read aloud none but Irish writers henceforth. She would have preferred to go on reading Charles Dickens or her favorite, Charles Lamb, who had filled our childhood years with their charming stories. But I condemned them now as spokesmen of the hated Sassenachs, the Gaelic name for the Saxons, which Michael and I took to calling the English. Although he was two years older, it was I who insisted on this ban. He was as fond of Wordsworth as Mother. But I insisted "Wordy," as I called him, and all other English poets had to go, to be replaced by Egan O'Rahilly and Owen Roe O'Sullivan and blind Raftery.

I can still see myself before the fire that last winter, reciting O'Rahilly's poem, "A Gray Eye Weeping," in which the penniless poet addresses one of the new English gentry. My heart almost burst inside me and tears streamed down my cheeks as I spoke the words.

> That my old bitter heart was pierced in this black
>   gloom,
> That foreign devils have made our land a tomb,
> That the sun that was Munster's glory has gone down,
> Has made me a beggar before you, Valentine Brown.

But on the day of May Eve, the day after Michael disappeared with Father's gun, I found it hard to think brave or angry thoughts as I lugged the basket of food down to Malloy's cottage. Her son's death in that foreign American land about which we heard so much seemed a dark omen for Michael, who was fascinated by America. He talked constantly of the help the Fenians would receive from our brethren who had fled there by the millions since the famines began in the 1830s.

As we approached Malloy's cottage by the lakeshore, after a mile's walk in the hot sun, I heard a sound that embarrassed me intensely. It was familiar enough, the wild mournful wail mingled with tumbling words in our own Irish tongue. Malloy was keening for her dead son. The peasants still retained the custom. But for educated folk like us, it was an embarrassment because it enabled the English to point to it and other habits of the peasantry, such as a love of strong drink, and sneer that we were still primitives, incapable of governing ourselves.

We stood outside the cabin, hesitating to interrupt the old woman, as the sad cry rose and fell. I could make out the words, full of the natural poetry of our people.

"My Grief! I have lost my dear boy, my warrior lad, who was rough in the fight.

"My Grief! His father gone before him into the dark ground, and his brothers and sisters scattered.

"My Grief! The portion of my old age, my one hope of joy. I knew by the voice of the crow on the lake that misfortune was at hand.

"My Grief and Ireland's grief, to have lost such a son."

At length her lamentation ceased, and we knocked on the door. Mrs. Malloy met us with her rosary in her hand. It always amazed me to see how easily the peasantry mingled the ancient pagan traditions and the Catholic faith. Old Malloy's face was like a withered apple now, but she still dressed herself with care. A fresh frilled cap was on her head, her homespun gown was spotless, and her plaid shawl was as fine as when she wore it on her wedding journey.

"Oh, Miss Bessie and Mrs. Fitzmaurice. I was hopin' ye'd come," she said. "And bring me a bit of bread and meat, too. I hadn't the heart to touch a match to a fire with the thought of poor little Peter dead over there in America. He was me youngest and best, ye remember the last letter he sent me with the draft for twenty dollars in it. I've been sittin' here thinkin', will he be waked and prayed for by a priest to lay his soul at rest? If not, ye know his fate will be to join the army of the old kings and live underground for all eternity as a slave to them heathens."

"I'm sure his friends said their prayers for him and a priest was at his side, Malloy," Mother said. "He was in an Irish regiment; you remember he said that in the letter he wrote you."

"Yes," Malloy said, dabbing at her eyes. "I do remember and thank God for it. But it's still a strange fate, isn't it, Mrs. Fitzmaurice, to go over the ocean to be killed by the bullet of a man you never had a quarrel with in your life?"

"America is a strange country," Mother said. "I'm not at all sure it's the best place for our young people to go."

"But they must go someplace, there's no work for them in their own land," Malloy said.

"Yes, that is Ireland's shame," Mother said with a sigh. "Our best young men—and women—leave us."

There was a sad story behind Mother's sigh. My older sister Annie had gone to America six years ago. She left as the bride of an Irishman who had come back to Limerick a rich man from twenty years in New York. He drove about the country in a Dublin coach pulled by four fine black horses. One of our Limerick town aunts, Mother's sister, had brought him calling on us, supposedly to show him the best-run farm in Ireland. He had been far more interested in Annie. His name was Kelly. He was hardly the sort of man to stir romance in a young girl. He was at least forty-five and fat in the neck and red in the face. But the offer of a wealthier, more interesting life than any local suitor could promise a bride persuaded Annie.

She arrived in New York to discover the stunning fact that her husband was already married and the father of four children. Kelly assured her that his political friends would have no trouble obtaining a divorce for him. The priest whom Annie consulted told her that the state of New York could do what it pleased, but the Catholic Church would never recognize such a decree, which meant that Annie would sin her soul—commit a mortal sin—every time she lay with him as his wife. She left him, but she could not stand the thought of returning home to be the laughing-stock of our village.

For a while her letters were frequent. She seemed to like America in spite of her awful disappointment. She made new friends who seemed to please her as much as she pleased them. She wrote of grand parties with enough silver on the table to buy dowries for all of Limerick county. Lately, though, her letters had dwindled. I knew that Mother often thought of her with that heavy sigh on her lips.

Listening to Malloy lament the hard necessity that had driven her son across the water, I found myself biting my tongue to prevent spouting angry words about what must be done to keep our youth in Ireland. The musket and the pike, the bullet and the shell, will do it, I wanted to say. Not prayers that God ignores or promises the British break. I found myself fearing less for Michael's fate and wishing only that I could share it with him.

"Has Mr. Dolan called upon you again this month, Miss Bessie?" Malloy asked, changing the subject with her usual disconcerting dexterity.

"No," I said, silently adding, *Thank God*.

"He's coming this afternoon," Mother said. "I thought it best not to tell her, because it would only give her more time to think of spiteful things to say."

Patrick Dolan was the merchant and moneylender of our village of Ballinaclash. We called him the gombeen man, from the Irish *goimbin*, meaning usury. He had inherited the business from his father, who was a Protestant like my own father. Patrick Dolan was no more than twenty-five or twenty-six and considered the catch of the countryside. Girls swooned at the mere sight of him, and more particularly at the thought of living in his house on the hill above the village, with Waterford cut glass on the table and a fireplace in each of the five rooms. But few had the dowry he could rightfully expect, except people as well off as the Fitzmaurices.

This was easy enough to understand, but I was amazed when he fixed on me as his choice. I thought sure it would be my sister Mary, who almost melted every time he looked at her. But he soon made it clear that I was more to his taste. He liked my "maturity," he called it, the confident way I carried myself. He carried himself in much the same fashion, I should add. He was a big, broad-shouldered fellow, with a wide brow and brown eyes that were clouded by a certain sadness yet retained a resolution to resist the envy and hatred that were often flung at him in the village. The people had no love for a gombeen man. In hard times when they could not pay what they owed him, he could take their land from them, seize their crops, their very furniture.

I told Patrick Dolan that I would never marry a man who made his living by tricking money from the pockets of poor men who needed it to feed hungry wives and children. "You may call it lending at interest, but I call it robbery," I said.

He smiled at me as if I were a charming child and said he was glad to see I did not accept him at face value. He assured me that he could dispose of my prejudices, if I would give him a chance. His money fed women and children who would otherwise starve when a man's crop failed or his cash ran short. His money sent younger sons and daughters to America, where they found jobs that supported half the families in the village.

I scoffed at his pretended benevolence and remained as disdainful as a duchess. I insisted he was part of the British system, an enemy of Ireland. He continued to call once or twice a month, while Mother, Mary, and Malloy urged me to be sensible. Lately Father had joined the campaign, telling me in his brusque way that I would never get a better offer. Malloy, perhaps prompted by Mother, returned to the charge now. "Sure I haven't a doubt you're to wed a rich husband. I've always seen it in your tea leaves. Get up tomorrow first thing and catch yourself a snail and your happiness is assured."

On May Day young girls were supposed to get up before sunrise to look for snails. If the creature was still entirely inside its shell, the finder could expect a rich husband. If the snail was outside his shell, beware poverty, if she married before the next May Day.

I told Malloy I would be sure to get up and find my snail. "But if he's inside his shell I'll pull him out by the nose to make sure I have naught to fear for another year."

Malloy laughed and said she always knew I had the devil in me. We left her looking through her food basket. Mother gently lectured me all the way back to the house. Where did I expect to find a decent husband? she asked. Did I want to end up married to some ignorant tenant farmer? Or an old maid like my Limerick aunts, her sisters? By the time we got to the house I was feeling quite desperate, and my turmoil was not alleviated by the sight of Patrick Dolan's assured smiling face. A sense of doom descended on me. I could see that it was only a matter of time before my resistance would crumble before the combined assault of his confident persistence and Mother's realistic logic. It was unquestionably true that eligible bachelors did not abound in our vicinity, especially bachelors who had some education and would not take to drink at the sight of a wife reading poetry.

Patrick Dolan suggested a walk. I said I had just walked my feet off. He suggested a ride. He had his jaunting cart at the back door. Mother said she had no objection, and we were soon jogging down the lanes past the green, sun-drenched fields. Mute Mick, son of Conn the plowman, waved to us as we passed. Down we went to the shore of the lake, a mile beyond Malloy's house, and across the causeway to Knockadoon Island, where the ruins of Earl Garrett Desmond's castle stood like a monument to Ireland's sad fate.

According to the legend, Lord Desmond made a pact with the devil to keep his power when the English came and the old gods put a curse on him. Once in every seven years he was doomed to gallop over the water and around the lake on a milk-white horse shod with silver shoes. Not until the silver shoes were worn out would be he loosed from the enchantment.

Patrick Dolan helped me down from the cart. We gazed up at the castle's battered walls, and I told him that this was a seventh year and time for Lord Desmond to circle the lake once more.

"You don't believe that old trash, do you?" he asked.

"No," I said. "But I think it's good for the people to remember the great old names. It will encourage them to fight for Ireland when the time comes."

"What time will that ever be?" Patrick Dolan said. "Do you think that men can fight riflemen with pitchforks? Will they make battleships out of the fishermen's curraghs and duel the British fleet? Face it, Bess, we're a conquered people and must make the best of it."

"Never!" I said. "I will never make the best of it. And I will never marry a man who thinks we should."

"Bess, Bess," he said, seizing my wrist and turning me to him. "Can't you see I'm dying for a kind look from your eye? Do you think a man with as much pride as I've got in me would come back again and again to take your insults and your temper if it wasn't for the love that was eating his insides?"

For a trembling moment I almost surrendered. But he made the mistake of carrying us back to the argument. "It's only common sense I ask of you, Bess," he said. "The common sense to see that there's no help for Ireland anywhere but in lifting herself up by slow degrees to where the British will respect us. I want to do that as much as you do. I honor your love for Ireland. I share it."

This was Father's thesis, almost to the word. My gorge rose all over again. "What kind of thinking is that for a man your age?" I said. "Isn't there a wish to strike a blow now, to right the wrongs of centuries instead of letting them go on and on? Sure I think you're as bad as

Lord Desmond. You've made your pact with Satan, too. But for you his name is Usury."

"I loan money but I'm no usurer," he said, his own temper rising at hearing that slur on my lips. "And I've made no pact with Satan. Unless his name is Love."

He picked up a piece of the shattered masonry from Lord Desmond's wall and flung it into the lake. "All right," he said. "Here's my last offer. I'll sell the business and we'll go to America. Forget Ireland."

"If I go to America," I said, "it will be to join the Irish there, the tens of thousands of them that are ready to fight for old Ireland. Some of them are already here, guns in hand. My brother Michael is with them this very moment in Limerick."

"God help him," Dolan said. "And God help me."

I didn't see, I wouldn't see, his torment. "It's from America that the help will come," I said.

"The kind of help your sister Annie got? Get the poetry out of your eyes, Bess. See the world as it really is."

"'Tis the poets who help us see the glory and the tragedy of life. See courage, faith, beauty, all the things money can't buy."

"Jesus God, Bess, will you stop seeing me as a man of money? Do I have the queen's head stamped on my face like a sovereign? I'm a man, Bess, a creature of flesh and blood, and I love you."

"You want to buy me," I said.

The word "love" aroused a blind anger and fear in me. I see now it was not fear of his love but of my idea of it as a prison that would turn me into a meek forgiver, like Mother.

"I would buy you if I could," he said. "I'd buy you to stop the thing that is destroying my sleep and my waking. But I know you can't be bought. It's what I love most about you, Bess."

A great dark thundercloud was moving down the lake from the direction of Limerick. I chose to look at it rather than at him. I would not let him buy me, either with his pleas or his money. I told myself the cloud was an omen; it carried within it the hosts of the air, the armies of the old kings and heroes. "Take me home," I said. "Can't you see it's going to thunder and rain?"

In front of our house, I sprang from the jaunting cart without a word of good-bye to him. I watched him drooping at the cart's head until he disappeared around the bend in the road caused by the cairn. This burial mound of the old kings had stood beside the road, covered with bright quartz stones, untouched for two thousand years for fear of the curse the ancient dead could lay on you. The conjunction of Patrick Dolan, the sad collaborator of defeated Ireland, and this silent symbol of our glorious past stirred wild thoughts in my head and wilder feelings in my heart.

A moment later I noticed how the sun was dwindling as the thundercloud mounted over lake and farmland like the frowning forehead of an angry god. Suddenly I knew what I wanted, what I must have, a love as wild and reckless as the one in the song that every Irish girl sang in her secret heart, while her mother frowned on her. "Donal Ogue," which is Irish for "Young Dan," was its title. I began to whisper it as the first drops splattered on the grass around me.

> *"Donal Ogue, when you cross the water*
> *Take me with you to be your partner.*
> *And at fair and market you'll be well looked after*
> *And you can sleep with the Greek king's daughter."*

Behind me came squeals of fright from the maids and the slamming of windows. They were rushing around in a terror, certain that one of the old gods was riding the thundergust. *Let him,* I prayed, *let him,* and went on with the song, with the words of the long-dead girl to her warrior lover, whom she knew to be faithless but whom she loved nonetheless.

> *"You said you'd give me—'tis you talk lightly*
> *Fish skin gloves that would fit me tightly*
> *Bird skin shoes when I went out walking*
> *And a silken dress would set Ireland talking."*

"Miss Bessie," bawled Bridget, the fat maid, "For the love of God come in. Lord Desmond himself could be in that wind, ready to seize your very soul."

I ignored her, letting huge drops of rain dash against my upturned face. "I'm not afraid of Lord Desmond," I shouted. I clung to the white pickets of the gate and chanted:

> *"To lonely well I wander sighing.*
> *'Tis there I do my fill of crying*
> *When I see the world but not my charmer*
> *And all his locks the shade of amber."*

A hand seized my arm. My sister Mary pulled me off the gate. "Good God, Bessie," she said. "Can't you let poetry alone for a bit? Hasn't Mother enough to worry about this day without you catching pneumonia?"

I whirled on her. "Let poetry alone? That's just like you, Mary, you keep poetry in a cage like your old bullfinch and let it hop out now and then. I've got it in my inside, all through me, and it comes out and in like breathing."

A tremendous bolt of lightning split the sky above the lake, and a crash of thunder followed it. "You can breathe in the house as well as out," Mary said. "Come on or I'll lambaste you one like I used to do when we were little."

"I'll submit to your pedestrian spirit," I said, holding out my arms to her. "Place the manacles upon my wrists and lead me to your dungeon vile. Tomorrow or the next day, Donal Ogue will come to liberate me."

Mockingly I chanted another verse from the poem:

"I saw him first on a Sunday evening
Before the Easter and I was kneeling
'Twas about Christ's passion that I was reading
But my eyes were on him and my own heart bleeding."

"That is the worst yet," Mary said. "Pure blasphemy. Pride rules your will, Bess."

Mary fled back into the house, abandoning me to Lord Desmond or pneumonia. By now the rain was starting to splash down in a torrent. I followed her into the parlor and felt contrite. Mother bustled in the kitchen, and Father read his paper by the oil lamp. I dried my hair and offered Mary a game of dominoes. We matched pieces while the storm beat on the roof and windows of our sturdy house. Hearing the wind howl, Peggy, the thin maid, wondered if it was the dwarf, Fer Fi, who haunts the lake, playing his magic music on his three-stringed harp. "Let's hope it's *gentraighe*," I said, using the Irish word for "laughter music." Fer Fi only played three tunes, *ceolsidhe,* wail music for mourning, *suantraighe,* sleep music for dreamers, and laughter music.

The door burst open and Michael reeled into the room, soaked by the storm, his boots streaming, his black hair in a wild tangle. "Father," he said. "You must help us. I have a man with me from America—"

The man himself stood in the doorway. He had the ripest curl to his smile and the whitest teeth and hair of the softest golden-yellow amber and the most reckless gray eyes I had ever seen. He stood well over six feet and carried himself like a soldier, his back straight and his shoulders squared.

"Dan McCaffrey," he said.

He wore expensive clothes, a stone-gray cloth-lined raglan coat and a dark gray suit that fit him beautifully. He closed the door against the storm and stood there while Michael told Father what had happened. McCaffrey was a major in the Fenian army in America. He had come to Ireland to help organize a rising. They had called a meeting of the Fenian circle, as their groups were called, in the cellar of a pub in Limerick. Only thirty men came, though a hundred had taken the oath. As they talked, a pounding of feet was heard outside, and the Peelers—the Royal Irish Constabulary—burst in through doors and windows. Someone had turned informer. McCaffrey had seized Michael's gun—the only weapon the circle owned—and cut down the first man who came at him, then drew a pistol and fought his way to the stairs, with Michael on his heels using the old hunting gun like a club. Only a few followed them; most of the circle were now captives.

Father groaned aloud and held his head in his hands. "Michael, Michael, you've ruined us," he said.

"What do you mean?" Michael said. "This has nothing to do with you."

"We need horses, Mr. Fitzmaurice," McCaffrey said. "There'll be a boat in Bantry Bay in five days to take me back to America. I'll take Michael with me."

I listened, fascinated. It was the first time I ever had heard an American talk. It sounded utterly strange. He said "hosses" and "Baantry Baay."

"Take him with you?" Father said bitterly. "Just like that? Take a man's only son, and leave him in his old age with a wife and daughters to support and no farm to his name?"

"What do you mean, no farm?" McCaffrey said.

"They'll take this farm and any other I can get."

"Where my father's people came from, County Mayo, they had men who wouldn't let that happen. The Molly Maguires."

If he had tried for a month, Dan McCaffrey could not have chosen a more offensive topic. The Mollies, so called because they sometimes wore women's clothes on their midnight forays and signed the single name Molly Maguire to their warnings, were a menace to the peaceful, law-abiding Ireland Father yearned to see. He had denounced them at our dinner table more than once and now proceeded to do so again, in even more sulphurous terms.

"In my most desperate hour, I'd never turn to the help of such scum," he roared. "I'll have nothing to do with men who murder their fellow creatures and maim cattle in the dark."

"My Dad said they fought for Ireland," Dan McCaffrey said. He was angry but also puzzled. As I soon discovered, his knowledge of Ireland was nothing but a patchwork of his father's nostalgic memories.

"They fight for their own empty pockets," Father shouted. "Lazy tinkers, most of them, who wouldn't do a day's work for double a blacksmith's pay. Like every Connaught spalpeen I've ever hired."

I shuddered to hear from my father the terrible prejudice that the different parts of Ireland bear against each other. The men of the west, like the day laborers (spalpeens) from Connaught that my father was talking about, were regarded with severe disfavor by us of the south. But we reserved our worst words for the "Fardowns," as the men of the north were called.

McCaffrey looked like he wanted to avenge Father's insult, but he was in no position to do so. "Will you give us the horses, Mr. Fitzmaurice?" he said.

"Yes," my father said. "Of course I'll give you the horses. You've taken my son. You can surely take my horses."

"You must have food for the road," Mother said. She drew me and Mary with her to the kitchen and put us to work with the maids. I could see that she did not like the way I was staring at Dan McCaffrey. Another verse from "Donal Ogue" leaped into my mind.

You might as well let him have me, Mother,
And every penny you have moreover;
Go beg your bread like any other
But him and me don't seek to bother.

Slicing meat by the door, I was able to hear the conversation of the men in the parlor. Michael tried in vain to impress Father with the certainty of victory in the crusade that McCaffrey and others were launching. The Civil War had ended in America, and there were fifty thousand Irish veterans ready to fight England. There were Irishmen of wealth, with mansions as great as any English lord's, ready to pledge their fortunes for Ireland's freedom.

"And how will the fifty thousand men get to Ireland?" Father asked. "Will you launch a navy strong enough to fight the British fleet?"

"Could be we'll get the American fleet, now that the war's over. The Union government's real sore at the lime-juicers for the way they backed the Confederacy. There's talk they're goin' to sell us half their fleet for a few bucks," Dan McCaffrey said.

I'm sure Father had never heard "sore" or "a few bucks" before, but he got the general meaning. He shook his head. "The cost would beggar any group of men. None but a government can pay the monstrous expenses of a fleet and army."

"We got a government," Dan McCaffrey said. "The Fenian Brotherhood's got a headquarters on Union Square in New York, a mansion big as the White House. The head center and the council operate from there, like the president in Washington, D.C. They're raisin' money by the ton."

"It's the love of Ireland working in their hearts," Michael said. "Major McCaffrey says if anything it's stronger among those born in America like himself."

"Our fathers taught us to hate the lime-juicers." McCaffrey said. "My old man saw four brothers and two sisters die in the famine of '31. He was half dead himself when he got to America, but free air and good money made a new man of him. What can be done for one man can be done for a country. Stick a pin in that."

This last, a favorite American phrase, baffled Father. He asked Major McCaffrey what part he had played in the Civil War in America.

"I was a major under Jeb Stuart," he said. "The best cavalry in the Confederacy."

"The Confederacy?" cried Father. "You, an Irishman, fought to keep slaves? And now you're coming to free Ireland. What sense can a man make of that?"

Dan McCaffrey admitted it sounded confusing, but the war had not been fought over slavery, he said. The Irish in the Southern army were supporting their section of the country against the oppression of the North. Now the South was an occupied land, like Ireland. This was hard for the South but good for Ireland. It made the war-hardened Irish veterans of the South ready to throw in their lot with Ireland's army of liberation.

Father was unimpressed. He talked passionately of his youth, when he heard the greatest Irishman of the century, Daniel O'Connell, denounce slavery and hold out the hope of an Ireland in which Protestant and Catholics could live as equals. From O'Connell Father also came to believe that Irishmen could win their fight against England without bloodshed, if they united and relied on moral force and legal protests against injustice.

Dan McCaffrey scarcely knew what he was talking about. Daniel O'Connell was a dead forgotten name to him. "Here's the only force that England understands," he said.

From within his coat he drew a great black revolver. I never thought that in our modest parlor I was seeing the argument that has broken heads and hearts not just in Ireland but the world over. Now I know that my father and McCaffrey stood for two different ways of thinking and feeling, two different attitudes toward the world. All I knew at that moment was how irresistible that gun looked in the fading light of May Eve. Within me a voice began whispering:

> *Donal Ogue, when you cross the water*
> *Take me with you to be your partner.*

Hurrah for the Outlaw's Life

In the same moment I saw that Michael's plan of escape was all wrong—to leap in the saddle and gallop to the shore of Bantry Bay was folly. The sleepiest village policeman could not fail to notice two men on fine horses, and there was no hope of any horse outrunning the steam engine and the telegraph. I flung aside my bread knife and strode into the parlor.

"Listen to me," I said to Michael. "You must forget the horses, if you don't want to end in a dungeon in Dublin Castle."

Michael turned scornfully on me. "We'll settle this without any help from you, Bess. 'Tis a man's business."

"It's Ireland's business," I said. "And a man on the run can't think clearly." I turned to Dan McCaffrey. "Will *you* listen to me?" I said. "A man as well dressed as you will have as little chance of escaping notice as a donkey in a cow herd. Add the thunder of a fine horse and you might as well take along a brass band to guarantee your capture. Don't you know there's a policeman in every village and a telegraph in every railway station? They'll have a regiment waiting for you at Bantry Bay."

"Bessie, your mother needs you in the kitchen—" my father said.

"Wait a sec," Dan McCaffrey said. "What do you think we should do?"

"Go slow instead of fast," I said. "Take three or four days to reach Bantry Bay. Shed your fine feathers and go off as a spalpeen with a spade on your shoulder. Michael should do the same. I'll go with you and scout the towns and find the guides we can trust to take us safely to Bantry by mountain tracks and byroads. Neither of you will be able to show your faces in a town by morning. There'll be descriptions of you posted up in every pub and post office."

"We sure could use you," Dan McCaffrey said. "But will your dad let you go?"

"He will not," my father said.

"I'll go, with or without his permission," I said.

Father sprang up in a rage and ordered me to my room. I refused to move a step. For an instant Father's hand twitched at his side. I thought he was about to strike me, something he had never done since I was born. Michael stepped between us. "She's right, Da," he said. "We do need her help."

Suddenly the bad blood that had been thickening between Father and Michael and between Father and me was no longer a desultory quarrel. It was a deep, blazing difference, into which all our resentments poured like boiling lava. Michael's resistance to Father's determination to make him a farmer, my anger at his curt advice to take Patrick Dolan's offer, fused with our detestation of his passive attitude toward Ireland's agony. "It's time you faced up to something, Da," Michael said. "We're not like your cattle, to be disposed of as you see fit. We intend to live our own lives."

For a long moment we stood there, frozen in opposition. Father glared from Michael to Dan McCaffrey. It was his American presence, his massive physique, that made the difference. Suddenly Father was no longer master in his own house. He stumbled back to his chair by the fire. "Do what you please," he said.

"Get them old clothes," Dan McCaffrey said to me. "We need to put some miles between us and this place by dawn."

I took his coat and ran down through the storm to Conn the plowman's hut. Lightning danced across the twilit face of the lake. Thunder crashed overhead. At the door a clap that sounded like the fall of a hundred tombstones made me tremble. I suddenly remembered the day they had carried poor Conn to this door, broken and moaning after the plowhorse had suddenly gone mad with the heat and trampled him. My old horror of violence and wounds awoke in me. For a good year after Conn's death I could not even see a galloping horse without feeling a sticky weakness spread through my body. I told myself I was breaking the bonds of these childish feelings, leaping the pasture where I had toiled and obeyed and feared and trembled. Was I trampling those I loved? I thrust the question aside.

In the hut, I found Conn's sons, Mute Mick and Johnny, enjoying a bit of poteen. They started back, sure I was a banshee in my black cloak. The terror made them obey me without question, even when they saw it was

my familiar self. I was soon on the way back to the house
with an outfit for Dan McCaffrey, complete to a pair of
ruined boots.

As I came back into the house, Michael was talking to
Father. "All will end well, Da," he said. "I'm sure of it.
We'll come back here a victorious host and install you in
the mansion house as lord of Ballinaclash."

"You mean install yourself," Father snarled. "That's
what's behind all your poems and your talk, a greed to get
your hands on enough money and land to save you from
honest toil. You're nothing but a lazy book-dreaming lout.
Get out on the road where you belong, and take your slut
of a sister with you."

A great wound was inflicted with those words. I felt it
like a knife thrust in my throat. I saw it strike Michael
like a bludgeon in his face. In the kitchen, Mother, her
face like a grave, stuffed food into knapsacks and handed
them to Michael and Dan McCaffrey. Michael had put
on the ragged pants and red shirt that he wore when he
worked with Father in the fields. Dan McCaffrey was
wearing one of old Conn's shirts, a riddle of rips and
patches, and trousers that were as dirty and torn as those
on the poorest spalpeen walking the roads. I borrowed a
filthy housecleaning dress of peasant homespun from
Bridget and took my old calico shawl and slashed it with
a scissors until it was little more than a rag around my
shoulders.

I told Mother I would be home in a week and kissed
her. She saw the lie in my eyes and wept. I was torn by a
terrible weakening love for her and almost lost my resolution. But I thought of what Father had called me and
knew I could not stay back now. In the parlor, Father
stared into the fire. His face was like the stone visage on
a tomb. But I was shocked to see that slow, bitter tears
were trickling down his cheeks.

I had never seen Father weep, never seen him in a situation where he was not in command of himself and others. Later I realized our farm beside Lake Fergus was a kind of enchanted island. We had grown up here surrounded by Mother's love and Father's strength only hearing like distant thunder the groans of the dangerous suffering world of the real Ireland that surrounded us. Father wept out of fear and knowledge of this world. In the end it had made him weak when he most wanted to be strong. Then I only knew the wounding words he had inflicted on me and Michael. I did not speak as we went out the door.

The storm was dying away as we reached the road, but it served its purpose for us, driving everyone indoors until the twilight had deepened into dark. We trudged along, Michael and Dan McCaffrey hefting spades on their shoulders to better play the spalpeen. I warned McCaffrey that his American speech would give us away in an instant. It would be better if he pretended to be mute, like Conn's son Mick.

"So much for precautions. Henceforth we shall enjoy ourselves," I said.

My heart was soaring like a wild hawk in the night. With one stroke my love of Ireland had burst the bonds of daughterhood and the polite, safe, boring future offered me by Patrick Dolan. I was launched on a wild gamble, and for the moment I knew only its strength, its excitement.

The thunder rumbled distantly in the west, the direction we were taking. "Do you hear it?" I said. "It's the army of the old kings. Perhaps we'll hear their cry."

Dan McCaffrey did not know what I was talking about. I explained that according to the country people, once or twice in a decade, over the mountains from south to north rolled the old kings' cry, shaking the ground like an earthquake. From east to west the land heaved and broke. From the clay rose the army of the dead, old warriors on their great horses and trumpeters and harpers and foot soldiers by the thousands in ghastly array. They raised their shields and spears and gave an answering shout to the kings' cry. They were calling on the living to come out and fight for Ireland.

As I told the story, Bel fires began to leap on the surrounding hills. I explained these to Dan McCaffrey, linking them to the old kings. Bel was the god the kings had worshipped, the pagan lord of the sun. I did not believe in Bel anymore than I really believed in the kings or their ghostly host. I knew those shouting warriors were a dream in the minds of the peasantry, born of poteen and the wind that howls up the Shannon from the Atlantic. But the turmoil of the day had loosed my mind and heart and made me ready to accept every kind of magic.

"Listen now," I said to Dan McCaffrey. "Any moment we'll hear the rattle of the warrior's spears."

"Spears ain't gonna help Ireland," Dan said. "We need repeatin' rifles. Carbines. And fightin' men."

He spat out his disgust at the condition of Ireland. The well-off were like Father, too ready to bow their knee to Queen Victoria and praise her for their prosperity. The poor were so wretched and beaten down, it was impossible to believe that they could stand in the field against trained British troops.

"But they believe in Ireland," I said. "Give them a green flag and they'll die for it."

"A soldier's got to believe in himself first," McCaffrey said. "He's got to have some pride, some honor, to give him the courage to stand and fight."

"We'll have to give them Ireland's honor," I said.

"How in hell do you do it?" McCaffrey said. "That's the question."

"Were there Irishmen who fought beside you in the war in America?"

"Thousands of them."

"Where did they get their pride, their honor?"

"From the free air of America. From their leaders, men like my commander, Jeb Stuart, who had pride and honor bred into them from the cradle."

"I want to go with you to America and find a way to bring those ideas back to Ireland."

"What the devil are you talking about, Bess?" Michael said. "There's no place for women in this work."

"No place for women? If it wasn't for this woman, you'd be riding down this road to your own sure destruction."

Dan McCaffrey likewise shook his head. "I'm not goin' to give your old man a chance to say that I—"

"What my old man says no longer matters. You heard what he called me as we went out the door. I'll never go back to him, no matter what happens. If you won't take me, I'll go to London and sell myself on the street until I get the passage money to America."

Dan McCaffrey laughed. It was a great dark gust of sound, as black as the night from which it came. In spite of my brave words, I felt a momentary fear at the recklessness I heard in that mirth. For a moment I wondered if he were one of the ancient warriors, returned to earth to live with the same mad courage as of old. I remembered another verse from "Donal Ogue."

Black as a sloe is the heart inside me
Black as a coal with the griefs that drive me
Black as a boot print on shining hallways
And 'twas you that blackened it ever and always.

"All right," Dan said. "You can come with us. Contrary to what Michael says, a woman with good nerves can do plenty for us. She can make friends for us in high places, play the spy in London and Dublin, carry messages between America and Ireland."

It began to rain in sheets again. There was no getting

shelter from anyone on May Eve. Every door and window was shut against the wayfarer for fear of the little people. We had nothing to do but trudge through the downpour until about midnight, when we reached the village of Knocklong. Following our plan, Michael and Dan waited on the outskirts while I approached the public house and scouted the danger.

The house was run by a woman, a little old sparrow of a thing who looked like she'd take fright at the mere thought of a gunman.

"Have you heard anything of men on the run from Limerick?" I asked. "I have a cousin who went off that way singing a war song."

"There's two proclaimed for murder," said the landlady, pointing to a notice on the wall. "The telegraph clerk came down with a constable to post it up a half hour ago. They're offering a hundred pounds reward and watchin' every road between here and Cork."

I made a great show of reading the descriptions on the notice. They were very close to the truth of Michael's looks, and they had everything right for Dan but the color of his hair.

"What do you think of these things?" I asked the landlady.

"I think everyone must do what he can for Ireland," she said. "If they're out there in the storm, go tell them there's warm food and dry beds here, and no money will be taken from them."

We entered the house by a back door and soon had a good dinner of beef and bread in our stomachs with liberal amounts of John Jameson's whiskey to burnish it. The men ate wrapped in blankets, their wet clothes drying by the fire. I wore an old nightgown that the landlady had given me. Dan McCaffrey looked at me with new admiration. "Bess," he said, "you might convince me that there's a chance for a rebellion here in Ireland, after all."

"Can I stick a pin in that?" I said.

"Sure," he said. "But what's so funny?"

"It's American talk. I've never heard anyone say that before."

It was such an everyday phrase to Dan he was not even conscious of it. It was a sign, albeit a small one, that the Irish-Americans and the Irish were different people. That was a discovery we each were to make to our individual griefs.

Michael began to sneeze and sniffle, and I told him to go to bed. He hesitated, not wanting to leave me alone with Dan McCaffrey. "It's all right, Michael," I said. "You're not my keeper. We're done with that sort of thing."

Michael went off, surly and snuffling. I turned to Dan McCaffrey.

"You can have me now if you want me," I said. "I know it's a sin. But everything we're going to do together will be a sin. It's a sin to hate the English. It's a sin to kill people. It's a sin to disobey your father and mother. It's a sin to—"

His lips were on my mouth, sealing my dark loosed passion with his man's desire. I was living the old poem; I was the girl in "Donal Ogue," mad with love for the warrior who had returned to the land of his ancestors from across the water. He lifted me and carried me across the room to the bed. The blanket dropped from his shoulders, and for a moment I saw him all golden and bronze in the firelight, his yellow hair gleaming. He raised the nightgown above my head and lay down beside me, his hand on one of my breasts. With a soft cry I drew him to me, wrapped him with my arms into my dream. I was Ireland, dark Rosaleen welcoming my hero-lover; he was one of the Fianna, blindly embracing his hope and his doom. But above all he was Young Dan, Donal Ogue, with promises of love and glory, gifts and treasures, on his lips. Joyously I whispered to him.

"Ah, Donal Ogue, you'll not find me lazy
Like many a high-born expensive lady;
I'll do your chores and I'll nurse your baby
And if you're set on I'll back you bravely."

So we loved half that May Eve away, while the Bel fires leaped on the hills and the old kings rumbled above or beneath the earth. But in the morning it was the real world of Ireland in 1865 that confronted us again. The landlady glared at me when I opened the door and wanted to know why I had not slept in the bed she had made up for me. I gave her a story about Dan being my girlhood love who had come home to marry me. I'm sure I was not very convincing. Her angry old eyes were like a reproach from my mother, awakening guilt in my Irish Catholic soul. I suddenly saw our pastor, lean old Father Dennis McHugh, glaring down at me from the pulpit of our parish church, warning us against "the dirty filthy sins of the flesh." I heard Father's farewell. *Take your slut of a sister with you.*

Worse, Michael's reproachful looks all but shouted the truth as I spoke. Only with the greatest difficulty did we persuade the landlady to lend us her son, who led us into the Ballyhoura Mountains on the border of Cork and Limerick counties. It was a rough track, and the lad left us in the late afternoon with little more than the hope that we might find shelter for the night. We found a goatherder's hut as the dusk came down and were offered the hospitality of the bare floor and whatever was in the pot for dinner. Dan played the mute and Michael said as little as possible while I produced a Kerry brogue to explain our journey. We took food from the pot though it almost choked us. The new crop of potatoes was not yet ready for digging, and the poor people were living on stirabout, made from the siftings of flour more than half bran. There were the man and his wife, three children, and six goats in the cabin. In the morning we spent the better part of an hour picking the fleas and lice from our hair and clothes.

Around midday the rain began to pour again, and we decided to seek shelter for the night in a public house outside Mitchelstown. Once more, I was sent ahead to reconnoiter. As I entered the front door, I found the landlord talking to a policeman. The constable took one look at me and said in a rich Cork brogue, "Sure that's one of them." I whirled and ran for the open road. The rain had slackened to a drizzle. I reached Michael and Dan as the policeman and a half dozen supporters emerged from the town. "There's where we'll spend tonight," I said, pointing to the blue mists of the Mitchelstown Mountains a good four miles away.

We set off on the run and kept a half mile between us and our pursuers until night fell and the policeman quit the chase. Had the old lady informed on us? Or had the police noticed my absence when they searched our house, and surmised our plan of escape? Either way, it meant we were now a hunted trio.

The rain drizzled down in the chill dark, and Michael began to shiver and sweat with fever. He had always been a delicate lad growing up. We found an empty cabin on a mountain slope and spent the night in it, our clothes soaked, the wind creeping in at us from a hundred cracks in the walls. By morning, Michael was so weak he could barely stand, and still the rain came down. We ate the last of the food we had taken from home and half carried, half dragged Michael through the mountains toward Kilworth.

Toward the end of the day, we came down from the mountains and crossed the River Funcheon about a mile above Kilworth. The river was in flood, and the only bridge was a great fir tree that had fallen across the stream. We teetered across it in single file like Indians and trudged onward in the rain. No shelter was to be found until eleven o'clock, when we all but forced our way into another lonely cabin. This one had man and wife and two children in it. The inevitable pot of stirabout was on the fire, but Dan could not eat another mouthful of the disgusting stuff. Looking up, he saw a hen perched on a beam overhead. He offered to buy it, but the owner, angry at the way we had pushed through his door, said no. Dan took out his pistol. The hen was promptly sold for two shillings and consumed within the hour.

The next day brought rich sunshine. Michael felt better. We decided to chance the road again and found a farmer driving a wagonload of corn to Cork. He spoke only Irish, and I had to act as our interpreter. I liked the look of the man—he was young and burly, with a great shock of red hair—and told him who we were. He immediately offered us his wagon and corn crop, if we but told him where we would abandon it, that he might go claim it when we were safely at sea. Dan McCaffrey was so touched by his patriotism, he insisted on giving him ten guineas in case he could not recover his wagon.

We put Michael to rest beneath the corn and turned the horse's head west from the Cork road to Bantry. When we grew hungry, we took some of the corn and roasted it by the road. At night we drove the wagon off the road and slept in it. Our fears vanished, and the journey became as gay as a vacation jaunt. I chanted a poem by Doheny, one of the rebels of the rising of 1848, as we rode along.

> *"Hurrah for the outlaw's life!*
> *Hurrah for the felon's doom!*
> *Hurrah for the last death-strife!*
> *Hurrah for an exile's tomb!"*

Beyond Dunmanway, approaching County Kerry, we drove through the pass of Ceimenagh in the Shehy

Mountains—one of the most majestic routes in Ireland. The road wound into the very bowels of the mountains. Dark rude outlines of rock masses rose hundreds of feet above our heads on either side. Dan McCaffrey saw the scene with a soldier's eye. "A hundred men with re-peatin' rifles could stop an army on this road," he said.

" 'Tis the beauty of it I love," I said.

We came down from the pass to Ballingeary, on the banks of Lake Lua. There, I insisted on halting to show Dan one of my favorite spots—the island in the center of the lake where the poet Callanan wrote some of his loveliest poems. We walked through the ruins of an old monastery, past gigantic forest trees, bowing their aged limbs into the clear water, while the shadows of the frowning mountain fell awesomely across the lake. From the distant crags came the eagle's scream.

I asked Michael to speak the lines Callanan wrote here. Softly he repeated them.

> *"I too shall be gone, but my name shall be spoken*
> *When Erin awakes and her fetters are broken.*
> *Some ministrel shall come in the summer eve's*
>   *gleaming*
> *When Freedom's young light on his spirit is*
>   *beaming—"*

Dan interrupted Michael with a gesture of impatience. "Bess, when we take Ireland, I'll build you a mansion here. We'll clear the land along the shore and turn the whole place into a park. It'll be the biggest and best es-tate you ever saw. Dukes and duchesses will fight to visit us."

"No, no," I said. "It should stay exactly like this, wild and lonely and ruined."

"That's an Irish way of lookin' at things," McCaffrey

said. "You're goin' to America, Bess, where people take a practical approach to life. You know why I'm doin' this—riskin' my neck over here?"

"To free Ireland, I thought."

"Sure. To settle my old man's score with the goddamn lime-juicers. But the men who free Ireland, Bess, the Americans who free her, expect to get a slice of it—a damn good slice—as their reward. An American don't risk his life—an American like me—for an idea."

He reached into his knapsack and pulled out a leather purse. Yanking the drawstring, he showed us a heap of glittering gold sovereigns. "There's what America teaches a man to respect. There's tens of thousands more where these came from. The Irish in America will pour them into the pockets of any man ready to fight for Ireland."

I saw disgust on my brother Michael's face. I felt it in my own heart. But I refused to yield to it. I told myself that I would teach Dan McCaffrey the power and the glory of the idea of a free Ireland, the nobility of sacrifice for it. I would teach him to love poetry and the wild beauty of lake and mountain—gifts I thought as natural to an Irish man or woman as breathing. America seemed to have strained them from his blood.

A day later we were approaching the town of Bantry. We planned to leave the wagon on the outskirts and hire a boat to cruise the bay in search of the ship that was to meet Dan. We felt secure in our wagon, while the constabulary watched the roads for three runaways on foot. There was also no reason for them to think we would strike for Bantry, a petty port compared to Cork or Kenmare.

A half mile from the town, security vanished. From a wheat field sprang a sergeant and a half dozen policemen with rifles at the ready. The Irish-speaking farmer had decided to collect the hundred-pound reward to add to the ten guineas he had gotten for his wagon.

The sergeant was a perfect twin of my mother's nephew, Barry MacNamara, tall and red-faced with a button nose and a big square chin. He was as Irish as I was. So were the rest of the Peelers, as the police were sometimes called. "Divide and conquer" had been the British motto ever since they came to Ireland, and these men were living witnesses to how well it had worked.

Dan handed the reins to me. "Whip that nag when you see me drop," he said. I didn't know what he was talking about. My heart thumped in my body like a fist pounding a drum. I looked back at Michael, who was spread low in the corn. "Get ready," I said.

Dan jumped off the seat and walked toward the sergeant with his hands held high. Slowly, carefully, I fastened my hand around the handle of the whip on the seat beside me. Now! Dan dropped to a crouch and shot the sergeant in the middle, and two of the policemen behind him. I never saw him draw his gun. It leaped to his hand like a magical thing. The others blazed at him, but their bullets whizzed past him and me, except for one that struck the metal rim of the wagon's right wheel with a clang like a blacksmith's hammer. All in the same instant I was wielding the whip on Dobbin's back. The big plow horse sprang forward like a cavalry charger.

Michael jumped up to fling a volley of corn ears at the surviving police, a brave gesture to disrupt their aim. Dan leaped for the rear of the wagon as we rumbled past him and vaulted into the corn. The policemen scattered like chickens before our rush, but they quickly reformed and trained their guns on us. Dan dropped another one with a single shot from his pistol, and the rest fled for shelter.

Our one hope now was to put distance between us and our pursuers. Through the town of Bantry we rampaged, while strollers gaped in amazement. Michael gaily bombarded them with cornstalks, and Dan sent them scampering with a wave of his gun. For another mile or two we raced bravely along the shore of Bantry Bay. Without warning our gallant steed stumbled, strove once to right himself, and came crashing to earth. A bloody froth bubbled from his nostrils. One of the police bullets had struck home. Dan put him out of his misery with a bullet in his head.

We fled into the mountains above the bay. A fog rolled in with the dark, and we wandered through it like lost souls, utterly ignorant of our direction but for the needle of Dan's compass, which he said had saved his neck more than once in the Civil War. We groped along, climbing up and sliding down for hours, Dan ahead and Michael behind me. Michael finally persuaded us to stop. His legs were like cornstalks, he said.

Morning found us a good five miles from the town of Bantry. As the sun rose and burned away the fog, we saw a lonely cabin tilted on the bare rock, high above the bay. Michael, who had visited the coast with friends from the university, said the place was called Priest's Leap in honor of a priest of the previous century, when the Catholic clergy were hunted like criminals in Ireland. According to the legend, the priest was trapped on the cliff and bounded above his pursuers with the aid of divine grace to land on the deck of a Spanish man-of-war in the bay.

"We sure could use legs like that," Dan said, gazing out at the tossing water. Far to the west, the dark green Atlantic heaved. Below us curled whitecapped Bantry Bay, with its waves dashing against stupendous cliffs. On this coast, Ireland was like a great rock-fanged monster facing the enemy ocean. It was hard to believe anyone ever could have conquered her.

We approached the cabin and found within it a man, a woman, and a single child. The man wore shreds of flannel, which might once have been drawers, and a tattered shirt of unbleached linen. The woman had an old blanket drawn around her shoulders, and her skirt was a mass of shreds, but she carried herself with uncommon pride. The way she touched her matted hair and rearranged the rags on her body announced that she had once fired men's hearts and eyes. Her bare feet and ankles were as faultless as a Greek statue of Diana, but her lofty brow was furrowed and wrinkled, her eyes dilated with despair and disdain.

The child, however, was well dressed. She wore a homespun jacket and skirt of sparrow color and good laced-up boots. Although she was no more than seven, her face was clenched and fierce, giving it a strange look of age, even of evil. Her name was Moira.

I decided that our best hope was to tell them the truth, even though they were the very faces and figures of Ireland's degradation. "We're on the run, and there's a price on our heads," I said. "Out there in the bay is an American ship. We don't know its shape or size. All we know is the name, the *Manhattan*."

I pointed to a half dozen ships swinging at anchor off the town of Bantry. The woman spoke rapidly to her husband in Irish, assuming that we did not understand it. She asked him if he thought they could get more money by betraying us. He answered that he was indifferent as to the choice. Why not bargain first and see?

I instantly changed my ground. Switching to Irish, I said: "We're going to America. We'll take your little one with us. This man is rich. He'll raise her like a queen."

The mother's violent eyes came aglow. She studied our ragged clothes and said we looked as poor as she was. If Dan was so rich, where was his money?

"Dan," I said, "count out every sovereign you've got."

In two minutes the sovereigns were on the crude table, a heap of glittering gold that made the couple's mouths gape. "Half of it is yours," Dan said, dividing it and pushing it across the table toward them. "But you won't get it until we step into the boat that takes us to the *Manhattan*."

The woman shoved the money back to Dan and said in Irish to me, "Swear by God and the devil and the fairies that you'll keep your promise."

"I swear," I said.

"Keep the money and spend it on her in America."

"We will," I said.

I told Dan what I'd promised. "'Tis the only bargain she'll make," I said.

A look passed over Dan's face that I did not like. There was something cunning and cruel in it. "Okay," he said.

The woman did not know what that American word meant. I scarcely did myself. But the moment I told her the promise was sealed, she began barking orders at her husband. He was to equip himself with one of the sovereigns and visit every public house in Bantry if need be to discover which ship was the *Manhattan*.

We spent the rest of the morning with the woman and her child. The mother spoke only Irish to the child, who did not seem to understand anything else. She told the little one that she was going to America, a land of gold and riches where she would never be hungry again. Irishmen there had their pockets full of money, like this man, who would be her father, and this woman, who would be her mother. Someday she would come back to Bantry, wearing clothes like a queen, and she would come up to this cabin with a dress of blue silk and a rope of pearls for her mother. Together they would parade the streets, giving the laugh to all those who sneered and called "Finey" after her, because she had kept her pride, though she had married low.

As I listened, I found myself wondering if I was as childish as this woman in her own way. I did not believe that all Irishmen in America had pockets full of gold. Dan McCaffrey had told me that those sovereigns did not belong to him. They had been collected from thousands of Irish in America for the Fenian cause. But I was trusting these nameless, faceless men, putting my faith in their love of Ireland, in spite of hints that their love was far from pure. The more I thought of it, the more I was glad that we were taking the little girl with us. I wanted this small creature with her nightbird face as a talisman, a reminder of Ireland's bitter truth, something that would prevent America from changing me as I feared in some deep way it had changed Dan McCaffrey.

Toward noon, the husband returned from Bantry town soused on Dan's money. He had located the ship *Manhattan*. According to report, it would sail with the morning tide. It was the last in the line of ships moored off the town. Beside her were two English steam frigates—ships of the Royal Navy. Worse, the town was alive with the talk of us. Lord Bantry himself, whose great estate of Glengarrif was nearby, was organizing a search party from his tenants and retainers to scour slopes and shore for us tomorrow.

Our one chance was to get a message to the *Manhattan* before morning. I said I would try it. To resemble a country girl, I blacked two of my teeth and smeared dirt on my cheeks. I tied up my hair beneath an old sunhat that the woman produced from beneath some rags in the corner. Finally I demanded Dan's gun and trudged to town. On my shoulder I carried a bundle of sticks that people might suppose I was hoping to sell for two pence. It was not unusual for a country boy or girl to walk ten miles to earn two pence in the Ireland of those days.

In town I went from house to house trying to sell my fuel, exposing myself dangerously, you might think. But it is well known that the smallest change in a person's appearance, if carried off with boldness, can baffle the most

alert pursuers. I spoke only Irish, convinced in spite of
the treachery of the Gaelic-speaking wagon man that an
Irish tongue, especially in a town, denoted a love of Ireland. Townsmen of this period had abandoned their native speech to ally themselves with the English. Most
people simply shook their heads and shut their doors, but
one broad-shouldered gray-haired man answered my
Gaelic good day with an equally Gaelic reply.

"God's grace shine on you, my girl," he said. "There's
enough turf hereabout to give us all the fire we need."

"I'm not selling these sticks," I said. "I'm showing
them about the country as a sign."

"Of what?" he asked, no doubt wondering if he was
dealing with a madwoman.

"Of Ireland," I said. "Alone, they can be broken by a
child's hand." I snapped one of them. "Together it would
take a giant to break them. And when a strong hand
grasps and fires them, they make a mighty blaze."

He looked up and down the street. "What do you
want?" he said.

"A boy to row out to the *Manhattan* and tell them to
have a boat at the foot of Priest's Leap before dawn."

"Consider it done."

"I will only consider it done when I see the promise in
the captain's handwriting," I said.

I slipped the gun from beneath my dress and aimed it
at his breast. "We've been betrayed enough. If you fail
me, I'll shoot you first and then myself."

"You have nothing to fear," he said. "Come round the
back of the house."

I went to the back of the house and was welcomed
with hot tea and fresh bread. The man's oldest son, a boy
of about sixteen, declared himself ready to take the message to the *Manhattan*. For two hours we sat there talking about Ireland. The older man did not think the
Fenians could succeed. Like Father, he thought the

British fleet was too strong to pass, and this made all the strength and money in America useless.

"If I were a young man I would go to America, not to fight for Ireland, but to start a new life," he said. "My son will go with my blessing."

The boy returned with a scribble from the captain of the *Manhattan*. The British were patrolling the waters of the bay in cutters. To deceive them, he would hoist sail tomorrow morning and stand out to sea. Then he would come about and steer as close to shore as he dared, before lowering a boat. We were to be waiting on the rocks at the foot of the cliff.

We slept that night on the bare floor of the cabin. The woman was up at dawn dressing the child and ordering the husband to get the fire going beneath the pot. We went out on the windswept cliff and saw that the *Manhattan* was still at her mooring. As Dan began cursing the captain, I saw something far more alarming down the coast. Some five hundred men were moving toward us, spread in a long line from the cliff's edge a good mile inland. It was Lord Bantry and his search party.

Dan studied them with a soldier's eye. "They're three miles away," he said. "It'll take them an hour to reach us."

"There go the *Manhattan*'s sails," Michael said.

The sails were indeed shaking out to the wind. She loosed from her anchor and swung toward the open sea on the tide. In half an hour she was opposite us. True to his promise, the captain put the helm hard over and bounded toward us on a stiff southeast breeze. But to our dismay, he hove to a half mile off and began lowering a boat. It would take them thirty minutes at least to row that distance.

"He's afraid of the rocks," Michael said. "And with good reason. They could tear his bottom out."

Over our shoulders, we could see Lord Bantry's line

of searchers, moving toward us at the same methodical pace. Lord Bantry himself had joined them on a big black horse. It was not at all clear who would reach us first, the boat or Bantry's men. As we watched, another horseman rode up to Lord Bantry and pointed to the ship. His Lordship pulled out a pistol and fired it in the air. The searchers on the mountainside came swarming down to join those on the shore, and all quickened their pace in our direction. The other horseman rode off pell-mell for the town of Bantry to alarm the British steam frigates.

"Get down on the rocks," Dan said to me and Michael. "I'll hold them off from here."

He pointed to a narrow path that wound down the face of the cliff to the wave-lashed rocks at its foot. The woman handed the little girl to me. With a growl Dan snatched her out of my arms and thrust her back to her mother. "We're not takin' that kid," he said.

"We promised. I swore," I said.

"I don't give a damn. Get goin'. It'll take you ten minutes to get down that path."

"Come on, Bess," Michael said, already beginning his descent. "Do what he says."

I turned to the woman and said in Irish, "There is nothing I can do. He's an American."

The woman's face turned black with rage. Her eyes seemed about to leap from her head. In a low hissing voice, she laid a curse on us. "May seven devils haunt you night and noon. May you wander the world like thieves and murderers, with the mark of Cain on your foreheads! May you die a dozen times by knife thrust and gun before death finally takes you! May those you love most betray you!"

For a moment I saw a great coiled snake within her rags. Fangs leaped from her hate-twisted mouth. I was paralyzed by dread.

"What's she saying?" Dan asked.

"She's cursing us," I said.

"To hell with her," Dan said.

With a scream of rage, the woman whirled and raced toward the oncoming line of Lord Bantry's men. In the rush of the wind we could not hear her words, but it was plain from her pointing arm that she was shouting the news of our identity. The child meanwhile stood gaping from her mother to me to Dan. For the first time I realized from the incomprehension on the small clenched face that the little creature was an idiot.

"Jesus God, come on, Bess," Michael said, fairly dragging me onto the path down the cliff. As we descended, we could see some of Lord Bantry's men running along the cliff edge, their guns in their hands. On the water the boat from the *Manhattan*, with six men at the oars and a coxswain at the rudder, pulled steadily toward us. The wind whipped around us, bounding off the cliff face, adding its hollow sigh to the thunder of the waves below us.

In ten minutes we were on a small ledge with the sea foaming around our knees. Spray leaped from nearby rocks, drenching us. The boat was only fifty feet away now. Behind the oarsmen, the captain of the *Manhattan* was risking his ship to edge closer to shore. He had a man with a lead line in the bow, sounding every foot of the treacherous rock-filled water.

Gunfire crackled on the cliff above us. I turned my head in time to see Dan McCaffrey halfway down the path, exchanging shots with a rifleman on the cliff edge. The rifle bullets sent chips of stone flying inches from Dan's face. His pistol spoke once more. With a cry the man dropped his gun and pitched back, vanishing from my sight as if he had toppled into an abyss. His rifle went clattering down the cliff to disappear into the seething waves.

The men in the boat shouted that they could come no closer. They were almost on the rocks, backrowing for their lives. Michael and I plunged into the foam. Dan threw his pistol to the coxswain and plunged after us. The sailors hauled us into the boat, all the while looking fearfully at the cliff above them, which was now lined with riflemen. Dan seized his revolver and sent them scampering with the last three bullets in the cylinder.

The sailors pulled with all their might for the ship while Dan brandished his empty pistol. What a figure he made beside the coxswain, his wet shirt plastered to his broad back, his yellow hair streaming in the sun. He kept the riflemen at bay until Lord Bantry himself rode up and, judging us to be out of pistol range, bravely exposed himself to rally his retainers and order a volley. The bullets fell a hundred feet to the west of us.

"Jesus," Dan said. "I've never seen such bad shootin'."

"They're Lord Bantry's men, but they're Irishmen," Michael said. "I doubt they want to hit us."

"The guy shootin' at me goin' down the cliff must have been English," Dan said.

"My God, look," I cried.

The woman had burst through the line of riflemen on the cliff's edge. She had the child in her arms. With a howl that reached us over the wind, she flung the little girl down upon the foam-drenched rocks below.

"Dear God, dear God, forgive us," I said.

"Why did she do it?" Dan said.

"They put her under arrest, no doubt," Michael said. "It was impossible to deny she'd sheltered us."

"It meant leaving the only thing she loved," I said.

"What a crazy country," Dan said. "You're better out of it."

"I wonder if we'll ever be out of it," I said.

Hail the Conquering Heroes

Aboard the *Manhattan*, all was confusion and roaring and cursing as we were hustled to the deck, the boat was hoisted aboard, and they laid on every scrap of sail to clear Bantry Bay before the British frigates caught them. We were led to the captain's cabin, and there I tasted my first cup of coffee. A bitter, scalding brew, I thought it, but Dan McCaffrey gulped it gratefully and said it made him feel at home already.

We looked like three half-drowned rats. The captain appeared and said as much. New York born, he was a big, broad man with a beard like the Lord Jehovah. His name was Dennis O'Hickey. He was a Fenian Republican to the eyes; he'd taken the oath and was ready to risk his ship for Ireland's freedom. He rarely spoke in less than a roar, even in his cabin.

"As a true O'Hickey," I said, "you should be consoled that you've saved two descendants of the O'Briens, as your ancestors no doubt saved thousands."

Neither he nor Dan McCaffrey knew what I was talking about. I explained to them that in the old days, when the O'Briens ruled Thomond, they never strayed a mile without an O'Hickey, because they were the hereditary doctors to the O'Briens. I told how Tom O'Hickey, one of our farmers, still had the old urge in him, without knowing it. Once, when my father had influenza, Tom had walked ten miles to get blood from an old Mr. Keogh. Like many, Tom believed that a Keogh's blood had a charm in it because a Keogh had once given his life to save a hunted priest.

"We have a Keogh aboard, as scrawny a bit of scrimshaw as you've ever seen," thundered Captain

O'Hickey. "I doubt if we could get blood out of him, any more than I can get work out of him. But I'll undertake to do a bit of doctoring for the three of you here and now."

He got out a bottle of John Jameson's and poured liberal amounts of it in the coffee, improving its taste no end. "You go to bed," he said to Michael, who was beginning to shiver, "and take this with you." He handed him the remains of the bottle. "I'll have some dry clothes sent up for you. Though I'll be damned if I have anything but a sailor's blouses and drawers for you, Miss."

"Anything warm will do nicely," I said.

"Will we make open water, Captain?" Dan said.

"Come see the race," O'Hickey said.

In five minutes a scrawny sailor appeared with dry clothes for us. He had a sad, solemn face. "I'll bet you're Keogh," I said.

"I am," he said.

"I've never seen a Keogh with a smile," I said.

We retreated to separate cabins off the main stateroom and changed into our sailor's clothes. They were so tight, I blushed to look down at myself. It was like wearing underclothes in public. Out on deck, I was relieved to find that no one so much as glanced at me. They were too busy in the dash for the sea. We mounted the captain's poop deck on the stern and watched the British frigate, steam pouring from its funnel, getting under way. Bantry is a long deep bay, and we had some sailing to get beyond Ireland's coast into international waters. The steam frigate gained steadily on us, but Captain O'Hickey remained unworried. In an hour we were at the entrance of the bay. The great heaving swells of the Atlantic tilted the deck beneath our feet. The *Manhattan* bit into them like a greyhound, sending great spumes of spray over the bow.

I turned to have a last look at Ireland. Beyond the

cliffs the land lay in the morning sunshine, a rich, royal green. The color of hope, I told myself. The color of loyalty and faith.

"We'll come back, I promise you, Bess. We'll come back," Dan said, apparently forgetting what he had exclaimed an hour ago about being glad to be out of it.

"Goddamn the bugger, he's giving chase," roared Captain O'Hickey, seizing his spyglass.

The British steam frigate was coming out of the bay, biting as furiously into the Atlantic swells as the *Manhattan*.

"He's clearing his decks," O'Hickey said.

"You ready to fight for your ship, Captain?" Dan asked.

"I'm as ready as the next man, but what good are rifles against cannon? He can stand off and blast us to driftwood," O'Hickey said.

"Let's pretend we'll fight, anyway," Dan said.

Captain O'Hickey began bawling orders. In five minutes every man in the crew—there were about twenty of them—had a rifle in his hand. The British frigate was closing on us with every passing minute. Finally there came a puff of smoke from her bow and the boom of a cannon. A round shot splashed a dozen yards behind us.

"I'll come about. You take charge of the men," O'Hickey said to Dan.

We hove to and wallowed in the swell while the frigate approached. Amidships an officer with a brass trumpet to his mouth bellowed, "Captain ahoy. We have reason to believe you have fugitives from justice aboard your ship. We demand their immediate surrender."

Captain O'Hickey put a similar brass trumpet to his mouth, though his tremendous voice needed no artificial expansion. "We have people who have paid for their passage to America. I intend to take them there. We are in international waters, and any attempt to board my ship will be resisted to the last man of my crew."

Captain O'Hickey gestured to a sailor by the after mast. "Break out the flag," he said.

Up the mast in the sunlight ran America's red, white, and blue banner. How bold it looked, whipping and crackling in the Atlantic wind, opposite John Bull's Union Jack. As long as I live, I will never forget my first sight of Old Glory.

"If you fire a shot at that flag, Captain," O'Hickey thundered, "I guarantee that it will be repaid a thousand-fold within the year. This is an American ship, manned by American citizens."

There was silence from the British frigate while the captain conferred with his officers. Then he raised his trumpet again. "We appeal to you as law-abiding citizens of a great nation. The criminals you are sheltering have killed three people and wounded several other persons."

I was struck with a pang of remorse, thinking of the sergeant who looked like my MacNamara uncle. I was sure he was among the dead. Dan had shot him point-blank.

"I was born in America of Irish parents," Captain O'Hickey replied. "They told me enough about British justice to prevent me from ever surrendering a fugitive to its vengeance."

Up in the bow, Dan McCaffrey shouted an order. The sailors lined the rail, their rifles leveled at the frigate. We could see the ugly snouts of the British cannon through their open gunports, the crews standing ready to fire. It was hardly a contest, if they chose to attack. But after another minute of indecision, smoke belched from the frigate's stack and her bow swung away from us, back toward Ireland. Captain O'Hickey ordered the helmsman to set a westerly course, and we were on our way to America.

That night in Captain O'Hickey's cabin we celebrated royally. The John Jameson's flowed, and we toasted the

United States of America more than once. We had been
saved from the gallows by the American flag, and I was
mightily disposed to love it and the man who flaunted it
as his emblem. I did not understand the divided feelings
Dan himself bore for that flag. I was scarcely aware of
the effect of these feelings on his heart and soul. It was
enough, at first, that we were safe and free and on our
way to rally the Irish of America. I vowed to redouble
our joy with a love that lived up to the promises I had
made to him when I lay in his arms for the first time.

Double and redouble we did, on the stout ship *Manhattan*. Our voyage was a kind of dream. The sun shone
on us every mile of every day. Even the creatures of the
deep seemed kindly disposed. Great whales surfaced one
day off Iceland and spouted mightily into the blue sky,
flipping their tails like children at play. The wind bowled
us along at a brisk ten knots, and Captain O'Hickey was
soon saying he had never seen a better passage. He had
always thought women were bad luck at sea, but he was
ready to change his mind.

A ship is a kind of island, a separate world with its
own ways and customs. We fit smoothly into it, almost
forgetting any other kind of world existed. It was a little
like the land of the Ever Living, the heaven of the old
Irish heroes, where there was nothing to do all day but
sing and feast and recite poems and make easy love
without fear of babies or bill collectors. Captain
O'Hickey was like a laughing God the Father with his
great beard and his stories of shenanigans in a hundred
ports around the world. Michael was our poet and musician. Dan was Oisin, son of Finn, noblest of the old Fenians. I was Niamh, queen of the Country of the Young.

I remember best the night that a full riding moon
spread a hush over the face of the ocean. There was only
the lazy sigh of the ship's prow in the rushing water, the
faint creak of the masts and booms, the occasional rustle

of a sail. Michael and I sat on the deck surrounded by the crew, save the helmsman, and told Fenian stories from the heroic days.

The night ended with Michael speaking our favorite Irish poem, the first he had recited to me when he came home from the university. In it, Red Hugh O'Donnell, the greatest hero of the sixteenth century, addresses Ireland.

> *O my Dark Rosaleen*
>   *Do not sigh, do not weep!*
> *The priests are on the ocean green,*
>   *They march along the deep.*
> *There's wine from the royal Pope,*
>   *Upon the ocean green,*
> *And Spanish ale shall give you hope,*
>   *My Dark Rosaleen!*
>   *My own Rosaleen!*
> *Shall glad your heart, shall give you hope,*
> *Shall give you health, and help, and hope,*
>   *My Dark Rosaleen!*
> *Woe and pain, pain and woe,*
>   *Are my lot, night and noon,*
> *To see your bright face clouded so,*
>   *Like to the mournful moon.*
> *But yet will I rear your throne*
>   *Again in golden sheen;*
> *'Tis you shall reign, shall reign alone,*
>   *My Dark Rosaleen!*
>   *My own Rosaleen!*
> *'Tis you shall have the golden throne,*
> *'Tis you shall reign, and reign alone,*
>   *My Dark Rosaleen!*

I prayed that those noble words would take root in Dan McCaffrey's soul and lift his fight for Ireland above crass hope of gain or lure of profit. I believe for a while it did work a change in him. He felt the pull of his Irish blood. He asked me to recite the poem to him again the next day and wanted to know what happened to Red Hugh O'Donnell. "The British poisoned him," I said. "He went as an ambassador to seek help from Spain, and the British sent a secret agent there and poisoned him."

Instead of awakening Dan's anger, as I hoped it would, the story of Red Hugh's fate only seemed to make him sad. He began talking in a disconsolate way about the hard luck of being on the losing side in a war. I realized how little I knew about his American life and asked him to tell me the story.

"Like I said, my father left Ireland in 1831. He went to Boston, like most Irish at that time. But he hated the place. He called the Protestants 'the icicles of Yankeeland' and said they were worse than the English in Ireland. They despised Irish Catholics. While he was there, they burned a convent full of nuns. They called Irishmen 'white niggers' and never gave them work if they could help it.

"Dad saw there was no future in New England and went south. He ended up buildin' railroads in the Louisiana swamps, up to his neck in freezin' water, bitten by a million insects, never knowin' when some snake would finish him."

"I thought the Southerners had slaves for such heavy work," I said.

"You wouldn't risk a slave in them swamps. Slaves were too valuable. Worth a thousand dollars a head. An Irishman was worth nothin' but the five or six dollars you paid him each week. When he died you just buried him there in the swamp. A lot died. A lot came out like my dad, shakin' with malaria. He went north and laid more track into Tennessee. He broke down with malaria there. While he was sick he met my ma. Her people had come down the

Cumberland from Virginia when there was nothin' but Indians in the state.

"They got married along about 1840. Ma's people had some money, and Dad borrowed some to add to what he'd saved on the railroad and opened a tavern with another Irishman in a town named Pulaski about a hundred and fifty miles from Memphis. That's where I grew up."

"Tell me what's it like," I said.

"Beautiful country. Rollin' hills. Stands of trees along the river bottoms. Dad says he settled there because it reminded him of Ireland. And because he met an Irish beauty. Ma's maiden name was O'Gara. Our grass ain't as green as Ireland. Bluegrass, we call it. But it's rich soil, good pasture for cattle and horses. Dad started raisin' horses with the money he made from the tavern. Then he built a sawmill. Pretty soon he was close to the richest man in Pulaski. He got into politics with the Democrats and went to the legislature at Nashville. He decided he wanted me to be a gentleman. Wanted me to have a good education. So he sent me to the University of Virginia. I was there a year when the war started.

"Dad didn't see nothin' wrong with ownin' slaves. Most of his friends in the legislature were from West Tennessee, down around Memphis, where they owned 'em by the hundreds. He said he'd never seen a slave treated as bad as he'd seen the Irish treated in Boston. So he threw in with the Confederates and told me to do likewise in Virginia."

"So you were in it from the start."

"Right from Bull Run," he said. "One of General Stuart's cousins was in my class. He introduced me to him and I got a commission in his cavalry brigade. That's where I spent the war, in Virginia with Stuart. He was the bravest man and the finest officer I ever saw. For a while we had a good old time. The ladies couldn't do enough for us. General Stuart made sure we had the best of everything. We whacked the Yankees almost every time we felt like it. But they wouldn't quit. They kept findin' more men, no matter how many we killed or captured. Pretty soon they had officers, veterans, who knew how to maneuver cavalry as good as General Stuart. Our last fight was at Yellow Tavern, about six miles from Richmond. There were only four officers left in our regiment. The men and horses were half starved. The Yankees tore us apart, and one of their troopers killed General Stuart with a handgun. I carried him back to his tent. That was the saddest day of my life.

"The second saddest was the day I came home to Pulaski. I'd known what was happenin' in Tennessee. The state split up, the east end goin' with the Union, the west with the Confeds. In Middle Tennessee, where we were, people split off both ways. That made for a mean war, sometimes brothers from the same family goin' on opposite sides. Old friends turnin' enemies. But I never expected what I saw when I got off the train. Our tavern, our house, just heaps of burnt-out timbers. A Union mob'd done it, right after the Union Army come through, in 1862. Dad never told me. He figured I had enough trouble of my own. Then the Union politicians went to work on him. They dragged him in front of some court and convicted him of being a traitor and confiscated our horse farm, our sawmill, everything we owned. It broke Dad's spirit. He died just before the war ended. His friends had to bury him with borrowed money."

"Dear God, Dan, what you've been through," I said. "How did you come to the Fenians?"

"I didn't have a cent. A friend of Dad's sent me to John O'Neil, in Nashville. He was a Union officer, a cavalryman, runnin' a pension agency for the Yankee army and recruitin' Fenians on the side. He said I was just the sort of man they wanted and sent me to New York."

We were alone on the *Manhattan*'s bow as Dan told

me this story. My heart swelled with a great pity for him, as well as a kind of awe. He was only twenty-five years old, but he had seen more death and tasted more bitterness than most men of fifty. No wonder he dreamt of a great estate in Ireland if we were victorious. Life had raised him up and cast him down. Without the Fenians he would have to go back to where his father had begun, toiling at hard labor for a few dollars a day. How could I find fault with him when I compared my soft safe life with his perils and sufferings? I put my arms around him and vowed to love him more wholeheartedly.

"'Tis time surely for your luck to turn," I said. "And with it, Ireland's. You may be a good luck charm, without knowing it."

"You're the first piece of good luck I've had in a long time, Bess," he said. "In fact, you're too good to be true."

"I'm true as the oak of this deck," I said, stamping my foot on the solid wood. "Will you be?"

I said the words lightly, but my mind flashed to the broken promise to the woman at Priest's Leap. For a moment a darkness fell on his face, as if he sensed what I was thinking. But he only laughed and kissed me and said, "What do you think?"

Later that day, I climbed into the rigging to contemplate the sea from the crow's nest. For this kind of exercise, I wore my sailor's costume. High above the water, I gazed at the world's immensity and felt very small. I thought of Dan's story and brooded on how little we controlled our lives.

I was so absorbed, I scarcely noticed the arrival of my brother. He had a similar fondness for this perch. Dan, on the other hand, seldom joined me here. He disliked heights. They gave him "the creeps," he said, an American word that needed no translation.

"Are you going to marry him?" Michael said.

"If he asks me," I said.

"What if I ask him?"

"I'll have your head," I warned him. "I haven't gone through the grief of defying Father, for all my love of him, to discover another father in you. Contrary to your assumption, the mere fact that I'm female and you're male gives you no authority over me."

"He's not worthy of you, Bess. He has no education, no spirit but that of a mercenary."

"If you knew his life, you wouldn't be so quick to find fault," I said, and told him the story of Dan's past. It shamed him into temporary silence, but he refused to change his mind.

"Remember how the song ends, Bess," Michael said.

"What song?" I said, trying to pretend I had no idea what he was talking about.

" 'Donal Ogue,' " he said, and recited the final verse.

"For you took what's before me and what's behind me
You took east and west when you wouldn't mind me.
Sun and moon from my sky you've taken
And God as well or I'm much mistaken."

"It won't end that way," I said. "God won't let it."

How strange it was, that while I was sinning my soul and defying my father and the precepts of the Catholic Church, I remained convinced that I was doing a holy thing to risk my salvation to free Ireland. Revolutionaries are strange creatures, and Irish revolutionaries perhaps the strangest of all.

That night, Dan bought a bottle of John Jameson's from Captain O'Hickey and got drunk. It was the kind of drinking I had never seen before, a dark plunge into whiskey as a kind of oblivion, without laughter or pleasure. But it loosed his tongue to speak to me for the first time with his feelings. Even when he took me in his arms, he said little by way of endearment. He never used

the word "love." "You're a beauty, Bess," he would murmur. He let me do all the talking about love.

Now, as he reached the bottom of the bottle, he looked
at me and shook his head. "Go 'way, Bess. When we get
to New York, go 'way from me. I specialize in lost causes.
Always on the losin' side. This thing—Ireland—losin'.
There's nothin' there, Bess. No spirit. No hope."

"'Tis my cause more than yours," I said. "You can't
tell me to go away from it. Any more than you can tell
me to stop loving you."

"Lovin'—me?" He shook his head. "You keep sayin'
that. You don't know what you're talkin' about. I haven't
got a dime, Bess. Girl like you—can get anyone she
wants, almost."

"I've got the only one I want," I said, putting my arms
around him. His obsession with money, with his poverty,
both touched and appalled me.

At this moment bad fortune brought Michael into the
cabin. "Excuse me," he said with heavy sarcasm when
he saw my arms around Dan.

A lopsided grin on his face, Dan lurched to Michael
and threw his arm around him. "I'm tryin' to tell your
crazy sister to stop lovin' me. You agree?"

"Definitely," Michael said.

"Whaaat?" Dan said. "You jokin'?"

"I am not," Michael said, with a courage that was
close to madness, considering Dan's size and strength.
"I'd like to see you part. I think you're ill-matched."

The arm of friendship around Michael's shoulder suddenly became a vise of rage. Dan seized the back of the
collar of Michael's shirt and flung him across the cabin.
His head struck the wooden bulkhead with a sickening
crack. Dan lunged after him, his fist held high.

I caught his arm, crying, "He didn't mean it, Dan."

He shook me off as if I were a fly, but I dodged past him

and threw myself in front of Michael, who was crumpled against the wall, groaning and holding his head.

"Will you strike me first?" I said.

"What kind of a goddamn game are you two playin' with me?" Dan snarled.

For a moment I thought he might kill us both. I saw nothing but blind drunken hatred on his face. All trace of the buoyant, reckless warrior had vanished. He looked old, with his eyes squeezed and his mouth clenched; old or possessed of some evil spirit. I shuddered, remembering the curse the woman had laid on us at Priest's Leap.

"We're playing no game," I said. "Go to bed now, and tomorrow we'll laugh at it all. Michael spoke without thinking. It doesn't alter in the least my feeling for you."

Two lies in one breath, I thought. But Dan lowered his fist, seized his bottle, and lurched out of the cabin onto the dark deck. I put Michael to bed with a cold cloth on his forehead and the next day forced him to shake hands with Dan. Neither displayed much enthusiasm for the gesture, but it was done in a manly way on both sides. I hoped that I had buried the enmity. It was just as well that I did not know it was a bitter seed and burying it meant only a later and more terrible harvest.

The next day, we sighted several ships on the southern passage to the West Indies. Captain O'Hickey said it meant that we were drawing near New York. Dan began preparing a report of what he had found in his journey through Ireland. There was not much good news in it. Although the Fenians had been secretly organizing for three or four years, they did not have more than ten thousand members. The movement was built around the local circles led by a center. Many circles had lost membership recently. In some cases, the center himself had quit. Few of the circles had guns. When they met, they spent most of their time talking about revolution and little of it in drilling. What worried Dan most was the lack of strength in the countryside. The active circles were in cities like Limerick and Dublin. But Ireland was a country of villages. Most of the people lived upon the land. Dan lamented the crushed and fearful state of the peasantry, almost all of them terrified at the thought of arousing the landlord's wrath.

"I remember the stories my father told me about Mayo—the Molly Maguires had the whole county paralyzed," Dan said. "Anyone who evicted a farmer or arrested a man for debt wound up with his throat cut or his cattle maimed. What happened to them?"

"They're all in America," Michael said. "Or in Australia or Canada. I've heard my father talk of the Mollies. They were the poorest of the poor, fellows with nothing to lose. Those that didn't die in the great famine of '48 fled the country."

"Mollies, Ribbonmen, Lady Clares, Whiteboys," Captain O'Hickey said. "They had different names in the different counties. But they weren't revolutionaries. All they thought to do was protect their own little bit of soil."

"With all due respect for your father," Michael said to Dan, "I think he was exaggerating the Mollies. Distance and time tend to expand the imagination at the expense of the memory. You can't blame the peasantry. They see no leaders but the parish priest, whose bishop tells him to damn all revolutionaries, and men like my father, who have taken the King's shilling, in his case from honest conviction."

Far from lending enchantment, the more we looked at Ireland from a distance, the more difficult our task became. We were in far from sanguine spirits as we approached the American coast.

Soon after the continent became a brown blur on the

horizon, we were hailed by a steam tug. "*Manhattan* ahoy," shouted a man in the bow, wearing a gaudy checked suit. "Are you the ship with the Fenians aboard?"

"What business is it of yours?" boomed Captain O'Hickey through his trumpet.

"I'm Pickens of the *Herald*," was the answer. "Let me come aboard. I'm here to get their story."

Captain O'Hickey came about as promptly as if Pickens had fired a shot across our bow. A rope ladder was flung down. Pickens leaped from the tug with the agility of a monkey and scrambled to the deck. He had a small, narrow face that seemed as innocent as a child's until you noticed his eyes. They flickered like the eyes of a bird, up, down, around, missing nothing.

"George Pickens is the name, folks," he said "I'm here by order of my editor, James Gordon Bennett. I've been cruising back and forth every day for a week to get your story. Where's the Fenian girl? This must be her, unless they're making sailors a lot different from the standard model these days."

He gazed at me for a moment, then made a smacking sound with his lips, as if he were contemplating a good dinner. "I don't know about your friends, but we're going to make you famous."

We were totally amazed. "How do you know anything about us?" Michael asked.

"The British papers wrote you up—or down, to be more exact. They arrived in New York by steamship ten days ago. We want exclusive rights to your story. How much is it worth to you?"

"Worth?" I said dazedly. "What do you mean?"

"I'll give you a hundred dollars each now and another hundred tomorrow if you promise to refuse to talk to any other reporter for twenty-four hours."

"That's twenty pounds," Michael said. It was a fortune

in Ireland, more money than most farmers could clear in a year.

"A hundred dollars U.S. currency, greenbacks of Uncle Sam," Pickens said. He yanked a wad of money out of his pocket and began to peel off bills.

"It's a deal," Dan McCaffrey said, and held out his hand. Pickens counted three bills, each worth a hundred dollars, into it. He turned to O'Hickey and handed him an identical bill. "I'd appreciate it, Captain, if you ignored any other ship that hailed you. These people are the talk of New York. A lot of other reporters will be looking for them."

We went into the main cabin, and Pickens asked us dozens of questions about our escape from Ireland. We told him the truth, and he was shocked by some of it. "The honest farmer betrayed you? I thought Ireland was united to a man behind the Fenians," he said.

He also seemed disappointed that neither Michael nor I had shot anyone. "You're sure you didn't use Dan's gun, especially in the fight on the cliff?" Pickens asked.

"Why should we do something so foolish? I've never fired a gun in my life," I said. "Our lives depended on Dan making every bullet count."

"Ireland needs a Joan of Arc," he said. "You could be it."

I was too astonished to answer him. He asked Dan what he thought of the Fenians' chances of success in Ireland. Dan told him the dolorous truth. Again Pickens was annoyed. "Only ten thousand Fenians in Ireland? Over here they're talking about two hundred thousand."

Pickens took me to the bow and sketched me on a pad he carried in his coat, reminded us of his promise to pay another three hundred dollars if we kept silent, and hailed his steam tug, which had been plowing alongside us while we talked. The moment he stepped aboard, the tug's engines began pounding mightily; smoke gushed from its funnel, and it was soon far ahead of us on the way to New York harbor. We watched him go, not quite able to believe our good fortune, as it seemed to us then.

"Three hundred dollars," Dan said, looking at the bills in his hand. "That's a good day's pay."

"Don't forget two hundred belongs to us," Michael said.

With icy contempt, Dan handed him one of the bills. He started to give me the other one, but I told him to keep it. Half jokingly, I remarked that they might not be real. I found it hard to believe Pickens's story that we were the talk of New York.

Captain O'Hickey was inclined to believe him. He said that the *Herald* was the biggest newspaper in the country. Its support could mean great things for the Fenians. The government of the United States trembled when the *Herald* attacked it. Michael and I found these ideas almost incomprehensible. Newspapers in Ireland attacked the government only at the risk of their existence. The idea of a newspaper having power was strange to us.

By midday we were passing the Narrows, the headland that guards New York's great bay. We paused there to let two quarantine officers board us. They were both Irish and asked in thick country brogues to see "the Fenian girl." I was duly exhibited to them, to my growing bewilderment. The formalities of quarantine and inspection were brief. The *Manhattan* was a small ship, and we were the only passengers. Within the hour we got under way again for the inner harbor. Soon the city of New York was open to our view.

It looked immense, squatting there on its island with the broad shining river streaming past. A thin cloud of light gray smoke hung above it, from burning coal that drove machinery in the factories. In winter, when furnaces consumed coal by the ton to keep the citizens' houses warm, the cloud was often much thicker, Captain O'Hickey said.

Suddenly, from a round fort on an island at the foot of the city, a cannon boomed. For the first time we noticed that there were a dozen boats cruising back and forth near the fort. Now they wheeled and headed for us. Most of them were sloops under sail. One or two had steam engines. As they drew closer, we saw that they were flying green flags, decorated with gold harps and sunbursts. Their decks were lined with men, many of whom fired pistols and rifles in the air. Pickens was right. We were being greeted like conquering heroes.

Truth vs. Publicity

Several boats ran alongside the *Manhattan,* and voices shouted: "I'm Wiley of the *Tribune.* I'm Case of the *Sun.* I'm Jones of the *World.*" But Captain O'Hickey, true to the promise that he had made to reporter Pickens, ignored the other newshounds and made steadily for his regular berth at Halsey's Wharf in the East River. There, as the ship was nudged against the pilings by a waiting tug, we encountered another amazing scene. The wharf and the street beyond it were crowded with cheering people waving green flags. A brass band was booming out "The Wearing of the Green." I found myself wishing mightily that I had something to wear besides my peasant rags.

On hand to greet us were no less than the mayor of New York, the Honorable C. Godfrey Gunther, a barrel-shaped German, and sundry other politicians. With them were numerous Fenians, led by John O'Mahoney, a burly, deep-browed man with a full graying beard and long hair of the same color. The mayor made a speech, in which he claimed that all New York was waiting to welcome us. We were the vanguard of the Irish army of liberation that would soon rise to plant the green flag over an Ireland as free and prosperous as the United States of America. Although he was not of Irish blood, the mayor said, he was ready to enlist in that army and carry a musket in the ranks.

I thought the mayor was vastly misinformed to call three fugitives an army of liberation. I was even more amazed to hear O'Mahoney say the same thing in a briefer speech. He added that the Irish were deeply gratified by the encouragement they were receiving from their "American brethren" to fight England, the enemy of both nations. We were then shepherded down the wharf to a carriage waiting in the street. All around us the immense crowd cheered, and the band blared out "The Wearing of the Green."

As we walked, a tall, very well-dressed man wearing a high black hat fell in step with me. "Your sister Annie sends her love and hopes to see you soon," he said.

"Where is she?" I said, much excited.

"She lives at the Metropolitan Hotel. You may go see her there anytime."

"What is your name?" I asked.

"Connolly," he said. "Dick Connolly. I'm Annie's closest—friend."

He smiled in a knowing way, as if he expected me to understand something in the way he paused before saying "friend." I understood nothing and simply thanked him. "I'll come see her as soon as I can," I said.

"By all means do—soon. You're famous, you know. We want to help you make the most of it."

At the carriage, reporters rushed upon us from all sides, shouting questions. O'Mahoney and the other Fenians shoved them away and said they would have to wait until we made our official report to the Fenian government. In

the carriage, the first thing we heard from the Fenians was
a denunciation of Mayor Gunther as a vote grabber. He
was thinking about running for reelection, even though the
Democrats no longer had any use for him, and he had
come down to welcome us to improve his chances with
Irish voters.

"What did that fellow Connolly want with you, my
girl?" John O'Mahoney said. He had a rough, blunt way
of speaking that reminded me of my father.

"He was telling me where I could find my sister. She
lives in New York."

"Where?"

"At the Metropolitan Hotel."

"Not the best address," said the man sitting next to
O'Mahoney. He introduced himself as Patrick J. Meehan, owner of the *Irish-American,* the city's leading Irish
newspaper. He was short and dapper, with brown hair
slicked tightly on his wide head. Beside him sat a bigger
man with a thick black handlebar mustache. He was introduced as Colonel William Roberts.

"Why isn't it a good address?" I said.

"Never mind, my dear," O'Mahoney said. "As a newspaperman, Mr. Meehan is naturally malicious. I prefer to
think the best of every man and woman until I find out
the contrary. For now let us celebrate your safe arrival."

"The devil with celebrations," replied Meehan. "I
want an interview for my paper. I want it now."

"I don't see how we can do that," Michael said. "We
promised the reporter from the *Herald,* Mr. Pickens, that
we'd give no interviews to anyone for twenty-four hours."

"Goddamn it," snarled Meehan, "where did you see
him?"

We told him and got even worse cursing for a reply. "I
suppose he paid you for it?"

We admitted as much, and Meehan instantly ordered
us to hand over the money to the Fenian treasury. O'Ma-

honey murmured that this was not necessary, but he accepted our cash. Colonel Roberts took from his pocket a wad of bills even larger than the one flashed by Pickens, and handed us a hundred dollars each to spend as we pleased. O'Mahoney said that, too, was unnecessary; we were agents of the Fenian government and would have all the money we needed. Colonel Roberts ignored O'Mahoney and said the money was a gift from him, to express his appreciation of our services. O'Mahoney muttered disagreeably into his beard but made no further objection.

Meehan insisted on interviewing us for his paper. Dan and Michael stuck to our bargain with Pickens and refused to tell him a thing. I let the men do the arguing while I studied the sights of New York. We were moving into the crowded part of the city. All around us swarmed a mass of hurrying people, dressed in the wildest variety of costumes, from well-groomed gentlemen in frock coats and high hats to ragged workmen. On almost every street corner, little girls stood barefoot, crying out the hope that someone would buy some hot corn from them. Around them four or five boys waved newspapers and screeched something about the trial of "the Southern conspirators."

I looked worriedly at Dan and asked if the government was trying the rebel Southerners for treason. Everyone laughed. "No," O'Mahoney said. "Just the fools who assassinated Lincoln."

Soon the street was perfectly jammed with carriages and wagons. Through our open window came a dreadful smell, a mixture of manure and a hundred other species of decay. The day was warm, and the heat seemed to redouble the odor. Though I had grown up on a farm and knew the smells of the barnyard intimately, I had never inhaled anything like this stench. I said as much to Colonel Roberts, who laughed and said I would get used to it. He no longer

even noticed it: O'Mahoney said he would never get used
to it. He'd grown up breathing Ireland's sweet air, he said
with a sad smile, and the hope of breathing it again was the
chief reason he remained a revolutionary.

After creeping along for a half hour we reached Broadway, where our progress stopped entirely. The street was
packed not only with carriages and wagons but with great
long omnibuses drawn on metal rails by teams of horses.
Nothing moved except the pedestrians on the sidewalks.
The air was full of the cracking of whips and neighs of
horses and the profane shouts of drivers. Our hosts were
unperturbed. They said such a pace was normal for New
York at this hour, when many offices and factories quit
for the day and ladies who had completed their shopping
were going home.

I was content to enjoy the view. Broadway was the one
street in America I had heard about—as had almost
everyone around the globe. My first impression was of a
totally artificial world of bricks and mortar. There was
not a tree or a blade of grass in sight. On either side,
huge stone buildings confronted each other. A single
person standing in front of one of these monsters would
have been dwarfed, but this impression was lost in the
mass of the crowd. Up and down both sides of the street
they rushed, at a pace that left me bewildered.

Mr. Roberts pointed out Alexander Stewart's palatial department store, which we could see a block or two above
us, opposite City Hall Park. It was fronted with cream-
colored marble. Roberts discoursed on the tremendous display windows, the first of their kind in the world, over
twelve feet long and seven feet high. He recited to us other
startling facts—the store employed three hundred sales-
man and clerks, twice as many people as lived in our little
village in Ireland. Seven million dollars changed hands
within those marble walls each year.

Eventually we began to creep along once more and finally reached our destination as dusk descended. Sweeney's Hotel was to be our home. A huge Fenian flag flew from a staff on the roof. The lobby was crowded with cheering, smiling Irish, shouting, "God bless you! Up the Republic! Three cheers for Ireland!" Our host, Mr. Sweeney, a small, excitable man with an odd bend to his nose, led us to the elevator. It was our first experience with one of these magical contraptions, and Michael and I were suitably amazed by its silent rise to our rooms on the fourth floor. The Irish-Americans were delighted by our exclamations. Apparently we greenhorns were performing exactly as expected.

In our suite, we found a dozen other Fenian leaders waiting, with their wives. I was both pleased and embarrassed to see these ladies, all elegantly dressed in the latest fashion. Mrs. Roberts, a large, big-bosomed woman of about forty, which I guessed to be her husband's age as well, took charge of me. "If we're to display this Irish beauty to her best advantage," she said, "we can't let her stay another moment in these peasant rags."

With a smile she told me that the ladies had brought along a selection of their own wardrobes, which they were determined to share with me until I was able to buy some clothes of my own. Not being sure of my size, they had even brought along a sewing machine, which they had set up in an adjoining room. With that declaration, the women swept me away with them, leaving the men to enjoy the numerous bottles of champagne that they were busy opening.

These women were as strange and exotic to me as so many Chinese. They were elaborately dressed, with innumerable ruffles and bows on sleeves and skirts, and fingers glittering with rings. Most amazing were their huge skirts, which were stiffened with great iron hoops. These were utterly unknown in the Irish countryside. I also was puzzled by the stiff way all the ladies moved, their upper bodies rigid, like soldiers on parade. I soon discovered the rigidity was caused by corsets laced so tight the wearer was in constant danger of suffocation. On their cheeks were bright patches of rouge against a deathly white background of powder. Most remarkable to me was their hair, piled in intricate coifs and curls that stayed miraculously in place and had a bright pleasing sheen.

They could not have been nicer to me. In fact, their sympathy was extravagant. "Oh, my dear," cried Mrs. Meehan, the pretty red-haired wife of the owner of the *Irish-American*, "how did you ever survive on that ship for weeks without a woman to talk to?"

"I don't know, I think I enjoyed having two dozen men all to myself," I said.

"Now, now," said Mrs. Roberts, "even though we're among friends, let us not be risqué."

With this remark, I caught a glimpse of the delicate line I would have to walk with Fenian women. They were utterly ignorant of the hard, rough world in which their men moved. I turned to outfitting myself. To my delight, Mrs. Meehan's dresses fit me almost exactly. They only needed a little tucking around the waist, which we were able to do quickly, with a needle and thread. The sewing machine went unused, but they gave me a demonstration of it anyway, as one of the wonders of the age, freeing women in America from endless hours of drudgery.

While I dressed, they plied me with artless questions about my adventures in Ireland. Was it true, they asked, that I had stabbed a British policeman to death when he was about to molest me? Was that why I'd had to flee with Dan's help?

They looked disappointed when I denied it and added that there were no British policemen in Ireland, they were all Irish. But wasn't there a reign of terror raging in

Ireland? That is what they heard. No woman was safe from the lust of the local landlord or his bailiff. Again, I disappointed them by knowing nothing of such things. Our landlord, Lord Gort, was in his seventies and had never shown an interest in Irish women. He spent most of his time in London. "Ireland's chief woe," I said, "is the landlords' lust for money. It's what drives so many poor to join their fellow exiles in England, America, and Australia."

"Exiles?" said Mrs. Roberts. "My dear, we're not exiles. We're *Americans,* as proud of that fact as any descendant of the Pilgrims. Those of us who have made their *fortunes,* here in America, like my husband, have no interest in returning to Ireland. We merely want to right a great wrong."

The other ladies all nodded vigorously. One of them added that as long as Ireland was beneath the British heel, it made the Irish in America feel ashamed of their names and blood. It was why so many Irish changed their names to English ones. Casey to Case, Harrigan to Harrison. Ireland's degradation was the reason so many Irish in this country were treated badly. This was all new and startling doctrine to me, awakening once more my sense of a gulf between the Irish and the Irish-Americans.

But I had no time to worry about that now. I was busy putting on petticoats and a gray taffeta dress complete with a hoop skirt. "How do I look?" I asked. Everyone assured me I looked lovely. My only unhappiness was the whalebone corset, which threatened to strangle me. I thought it was superfluous for me, though it was no doubt vital to keep some figures in place. But Mrs. Roberts insisted I had to get used to it. Every fashionable woman wore one, no matter what her age.

When we returned to the sitting room of our suite, the champagne was flowing, but Patrick Meehan was looking more disgruntled than ever. Everyone was standing in groups of two and three, reading newspapers. "The *Herald* put out an extra for you," Meehan growled. "Listen."

He led me to the window. Above the noise of the traffic on Broadway rose a newsboy's cry. "*Read about the Fenian girl!*"

"What does it say?" I gasped, my head beginning to spin with the upheaval of the day.

Michael handed me a copy of the paper. I saw myself sketched on the edge of the cliff at Priest's Leap. It was a fairly good likeness of me. Pickens had gotten that much from his shipboard visit. But I was aiming a revolver at a charging British soldier, shooting him at point-blank range while Dan and Michael cowered behind me on the precipice. It was hard to tell which was Dan, but one of the men was wounded and was being carried by the other man. This apparently explained why I was wielding the revolver.

Pickens's story was a romance. It told how I had grown angry at defending my virtue against the constant assaults of the British soldiers stationed in my village and had taken a vow to strike a blow for Ireland. Secretly I had sworn the Fenian oath, which I found in my brother's room, and waited my chance. When Dan McCaffrey was captured by the British, I had gone to the jail, shot the sentry, and freed him. My brother, Michael, had joined us, and together we had assisted the battered victim of British injustice—an American citizen tortured by the English in utter indifference to his rights—to flee the country. The climax was a desperate struggle on the cliff while the *Manhattan*'s boat waited to carry us to freedom. Not one but six British mercenaries had fallen before my deadly aim.

"Gentlemen," I said, flinging the paper aside. "None of that is true. I'm no more a heroine than—than your wives here. But there is a hero in this room. He stands there."

I pointed to Dan McCaffrey.

"I saw him—and my brother will attest to it—I saw him fight a dozen, then a hundred men, singlehanded. We told this reporter the truth. Why didn't he print it?"

"Because we've decided it's better policy to make you the heroine, my dear," John O'Mahoney said. "Major Mc-Caffrey needs no public adulation. It must be enough for him to know we appreciate his courage. But he's had the misfortune to fight on the losing side in the civil war just ended. It will be hard to make a hero of any Confederate officer for a long time to come. But you, my dear, with your beauty, your grace, your poise—you're a dream come true for us. You can portray Ireland both suffering and heroic."

"Exactly," said Patrick Meehan. "Exactly, Mr. Head Center. But where the hell do you get off giving her story to the *Herald*? It was supposed to be my story."

"The *Herald* is the most important paper in the country. It has a circulation ten times as large as the *Irish-American*'s," John O'Mahoney said.

"Who authorized you to do that? Did you confer with any of the council?" Meehan cried.

"I'm not under obligation to confer with the council on every small decision," O'Mahoney said.

"You will be from now on," Meehan said.

"Now lads, now lads," Colonel Roberts said. "This is supposed to be a celebration. We've won a victory over the British with this story, as important as the American triumph at Trenton in the Revolution."

"Colonel Roberts is right," O'Mahoney said. "Let's forget our quarrels until tomorrow." He raised a glass of champagne. "Here's to our Irish heroine."

Defiantly, I raised my glass to Dan McCaffrey. "Here's to my Irish-American hero."

After several more glasses of champagne, we descended to Sweeney's dining room, and I encountered my first American dinner. I never saw so much food set on one table in my life, nor such eating of it. Mrs. Roberts attacked an entire roast duck and demolished it to a few fragments. Her husband had steak, a veal chop, a lamb chop, and a battalion of side dishes ranging from vegetables to soup. Mr. Sweeney insisted we refugees should begin with gumbo filé, which he said was the favorite dish of General Winfield Scott, the conqueror of Mexico. It consisted of thirty or forty oysters with their accompanying liquor, cooked in powdered sassafras leaves within the gut of a boiled chicken. It was so rich, I could not eat a bite of anything else, which caused all the Irish-Americans to remark that my stomach must have shrunk from my years of starvation in Ireland. I replied that this was an insult to my father's reputation as a farmer, but no one paid me the slightest attention.

We returned to our rooms, Dan and Michael groaning like women in childbirth from the food they had stuffed down their gullets. John O'Mahoney came with us. He sat down in the parlor of our suite and talked to us like a father to his children. He told us the story of his life—how he had been deceived into committing himself to the Revolution of 1848 and found himself virtually alone in the field against the whole might of Great Britain. He became a fugitive, then an exile, and he vowed that the next time Ireland would have a thorough revolution or none at all. He would never deceive others as he had been deceived into risking their all without a united national front to sustain them.

"Yet you see me here in America, practicing deception. I can see the question on your young faces. You're asking, is this old man a double hypocrite or a fool? My only answer is the peculiarity of our situation here in

America. Our movement lives on American money. But the money is not forthcoming unless there is hope—dramatic evidence offered that Ireland is ready to revolt. So I must ask you not only to forgive me for the deception but to join me in it, for the sake of the cause."

He told me I had to be ready to sustain my role as the Irish heroine that Pickens depicted. Dan McCaffrey must teach me how to shoot a gun. "You must be ready to tour the country giving demonstrations of your prowess, to raise the money we need," he said.

He also talked frankly to us about the divisions within the movement. He was being criticized by Colonel Roberts and Patrick Meehan, who styled themselves "the men of action." They wanted to do something quickly, while the enthusiasm of the Irish-Americans was high. O'Mahoney insisted that it was wiser to wait and begin the fight only when we were reasonably sure of success.

We thanked him for his candor, and I told him that I was ready to do anything he asked of me. He kissed me on the cheek and said my story—the true one—had renewed his faith in the cause. Men with Dan McCaffrey's courage were what Ireland needed most of all. Dan reminded him of those lines from a favorite poem.

> "Yet trust me friends, dear Ireland's strength, her
>   truest strength is still
> The rough and ready roving boys like Rory of the
>   Hill."

The Men of Action Take Charge

Head Center O'Mahoney left us in an overfed, disillusioned daze. We were revolutionists, but we were also actors; we were conspirators both against England and against Irish-Americans who were supposed to be our shock troops. This was only the beginning of my American discoveries.

The next morning reporters swarmed to see us. Dan and Michael were ignored. They wanted to talk to no one but the Fenian girl. Patrick Meehan insisted that his man, a scrawny little redheaded fellow named Mike Hanrahan, be seen first. Hanrahan wore a green-and-white checked suit and a tilted derby and had a dead cigar in one corner of his mouth. His puckish face had the wisdom and not a little of the weariness of the world on it. He listened with barely concealed boredom as I labored through the tale Pickens had constructed for me.

"Do you expect anyone to believe that story when it's plain you don't believe it yourself?" Hanrahan said.

I almost burst into tears. "Ah," Hanrahan said. "You don't like being a professional liar?"

"No," I said.

"You must see yourself as an actress and the whole thing as a performance. All the world's a stage, remember? Fate has handed you a juicy part. 'Tis up to you to play it well."

"I'll try," I said halfheartedly.

"You'll do more than try, you'll succeed," he said. "Because you have Red Mike Hanrahan as your director and coach. Now. You can't drone out your tale. You must *live* it. You must take each of these penpushers with you, from the first line to the last. Those blue eyes of yours must flash with anger, defiance. Those rosy lips must tremble with fear and anguish, curl with scorn. Believe me, Bess, you'll charm them out of their socks. Now let's have a rehearsal."

For a good hour, while other reporters growled and grumbled outside, Red Mike put me through my lying paces. He pointed to holes in my story and gave me answers to probable questions. Where had I learned to fire a pistol? I told of stealing my father's gun and retreating to a wooded glade in company with my brother. How did I feel about killing a man? A pause. My eyes grew stormy, my brow furrowed. If he was a British soldier, I did it without a qualm. Ghengis Khan could not have sounded more bloodthirsty.

At last, the other reporters were admitted, and I performed under Red Mike's approving gaze. There was not a single hostile question. I answered the friendly ones, all anticipated by Mike, without a blink of hesitation. This prepared them to swallow my really gorgeous lying about the Fenian legions in Ireland. They were a host, waiting only for arms and ammunition from America. Given these, they would rise like an irristible tide and sweep the British into the sea. There were Fenians everywhere, in the schools, the army, the constabulary, even the priesthood. The reporters believed every word of it and it was in the newspapers the next day.

In spite of Red Mike Hanrahan's clever reasoning, I found myself inwardly sickened when I read my lies in print. It was demoralizing to see them embellished by even more fantastic lies from the imaginations of the reporters. One had me dueling saber to saber with a British cavalryman. There was simply no absurdity to which they would not stoop, especially when it made a good illustration. I grew to wonder what purpose was served by the amazing number of American newspapers, beyond the entertainment of their readers.

The next day was absorbed by Mrs. Roberts and Mrs. Meehan, who took me shopping for a wardrobe. Most of this we acquired in A. T. Stewart's new uptown store, at Astor Place. I was properly amazed at the dimensions of the building. At its center was a vast arcade over a hundred feet high, with a glass roof through which the sun streamed. Surrounding it on all sides were six tiers of counters and shops, each of which specialized in selling a certain item, such as shawls.

It was a vertical village within the city, in which all the beauties of the world of cloth seemed assembled. I could not believe the endless variety of colors, weaves, fabrics. Gloves, hats, jewelry, stockings, everything a woman needed to become a bird of paradise was there, with the prices clearly marked. I was staggered by the lavishness with which Mrs. Roberts laid out money. A dozen pairs of stockings when a half dozen would have been ample. Material for a half dozen summer and a half dozen winter dresses, an exquisite fur-lined damask cloak and a silk pelisse, two pairs of unbelievably soft black kid boots. We stopped in a notion shop and bought rouge, powder, and macassar oil for my hair and fragrant soaps for the bath. It all must have cost several hundred dollars, but Mrs. Roberts never ceased handing out the greenbacks. When I wondered if there was no end to them, she laughed and said it was all being paid for by the Fenian treasury.

Back in the hotel, the ladies showed me how to apply the macassar oil to my hair, to get the sheen that I noticed and envied last night. A seamstress was summoned from one of the side streets off Broadway, a smiling gray-haired Irishwoman who took my measurements and myriad instructions from Mrs. Roberts and departed with the cloth we had bought at Stewart's.

A short time later, Dan and Michael arrived with Red Mike Hanrahan. My fellow refugees were wearing ready-made clothes, which they had bought at a store not far from the hotel. They did not fit too well, but both considered it a marvel that you could walk into a store and find shirts, coats, and suits, all sewn together and ready to wear. Mike Hanrahan said the manufacturer was a man who had made uniforms for the Union Army during the war. "I warned these lads that their pants may split up the back as mine did at Bull Run. The crook never made an honest garment for a soldier in the whole war, and I can't believe he's starting now. Shoddy was his middle name, the thieving Yankee swine."

"I told Mike maybe somethin' else made his pants split at Bull Run, like runnin' too fast," Dan said.

"You Confederate blackguard, do you dare to insult the honor of the Fighting 69th?" Mike said. "Defend yourself now."

He began dancing around Dan like a terrier around a mastiff. Dan stood with his hands on his hips. Mike hurled a punch, which struck Dan in the chest. "Jesus God, it's broke," Mike cried, stumbling back, clutching his fist. "The man's made of metal."

I laughed heartily, but Mrs. Roberts did not approve of such disorderly conduct. "I hope you took them to my husband's tailor," she said. "To make sure they will be *properly* dressed."

"We spent a good two hours there," Mike said. "The man serves the best Irish whiskey in New York while you wait. About this time of day, though, he has trouble threading a needle."

Mike gave a funny imitation of a drunken tailor trying to sew on a button. This time he drew a smile from Mrs. Roberts, and Mrs. Meehan almost died laughing. Dan meanwhile was ordering champagne sent up. We were soon esconced in our sitting room like royalty, enjoying vintage Moët & Chandon.

Looking back on those first days in America, I can

only lament how childishly greedy we were. We thought there was no bottom to the Fenian treasury. We never stopped to ask where the money was coming from. Red Mike Hanrahan was telling us about his misadventures in the Civil War when a visitor arrived to disturb our complacency.

There was a knock on the door. Michael opened it and backed away, temporarily speechless. A husky, solemn man in a black cassock edged with red strode into the room. On his breast glowed a small gold crucifix. He had the youngest, most innocent-looking face I had ever seen on a man. Although he was in his middle years, he seemed to have passed through the world without a taint of age or corruption, except for a strange patina of sorrow in his eyes. It made him look like he was on the verge of tears.

"Archbishop McCloskey," gasped Mrs. Roberts. She struggled to her feet, spilling champagne down her front, and fluttered across the room to kneel before the archbishop and kiss his ring. Mrs. Meehan swiftly imitated her. "I am Mrs. William Roberts," she said. "My husband is Colonel William Roberts."

"I know who he is," McCloskey said in a mild gentle voice. "I'm looking for the Fenian girl and her friends."

"You've found them," I said, remaining stubbornly in my seat. I had never met a bishop before in my life, except at the altar rail when I received my confirmation, and I found myself disliking intensely the idea of kneeling before him to kiss his ring.

"Hanrahan of the *Irish-American*," Mike said. He bobbed to one knee and kissed the extended ring.

"Michael Fitzmaurice," Michael said, and repeated the obeisance.

"Dan McCaffrey," Dan said, sticking out his hand. The archbishop shook it.

"Are you a Catholic, my dear girl?" the archbishop said, fixing his sad eyes on me.

"I was raised one," I said.

"Then you must know that you're committing a serious sin, consorting with Fenians and recommending others to take the Fenian oath."

"My conscience does not admit to that sin, my lord," I said, calling him by the name we gave bishops in Ireland.

"No, I suppose not," he said in his mournful way. "I'm not a lord, like bishops in Ireland. Over here, we're merely called bishops. As Mr. Hanrahan will tell you, we're sometimes called much worse. By our fellow Catholics. Fellow Irish."

Mike looked uncomfortable. "It's a free country, Bishop," he said. "Besides, most of those compliments were paid to your beloved predecessor, as you insist on calling him."

"He means Archbishop John Hughes. He died last year. Have you heard of him?" McCloskey asked, sitting down opposite me.

"I met him when he visited Dublin in 1863," Michael said. "He talked to a group of us students. He sounded more like a revolutionary than anyone we had heard in Ireland."

Archbishop McCloskey nodded and smiled ruefully. "He was speaking to you as Irishmen, not Americans. He was a very emotional man. He was born in Ulster. He knew what British oppression was like, firsthand. I can't make that claim. I was born in this country. I can only tell you why I think the Fenians don't belong in America. You're in a different country now, with its own destiny—a great one, I hope and pray. But you'll soon find out that the Irish are not wanted here. It's a Protestant country."

"You can stick a pin in that," Mike Hanrahan said.

"Before the Civil War, there was a political party called the Know Nothings, who were determined to drive us out of American life. They beat nuns and priests on the street. They elected hundreds of candidates to state legislatures and Congress to pass laws against us. Here in New York, Archbishop Hughes had to station three thousand armed men in our churches on election night," McCloskey continued in his mournful, almost apologetic way. "To overcome this kind of prejudice is not easy. We have to teach our people to save their money, to control their fondness for liquor, to work hard. The Fenians are distracting everyone with an impossible dream, a shortcut, the idea that freeing Ireland will give us instant respectability. This champagne you're drinking. Do you realize it's been paid for by poor servant girls and day laborers who might have given us the money to build schools and educate priests to get the next generation out of slums like the Sixth Ward?"

"Maybe there would be no slums, or exiles in them, if Ireland were free," Michael said.

"That's very good revolutionary rhetoric," McCloskey said. "But what does it really mean? Ireland isn't free, and there are slums. These are the realities we must face. Do you remember what Archbishop Hughes said to your fellow Irish revolutionaries in Dublin? If you undertake a revolution and have not measured your strength so you know you have at least a chance to win it, you commit a great crime. I believe that, too. I'll tell you what else I believe—or at least fear: that the Fenians will destroy the respect that the Irish have won here in America for the fighting they did in the war. The Irishmen who died in Union blue wiped out the disgrace of the Revolution of 1848. You can't believe how the Americans laughed at us over here for that fiasco. A revolution that began and ended with a skirmish in a cabbage patch. Archbishop Hughes could barely talk about it without weeping."

Michael was more and more shaken by this man. So was I. He was so different from our priests in Ireland. He sat there in the chair, talking to us as equals. In Ireland priests—and above all bishops—did not converse. They orated. They issued pronouncements. They had none of this man's gentleness, nor his sadness. All was fierce discipline and warnings of hellfire.

"Let me ask you this, Bishop," Red Mike Hanrahan said, jollity gone from his voice. "Here's an Irishman who risked his life to make the South free." He clapped his arm around Dan McCaffrey. "To give her the right to escape the tyranny of the North, of the icicles of Yankeeland, just as Ireland seeks to be free from England. What do you say to him?"

"That he fought well for a bad cause," McCloskey said. "You and I don't agree, Mike, and you'll no doubt attack me as you attacked John Hughes. But the argument doesn't work. Ireland is a separate country. The South never was. You're mixing things up, Mike. You can't decide whether you're an Irishman or an American."

"I'm a man opposed to tyranny wherever I see it," Mike said. "And I welcome this man, this so-called traitor, by your lights, this rebel, as a Fenian brother. If you and your clerical kind were true men, instead of truckling to every government that throws you a crumb of power, you'd have stopped Irishmen from raising a finger to help the North, and the South would be free today, ready to support Ireland's cause."

"That's moonshine and you know it, Mike," McCloskey said. "Who was the South's chief ally? England."

My head was starting to ache. I was finding out how many twists and turns history had, and how ready emotional men like Mike were to overlook them. I was also discovering how many savage feuds and arguments existed among the American Irish as well as between them and the Americans. Perhaps Archbishop McCloskey saw some of this confusion and dismay on my face. He again turned his attention to me.

"Mike and I are old antagonists. But I'm here as your friend, my dear girl. I dread the thought of what may happen to you if you persist in playing the part they've assigned you. They'll drag you into their dirty politics and use you and then discard you."

"No one's goin' to discard her, Bishop, long as I'm around," Dan said.

Everyone, including Archbishop McCloskey, knew what those words meant. For me they were a declaration and a summons. I fought the pull of guilt and fear, the recognition of genuine caring that drew me to this sad-eyed, sad-voiced man with the crucifix on his breast. I told myself that once and for all I was joining those ancient Irish heroines who relied on nothing but their warrior lovers' strength.

"I appreciate your concern for me, my lord—I mean, Bishop," I stumbled, "but I must go the way my soul—my Irish soul—calls me."

The archbishop sighed. "All right," he said. "But if you ever need help, remember, I'm your friend, no matter what happens."

He departed as quietly as he came, leaving us in a most uneasy frame of mind. "He's a smooth one," Mike Hanrahan said. "Arguin' with him is like tryin' to wrestle with a greased ballet dancer. I liked Old Hughes far more. We called him Dagger John. When you hit him, he hit you back. It was a nice clean donnybrook. This fellow is always floatin' away from you, makin' you feel guilty over the rotten thing you just said to him."

Dan McCaffrey shook his head. "Now I know why my dad said he was glad to leave the priests behind when he settled in Tennessee."

"I *hope* Mr. McCaffrey's statement implied nothing more than friendship," Mrs. Roberts said.

"No, ma'am. Nothin' more," Dan said, winking at me. I smiled bravely back, but it was not a joke to me.

"Remember, my dear, you have become a symbol of Ireland," Mrs. Roberts said.

Mrs. Meehan, who I now decided was pretty but stupid, nodded emphatically. The ladies gathered their shawls and bonnets, and departed. The door had barely closed behind them when Michael said, "She's right, you know."

There was a bit of the priest in Michael, as there is in many revolutionaries, and Archbishop McClosky had aroused it. Michael began lecturing us on the danger of scandal. He ended by declaring I should move elsewhere, perhaps become a boarder with some respectable Irish family.

Dan grew more and more enraged. He expressed it in his usual fashion, grabbing Michael by the shirt and lifting him a foot off the floor. "Won't you ever learn to keep your mouth shut?" he snarled.

Red Mike Hanrahan quickly intervened. "Boys, boys. Save your fire for the Sassenachs. We're as safe from gossip here in this hotel as we would be on Robinson Crusoe's island. No one ever stays here but Celts. And ninety percent of them are Fenians. But to make matters more circumspect, we'll issue room keys to each of you, and no one but yourselves will know whose inside doors are locked and whose are open."

That was the end of my moving elsewhere. That night we resumed our American education. John O'Mahoney took us to dinner at the home of a rich Irishman on Clinton Avenue in Brooklyn. His name was George McGlinchy, and he had built part of the great aqueduct that brought water to the Croton Reservoir on 42nd Street, which made it possible for so many hundreds of thousands of people to live in New York. We thought McGlinchy would want to hear about Ireland, but after a few words on the subject, he spent most of the time talking about New York politics. He interwove the story of his life through the discourse, telling us how he had started as a hod carrier, saved his money, and launched his own construction company. He sent his brother-in-law into politics to obtain the government contracts that had made his fortune.

While he talked, Mr. McGlinchy ate like he expected a famine. The table was covered with dishes—steaks, chops, roasts, in almost as much profusion as Sweeney's Hotel. No wonder he was fat to bursting, and Mrs. McGlinchy the same way.

McGlinchy advised me to look up his brother-in-law. There was no one who knew how to show someone a better time in New York. His name was Richard Connolly. "We met him at the wharf," I said, "when we landed. He said he knew my sister Annie."

"Annie?" said McGlinchy, looking at me with new interest. "Anne Fitzmaurice. Sure I know her, too. Queen Anne, we call her for her manners. And her looks."

"Who is this, love?" asked Mrs. McGlinchy.

Mr. McGlinchy seemed suddenly at a loss for words. "A friend of Dick's," he said. "A charming woman. It seems she's Miss Fitzmaurice's sister. How's that for high?"

I had to ask for a translation of that American phrase, which meant extraordinary.

O'Mahoney finally managed to change the subject to the Fenians. He began telling McGlinchy the good news that Dan McCaffrey had brought back from Ireland. The Fenian legions were ready to rise. While the men pursued this fiction over coffee, Mrs. McGlinchy and several lady friends entertained me in the parlor. The room was lavishly furnished. There were lace curtains on the high windows, and heavy green damask overcurtains. The chairs and the settee before the marble fireplace were all plush and velvet, with gold fringes and tassels. On the walls were over a dozen brightly colored pictures, which Americans called chromos.

Sitting in the middle of this luxury, the women only wanted to talk of Ireland. "Doesn't she have the look of the old sod?" Mrs. McGlinchy said. She had been born in Cork, but she remembered little of it, having come to this country as a child. Several of them, who were as well dressed and probably as rich as Mrs. McGlinchy, had returned to Ireland for visits. They talked of the beauties of Killarney, the Kerry coast. I talked of the poverty of the people. I told them how stirabout tasted in a cabin pot. I saw that it made them uncomfortable.

"Why would anyone stay in such a country? Why don't they come here or go to Australia or Canada?" Mrs. McGlinchy said.

"I think we have enough Irish here," said another woman, who was even fatter than Mrs. McGlinchy. "Go visit the Sixth Ward, and you'll agree with me."

"I keep hearing about this Sixth Ward. I must go see it," I said.

"It wouldn't be safe to go by yourself," Mrs. McGlinchy said. "Above all after dark. They have a saying there. A murder a night."

"And they're Irish?" I said incredulously.

Mrs. McGlinchy nodded. "The kind of Irish who eat stirabout in Ireland. There's a bad streak in our people. A laziness, a carelessness."

"'Tis none of those things," I said. "It's a despair, a hopelessness that kills the spirit in a person. That's what must be changed."

"You'll change your mind, once you see the Sixth Ward," Mrs. McGlinchy said, with impenetrable complacency. I thought of the sadness in Archbishop McCloskey's eyes and hoped she was wrong.

On our way back to New York in our carriage, John O'Mahoney drew from his pocket a check that McGlinchy had given him. It was for ten thousand dollars. "For the privilege of meeting the Fenian girl," he said. "I've been trying to get to see that old crook for six months and he always put me off. You're going to open many doors for us, my dear."

"Did you call him a crook?" I said.

"From what I hear, he stole a half million dollars from the Croton Aqueduct alone," O'Mahoney said.

"Do we want money from the likes of him?" Michael said.

The carriage approached the Brooklyn ferry. We debarked and boarded the boat, which soon set out, its bell clanging. O'Mahoney led us to the prow, and we looked across the river at New York. The great city glowed with thousands of lights in windows and on streets, like a thing out of fairyland. "Michael," said O'Mahoney, "when I began this business, I believed, like you, that right could conquer might. I believed that the truth was a sword. I believed that every man loved my country as I did. Now I know differently. Only a rare few are that way. And truth—I've seen it cut down by the sword, or by a pen, hired by the sword—a thousand times. I've seen might, power, grind righteous men into the dirt. Now I think of it as a dirty business—with a glorious goal. That's the only thing I've been able to preserve—the goal. An Ireland worth dying for."

Those were sad words. I have never forgotten them, nor have I ever forgotten that sad man, John O'Mahoney, speaking them as he gazed across the water at the city that had corrupted him and the people he loved.

What I heard as sadness, Dan McCaffrey heard as weakness. Back in our rooms at Sweeney's Hotel, he flung aside his coat and poured himself a drink. "Hell," he said. "We're never goin' to have a revolution any-where with that worn-out old sobber runnin' it."

"Give him credit for being honest, at least," Michael said.

"What the hell has honesty got to do with runnin' a revolution—a war?" Dan said. "In a war, you spend ninety percent of your time tryin' to trick the enemy into thinkin' you got twice as many men as you really got, or feintin' toward his left flank and hittin' on his right flank. You hire spies to go and steal secrets and lie for you; you raid his supply depots and steal his guns and horses and ammunition. It don't matter whether you shoot him in the back or the front, the point is to kill him and win the goddamn war."

"A revolution is not the same as a war," Michael said. "A revolution aims at creating a nation. It has to worry about the kind of nation it will create if its revolutionary acts are unworthy of Christian men."

"Jesus Christ, you're a goddamn preacher, you know that?" Dan said. "Take my advice, go get a job runnin' a Sunday school. Bess here has more guts and brains than you'll ever have."

I retreated to my bedroom and left them arguing. I could hear their voices rising and falling. It was all a waste of breath. They were totally different men, who would never agree on anything. Gradually my attention shifted to the sound of the city outside my window. It was as strange and unnerving to me as the events and argu-ments of the day. It seemed like the breath of a huge snuf-fling monster, being drawn and exhaled, drawn and exhaled. It would stir into more active life as a horsecar or a carriage passed, then dwindle to sibilant sighing once more. There was a kind of vigilance to it. Though I knew it was absurd, I felt it was watching me. I felt observed, under scrutiny, by too many people, from Dan to Mike

Hanrahan to Mrs. Roberts to Archbishop McCloskey to legions of faceless, nameless newspaper readers.

Suddenly Dan was beside my bed, whispering, "How's my wild Irish girl? Ready for a little lovin'?"

I was appalled, even frightened, by my reluctance. The lovers' world of the good ship *Manhattan* was beyond recall here in the center of the real Manhattan. It was equally hard to summon the spirit of my long-dead Irish heroines to this hotel room, three thousand miles away from Bel fires and Ireland's mystic darkness. Yet how could I say no to him? I had chosen him before the sad eyes of Archbishop John McCloskey.

Dan sat on the edge of the bed, taking off his clothes. "Where in hell did you get him, Bess? Your brother. He's an idiot."

"Try to be patient with him," I said.

"Yeah," Dan said perfunctorily. "Just don't you listen to him, Bess. You stick with me in this thing. We're goin' to win this war—and have ourselves a good old time in the bargain."

I thought of the drunken truthteller on the *Manhattan* and wondered if he was talking to encourage himself as well as me. I remembered the bitter defeated soldier facing his poverty. I saw his need to believe those brave words. I wanted to love him, but as I opened my arms to him, I could see and hear nothing but reproachful eyes, condemning mouths. I could only think of the distance between Ireland and Tennessee.

Why Should Not She a Countess Be?

The next morning I awoke in a disconsolate mood. After Dan left me I had lain awake for hours. He seemed unaware of the halfhearted way I had responded to his kisses and caresses. After breakfast, Mike Hanrahan arrived with another group of reporters, mostly from magazines that came out weekly or monthly. They sketched and questioned me for the better part of two hours. I could never have endured it without Mike's philosophy of playing a role. He took one look at me and knew there was something wrong.

"Bish' McCloskey's still botherin' you, eh?" he said. "Just remember the old adage, the show must go on. A good actress plays her part whether it's comedy or tragedy, no matter how she feels."

"How do you know so much about acting?"

"I did a turn or two before the footlights until I realized no woman was ever goin' to worship my ugly mug. It's the handsome boyos who get the girls—and the money."

I got through the interview without mishap and the scribblers departed. Mike said I was "at liberty" for the rest of the day. Michael and Dan had gone off to Moffat House, the Fenian headquarters. I decided to use my freedom to find my sister Annie.

Sweeney gave me directions to the Metropolitan Hotel, which was only a dozen or so blocks up Broadway. It was a day of bright sunshine, and I set out in high spirits, glad of the chance to stretch my legs. Even at this hour, about eleven in the morning, Broadway was thronged with carriages and white-topped omnibuses and hackney coaches. I was fascinated by the carmen, who wore white canvas smocks and drove big two-wheeled carts while standing on a narrow platform in front. It was amazing, the way they kept their balance on this lurching, tipping slab of wood.

Within a half hour I was at the Metropolitan Hotel. It was impossible to miss it. The place filled an entire block on Broadway, a great brownstone cliff of a building just north of an even larger and more spectacular hostelry, the St. Nicholas, also a block long and fronted in white marble. Inside I found myself in an immense hall with a marble pavement and tremendous Corinthian pillars of black basalt. I wandered about like a lost soul for a few minutes while people trod confidently past me. Suddenly I was face to face with a black man—my first sight of a Negro. He was as tall as Dan, and he looked as strong. He was carrying a half dozen bags under his long arms.

"Can you help me?" I asked. "I'm lost entirely."

"Why sho, Miss," he said. "You lookin' for someone?"

I explained, and his face broke into a cheerful smile. "I know Miss Fitzmaurice. You just wait here until I get these bags into a hack."

From behind me, a man's voice shouted, "Come on, boy, let's go. I got a train to catch."

"Yes, suh," said my black friend. He was back within sixty seconds, shaking his head, looking at a coin in his hand. "Seven bags and he give me a nickel," he said. "Just like a Yankee. Never get a good tip from no man north of the Connecticut line."

Some of the things he said reminded me of Dan's accent. I asked him if he was from Tennessee. "How'd you know that?" he said. I told him I had a friend who came from the same place.

While we talked, he led me rapidly through the immense hall to several rooms beyond it. Here I found remarkable numbers of well-dressed women sitting on couches and chairs, looking bored. Lesser but still considerable numbers of children sat beside them looking equally bored.

In a last, smaller room at the rear of the building, a dark-haired woman sat playing a piano in the far corner. "There she be," said my black guide. "She come down here and play real nice music every mornin'."

I recognized the back of Annie's lovely head, her graceful neck, at the same moment that I remembered the tune. It was "The Nut Brown Maid," an old song that Father liked to sing to us. I gave my black Tennessee guide a dollar and tiptoed across the room. Standing just behind Annie, I sang the words.

> *"The country maid*
> *In russet clad*
> *Does many a time surpass*
> *In shape and air and beauty rare*
> *The court or town bred lass*
> *Since none deny*
> *This truth then why*
> *Should love be disobeyed?*
> *Why should not she*
> *A countess be*
> *Tho' born but a nut-brown maid?"*

"Bessie," Annie cried and sprang up. We flung ourselves together in a heartfelt kiss. She stepped away from the piano, gazing at me, shaking her head. "I can't believe it," she said. "My little sister."

I had been a gawky thirteen-year-old when Annie went to America, six years ago. It took an effort for me to realize how different I looked to her. She, on the other hand, did not look so different to me. She was only more beautiful now. Her figure was fuller, and there was a graver, yet not unpleasant, cast to her mouth. Her skin

was the same pure MacNamara white, without a freckle
or a blemish. Her thick black hair, set in a series of pi-
quant ringlets on her forehead with a glowing fall at the
back, was still a crown of glory. She was wearing a delicate touch of color on her cheeks and lips, which perfectly set off the skin and hair.

"I've done nothing for two days but read about you. I
think the only paper that hasn't carried your story is the
Times, but they hate the Irish and would never publish
anything good about them. Where did you learn to shoot
a gun? Has Father turned into a Fenian warrior? Where's
Michael? Why isn't he with you?"

"Michael is the Fenian warrior," I said, and did my
best to separate the truth from the fictions published by
the papers. I made no secret of Dan McCaffrey being the
true hero of the tale.

"Is he from New York?" Annie asked. "I don't know
him."

"From Tennessee," I said. "I'm—in love with him. But
I don't know exactly what to do about it. Not that I haven't
already done—a great deal. I need advice, Annie."

"Of course you do. That's why I told Dick to go down
to the dock to meet you. But let's not talk here. There are
too many eyes and ears."

I looked around and noticed that all the women in the
room were staring at us with the greatest fascination. Annie led me out to the main lobby and the elevator. In five
minutes we were in the sitting room of what she called
her "apartment." It was as elegantly furnished as Mrs.
McGlinchy's living room in Brooklyn, with a red velvet
sofa and dark purple armchairs. On the walls were not
chromos but real paintings of rural scenes. Beyond the
sitting room were two more rooms, fitted out as sleeping
chambers, with handsomely carved fourposter beds.

"Who pays for all this?" I said. "Have you become an
actress?"

"My innocent little Irish sister," Annie said. She took a bottle of champagne out of a cabinet and pulled a long velvet cord by the window. A black man in a red uniform appeared within seconds, so it seemed. His name was Washington Jones. She introduced him to me and said, "Get me a bucket of ice, will you, Wash?"

Wash was soon back with the bucket, into which he cheerfully twirled the champagne. Popping it open, he poured the first round into our glasses, accepted a tip from Annie, and departed. *"Sean ait aboo,"* Annie said, raising her wine to Father's family salute, which meant "Hurrah for the Old Place." She took a swallow that all but emptied her glass, and refilled it before continuing with her answer to my question.

"I haven't become an actress, little sister," she said. "But I've become a wiser woman since I saw you last. You know what that skunk Kelly did to me. When I wouldn't marry him, he threw me out on the street without a cent. That was my first mistake, not marrying him. But I didn't know that six years ago. Jesus, it seems like a century."

"But you told us it would have meant sinning your soul with him every time—" I said.

"Yes, I remember using that quaint phrase," Annie said. "Sinning my soul. I soon found out that sinning your soul was the favorite sport of every man in New York. I went looking for work. Honest toil, as our late Archbishop Hughes called it. I thought I could become a governess—the town is loaded with millionaires looking for governesses. But no one with an Irish name can get any such job. For an Irish girl, it's down on her knees with a scrub brush in her hand."

"Did you do that?"

"Yes. At the Jeromes. One of the very best families, you know. I'll show you their mansion. The master of the house, Leonard Jerome, is one of the richest men in New

York, worth at least ten million. At the ball he gave to open the house, he decorated the ballroom with five thousand orchids. In the center were two fountains, one spouting champagne, the other eau de cologne, all night. A few weeks after I arrived, he passed me in the upper hall, where I was scrubbing away. He told me to stand up and looked me over like you would a prize horse."

Annie rose and poured herself more champagne. She filled my glass as well. Again she all but emptied her glass in a single swallow. I soon understood why she needed reinforcement, as she continued her story. Two nights later, Leonard Jerome summoned her to his room. It was past midnight. He was in bed with the belle of the season, Mrs. Pierre Lorillard Ronalds. They were both naked. Jerome sat on the edge of the bed, fooling with himself. "Take off your clothes," he said to Annie, "and get into bed here. We're not having any fun this way."

Annie refused. Jerome glared at her and repeated his order. "Oh, Leonard, you're just drunk," said Mrs. Ronalds. "Let the girl go to bed."

"I gave her an order. She'll obey it," Jerome roared. "Take off your clothes."

Annie was too terrified to speak. She could only shake her head, again refusing. Jerome lurched from the bed and tore her robe and nightgown from her body. He grabbed her by the hair and flung her into the bed. The excitement aroused him, and he raped her with consummate brutality. Then he swung over and began a similar execution on the elegant Mrs. Ronalds, who permitted him to do his worst, while she mocked him. "Defile me, Leonard, that's all men like you can do," she said. "That's all you're good for, creating disgust. In the end you may even enable me to tolerate my husband."

"Bitch—bitch—bitch," Jerome snarled with every stroke. "You should be downtown with the rest of the whores. That's where you belong."

"I know," she said. "Do unto me what you've done to them, Leonard. Do it all."

In retaliation, Jerome withdrew from Mrs. Ronalds and again took Annie. "You see how considerate I am," he sneered. "I withhold the best of myself. Does it make you sick with longing?"

"No, only sick with pity for that poor girl," Mrs. Ronalds said.

She watched, expressionless, as Annie writhed in his arms and succumbed with a shudder to his consummation. "Now get out," Mrs. Ronalds said to Jerome. "Go sleep somewhere else in this marble kennel."

Jerome departed with a snarl. Annie lay sobbing hysterically. Mrs. Ronalds gently soothed her, revealing a womanly tenderness she had withheld from Jerome. She led the weeping girl into the private bathroom of the bedchamber and ran water in the tub for her and showed her how to use a syringe to cleanse the inner part of her body and avoid a baby. She sat beside the tub, telling Annie she was very beautiful and she must not allow this experience to shake her faith in her beauty. Leonard Jerome saw her only as a scrubmaid, but there were other men in the city who would see her as a princess. Annie wondered how or why and sobbed out the story of her first betrayal. Now she was doubly ruined.

"You must stop thinking in that old-fashioned way," Mrs. Ronalds said. "A woman is never ruined until her spirit is broken. Keep your inner heart inviolate and that will never happen."

She told Annie the story of her own life. She had deliberately married Ronalds, a much older man, whom she saw she could dominate. Her defiant spirit infuriated men like Jerome, who believed that every woman—and most men—should grovel before them.

Annie still had no idea what she should do. She threw herself on this woman's mercy. Staying in Jerome's service was out of the question. Mrs. Ronalds told her to pack her things and come home with her. The next morning she received Annie in her bedroom, and they discussed her future.

Mrs. Ronalds offered her the following alternatives. She could get Annie work as a hostess at one of the finest concert saloons, such as the Louvre. There she would be on display to some of the best and richest men in New York, men who appreciated beauty and—in some cases—knew how to treat a cultivated woman. Or she could procure her a place in one of the best parlor houses, where a select clientele of wealthy men went to enjoy the women who lived there. As a resident she could look forward to earning as much as two hundred dollars a night—and more important, the possibility of meeting a man who found her so much to his liking that he became her protector. Or she could attempt a career on the stage. The chorus lines of several theaters were open to girls with her beauty.

Annie decided that she preferred the concert saloon. Becoming an outright lady of the evening was repugnant to her. For the theater, she felt she had small talent and little interest. So, with Mrs. Ronalds's intercession, she soon found herself ensconced as a well-dressed hostess in the Louvre, the best of the concert saloons. Her purpose was to charm the guests, persuade them to buy only the most expensive champagne, and make sure the pretty waiter girls behaved with reasonable decorum.

Her beauty made her an immediate success. She was soon being squired to all the best shows and seated on the right hand of millionaires at restaurants such as Delmonico's. At the end of the evening, she would sometimes respond by showing her "appreciation." It was not bestowed casually, and it thus was all the more ardently sought. Gifts of jewelry, gowns, furs, invitations to Europe were showered upon her. Still, she remembered her mentor's injunction and kept her inner heart inviolate.

"Then I met Dick," Annie said. She got up once more to replenish her champagne and discovered the bottle was empty. With a pretty little hiccup, she turned it upside down in its melting ice. "Dick Connolly. The man you saw at the wharf when you landed. He made me forget Mrs. Ronalds's golden rule, always do unto a man what he wants to do to you."

Annie giggled and flopped into her chair for a moment, then sprang up. "Let's go look down on Broadway," she said. "I need some fresh air."

In a few minutes the elevator took us to the Metropolitan's "sky parlor." It was almost empty, because it was nearly time for dinner, which Americans, for some reason I have never fathomed, call lunch. They moved dinner into the evening and banished our old word, "supper," almost entirely.

The view from the sky parlor was breathtaking. We could see up and down Broadway for a mile in either direction. The street was jammed with carriages and omnibuses and wagons as always, with subsidiary swarms of people scurrying along the sidewalks. South of us, the East and Hudson Rivers met at the Battery and formed the great shining bay. To the north the city grew wider, with residential streets stretching out like the grid of a great electric machine, interspersed with the green of Central Park and other parks, and the Egyptian immensity of Croton Reservoir at 42nd Street. Directly east of us a vast jumble of houses and streets lay like a netherworld, stretching to the river.

In this lofty perch, Annie continued her story. Two years ago, after four years of triumphs at the Louvre, she had met Richard Connolly. He was a politician, born in Ireland and brought to this country as a boy. Something about him penetrated the armor she had sought to forge around her heart. At first she thought it was his wit. Then she thought it was his looks. But she had dealt with handsome, witty men before. She finally decided it was her discovery that he was a serious man and he was seriously in love with her. Farewell, armor. She allowed him to persuade her to leave the Louvre and become his exclusive mistress. She had been living with and loving him here at the Metropolitan Hotel ever since.

"But you haven't married him?"

"He's married already. That's the great sorrow of my life. If she died—I'd marry him tomorrow. But I don't wish that on her. She has three small children. She's such a horror. She does nothing but denounce Dick and tell him he'll come to a bad end. A religious virago. She gives away half his money to priests. She doesn't understand what Dick is going to do."

"What's that?"

"He's going to take this city away from them. Away from the Jeromes and the Schermerhorns and the Stuyvesants and the Astors. He's going to have as many millions as they've stolen down on Wall Street—and something more. He's going to control City Hall. He can make them come begging to him for the safety of their mansions. He can make this city their graveyard, with a snap of his fingers."

"How?" I asked, utterly amazed.

"You see that?" she said, pointing down Broadway and across it toward the East River. "You see those slums? An army lives down there. An army of Irishmen who can slug and shoot better than any army the rich can find. Dick Connolly and his friends Peter Sweeny and Bill Tweed are its commanders."

She sat back in her cushioned chair, glaring out at the city, a frown all but destroying her beautiful face. "We'll see who owns New York," she said. "We'll see."

" 'Tis a pity we can't use them to free Ireland," I said. "That's where I've cast my lot."

"We must talk to Dick about that, tonight. We must arrange to get you out of the hands of those Fenian chiselers. That's all they are. Small-time chiselers, Bess."

"I think some of them are honest men," I said. "The old man, the leader, John O'Mahoney."

"I've never met him," Annie said abruptly, "but if he honestly thinks he can free Ireland, he's crazy. That's what Dick says. Anyone who wastes his time on something as crazy as that has got to be nuts, cuckoo, birdcage. Do you get me, kiddo?"

"Yes," I said, amazed by her American slang. "But I'm not a child, Annie. I must make up my own mind about it."

She shook her head. The champagne had made her a little drunk and impervious to argument. "Now is the time for you to move, Bessie. You're famous. There's a half dozen men I've got in mind for you. Now you can have your pick. You might even get one to put his name on a marriage license."

I said nothing, but for the first time I felt uneasy, fearful—not for myself but for Annie. She had revealed something that she herself did not want to face. She seemed to sense it, in spite of the reassuring champagne. "Let's go have lunch," she said, in a duller, emptier voice.

The Bloody Ould Sixth Ward

I thought we would eat at the Metropolitan Hotel, but Annie led me to a hackney coach and told the driver to take us to the Fifth Avenue Hotel. It was far uptown at 23rd Street facing Madison Square. In Broadway's heavy traffic, it took us a half hour to get there.

"This is where I want to live," Annie said, as we got out of the coach. I could see why. The front was gleaming white marble, six stories of it. Inside was more marble, on the floors, at the reservation desk, in a staircase wide enough for a palace. We went up the stairs to the second floor, where a dining room that seated several hundred opened before us. Crystal chandeliers dripped from the ceiling. We were led to a table where almost a dozen people were already seated. It was the Fifth Avenue's custom to dine in groups of twenty. The idea appealed to Annie, who said she was bored with eating alone at the Metropolitan.

"Have you made no friends?" I said.

"Men, yes; women, no," Annie said. "It's not easy to make friends when every woman you meet, almost, is a potential enemy. There's hardly a woman in New York, married or unmarried, who wouldn't like to take Dick away from me."

The food was good, but too plentiful. I asked Annie how she had kept her figure, faced with such monstrous amounts of vittles. She laughed in a short, hard way and said it was easy when your future depended on it. She ate only nibbles of the six or seven main dishes and twenty or thirty minor dishes but insisted on having another bottle of champagne. I drank very little of it, but she finished it handily.

The conversation of the other women at the table

seemed to be mostly about millionaires. There was great debate about how much various men were worth, five, ten, or twenty millions. Much attention was given to new millionaires, two in particular, named Fisk and Gould. Several women—all the diners at our table were female—bragged of their husbands' acquaintance with these gentlemen. They discussed the extravagances of various millionaires, their mansions, their yachts, their horses. Each conversationalist strove to top the previous one with a more sensational item.

"Most of their husbands are probably clerks on Wall Street," Annie muttered to me.

I asked Annie if it was common for married women to live in hotels. She said it was becoming a custom. Women gave birth and raised children in them. The living was cheaper than the cost of buying and furnishing a house. The Civil War had driven the price of everything out of sight. An apartment in the Fifth Avenue Hotel cost about a hundred dollars a week for two, including no less than four meals a day. The fourth meal was served late in the evening, as an attempt to seduce those who had not gorged themselves on the first three. Annie said the rooms were beautifully furnished, and, most remarkable, each suite had a private bathroom.

To our amusement—at first—our tablemates began talking about the Fenian girl. Several had read her story in the paper. One large, severely plain woman shook her head angrily. "My husband says we ought to send them back to the British for hanging."

"My husband says we ought to send all the Irish back to the British," said a plump younger woman with straw-colored hair.

"It would certainly improve New York," said the severe woman. "My brother-in-law was robbed of a hundred dollars by one of them last week. Not ten blocks from this hotel."

I could feel my temper rising, but Annie motioned me to be silent. We sat there, finishing our tea, while they denounced the Irish as lazy, thieving, superstitious. The severe woman said she would never hire one as a servant. At her husband's bank, they had hired an Irish clerk. The other clerks threatened to quit, and the Irishman was dropped. Everyone agreed that these were excellent tactics. Only a united front among the Americans could keep the Irish out. They were as bold as they were greedy, ready to barge in anywhere.

After lunch we sat in one of the public rooms of the Fifth Avenue Hotel. I was fuming. Annie was amused at my anger. "You'll hear a lot worse than that if you stay in America," she said. "Remember it when your Fenian friends start telling you that this country is behind Ireland heart and soul. The politicians hand out that sort of blarney around election time to get the Irish vote."

Annie took a small watch from her purse. Its gold frame was encrusted with diamonds. Dick Connolly had given it to her for her birthday. "Two o'clock," she said. "We've got a whole afternoon to kill. What would you like to do, my Fenian girl? Visit Barnum's Museum?"

"See the Sixth Ward," I said.

"What?" Annie said. "There's nothing to see down there."

"Then why does everyone talk about it?" I said.

"It's worse than Hell's Kitchen—and that's saying a lot."

"Hell's Kitchen," I said. "Let's put that on the itinerary, too."

"We may see some of that tonight," she said. "We'll do the town, you and I and Michael and Dick." She hailed a hackney coach and told him to take us to Tammany Hall. The driver nodded. Apparently there was no need for an address. As we rode downtown, she warmed to the idea of my tour. "Maybe you should see the

Bloody Ould Sixth, as they call it. See all the lower wards. Then you'll understand a little more what we're up against."

As we rode along, Annie explained that Tammany Hall was the headquarters of the city's Democratic Party. Dick Connolly was a member of the Central Committee as well as a leader of the Twentieth Ward. The odd name came from an old Indian, Chief Tammanend, who was a kind of god to the Delaware tribe. He performed great feats in the misty past, like some of our Irish heroes. Every Irishman in the city worth his salt voted behind Tammany. Without the power of party, there would be no jobs for them at City Hall or on the police force or anywhere else in the government.

Our journey took us far downtown, to the corner of Nassau and Frankfort Streets, where stood a somewhat dingy looking five-story building. A squad of burly fellows was lounging against its redbrick front. Annie took a calling card from her purse and hailed one of them. "Take this to Dick Connolly," she said. "Tell him I'm waiting outside."

In five minutes the same tall, smiling man with the stately nose and clean-shaven face whom I had met at the dock emerged from the door and greeted us cheerfully. He gave Annie's hand an affectionate squeeze and bowed low to me. "I hardly know what to say, finding myself face-to-face with such fame," he said. "Reading your story made me think Ireland might yet be free, from the center to the sea, as the old lady said in the song."

"Annie just spent a good hour telling me you think the idea is nonsense," I replied.

"A politician is like a woman. He changes his mind twice a day, when the newspapers come out," Dick Connolly said.

"We're here to settle our evening schedule," Annie said, "and to get an escort. Bess has heard so much of the beauties of the Sixth Ward and points below, she wants to see them for herself."

"I doubt if I can call out the 69th Regiment on such short notice," Dick said. "But perhaps Tiny Tim will do."

He turned and spoke to a man by the door, who in turn bawled a summons inside. In a moment there emerged the biggest man I had ever seen. He was at least six feet five and perhaps four feet wide. He wore a long black frock coat and loud checked bell-bottomed pants.

"Tim," said Dick Connolly, "these ladies want a tour of the Sixth Ward. Bring them back without so much as a curl on their lovely heads disturbed."

"Don't worry about a ting," Tim said. He tipped his high beaver hat to us and got into the cab, causing it to tilt alarmingly until he settled opposite us. Tim's name was Mulligan. He said he knew "de Sixt' ward" well. He was born "dere." But now he lived in "de Twenniet." His "mudder" had advised him to get out of the Sixth Ward as soon as possible. In the same strange accent, Tim told me how much he enjoyed reading how I had "plugged" the lime-juicers in "Iland."

Soon we were in a spidery tangle of streets with strange names, Bummers' Retreat, Cat Alley, Cockroach Row. The stench was unbelievable. Annie put a handkerchief over her nose and mouth and remarked that some rich New Yorker had described the odor as a mixture of rotten eggs and ammonia. She explained that most of the houses had no bathrooms, and people simply threw their slops in the gutters. Soon we were among the tenements, tall wooden buildings crammed side by side on the narrow streets, shutting out the sun. The air that came out of the doorways had the stink of the grave. Every ten feet there was a wretched little saloon in the basement or on the first floor.

The people who looked out from the windows or sat on the steps of the tenements all had the mark of death on their faces. It reminded me of stories I'd heard about the famines in Ireland. Worst were the children, scrawny, fierce-faced little creatures. Annie said many of them lived on the streets, without father or mother. One newspaper said there were thirty thousand of these urchins.

"Dear God," I said. "Wouldn't they be better off in the poorest village in Ireland?"

"You agree with our friends at lunch?" Annie asked me sarcastically.

I thought of Mrs. McGlinchy, fat and self-satisfied in her velvet parlor, and wondered how she could live so well while Irish men and women were living like this only a mile or two away. Now I knew the source of the sadness in Archbishop McCloskey's eyes. These were his people, but what could he do for them? He seemed as incapable of easing their misery as everyone else, even though he was not as indifferent.

"Lookit 'at," Tim said. He pointed down Bixby Street. "Shylock Boik's trowin' out anudder one."

Burke was a landlord. Annie said he owned a whole row of tenements on Bixby Street. He was well known for his heartless evictions. He never let anyone stay longer than a week without paying the rent. His victim today was a young red-haired woman with four small children. She wept and cursed, and the children wept, too, as the burly, bald-headed Burke piled their pathetic sticks of furniture on the sidewalk. The mother fell into her only chair, crying and coughing. One of the children, a boy not more than ten, ran into the nearest saloon and came out with a glass of whiskey.

"I know huh," Tim Mulligan said. "Red Mag O'Toole. Married Mickey Maloney. He got it in d'head at Gettysboig."

"Can't we do something?" I said.

"Y'could pay huh rent for anudder week," Tim said.

Annie thrust a bill into my hand. I jumped from the

cab and ran down the street. I gave the bill—it was ten dollars—to the mother. "I wish it was more," I said.

"Are yez from de mission?" she said. "Y'can keep y'goddamn money. Y'ain't gettin' me kids. Y'ain't gettin'm!"

I didn't know what she was talking about. Suddenly there were faces at a dozen windows, shouting curses at me. A bottle sailed down and smashed near my feet. Another missed my head by an inch. Tim Mulligan came legging down the street yelling for them to stop.

"She's okay. She ain't no Protestant blackleg. She's Irish. D'Fenian goil," he roared.

Instantly there was a rush into the street from every house. In a twinkling there were two or three hundred people around me. I found it hard to believe that the single row of tenements, no more than eight or nine of them, held so many. Annie later told me they were jammed in there, five or six to a room. Not a face or a hand had seen soap or water in a month. They smelled almost as bad as the slops they threw in the streets. Some of them were as ragged as the peasants I saw in the cabins in Ireland.

"She come down here t'see de Sixt Ward," Tim Mulligan said. "She hoid about it in Iland, right? D'toughest ward in New Yawk."

"Sure there's no gettin' over d'Sixt," cackled one withered old woman. "The glorious fights I seen down here. "T'would put Finn and the Fianna to shame, they would."

"Now we must unite and fight for Ireland," I said. "Instead of fighting each other."

"Give us a chance and we'll do it sure enough," shouted one scrawny fellow, who had only two or three teeth left in his mouth.

We heard a cry from the end of the street. Mulligan whirled and burst through the crowd, knocking men and women pell-mell. I saw a man struggling with Annie at the door of the cab. Mulligan got to the fellow before he knew what was happening and seized him by the collar of his shirt. He spun him around and struck him a punch that sent him flying twenty feet. He sprang after and kicked the fellow again and again until he lay whimpering in the gutter.

"He tried to steal my purse," Annie said.

"He won't steal nuttin' for a while," Tim said.

The citizens of Bixby Street had emerged from their narrow alley to examine the moaning thief. Two or three boys ran over and peered in his face. "It's Mickey Condon," one of them yelled.

"He says his ribs is busted," yelled another one.

"Y'Tammany plugger, Mulligan, did y'have to bust his ribs?" shouted a third.

"Whip dat nag," said Mulligan to the cabman.

A rock struck the cab, then a splat of mud. The cabman's whip cracked, and we departed the scene of my attempted benevolence under fire from whatever the Sixth Ward could find lying loose in the streets. Once safely out of range, the cabman slowed his horse, and we proceeded uptown to view what Annie called "more pleasant sights." We passed a handsome park named after President George Washington and found ourselves on Fifth Avenue.

There, block after block, stood the mansions of the rich. By and large they were disappointing from the outside, all dull, drab brownstone with high stoops and identical sets of windows and huge bristling cornices. Excessive show was not yet the fashion among America's "old rich"— those who had made their fortunes before the Civil War. But behind the staid exteriors was fabulous luxury, which Annie knew in amazing detail. The owners' names, Schermerhorn, Brevoort, Belmont, meant nothing to me but a great deal to Annie. To her descriptions of their parlors and ballrooms she added choice anecdotes from their lives, most of them uncomplimentary. I did not realize it at the time, but Annie had become a typical American, fascinated by the rich and their often bizarre lives.

Aside from the dullness of its brownstone fronts, Fifth Avenue was a lovely street, lined with huge shade trees and free from Broadway's furious commercial traffic. Crossing Madison Square we paused before the house Annie knew best, Leonard Jerome's mansion on the corner of 26th Street. He was one of the new rich who believed in ostentation. The house was a huge pile of red brick and marble with windows ten feet tall and double porches of delicate ironwork overlooking the square. Behind it on 26th Street were stables, which Annie said were as lavish as the house, with black walnut paneling, papered walls, and rich carpeting. On the upper floor was a six-hundred-seat theater, which Jerome had built to display Mrs. Ronalds's singing talents to the "upper tendom"—the wealthy ten thousand who constituted New York society. Our tour ended at 33rd Street and Fifth Avenue, where we examined the twin mansions of John Jacob Astor III and his younger brother William. These were unabashed palaces, with great Corinthian columns and double stoops of white marble. Inside, Annie said, were banquet halls and art galleries that equaled anything owned by Queen Victoria.

"How's dat for high?" Tim Mulligan said with frank admiration. "Dey say old Astor was wort' twenty million when he croaked."

After making us promise to pay no more visits to the slums, Tim left us in front of the Astor mansions. He had a "brudder" who worked as a groom for one of them, and he thought he would pay him a visit. We continued up Fifth Avenue to admire the immense walls of the Croton Reservoir at 42nd Street. I told Annie of visiting Dick Connolly's brother-in-law, McGlinchy, who had supposedly gotten rich building it. "I know him," Annie said. "He's the biggest skirt-chaser in town."

I was stunned by the contrast between the McGlinchys' comforts, the complacent wealth of Fifth Avenue, and the slums of the Sixth Ward. America was a bewildering country. "'Tis not much different from Ireland," I said. "The poor in their hovels and the rich in their mansion houses."

"Now you can see why some of us think we must do something here before we can do anything for Ireland," Annie said.

"Are all cities like New York?" I asked. "Are there Sixth Wards in Boston and Philadelphia and Chicago?"

"So they say. It's every man—and woman—for himself in this American life, little sister. Get that through your head."

This dog-eat-dog philosophy did not jibe with Annie's cry to do something for the American Irish. I began to suspect a deep confusion in her mind—perhaps in all American minds—between the wish to help others and help themselves.

We continued up Fifth Avenue past the site which the late Archbishop Hughes had chosen for a cathedral that was supposedly going to surpass Westminster Abbey. Only the outer wall, to the height of about thirty-five feet, had been completed when the Civil War broke out. We were soon at the entrance of Central Park. Here we saw fashionable New York on display. A dazzling variety of carriages and fine horses whirled along the winding roads of the park. Almost every vehicle was filled with brilliantly dressed women out to see and be seen. Annie pointed to one of the gaudiest carriages, all cream and gold, drawn by four magnificent black horses. A rather fat black-haired woman in a deep purple dress sat behind the two coachmen. "There goes Madame Restell," she said. "That's who to see if you catch cold."

"Is she a doctor?" I asked.

Annie laughed. "In a way. I keep forgetting how green

you are. 'Catch cold' is the polite American way to say miss your monthly. You know what *that* means, I hope?"

"Of course," I said, blushing nevertheless.

"Madame Restell knows how to make you regular again. Get rid of your cold."

"You mean the baby?"

"Right. She deals only with the best people, and she's made about a million dollars doing it."

"Have you been to her?"

"Not yet. Thanks to Mrs. Ronalds. I use my syringe faithfully. But it's no guarantee. I know a lot of women who've gotten caught, in spite of it. Which reminds me. Are you doing anything to play it safe with this big lug from Tennessee?"

"No," I said. "But he's not a lug."

"Okay. He's a hayseed."

"What's that?"

"A country boy."

"I'm a country girl. So are you."

"Not any more, little sister. Six years in New York teaches you more about life than sixty years in County Limerick. Bring your friend along tonight. Let me look him over."

I found myself disliking more and more Annie's assumption that she was going to take charge of me. At the same time, I was intimidated by her cool confidence and the successive shocks I had received since we landed in New York and met the Fenian leaders. I was only nineteen and realized I badly needed a guide. I meekly followed Annie into a pharmacy on lower Broadway, let her buy a vaginal syringe for me, and listened carefully to her instructions for using it.

Perhaps it was a heightened consciousness of the risk women take that made me rebellious when I found myself under masculine criticism a few minutes later. In our suite at the hotel Michael and Dan were talking with Colonel William Roberts, Fenian "man of action," husband of the imperiously respectable Mrs. Roberts. The men sprang to their feet and demanded to know where I had been all day. I explained curtly and advised Dan and Michael that we were invited out for the evening by Mr. Richard Connolly, sachem of the Tammany Society.

Colonel Roberts (it was his rank in the Union Army) immediately became agitated. "You shouldn't go near him," he said. "They've done nothing for us. He only wants to use you to get the Irish vote."

"I don't know what you're talking about," I said. "It's a purely social evening."

"The colonel's right," Michael said. You must remember who you are. Not just Bess Fitzmaurice, but the Fenian girl."

"I will nevertheless go where I please and do what I please," I said. "Furthermore, I met Mr. Connolly today, and he said he was changing his mind about the Fenians."

"Did he now?" Colonel Roberts said. "That's very interesting. Maybe you should go, and if I bump into you somewhere along the way, we could have a bit of a talk."

This sudden shift of ground left Michael bewildered. He weakly acquiesced. After Roberts left, Michael began damning him as a politician first and a Fenian second. "He came up here to talk us out of supporting O'Mahoney," Michael said. "He claims everyone on the council is disgusted with the old man."

"What'd I tell you last night?" Dan said. "That old boy's worn out. He's a good old dog, but he's worn out."

"He's given twenty years of his life to Ireland," Michael said. "Living here in a hole in the wall, on charity most of the time. I haven't the heart to turn him out because he's old. Nor do I think he's so wrong about what he says, that we must wait and plan before we strike."

"You don't keep an army waitin'," Dan said. "Waitin' rots an army."

"We don't have an army. We have detachments scattered here, there, and everywhere. Most of them without guns," Michael replied.

"You'll have an army soon enough," Dan said. "If we do what Roberts says."

"What's that?" I asked.

"Take Canada," Dan said.

There it was, the wild, daring idea that was to tear apart the Fenian movement and leave behind it a legacy of betrayal and hatred. Struck by its novelty, I listened while Dan told me why he favored it. There were fifty thousand Irish-American veterans of the Civil War armies in America, spoiling for a chance to strike a blow against England. To be brutally realistic, there was not much hope of getting them to Ireland as long as Britannia ruled the seas. Canada was a different proposition. There was not so much as a fort on its long border with America. Already inside Canada were a million Irish who were ready to rise and cooperate with an invading army. The Canadians themselves were divided. The Catholic French hated the English and would welcome the Catholic Irish as liberators. There was no central government. The various provinces were ruled from London. All the Fenians needed was the cooperation of the American government. To get that cooperation, they needed help from politicians—which no doubt explained Colonel Roberts's sudden change of mind about Dick Connolly.

Michael kept frowning and saying he had grave doubts about the whole scheme. I left them arguing and retired to my bedroom to dress for dinner. There I was delighted to discover that the seamstress had finished two of my new dresses and delivered them. One of them was a dinner dress, which I promptly tried on. It was a rose-colored satin, brocaded in white velvet with a deep flounce of blond lace, a half yard wide. There was satin on each side below the waist, and the whole thing was lined throughout body, skirt, and sleeves with white silk. I strolled into the sitting room and displayed myself to Dan's admiring eye.

"Hey," he said, "you're ready for Fifth Avenue in that number."

Facing myself in a mirror inset in one wall, I liked what I saw. I was not as beautiful as Annie, but I was certainly more than passable. Then I thought of those ragged Irish in the Sixth Ward and felt a terrible, confusing guilt, to be standing here in satin and silk. Knocking on Michael's door, I pretended I wanted to show him the dress. I sat down and told him where I had been, what I had seen this afternoon.

"We're in a strange country, that much is certain," Michael said. "For the time being we must follow its customs. When in Rome, as the saying goes. But the more I see and hear, the more I think the Irish and the Americans are deadly different. This scheme to oust O'Mahoney is an American thing from start to finish. 'Tis too much trouble and difficulty to help Ireland, so we'll all go up and rob land in Canada instead. O'Mahoney tells me the Americans have been smacking their lips over Canada since the century began."

Then he dropped politics and asked, "How is Annie? As beautiful as ever?"

"More, if possible," I said.

"What's this fellow Connolly to her?"

"Her man. She's married to him—in all but name."

"And he's married in name to someone else?"

"Don't blame her, Michael, until you know a bit more of New York and what's happened to her."

I told him about Leonard Jerome. His eyes bulged in

his head. "She made that up," he said. "She made it up to justify herself. Just as you've used the Fenians to justify throwing yourself into McCaffrey's bed."

"I have not thrown myself anywhere," I said. "If you had a brother's heart, instead of the head and tongue of a canting monk, you'd rejoice that Annie's found herself a protector. As for me, it's simply a matter of you minding your own business."

I stormed through the sitting room past Dan without looking at him and burst into tears when I reached my bedroom. Dan came to the door and knocked. "Are you okay?" he asked.

"Yes," I said.

"You sure?"

"Yes. Go away."

It was a thoughtless phrase. I would soon regret it.

A Good Old New York Bender

We waited in the lobby of Sweeney's for Annie and Dick Connolly. They arrived at seven, as promised. Our Tammany sachem had hired an open carriage, perfect for a warm summer evening. Michael and Annie exchanged enthusiastic kisses. I had warned him that if he said a word to spoil the evening I would kill him. Dick Connolly gazed approvingly at my gown and said in his dry way, "The Fenian girl has become the Fenian lady."

We drove uptown for a drink at the Louvre, the concert saloon where Dick and Annie had met. A stroll through it was equal to a visit to Versailles. Never have I seen so many crystal chandeliers and marble columns. The walls were paneled in gold and emerald. There were baskets of fruit and bouquets of brilliant flowers on the marble-topped tables. The grand hall had a mirrored bar at least two hundred feet long. In the quiet lounges off this hall sat some of the most beautiful women I have ever seen. Many of them smiled winningly at Dick Connolly, and one ran over to give him a message for "Peter." No wonder Annie felt threatened by her own sex.

We drank a bottle of excellent French champagne, and Dick Connolly talked of the happy day he walked into this room and met Annie. "I looked at her and thought, 'There's a true Irish beauty to warm an exile's heart,' " he said. "But would she be interested in a spavined old politician like me?"

"I took pity on him," Annie said. "He was so lonely, only surrounded by a dozen or so of his pals."

"I got rid of them the moment you smiled at me," he said.

"You mean most of these women are hired by the management?" Michael asked in his most severe moralist's tone.

"Some are," Annie said.

"They had a wedding here only last week," Dick Connolly said. "An Astor nephew married a girl he'd met in this very room."

I noticed Dan was staring at one woman, a tall blonde, with uncommon interest. "We may have another," I said, "if Dan keeps looking at that girl over there."

"The countess?" Dick Connolly said with a smile. "You need a loaded wallet and a loaded gun to play games with her. She's German. Claims her father was lord of the bedchamber to King Ludwig of Bavaria."

Dan gave me a glower. My Donal Ogue was in a surly temper, and I did not know why. He drank his champagne and said nothing while Michael drew out Dick Connolly. He had been born in Banta, not far from Cork. A few years before the famine of '47 he was brought over by an older brother. He soon saw that there was no way for an Irishman to rise but by politics. But he also determined that when he rose, he would know where and when to challenge the Sassenachs. He entered a bank and acquired enough knowledge of that arcane business to become an officer. Every spare hour, night and morning, he devoted to politics, and soon was a Tammany sachem and a leader of the Twentieth Ward. He and men we would soon meet had spent the last five years eliminating from the topmost posts in Tammany what he called "croakers," men who complained and quarreled and divided the ranks. Now Tammany was united for the first time in a decade. "Which means," he said in his wry way, "if all goes well in the elections this November, we'll be ready to reap the harvest."

"A harvest of what?" asked Michael.

"Dollars," Dick Connolly said. "We're going to get our money out of City Hall the way the Sassenachs get it out of Wall Street. We're going to use it to do what they did—buy real estate, start banks. We're going to own our share of this city. Maybe own it all, before we're through."

We listened, amazed by his boldness, too ignorant of American life to know that we were hearing a plan that would bring disgrace and ruin on Dick Connolly and many others and smirch what little reputation the Irish had in America. Dan was as silent as me and Michael. The ways of New York were as strange to a man from Tennessee as they were to us. If we had any doubts, Annie stilled them for us with her wild enthusiasm. She raised her glass and said, "A toast. To the conquest of New York."

We drank heartily to it, though it occurred to me that we ought to be drinking to the conquest of Ireland. Matters were becoming extremely confused in my head. Having finished our champagne, we strolled across

Madison Square to the corner of Fifth Avenue and 23rd Street and entered a formidable building, fronted with marble. "This is the Blossom Club," Annie said. "Where the big-shot pols relax."

"And potshot each other," Dick Connolly said.

We entered an elegant reception hall. The Turkish carpets were so thick, you could have struck a sledgehammer on the floor without making more than a faint thud. Paintings hung from the oak-paneled walls. Dick Connolly pointed to one in particular. It was on our right beside the entranceway. Frame and all, it was at least ten feet high. The subject was a man with a huge head and vast front, wearing an expensive brown suit. In his tie glittered a magnificent diamond. His mouth and chin were covered by a mustache and beard, but a small smile was visible on his lips, and his eyes glittered with a mocking humor. Dick Connolly took off his tall black silk hat and bowed low before the portrait. "We must pay obeisance to the ruler of the universe," he said.

"Who is he?" Michael asked.

"That is the Honorable William Marcy Tweed, member of the Board of Supervisors of the City of New York, deputy street cleaning commissioner, and grand sachem of Tammany Hall. If you wish to shorten these titles, simply call him God," Dick Connolly said.

"It's a good likeness," Annie said. "When did they hang it?"

"Only a day or two ago."

"The hell with being God. He never has time to enjoy himself," roared a voice behind us.

We confronted the man himself. He was almost as mammoth in the flesh as he was in his portrait, the same vast front, with a more pronounced paunch and the chest and arms of a wrestler. He weighed at least three hundred pounds and stood over six feet. He swept Annie off her feet in a tremendous hug and called her his favorite Irish princess. "And this is the Fenian girl?" he thundered, turning his attention to me.

"None other," said Dick Connolly. "And her brother, Michael Fitzmaurice, and Major Dan McCaffrey of the Fenian army."

"I salute you all," roared Bill Tweed, bringing his hand to his balding head. "The Blossom Club is at your disposal. Consider yourselves my guests. Except this Irish Scrooge here, who will pay for everything he eats and drinks, or else." He prodded Dick Connolly in the chest with an enormous fist.

"Or else what?" Dick Connolly said.

"Or else I'll pay for it, as usual. Come along, let's have a few drinks." He opened his arms wide and literally swept us before him to the bar, on the left of the reception hall. Dozens of well-dressed men were standing at a long, gleaming crescent of dark wood, glasses in their hands. "Gentlemen," boomed Bill Tweed at the entrance. "We have a guest of honor tonight. The Fenian girl and her compatriots."

The room exploded with cheers, and a hundred glasses were raised to toast us. In the midst of the uproar, I heard Dick Connolly say to Tweed, "Has Sweeny seen Roberts?"

"He's talking to him now, upstairs," Tweed said.

We retreated to a corner table and a bottle of French champagne was speedily placed before us. Bill Tweed drank a toast to us and cheerfully asked us how much of my story was true. I told him none of it and pointed to Dan as the real hero of the adventure. "Where are you from, Major?" asked Tweed.

"Tennessee," Dan said.

"You're a long way from home. Were you in the war?"

"Stuart's cavalry."

"A rebel. Or should I say Democrat? Here's to you and your gallant cause."

Tweed began talking of the Civil War as the South's greatest mistake. Once they had fired on the flag, the Democrats of the North had to go against them. If they had forsworn the gun, they could have ruled the country in alliance with the Northern Democrats.

"We could have kept the nigger in his place forever," Tweed said. "And given honest Irishmen a chance to earn their bread."

"It seems to me, sir," said Michael, "that an honest Negro and an honest Irishman should have the chance equally."

"Ho? What's this?" roared Tweed. "An idealist? Go down to the Sixth Ward and preach that doctrine to your fellow Irishmen. I'll guarantee to pay for your funeral."

"Bill's a Scotsman," Dick Connolly said. "But he's learned to love Irishmen."

"I love them for the way they vote. Often," Tweed said. "Without them I'd be nothing. Did you ever hear of Big Six? That was my fire company. John Reilly, God rest his soul, and I organized it. Seventy-five stout boyos we had in it, every one of them ready to swing an ax or club for Bill Tweed on election day."

"I don't understand," Michael said. "What does a fire company have to do with elections?"

"Is this schnoozer bingo?" Tweed asked Dick Connolly, using New York slang to ask if Michael was drunk.

"He's just off the boat, Bill. Green as grass."

"I think it's growing between his ears."

Patiently, the grand sachem of Tammany explained that a fire company was a phalanx who remained loyal to their leader, not only casting their votes for him on election day but beating black and blue those who tried to vote for anyone else.

"There's not many of them left now," Tweed said, with a sudden throb in his rumbling voice. "Most of them joined the 69th Regiment or the Irish Brigade. They're

pushing up grass in Virginia while the goddamn abolitionists who started the war are riding around New York
in coaches and fours on the money they made from selling soldiers rotten food and cheap uniforms. I tell you,
the Democrats have got some scores to settle with those
buggers. And settle them we will, eh, Dick?"

"And how will Ireland be helped by all this?" Michael
said.

"That takes a bit of crystal-ball gazing," Dick Connolly said. "When Bill Tweed here becomes the most
powerful politician in America, a man who can go to the
Democratic national convention and nominate the next
president, he won't forget he started with Irish muscle
and rose on Irish votes. He'll tell that president that
America must help Ireland—or else."

"When will that be?" Michael said.

"The next presidential election is 1868. That gives us
plenty of time to work and plan," Dick Connolly said.

"Didn't I tell you he was an Irish patriot?" Annie said,
gazing worshipfully at Dick.

"Bill Tweed never forgets a friend—or an enemy,"
Tweed said. Something flashed in his eyes that made me
believe the last part more than the first.

Glancing at his gold watch, which he wore on a chain
across his paunch, just below a diamond that looked even
bigger than the jewel in his portrait, Tweed announced it
was time for supper, if we wanted to catch the show at
Tony Pastor's. We went up the wide carpeted stairs and
were met at the top by our old friend Colonel Roberts.
Beside him was a stumpy, beetle-browed man with a
brush mustache. He had a round Irish face and dark, uneasy eyes. Roberts and Tweed pounded each other on the
back in familiar style and introduced us to Peter Barr
Sweeny. "Call him Brains for short," Tweed said.

"How do you do," Sweeny said, taking my hand and
bowing low to kiss it. "I am honored to meet you."

In that needling spirit that I gradually realized was the standard mode of address for politicians, Tweed guffawed at Sweeny's manners. "When are you going to stop acting like a goddamned frog, Sweeny?" He turned to me and explained that Sweeny had taken a trip to France a few years ago and had been vastly impressed with Napoleon III, the ruler of the Second Empire.

Sweeny flushed and glared at Tweed with something like hatred. I suddenly wondered if all was as jovial as everyone pretended. "I wish I could do as much for Ireland as this young woman has done," he said.

"Maybe we'll give you a chance," Tweed said. "We'll make you a general in the Fenian army. How would that go down, Bill?"

"Name your price," Roberts said with a laugh. "A healthy contribution could work wonders."

"You're already soaking our contractors and aldermen. Fatso McGlinchy told me he coughed up ten thousand dollars last night, after a dinner with the Fenian girl here," Tweed said.

"I'm not a general," Sweeny said. "But I would be ready to serve Ireland as—say, her first president."

Michael stared in astonishment. It was plain that Sweeny was serious. The presumption of the American Irish was amazing.

We entered a private dining room where a squadron of waiters served us a feast. The cooking was mostly French, heavy with truffles and cream sauces. The dishes were as plentiful as an American dinner, ranging from beef to roast duck. The wines were superb, each bottle introduced with a flourish by Sweeny, who seemed to have supervised the menu. He discoursed on their age and flavor, until Tweed interrupted him in his brusque way. "Pour it, Brains, for Christ's sake, and let it speak for itself."

Beyond talking wine, Sweeny said little. Studying him,

noting his restless eyes and twitching hands, I concluded
he was mortally shy, a strange handicap for a politician.
Annie later confirmed this to me. In 1857, Sweeny had become district attorney of New York. When he rose to
speak at his first trial, he had lost the power to make a
sound, fled the courtroom, and resigned the office. He was
a graduate of Columbia College, a persistent reader of
books on history and philosophy. Tweed and Connolly
never made a political move without consulting him.

"Sweeny has a mind that can see around corners in the
dark," Annie told me.

For a while we feasted and joked, but soon the topic
came around to the main point, the Fenians and Tammany. I began to see that these men, for all their booming good humor, never wasted a moment of their time.
They thought, ate, slept, drank politics, and the great
splurge I had won in the press made them think that the
Fenians could become a very important part of their political engine. Colonel William Roberts had obviously
tried to convince them of this in the past without success.

"Colonel Roberts tells me that there's been a great
change in Fenian thinking. More and more men of action
are coming to the fore," Sweeny told Tweed. "He says
they see no point in waiting for a secret army to train in
Ireland or an escort of American men-of-war to carry an
American-Irish army across the Atlantic. Both ideas depend on too many imponderables."

Dear God, I thought. He talks like a statesman already.

"Colonel Roberts and his friends believe it makes better sense to use the Irish veterans of the Civil War as
soon as possible, before they settle into jobs and marry
away their futures. They want to fight now, and all they
need is a target."

"How about the British Embassy in Washington?"
Tweed said, chomping on a duck's carcass. "I went to a

party there when I was in Congress. They threw me out because I pinched some duchess's ass."

"Were you sober a day while you were in Washington?" Connolly asked.

"Maybe one," Tweed said.

"Colonel Roberts thinks fifty thousand men deserve a bigger target," Sweeny said. "Canada."

"Canada?" Tweed said, sucking duck fat off his fingers. "The whole damn country?"

"We'll start with the province of Ontario, the heartland," Roberts said. "Conquer that, arm the Irish there, and the other provinces will fall like tenpins."

Tweed pulled pieces of duck out of his teeth with a gold toothpick. He looked hard at Dan. "You're a brother of the blade," he said, using the slang for soldier. "What do you think, Tennessee?"

"It's a big country," Dan said. "You'd need a real army. Cavalry, especially. But I like the idea."

"You want a chance to use your barking irons," Tweed said. "If there's more like you around, it might work."

"What's a barking iron?" I asked Annie, sotto voce.

"A gun," she whispered.

"What do you need from us? We can't give you much help in Washington these days," Tweed said.

"We can make our own way in Washington," Roberts said. "There's a dozen votes on the Fenian council that you can influence. We need them to make this major change in policy." Roberts reeled off a string of names. To each, Tweed gave a small nod, as if to say, "I've got him."

"We need help in raising money and recruiting men," Roberts continued.

"Easy," Tweed said. "But what's in it for us? We need to win this election in November. Big John Morrissey's out to murder us. Sheriff O'Brien's lukewarm."

"Precisely why I think we can do business," Sweeny said. "They can help us rally every last Irish vote, and finish the croakers once and for all. If we go in with him, Colonel Roberts tells us the Fenian flag will fly over Tammany Hall. The Fenian girl here will stride the platform with our orators. Tammany and Fenian will be one in spirit and in strength."

"The devil they will," said Michael.

Astonishment spread from face to face. Was this mere boy daring to defy the most powerful politicians in the greatest city in America?

"What did that bingo say?" growled Tweed.

"The Fenian flag will fly only over two places—the Fenian headquarters here in New York and someday, God willing, over the soil of the Irish nation," Michael said. "It will never, as long as I have a voice, be used to dignify corrupt elections."

"Get that bulltrap out of here," Tweed roared, "before I loosen his bone box."

"Mr. Fitzmaurice," said Dick Connolly, "you are young in the ways of this world. If you want to grow older, I suggest you go quietly back to your hotel and meditate on your sins."

"You have the power to silence me here. But I'll speak out against you as long as I have a voice in the Fenian Brotherhood," Michael said.

"That may not be very long," said Colonel Roberts.

Michael glared across the table at me. "Are you not coming with me?" he said.

Dan McCaffrey rose beside me. "No," he said. "She's not comin' with you. Now get goin' before I finish doin' what I started to do to you at sea."

"Don't let them use you, Bess. They'll do to you what they've done to her," Michael said, pointing to Annie. "They'll make you a whore."

Moving with a speed that was amazing for a man of his

bulk, Bill Tweed lunged to his feet and careened down the table. He seized Michael by the back of the collar and lifted him two feet off the floor and dragged him to the door. With a heave of his immense arm, he flung him into the hall. "Get rid of him," he roared to someone out there.

"That young man is no gentleman," Tweed said, lumbering back to his seat. "Now, where were we?"

"We were arranging to invade Canada, and—incidentally—win the next election," Dick Connolly said.

"Oh, yeah," Tweed said, probing a tooth with his gold toothpick. "I like it. We'll help you raise the old balram. We'll boost you in the papers. We've got enough reporters on the take to form a reserve regiment."

Annie translated for me. "On the take" meant bribed. "Balram" was money.

"Somethin' else," Tweed continued, still probing his tooth. "General Grant's comin' to town in a couple of days. The city's gonna throw a big parade for him. No one knows whether he's a Republican or a Democrat. Be nice if the Fenians and Tammany marched together, don't you think?"

Roberts agreed to everything. He was especially enthusiastic about welcoming General Grant. "Could you help me obtain a private interview with him?" he asked. "I would like to offer him command of the Fenian army of liberation."

This wild idea made even Tweed blink. "That's pretty steep. I think the general figures he's got a lifetime job in the U.S. Army at the very least. But it might give him a good laugh."

Roberts looked discomfited. Tweed pounded him on the back. "Don't feel bad, Colonel. I've heard crazier ideas. That's enough politics. Let's show the Fenian girl and her knockout sister here a good old New York bender. On to Tony Pastor's."

Annie was smiling bravely, but there were tears in her eyes. Michael's cruel words had cut deep. Damn him, I thought. Annie was not a whore. It was not true and it would never be true, neither for her nor for me. At the same time, I could not help feeling a certain subtle gratitude for Michael's bluntness. He had demolished Annie's pretensions to mastermind me.

I had refused Michael's summons. I had stayed beside Dan. But as we descended to the street, he paid very little attention to me. Tweed had his big arm around Dan's shoulder, asking him how many cavalrymen the Fenians would need to conquer Canada. Dan's face was alive with pride and pleasure. He was reveling in the attention and admiration of these powerful men. I sensed danger in his eager acceptance of them. But I felt the excitement, too.

Come what may, I will take my chances with him, I told myself. And hope against hope that it will not end like the poem, with my heart blackened ever and always.

Bowery Millionaires

The trip down the bowery to Tony Pastor's Opera House was a show in itself. We went in a large open carriage, a landau, belonging to Bill Tweed. I soon saw why the Bowery was called "the Broadway of the poor." Immigrants of all nations thronged the sidewalks. Almost every second storefront bore a sign in German. There were German bands tootling on every corner. As we got lower down, there was a half-mile stretch of restaurants and saloons with gas lamps illuminating brightly colored signs in their windows.

A shocking number of the strollers on the sidewalk were drunk. Both men and women staggered and sang and shouted and swore. "The cheap whiskey will destroy us all," Peter Sweeny said. "I see the day when we must tax the price of it beyond the reach of the poor."

"Good luck getting that one through Albany," Dick Connolly said. "But we could use it as a bell ringer. The liquor interests would pay a cool million to see it killed."

Once more Annie translated for me. Albany was the capital of New York state, where laws for New York City were passed by a legislature. A bell ringer was an old political maneuver, whereby someone paid a handsome sum to stop a piece of legislation that would harm his interests.

"Ah," growled Tweed, "gettin' drunk is the only consolation the poor bastards have got. They'd cut our gizzards out if they ever caught us trying to take away their booze. And I wouldn't blame them."

Connolly and Sweeny were silent. I sensed once more that there was less than perfect harmony between them and Tweed.

Tony Pastor's theater marquee was ablaze with gas lamps. In front of it milled a crowd of undernourished little ruffians, who swarmed around us, yelling. "Hey, Mistuh Tweed. Me fadda's sick, can y'gimmy a buck?" and similar pleas. Tweed took a great roll of greenbacks out of his pocket, peeled off a dozen or so, and threw them up in the air. The ensuing scramble was ferocious. The urchins kicked and gouged and punched for the money. Tweed stood on the steps laughing at the melee. He joined us inside, saying, "There's some good sluggers there, Peter."

"Sure enough," Sweeny said, without enthusiasm.

I paid scant attention, because I was too busy admiring the lobby, which rivaled the Blossom Club in splendor. The carpets were inches thick, and the walls blazed with golden lamps. A great marble staircase ran up to the second floor. People paraded up and down it like dukes and duchesses on coronation day. Several were in evening dress.

"The swells are coming down here," Tweed said. "I've been telling them it's the best show in town."

Annie nudged me. "Up there," she said. "It's my friend Mrs. Ronalds."

She gazed down at us from the balcony, a look of mild amusement on her face. Two men in evening dress stood on either side of her. It was my first sight of an American aristocrat, and I will never forget it. She was tall and strongly built, with a full figure. Around her supple neck was a set of pearls that caught the glow of the lamplight and ringed her throat with white fire. Her dress was of white silk, finished with heavy gold cord and tassels. The bodice was low, with revers of green that matched the trimming on the skirt. Over her bare shoulders she wore a mantle of dark blue silk held with a gold clasp. Her dark hair was heavily crimped in front and dressed in a waterfall at the back.

But it was not the beauty of her clothes or her face and figure that impressed me. It was the cool disdain with which she looked down at the crowd of which we were a part. It was a multicolored mostly Bowery mob, dressed in the garish styles of the poor. I thought of the scene in Leonard Jerome's bedroom as Annie had described it to me and understood why she could madden a man. There was something withheld, inviolate, unconquerable about her beauty. I sensed she had judged this American world and found it worthy of nothing but bitter amusement.

Beside me I heard Bill Tweed mutter, "What a piece. I wonder how much it would cost to get into that?"

"They say it cost Leonard Jerome a million," Connolly said.

"Worth it," Tweed said.

"Why don't you say hello to her, Annie?" Dick Connolly said.

"I doubt if she'd remember me," Annie said.

"She'd remember the Fenian girl, if she reads the papers," Dick replied.

"I would like to thank her—once more," Annie said.

We went up the stairs—just the two of us, while the men stood in the lobby below, greeting fellow Democrats by the dozen.

Annie approached Mrs. Ronalds with the greatest timidity. "Good evening," she said. "I'm sure you don't remember me. Annie Fitzmaurice—from Mr. Jerome's house. I didn't expect to see you here. I felt I should say hello and tell you how well things go with me. Thanks to you, in great part."

"Of course I remember you," Mrs. Ronalds said in a throaty voice.

"This is my sister Bess," Annie said. "You may have read about her in the paper—she helped the Fenians escape from Ireland."

"How do you do," Mrs. Ronalds said. "I envy your adventure. Rodney." She turned to one of her escorts, a short, sharp-faced fellow whose head barely reached her shoulder. "Here's the Fenian girl, who made Your Majesty's troopers look so silly in Ireland."

"You don't say," he sneered.

"Rodney is the Viscount Gort," Mrs. Ronalds said.

Annie and I both gasped with the shock of hearing such a familiar name. His title told us that he was the son of Lord Gort, who owned our family farm.

The viscount glared at me for a moment, his hands behind his back. Then he turned to the man on the other side of Mrs. Ronalds. "Doesn't look the least different from any other Irish tart in London," he said.

"Careful, Rodney," Mrs. Ronalds said. "According to the papers she's a dead shot."

"Tell me another," Gort sneered. "She's a common vagrant. People like her don't know any more about a gun than they do about soap and water."

"I think you're a poor loser, Rodney," Mrs. Ronalds said.

"When I take a hand in Irish affairs," Rodney said, growing more and more angry, "you'll hear no more stories of Fenians or Mollies or anything else. There's a group of us my age, who expect to come into our lands in a year or two. We're going to give the Irish what they deserve, the bayonet and the noose. That's what kept them in their place for two hundred years, until people like my father became sentimentalists. It wouldn't surprise me if you find it necessary to do the same thing over here."

"I dare say you're right, old fellow," said his friend, who seemed half English, to judge from his accent.

"I won't dignify Lord Gort with an answer," I said. "Except to remind him that Irishmen can use bayonets, too."

Before he could reply, I turned to Mrs. Ronalds, thanked her for the help she had given Annie, and quickly withdrew. When we rejoined the men, Dick Connolly asked, "What was that little twerp saying to you?"

"That little twerp is Viscount Gort," I said. "He tried to insult us, but he didn't succeed."

"Who's the man with him?" Annie asked.

"That's Wee Willie Schermerhorn," Connolly said.

"He talks like an Englishman," I said.

"That's the way they all talk, the swells," Connolly said. "They worship the goddamn lime-juicers. You should have been here in 1860 when the Prince of Wales came to visit. The upper tendom crawled on their hands and knees to get an invitation to a ball or dinner where they could shake his royal hand."

"Kiss his royal ass, you mean," Bill Tweed said.

A short, swarthy man in evening dress rushed up to us. He was an employee of Tony Pastor, who was ill. Our host offered us a thousand apologies for this fact and escorted us to a box above the stage. The orchestra was striking up a sort of overture as we sat down. In a few minutes the same man appeared on the stage as the impresario of the evening. At a signal, the orchestra stopped playing, and he announced that he was honored to introduce two distinguished guests: "The grand sachem of Tammany Hall, the Honorable William Marcy Tweed. And his guest, Bess Fitzmaurice, the Fenian girl."

Roars and shouts and whistles poured down on us, along with stamping feet and beating hands. We both rose and accepted the tumultous applause. Opposite us in another box sat Mrs. Ronalds and Viscount Gort. I wondered what the viscount was thinking. My rage at him as the personification of England's arrogance obliterated what little worry I had about becoming the ally of William Marcy Tweed.

Having taken our bow and informed the public of our political liaison, we were free to enjoy the show. It was called variety, a new style that had come into favor in America during the war. Instead of a single play, there was a host of performers, each displaying some peculiar skill. A contortionist tied himself into amazing knots; a Chinese juggled glass balls, bottles, and horseshoes in the air while his dog leaped through the whirling circle; a family of acrobats in pink tights that revealed every secret of the male and female anatomy leaped and somersaulted around the stage; an Irishman named Donnelly made wondrous rattling music on a sort of guitar, called a banjo; and two other Irishmen, named Sheridan and Mack, blacked their faces with cork and grease and sang like Negroes. They were called "the Happiest Darkies Out," and they lived up to this notice, even though I could make little sense out of their drawling accents.

There was an Irish comedian who told funny stories in a brogue that was obviously fake and a "Dutch comedian" who did the same thing in what passed for a German accent. The hit of the evening was Miss Ella Weaner, "the Protean and Lightning Change Songstress," who raced off-stage and donned a new dress for every song she sang. The audience apparently considered the costumes more important than her voice, because they applauded each new dress before she opened her mouth. It was just as well. I had heard better singing at wakes in Ireland. Finally came a play, *The Liberation of Charleston,* which satirized the abolitionists in the Union Army as the most arrant thieves who ever lived, stealing anything they could seize from the hapless Southerners. The audience loved it and roundly booed the Negroes (Sheridan and Mack still in their black faces), who strutted about declaring themselves "de Gob-nor" and "de Sen-ator."

When the curtain fell, Tweed led me backstage to meet Ella Weaner. I was startled by the way both actors and actresses walked around in states of near undress. Ella's singing style had had a warbling sweetness to it, but her manner face-to-face was about as sweet as Conn the plowman. "Hello, kiddo," she said, out of the corner of her mouth. She sprawled in a most unfeminine way in her chair, and asked Tweed for a cigar.

"Not now, Ella," he said. "Get your glad rags on, we're showing this Fenian girl a New York bender tonight."

"You're on," she said. "I'm always ready for a little blue ruin."

While we waited outside Ella's dressing room, Tweed was besieged by stagehands and actors and actresses, all of whom seemed to want his help to procure a job for a relative. He listened with lordly patience to each suppli-cant and advised him or her to make an appointment to see him at Tammany Hall. At last, Ella appeared in a red dress that was as gaudy as anything she had worn onstage, her cheeks rouged and her lips a bright crimson.

In the lobby, we rejoined Dick Connolly, Annie, and Peter Sweeny, who had also found a female friend, Kate McGuire. She was short, plump, and rather ugly. Her taste in clothes ran to bright green. Tweed greeted her with a shout. "Hello, Kate, how about a rubdown?" As we strolled to our carriage, Annie explained that Kate had been a rubber in a Turkish bath, until Sweeny became her devoted admirer.

"We hate each other cordially," Annie whispered to me. "She's as mean and common as they come. She has a hold on Peter that no one can break."

We rode down Broadway past a dozen dark and silent theaters. Our variety show had lasted the better part of three hours, and it was now approaching midnight. The numerous concert saloons still blazed with light, and music resounded from them. Rainbow-colored transparencies advertised the singers and dancers who were performing inside. But we had seen the best of the concert saloons, the Louvre, and Dick Connolly dismissed the rest as "gin mills." We were going to "the most famous—or infamous—dance hall in the United States, Harry Hill's."

A huge red and blue lantern swung above the entrance, which was on Houston Street, not far from Broadway. A number of unescorted women were going in a separate entrance as we passed through the door Bill Tweed held for us. We found ourselves in a long, low room with a bar, which also sold oysters and sandwiches. Tweed ordered some oysters and champagne for us and led us through a rear door and up the stairs to the dance hall. A short, thick-set man with a frowning forehead and angry eyes met us.

"Hello, Harry," Tweed said. "Get us a table, will you? There's oysters and champagne coming up."

The room was jammed with men and women in about equal numbers. There were no decorations worth mentioning. The place was nothing but a large, shabby, two-story frame house from which the walls had been removed to make a single large hall. On a raised platform sat the orchestra, which consisted of a piano, a violin, and a bass violin. There were fifty or sixty couples on the floor doing a violent American dance, whirling this way and that, crashing into each other and singing away to the music. As we followed Harry Hill, he continually barked orders to his guests. "Less noise there! Girls, be quiet." Various rules were painted on signs, in poetry, such as:

> *"Let him who swears prepare to go*
> *Headfirst into the street below."*

> *"A man who sits while a woman stands*
> *Will leave his teeth in Harry's hands."*

Annie explained to me that Harry Hill fancied himself a poet. He was very religious and gave large donations to churches and charities. He insisted on standards of decorum, and he enforced them with his fists. Among his other rules was a requirement that a man must either dance or drink. Otherwise he was asked to leave. If he was shy about leading a partner to the floor, Hill chose one for him. Only the best-looking women, wearing respectable clothing, were permitted to enter the "ladies' door."

We finally reached a table in the corner. It was taken by a company of men and women, but Harry Hill coolly announced that it was "Bill Tweed's table," and all but one lanky, middle-aged man rose to withdraw. "Who in hell is Bill Tweed?" he drawled, in an accent that sounded like Dan's. Hill hauled him to his feet by his shirt and knocked him unconscious with one tremendous punch.

"Anyone who asks that question is too dumb to drink in my place," Hill said. "Get rid of him."

His friends hastily dragged the man away.

"How about singing us a song, Ella?" Harry Hill said as we sat down.

"Sure," she said. "As soon as I get some champagne down the old pipe."

"We got a bigger attraction with us tonight," Bill Tweed said. "The Fenian girl."

To Ella's indignation, Hill rushed to the orchestra, stopped their music, and announced my whereabouts to the house. A great crush surrounded us, and Bill Tweed rose to drink a toast to Ireland. It was returned with a roar and a tremendous clink of glasses. Tweed made a little speech, in which he cheerfully insulted all "you bingo boys and bingo morts" (drunks, male and female) who were content to drink to Ireland. What the Fenians needed was money, and he was going to see that they got it. To prove it, he hauled out his wad of greenbacks and told me to spread my skirt. He peeled off a half-dozen hundred dollar bills and threw them into my lap. Instantly began a stampede to imitate his example. Five mad minutes later, I was sitting there with several thousand dollars in my lap.

After the spontaneous offering of the crowd, we received a stream of more important visitors. A huge bearded man in black, John Morrissey, shook my hand and sat down beside Tweed for several minutes of intense conversation. He was a powerful Tammany sachem, leader of a ward, and a former heavyweight champion boxer. When he rose to leave, he asked with a mocking smile, "How much did Tweed give you?"

"A thousand," Tweed said.

"Here's two," Morrissey said, and dropped a handful of bills into my lap.

This inspired a hurried conference between Tweed,

Dick Connolly, and Peter Sweeny. "Is he ever going to take orders?" Connolly asked.

"I think he might for a while. He likes the Fenian idea," Tweed said.

Once more it was evident that these men never stopped working at politics. Colonel Roberts of the Fenian council was meanwhile gleefully counting the money and announced it came to over five thousand dollars. Tweed reached over and took a thousand off the top. "We get twenty percent of all the business anyone does with us," he said.

"We'll make it up out of our own pockets," Peter Sweeny said, glaring at Tweed.

"That's your affair," Tweed said.

A small, squinty-eyed man in a purple coat and yellow pants came weaving up to us. In his hands was a string of pearls of amazing size. "Wanna give these to thish Irish beauty," he said. "Jus' stole'm from the Metropol'tan Hotel."

"This is Dublin George, the best badger in town," Dick Connolly said. "Why not take them? I'm sure they came off the neck of some Sassenach queen."

A half dozen other prominent thieves, known by such picturesque names as Sheeny Mike, Big Nose Bunker, and the Doctor, made similar contributions of jewelry. The most striking of these charmers was William Varley, also known as Reddy the Blacksmith, a square-built, hard-featured man with a white coat and a Panama hat worn at a cocky angle. Speaking through a thick red mustache, he tipped his hat and assured me that he and his sister wanted to do their share. The William Varley Association was going to take up a collection in the Fourth Ward, and his sister was going to get her girls to contribute an entire night's earnings at her house on James Street.

"Morrissey just gave her two thousand, Reddy, how's that for high?" Tweed roared.

"We'll double it," Varley said.

I smiled and offered him a toast in champagne. When he swaggered off, I asked Annie what sort of a house his sister owned. "The worst brothel in New York," Annie said.

Through all this conversation and collecting, we were dining on oysters and champagne. After consuming half a bottle, Ella Weaner announced that the stuff had no kick to it and called for some of Harry Hill's absinthe. "Nobody should drink that poison," Tweed said. But Ella insisted, and Annie said she would join her.

Dick Connolly grew angry. "You promised me that you'd never drink absinthe again," he said.

"I like the feeling it gives me," Annie said defiantly. "There's not a worry in the whole world for a while. Besides, it's the drink of the house."

"Don't you know better than to argue with a woman?" Tweed said. He summoned a waiter girl and ordered a bottle of absinthe. Ella and Annie downed a glass apiece, but I only sipped my portion. I thought it tasted vile. Dan said he would try some and found no difficulty getting down more than his share. Annie said she wanted to dance and dragged a reluctant Dick Connolly onto the floor. Dan found me more willing, and we were soon careening around the place taking and giving physical punishment. It was like no dancing I had ever done.

We were interrupted by Harry Hill mounting the stage to shout, "Attention! Attention! A song from the incomparable Ella Weaner!"

Ella must have had another glass of absinthe while we were dancing. She was thoroughly drunk. Perhaps she had to be to sing her song. Its title was "Creep into My Bed, Baby," and all its lines enlarged on that suggestion. I knew we were in fast company, but such blatant abandonment of decency shocked me. I looked across the dance floor and saw Annie nuzzling Dick Connolly's neck. Everyone in the place laughed uproariously at the more risqué lines.

"Gives you ideas, don't it?" Dan McCaffrey said, slipping his hand under my arm and cupping it over my breast. I remembered Michael's warning words and wondered what was happening to me, to everyone.

"Yes," I said, "bad ones," and stalked back to the table. There we found Kate and Peter Sweeny well into another bottle of absinthe, and Bill Tweed deep in conversation with a short, slim man with a shock of wavy black hair, a heavy black mustache, and a well-trimmed beard. He wore a beautifully tailored dark blue suit and a sky blue necktie. A gardenia glistened in his buttonhole. Tweed introduced me to A. Oakey Hall, the district attorney of New York.

"I am delighted to meet a woman capable of putting a squadron of British troopers hors de combat," he said. "No doubt if they had brought their wives along you would have made them whores in combat as well."

Sweeny groaned. "Oakey," he said, "do you know what happened to the man who made too many puns?"

"He was severely pun-ished?"

"He was denied the nomination."

"Sweeny," said Hall, "you can't threaten a man who has prosecuted twelve thousand citizens of Crimeland. Few candidates have as many tried friends."

"Dear God," I said, "he really can't stop."

"No more than an Irishman can stop drinking," said Tweed. "Give us a quote from Shakespeare, Oakey."

"In Hamlet's words, a politician is . . . one that would circumvent God."

"Leave God out of it," Sweeny said. "You're more interested in beating the nominating committee, Oakey. But it won't work this year."

District Attorney Hall looked discomfited. I again perceived that behind the raillery serious politics were being conducted. Hall turned to Tweed. "Does this mick have the final say?" he asked, glaring at Sweeny.

"You need more ballast, Oakey," Tweed said. "Politics are too deep for you. They are for me, too, and I can wade long after you start to float. But the squire always keeps his feet on the bottom."

"In the mud, the congenial home of every Irishman," Hall said.

Peter Sweeny sprang to his feet and grabbed Hall by his silk tie. "Get out of here, you goddamned Know Nothing, before I wipe up the floor with you."

"In friendship false, implacable in hate / Resolved to ruin or to rule the state," Hall said, rescuing his tie.

"Is that Shakespeare?" Tweed said.

"No," said Hall. "It's Dryden. But it fits."

My feet had long since left the bottom of this political torrent, but I could see that there were fierce antagonisms among our Tammany friends. It did not take me long to learn that men like Hall and to a lesser extent Tweed feared the power of Irish politicians like Sweeny. Before the Civil War, Hall had been a Know Nothing, the political party dedicated to driving the Irish from America. Sweeny was a dark, brooding spirit, who never forgot an injury and treasured up his moments of revenge. Hall was seeking Tammany's nomination for mayor, and Sweeny was opposed to him.

Hall departed, and we soon followed him. Everyone was more or less drunk—the absinthe lovers more, the champagne swiggers less. Ella Weaner was staggering against Bill Tweed, and Kate was hanging on Sweeny's shoulder. Annie was skipping and singing around Dick Connolly as we reached the sidewalk.

"Armory Hall," shouted Ella. "Let's pay a li'l visit to ole Billy McGlory."

We piled into the carriage, with Kate bawling a song.

> *"I was born in Mullion in the County Cork*
> *Thirty-five hundred miles from gay New York*
> *My father never gave a good goddamn*
> *Because he was a real old Irishman."*

Billy McGlory's Armory Hall was on Hester Street, deep in the East Side slums. The streets were full of people; once more an astonishing number of them were drunk. As our carriage reached the door of the hall, it was flung open and two or three huge fellows pitched a man into the street. He was unconscious, and he sprawled helplessly in the gutter. Immediately he was set upon by the local inhabitants, who pulled off his shoes, coat, shirt, and pants. Tweed thought it was uproariously funny and stood laughing at the show.

"Hayseeds should stay out of Billy McGlory's. Remember that, Tennessee," Tweed said, grinning at Dan.

Dan smiled bravely, but he obviously did not like being called a hayseed.

Armory Hall was not much more dingy than Harry Hill's, but the patrons were strikingly different. Only a few men on the dance floor were well dressed, and the women had none of the beauty or sophistication of Hill's female patrons. McGlory himself, a squat, grinning barrel of a man, came bursting through the crowd to greet Tweed. "Hello, Boss," he yelled above the din. The band had four or five trumpets in it.

"Give us a table upstairs, Billy," Tweed said, "and we'll introduce my friend the Fenian girl to the house."

We repeated the introduction staged at Harry Hill's. This time I stood on a balcony, divided into a number of compartments by curtains, overlooking the dance floor. The patrons cheered lustily when Tweed gave me five hundred dollars, and a basket was lowered from the balcony for their donations. It was soon overflowing with greenbacks, watches, diamond bracelets, and strings of pearls. Roberts counted two thousand dollars, and this time he gave Tweed four hundred without waiting for him to take it. The jewelry we gave to Peter Sweeny, who said he would fence it tomorrow. When I looked baffled, they explained to me that there was a regular system of disposing of stolen goods in New York through people known as "fences" who passed them on at a profit to legitimate buyers.

I was tempted to ask if there was anything done honestly in America, but I was distracted by the show on the dance floor. The patrons seemed to relish our presence. They went at their prancing with more than ordinary vigor. Couples crashed into each other and were knocked sprawling. This led to fights, in which the contestants seemed well known. "There's Hell-Cat Maggie," Tweed said, pointing to one woman with dyed orange hair and a bloated face daubed with rouge and plastered with powder. "Hey, Maggie," Tweed yelled. "Show us your fangs."

Maggie strutted over to us and opened her mouth. Her teeth were filed to dagger's points. "Yez are gonna see some action tonight, Bill," she said. "Them whores from Battle Row is down here on a bender. We're gonna trow 'em outta here."

An altercation broke out on the floor. A huge woman named Battle Annie Welsh, not liking the way she was bumped by a woman almost as large, hauled off and smacked her. Her male escort smacked Annie, and the war began. "There's Gallus Mag," yelled Tweed, pointing to a six-foot female who charged into the fray wielding a club. She wore suspenders to support her skirt. Sadie the Goat was also cheered as she rushed into the melee, head down, butting opponents with ferocity. Other members of the Battle Row Ladies Social and Athletic Club, a collection of brawlers from Hell's Kitchen, rushed to support Annie Welsh, and the room was soon full of slugging, wrestling females, all of them fat burly creatures. The spectators cheered them on, Tweed and Colonel Roberts leaning over our balcony to get a better view. Joining them I saw the heads of a dozen other well-dressed people in the curtained compartments around us. "The better sort" sat up here to watch the denizens of the netherworld disport themselves below.

Hell-Cat Maggie sank her fangs into Battle Annie Welsh's arm, only to be butted headlong by Sadie the Goat, who in turn was clouted by Gallus Mag's club. Sadie rolled on the floor, holding her head, wailing like a banshee, while others kicked and stomped her. The moment anyone went down, she was fair game for feet. Frequently they were pounced upon by two or three, to be throttled and pounded from head to foot. The men fought, too, kicking and kneeing as well as slugging. All, male and female, screeched through clenched teeth with a fierce animal sound, pitched upon a single note.

Another sound pierced the uproar, the shrill burble of police whistles. A dozen husky men in blue surged onto the floor, and even wilder carnage ensued. They clubbed everyone indiscriminately, all but carpeting the floor with groaning semiconscious victims. Many of the combatants fled into the shadows, where no doubt convenient doors allowed them to escape into the streets. In five minutes it was over. The police were hauling carcasses to the jail or the hospital. Hell-Cat Maggie stumbled over to our balcony. Blood oozed down her bloated face from a gash on her forehead. She held up a trophy for Tweed to admire. It was a human ear. "It's Sadie's," she screeched. "I got her goddamned ear."

"You're one in a barrel, Maggie," Tweed said and threw her a greenback.

A waiter girl arrived with three bottles of champagne. At least, I thought "she" was a girl, because "she" was wearing a short skirt and wore about a pound of rouge on her cheeks and lips, but a second look revealed that "she" needed a shave and had thick black hair on "her" arms. "Hello, Gorgeous," Bill Tweed said. "Meet the Fenian girl. You're probably more interested in her friend from Tennessee."

Gorgeous fluttered his eyes at Dan. "He's a hunk," he said as he opened the champagne.

Dan could only gape in astonishment. I did the same. "Look at the greenhorn and the hayseed. They can't believe it," Sweeny's girl, Kate McGuire, said. Everyone had a laugh on us, and the champagne went around. In the hall outside there was a constant jingle of bells, which the waiter girls and boys wore on their boots. A stream of them passed us, arm in arm with customers, to enjoy themselves in other compartments on the balcony.

Ella Weaner was very drunk by now. She sat on Tweed's lap and sang, "Creep into my bed, baby." Kate McGuire was almost as drunk. So, I regret to say, was Annie. "Give us a little strip, Ella," Tweed said.

"Anything you say, Bill," she giggled.

Lurching up on the table, Ella proceeded to sing another round of verses from "Creep into My Bed" while taking off her clothes. In five minutes she was utterly naked, singing away, her breasts swaying and her belly vibrating before Tweed. On the floor below us dancing ceased. Everyone gazed up, transfixed by the spectacle, roaring approval when Ella made a particularly sensual movement with her pelvis.

Tweed suddenly turned to the crowd below. "Anyone want her down there?"

There was a roar of acceptance. Tweed rose to his feet, and with a sweep of his big arm he hurled Ella Weaner off the table and over the balcony. I rushed to the rail and saw a dozen leering, laughing men catch her and go crashing to the floor beneath her weight. The rest of them pounced on her, pawing at her breasts and thighs. "Whoa!" They roared and flung her high in the air and caught her again.

"Whoa!" They hurled her across the floor like a sack of meal. Then Billy McGlory himself hauled her down and danced around the floor with her, his finger probing deep into her sex while Ella gasped and giggled. Suddenly she pulled away and struck McGlory in the face. "Get your hands off me, you son of a bitch," Ella screamed. "I ain't one of your goddamn cunts."

McGlory looked up at Tweed. "Shall I teach her a lesson, Bill?"

"No," Tweed said. "She needs her face to make a living."

"Just one punch, Bill," McGlory said, circling Ella Weaner.

"Jesus, he'll kill her. Stop him," Tweed said, to no one in particular.

Before anyone else could speak or move, Dan McCaffrey vaulted over the balcony and sprang to a beam that supported some gaslights below us. He swung on it like an acrobat and dropped into the crowd only a few feet from Ella and McGlory.

"Mr. Tweed says no," Dan said.

"Screw Mr. Tweed," McGlory said and raised his fist to strike the blow that would have smashed Ella Weaner's face. But the blow never fell. Dan whirled McGlory around and punched him twice, once in the belly, then in the chin, and sent him flying into the crowd on his back.

A half dozen bruisers started for Dan, but they were frozen by a bellow from Bill Tweed. "Cut it," he thundered. "The man who swings at him will be floating in the river tomorrow night!"

Tweed threw down Ella's clothes and told her to get dressed. Several of the crowd kicked the garments to Ella's feet, and she put them on. We descended to the dance floor, and Tweed collected a sullen, weeping

Ella. As we emerged onto the street, we heard a bell clanging 4:00 A.M. from the west side of the city. "I think Trinity is telling us it's time to go home," Dick Connolly said.

Dan and I left them at Sweeney's Hotel, which was nearest to the bottom of Broadway. Upstairs in the sitting room, Dan kissed me drunkenly. "How about lettin' this baby creep into your bed?" he said.

For a moment all I could see was Ella Weaner's naked body being mauled by the drunken dancers on the floor of Billy McGlory's hall. I saw Annie dancing giddily with Dick Connolly. "No," I said. "Not tonight."

Dan stepped back, his face the sullen mask I had seen on the *Manhattan*. "You figure Roberts is a better bet? Or maybe Tweed himself? He was givin' you the eye all night."

"I'm figuring nothing," I said. "I'm tired and—a little sick from too much drink."

"The hell you're figurin nothin'," he snarled. "You seen how your sister's makin' out and you're gonna do at least as good."

"How can you accuse me of such a thing?" I said. "Did I ask you for anything on May Eve?"

"You were a country girl then. Now you're in the big city and learnin' fast."

"I'm learnin' fast about you," I mimicked him, losing all control of my temper. "The only thing that troubles you is your inability to get your hands on some of that money you saw tonight."

"I know what I want my hands on," he said. "And I'm gonna get it before daylight."

He strode to the door and slammed it behind him with a crash like a cannon shot.

I stood in the dark room in the middle of the night-shrouded city, weeping with bewilderment and anger and fear. Behind me a mocking voice asked, "Did you have a pleasant night of it?"

I whirled on my brother, Michael, a dark blur in the door to his room. "Shut up," I said. "I want no advice from you—nor any man."

No Man Shall Hurt Me

I fell into a troubled sleep and awoke to find late morning sunlight streaming in the window. The room was unmercifully hot. I opened the window and found it was just as hot outside. I was about to discover New York's tropical summer. I discovered something else when I ventured into the sitting room, on my way to the bathroom. A champagne bottle sat empty on a table, and a woman's dress, reeking of perfume, was flung on the couch. From Dan's room I heard a muffled male voice, then a female voice, laughing.

I fled down the hall to the ladies' bathroom, my face aflame, my heart pounding. I could not decide whether to weep or curse. I had given myself to this man, living out a poem, a dream of unselfish love, of heroic self-sacrifice for a noble cause. I was painfully learning that he was no unselfish hero and life was not a poem. I thought of the whirl of the past days, the stories and pictures in the newspapers, the respectable ladies in Mrs. McGlinchy's parlor in Brooklyn, the denizens of Billy McGlory's dance hall, Colonel Roberts greedily counting the money, Annie's drinking, Michael's insults—and now this betrayal by Dan McCaffrey. It was like a story I had read by the American writer Poe, "A Descent into the Maelstrom." I felt as helpless, as bewildered, as the victim in that terrifying tale. I could only hope that in the end some sort of explosion or upheaval would fling me up from the depths into which I seemed to be drowning.

When I returned to our suite, milady's dress was gone. I emerged from my room in time to meet her as she came out of Dan's room. She was not what I had imagined—a regal blond beauty like the countess at the Louvre concert saloon. She was short and red-haired and as Irish as I was, with a northern accent. "Good morning," she said. "I'm Nora. You must be the Fenian girl."

"I prefer my own name," I said. "Bess Fitzmaurice."

Nora tossed her head in the direction of Dan's room. "He told me all about you in his cups last night. You may know a thing or two about guns, but you don't know much about hangin' onto a man."

"When I need advice from the likes of you," I said, "I shall be in a bad way indeed."

"When you've been around this town a while, honey, you may change that tune," Nora said, showing her teeth. "Famous one day, forgotten the next, that's the way things go in New York. I've seen actresses livin' like queens one month and lookin' for jobs as waiter girls the next month. You'll find out, if the British don't do for you first."

I opened the door to the hall. "Good-bye," I said.

"We may meet again," she said. She strolled impudently to the door of Dan's room. "Au revoir, lover."

The reply was no more than a mumble. Nora blew him a kiss and departed. I sat on the couch, too unhappy to think about eating until past noon, when Michael appeared. He had gone down to Moffat House, the Fenian headquarters, and told John O'Mahoney about our alliance with Tammany and what he knew of our trip around New York with Tweed last night. O'Mahoney had given Michael a scathing opinion of Tweed and his partners.

They were totally untrustworthy. They were supposedly the friends of the poor Irish in New York, but in fact they only threw them crumbs from their political banquet table and used Irish votes to augment their power on election day. Irishmen in Tammany, like Dick Connolly and Peter Sweeny, were bloodsuckers ready to sell out their countrymen to line their own pockets with gold. An alliance with them would ruin the reputation of the Fenian movement with the rest of America.

"The head center"—he used O'Mahoney's official title—"has called a meeting at Moffat House this afternoon. He wants you and Dan to attend. We're going to settle this matter once and for all," Michael said.

"I'll leave it to you to rouse Mr. McCaffrey," I said. "I'm not speaking to him."

This was pleasing news to Michael, and he took even greater pleasure in dragging Dan from his bed. When he stumbled into the sitting room, I felt a pang of remorse. He was suffering from one of the worst hangovers in the sorry history of alcohol. His normally fair skin was a pale green; his eyes were slits.

"Coffee," he gasped. "Get me some coffee."

"Go get your own coffee," I said. "You're quick enough to go get other things for yourself."

Michael took pity on him, only because he was under orders to deliver him to Moffat House on schedule. He had a pot of steaming coffee sent up from the restaurant and all but poured it down Dan's gullet.

"I met Nora," I said, watching the show. "She's lovely."

"Thanks," he said.

"You talked me over thoroughly, I gather, and found me wanting," I said.

"Yeah," he said.

"The feeling is mutual," I said.

That was a lie. Behind my bitter words, my heart was a stone that felt nothing. I was numb with anger and pain.

We arrived at the Moffat mansion off Union Square around 1:00 P.M. A huge Fenian flag, with its gold harp and sunburst, flew over the door. The former home of a patent medicine millionaire, the house was well worthy of being the headquarters of a government in exile. The furnishings were palatial—immense gold leaf mirrors and brocaded velvet draperies, French empire furniture upholstered in gold and green. In the dining room, Head Center O'Mahoney and the members of the council were gathered around a large oval table. We sat off to one side, observers more than participants.

Pulling on his long beard, O'Mahoney began the game with a stiff demand for an explanation from Colonel Roberts. O'Mahoney pointed to me. "This young woman, who has become in a few short days the symbol of our movement, was seen last night all over New York on the arm of William Marcy Tweed."

"So she was," said Roberts coolly. He was obviously well prepared for this challenge. "My opinion of Mr. Tweed corresponds to yours. He's a corrupt politician. He's also the most powerful man in New York City and in the state. Proof of this, if you need it, is here in this satchel."

He put a small black bag on the table and opened it. Quickly he took out the mountain of greenbacks we had collected last night. The other members of the council gaped at the pile. "Nine thousand dollars, gentlemen. To be placed in our treasury. From one night's work with Mr. Tweed."

Roberts launched into an impassioned discourse about political realism. The Irish were accused of being dreamers and talkers, without practical ability. He heard it every day in business, and he had heard it in the Union Army. There was some truth to the charge. It was time to put an end to those stories by showing the world that we could deal with men like Tweed and others in Washington, D.C. "We're fighting a war, not conducting a tea party or organizing a gentlemen's debating club," Roberts roared. "Mr. Lincoln and his friends didn't win the war just ended by asking for a letter of recommendation from a soldier's pastor. They just asked: Will he fight? I asked Mr. Tweed that question last night, and his answer was yes. There's the proof."

He pointed to the pile of money.

The council looked to John O'Mahoney for an answer. He pulled at his beard and said he was no orator, much less a debater. He said he would let the question be decided by a majority vote of the council. A pleased smile spread across Roberts's face. He knew that with Tweed's help he now had a majority of the votes on the council. From that moment, John O'Mahoney ceased to be the leader of the Fenian movement in America.

"Wait!"

Michael sprang to his feet, his face aflame. "As a young man who's pledged his future to this cause, I think I'm entitled to be heard," he said. "I came to these American shores with a heart full of hope, with faith that in America purity of purpose and integrity of means were possible, because the degradation to which our people are subjected in Ireland was not operative here. But I now find a new kind of degradation threatening us, the degradation of too much wealth, of easy riches, of power that corrupts as it pretends to assist us."

For ten minutes Michael poured forth his natural eloquence in this vein. He said he stood with John O'Mahoney and they both spoke for Ireland. It was madness to expect Tweed or any other American politician to care seriously for Ireland. Only the Irish could do that in a sustained way. Only they could keep as their goal Ireland's liberation. "Don't be distracted by American schemes," he cried. "Don't be fooled by American promises."

The response of the council was angry and ugly. Roberts made a sneering, bullying speech that ridiculed Michael's pretensions to speak for Ireland or anyone but himself. I disliked that part, but I could not disagree with the rest of his argument. Without the help of the United States, there was no hope of striking a serious blow for Ireland in the near future. Now, now was the time to act, while veterans roamed the country in search of employment. At his close, Roberts pointed dramatically at Dan McCaffrey. "Ask this young man if he would risk his life for Ireland if we came to him five years hence, when he has perhaps married that lovely young girl beside him and is settled on his farm in Tennessee. No! It is unreasonable, impossible."

I gave my Donal Ogue a glare, which was intended to inform him that it was unreasonable and impossible to expect this lovely young girl to marry him in five years—or fifty. He ignored me and vehemently agreed with Colonel Roberts. The new leader—for that was what Roberts was swiftly becoming—declared that it was his intention to go to Washington, D.C., immediately and consult with the leading politicians there. "Let greenhorns from Ireland carp at America," he shouted. "I have faith in her devotion to freedom, her sympathy for the oppressed."

The council voted eighteen to two in favor of Roberts's policy. John O'Mahoney, the founder of Fenianism, became a mere figurehead, whom Roberts and his friends maintained in office for their own purposes. To soothe him, they agreed to send a diplomatic mission to Ireland, explaining the shift in policy to the Fenian leaders there. Patrick Meehan, the owner of the *Irish-American*, and a man named Dunne, fat and rather stupid looking, agreed to leave on the first available ship. Roberts meanwhile would depart for Washington, D.C. He asked the council's permission to take with him, as an "attention getter," the Fenian girl and Major McCaffrey.

I glanced at Michael. His glower spoke disapproval, but I had already declared my independence of him. I glanced more coolly at Dan McCaffrey and decided I was now independent of him, too. I would chart my own course, make up my own mind about this adventure. "I'm at your disposal," I said.

On the way back to our hotel, Colonel Roberts expanded on his plan. He wanted me and Dan to create a kind of variety act, which could be performed at Fenian meetings and rallies. It was to be based on our newspaper stories of me fighting off a horde of British troopers with Dan's pistol. He had arranged with Dick Connolly for me to take lessons in marksmanship at a shooting gallery on the Bowery, during the hours when the place was not open for business. Dan was to be my teacher.

Roberts took us directly to the gallery and introduced us to the owner, a cheerful, moon-faced Irishman named Slattery. Roberts slipped him a few greenbacks, and Slattery closed his doors to the public. He informed us that he was adjourning to the corner saloon and left me and Dan alone.

Mockingly, Dan picked up a big revolver not unlike the one he wielded in Ireland, and said, "This is a gun." He picked up a cartridge and said, "This is a bullet."

"Don't treat me like a fool when the folly is all on your side," I said. "I hoped I would be excused the task of ever saying another word to you. Now it seems we're thrown together again. Let's say only what's necessary, as plainly and as simply as possible."

That silenced him. Sullenly he shoved six bullets into

the cylinder and showed me how to squeeze the trigger. The target was an Indian, painted on paper and hung on the rear wall. The first shot I fired, the big gun bucked in my hand and went flying to the floor. The bullet went into the ceiling. Dan's condescending smile infuriated me. I seized the weapon with two hands the next time and minded his admonition to squeeze, not jerk, the trigger. I brought the Indian's chest in line with the sight at the end of the barrel and fired again. The bullet was only a foot or so wide of the mark. Slowly, over the next two hours, using my two-handed style, I improved until I was able to put an occasional bullet through the painted Indian. But I was still far from the markswoman described in the papers. Each crash of the gun made me flinch and tremble.

"Is there no lighter gun?" I asked. "This cannon is simply too heavy."

Dan shrugged. "What difference does it make? You're never goin' to learn to hit nothin', anyway, except when the law of averages gets in your favor."

He picked up the gun and put six bullets in the Indian's head. I stalked out in a fury. By the time I reached the hotel I was exhausted. The temperature was in the nineties, and it must have been 110 in the shooting gallery. I bought a copy of *Harper's Weekly* at a newsstand on the corner and spent the next hour absorbed by the grisly tale of the execution of Lincoln's assassins. It was not very cheerful reading. Paging through the advertisements, I came across one for "the National Revolver, the lightest gun in the world." It was being sold by George N. Hickcox at 54 Cliff Street.

I rode to Cliff Street in a hackney coach and found bewhiskered Mr. Hickcox in the process of closing his store. It was a veritable armory, with pistols and rifles of every shape and size on the walls. The National Revolver cost twenty dollars. I bought it, and three hundred rounds of ammunition, and went back to Slattery's shooting gallery on the Bowery. He was still closed, awaiting the business rush of the evening.

I set to work. The revolver fit neatly in my hand, and it did not buck or leap when I squeezed the trigger. Using bull's-eye targets, I fired deliberately and examined the result, learning to judge the drift of the bullet to the right, a peculiarity of the gun, no doubt. I grew more and more used to the bark of the gun. Slattery wandered in after I had been at it for about an hour. "Still here?" he said. "By God, you mean business." He watched me for a few minutes and declared himself amazed. I was learning fast. He gave me a few bits of advice about how to stand for better balance and letting my breath out before I fired.

I rode back to the hotel feeling proud of myself. In spite of male contempt and the blazing heat of July, I had taught myself to do a difficult thing. I felt a little more equal to dealing with this tumultuous, bewildering American world. And with Dan McCaffrey.

Walking down Broadway, surrounded by ladies wearing expensive, gaily striped dresses in the latest Paris fashion, I found myself reciting an old Celtic charm. "May I be an island in the sea. May I be a hill on the land. I shall wound every man. No man shall hurt me."

Riding History's Whirlwind

I was still in this bitter mood when I left New York for Washington, D.C., three days later with Dan McCaffrey, Red Mike Hanrahan, and Colonel William Roberts. Dan was equally sour and silent. Red Mike tried to cheer us up by telling us the story of his improbable life, from his birth in India, the son of an Irish sergeant in the British Army, through stints on the London stage, in the California Gold Rush of '49, and in the Union Army. When this failed, he tried reciting endless verses of "Brian O'Linn," a comic poem about an Irish idiot who always made the best of everything. This failed as miserably as his first effort.

Colonel Roberts, egotism personified, scarcely noticed our gloom. He was ebullient. A Fenian regiment had marched in the big parade that had welcomed General Grant to New York the previous day. They had worn the blue of the Union Army, with bands of green ribbon on their sleeves. Roberts told us that the general had noticed them and asked who they were. When he was told, he replied, "More power to them."

I struggled to raise my spirits by taking an interest in my new surroundings. It was my first trip on an American train. I had ridden trains in Ireland on trips to Dublin to visit Michael at the university, but nothing in their plain decor prepared me for the American parlor car. The seats were upholstered in deep carmine and golden-olive velvet plush. Each window had curtains of salmon-colored cloth, stiff in patterns of gold bullion. From the ceiling hung large double silver chandeliers. It was the last car on the train and had an observation platform on which you could stand to let the wind whip you.

We departed from Jersey City on the New Jersey Railroad. At New Brunswick, they uncoupled our car and attached it to an engine of the Camden & Amboy Railroad, which hauled us the rest of the way through the state of New Jersey. Its neat farms and prosperous towns were my first glimpse of America beyond New York. At Camden we rumbled across the Delaware to Philadelphia, where we changed trains entirely, this time to the Philadelphia, Wilmington & Baltimore Railroad. Our new parlor car was even more gorgeous. Instead of double seats, there were armchairs, upholstered in scarlet velvet. On the floor was a magnificent Turkish carpet, and each armchair had a small table beside it for magazines and books. A large, ornate fountain at one end of the car contained ice water, which we drank greedily. It was very hot.

I remarked that nothing in Ireland compared to such summer heat. Dan laughed briefly and said, "This is nothin'. You should visit Memphis in July."

"You will, if all goes well," said Colonel Roberts. He hoped to send us on a fund-raising tour around the whole country, from Boston to New Orleans and as far west as St. Louis and Chicago. He spread a map on his table and pointed to dozens of cities and towns. There were now over four hundred Fenian circles, and the membership had risen to twenty-five thousand. They hoped to double it within the year—with the help of the Fenian girl. They planned to enlist Irish women in an auxiliary called the Fenian Sisterhood.

Colonel Roberts talked roundly about the size and power of the United States. It was well on its way to becoming the greatest nation in the world. Already it had more railroads, bridges, and steel and textile factories than any other country except England, and it was only a matter of time before we challenged her power. The English knew this, and that was why they had attempted to wreck America by supporting the Southern Confederates. It was inevitable that America and England were going to fight for leadership of the world. Both countries knew it, and that was among several reasons why Colonel Roberts was convinced that we had a good chance to win American support for the Fenian invasion of Canada. He had been to Washington several times in the last few months, and numerous congressmen and influential generals had privately assured him that they favored kicking the British out of Canada as a first step to smashing them in the inevitable war.

Colonel Roberts had been a successful dry-goods merchant and had served in the Union Army's commissary department during the war. He had a head for figures, and he stunned us by rolling off his tongue spectacular summaries of America's immensity. From sea to sea, the nation now comprised 3,025,000 square miles. Of the 1,936 billion acres in the national domain, no less than a billion had not yet been settled. Stretching away to the Rocky Mountains and over them to the Pacific lay an empire three times larger than the entire country when it gained its independence from England in 1783. If this great wilderness were populated as densely as England, it would furnish homes for 539 million men, women, and children. In this year alone they expected to take $16 million in gold from the territory of Montana. The transactions of brokers in Wall Street for the year ending June 30, 1865 reached 6 billion dollars. A single block of land in New York had recently been sold for $500,000. The Internal Revenue Department reported that $7 million was spent each year in New York alone on theaters and restaurants. In the final year of the war, the North spent $3 billion to support its armies.

"I calculate that we can conquer Canada for ten million," Roberts said. "Chicken feed!"

"Red Mike Chicken, formerly Hanrahan, reporting for duty," cried Mike, springing up and saluting.

Arriving in Washington, D.C., in the late afternoon with these stupendous numbers rattling in my head, I expected to encounter a capital out of the Arabian nights, a metropolis of marble and gold, teeming with monumental magnificence. I was shocked to discover a shabby, dirty town, not much bigger than the city of Limerick. The public buildings, which were still draped with black in mourning for the fallen Lincoln, stood like absentminded fits of grandiosity in the midst of swamps and open fields. The one truly striking edifice was the Capitol, which Mr. Lincoln had insisted on completing in spite of the toils and expense of the Civil War. Its superb dome, topped by a statue of Freedom leaning on a sheathed sword, caught the breath. But all around this glorious building were blocks of crumbling old houses.

Pennsylvania Avenue, the main thoroughfare from the capitol into the heart of the city, was as full of ruts and holes as any country road in Ireland. As we reached an intersection in our open carriage, we were engulfed by a hot wind blowing a dust storm, known in Washington as a "Sahara." It almost choked us. The south side of the Avenue was lined with dingy buildings and an agglomeration of sheds and shacks that served as the city market. On the north side was one of the few sidewalks, and the town's hotels and restaurants. Immediately north of the Avenue, between the Capitol and the Executive Mansion, was the only part of Washington which was sufficiently built up to warrant the designation of a city. Houses, churches, school buildings were crowded here, but all seemed done in a small way, built without attention to appearance or comfort. There was an abundance of petty rooming houses and cheap restaurants and saloons to serve the poorly paid clerks who worked for the government.

Colonel Roberts, oblivious to the contradiction between his words and his previous statistical paean to

America, began damning Washington as the worst city
on earth. There was not a streetcar in the place. A few
straggling omnibuses and helter-skelter hacks were the
only public transportation. A pedestrian often had to
walk blocks before he or she found it possible to cross a
single street, so deep and pervasive was the spring and
summer mud. And the temperature! It made the heat of
New York seem like an autumn zephyr. We struggled to
our rooms on the third floor of the Hotel Willard and collapsed.

At dinner we were joined by new allies—the man who
had recruited Dan into the Fenians, Colonel John O'Neil,
and his wife, Margaret. He was a smashingly handsome
black-haired Irishman in his mid-thirties. His wife was
five or six years younger, a brunette, with a rather homely
mannish face and a solemn manner. The sight of O'Neil
did wonders for Dan. His surly mood vanished, and he
became an eager inquirer into the political and social do-
ings of Tennessee. He asked for news of friends, for
prognostications of the future.

Alas, Colonel O'Neil had little good to tell him. Few
of his friends, most of whom were Confederate sympa-
thizers, had stayed in the state. O'Neil's reply became a
kind of grim litany. "Confiscated, gone to Mexico. Bankrupt. Gone to California." The state was being ruled by a
man whom both O'Neil, who had fought for the Union,
and Dan seemed equally to despise, a Methodist minister
named William Brownlow. Middle Tennessee, where
Dan lived, and East Tennessee were still under martial
law, which meant a man could be shot for disobeying a
soldier's order. What was even more confusing to an outsider, this "Parson" Brownlow, who had supported the
Union, was a violent foe of President Andrew Johnson,
who was also from Tennessee. The two men had hated
each other for years.

The intricacies of American politics were truly

bewildering for an outsider. I said as much to Red Mike Hanrahan. He laughed and said most of the confusion was caused by the war. "Before that craziness began, everyone was either a Democrat or a Republican. But a lot of Democrats pitched in with the Republicans to fight the war. A good many simpletons like meself joined up for the same reason, to save the Union. The next thing we knew, we were fightin' to free the slaves. On those terms they wouldn't have gotten ten Irishmen into the army from Philadelphia to Boston. Now there's Democrats by the tens of thousands wakin' up like drunks the mornin' after a bender and vowin' to swear off Republicanism for life."

This, Colonel Roberts said, was Ireland's opportunity. President Johnson was a Democrat. Lincoln had chosen him to run with him on his Republican Party ticket to create a united front for the war effort. Johnson would listen to Irish Democrats from Tennessee. That explained Colonel O'Neil's presence.

Our spirits were high that night. We soared on hope and bid defiance to all other faiths but our own. John O'Neil raised his glass of bourbon, a drink much favored in Tennessee, and tried to make our optimism into an antidote to his wife's worries about the Fenian cause. "We'll make a convert of you yet," he said. His tongue loosened by the liquor, he told us how they had met, while she blushed and tried to silence him. In the winter of 1862, he had been carried into a Nashville hospital almost dead of a stomach wound.

"I thought I was in heaven for sure," he said. "There was the most beautiful creature I've ever seen looking down on me in a dress all of white, a rosary tied about her waist. 'Twas Margaret."

She had been a Sister of Mercy, working in a hospital founded by her order. They had opened their doors to the wounded of both sides. It was a horrible time. The dying filled the rooms and corridors. Her care had not a little to do with saving John O'Neil's life. During his convalescence, they fell in love. She was Irish, from Kerry, the same county from which O'Neil's parents had come. Finally she went to her mother superior and told her that she could no longer obey her vows. She was driven from the hospital like a scarlet woman. Colonel O'Neil, his health restored, instantly proposed.

With much sadness, we discussed the Catholic Church's blind severity toward those who refused to conform to all its dictates. So often, they seemed to want obedient automatons, rather than men and women who pledged their religious faith yet retained the right to think and act freely. They would have to change their ways if they wanted to keep the allegiance of Irish-Americans, Red Mike said. Colonel Roberts agreed. The success of the Fenians in the teeth of clerical opposition was proof of the power of American freedom. I studied Margaret O'Neil while this conversation went back and forth. She did not respond to it. I sensed a troubled soul.

"Are these the representatives of the Irish Republic?" asked a voice from behind me.

"Indeed we are," said Colonel Roberts to the trim, elegantly dressed man who asked the question. "And of the New York Democracy."

"A formidable combination," said our visitor, as Roberts rose to introduce him.

"Ladies and gentlemen, the honorable Fernando Wood, congressman from New York and former mayor of our fair city."

"I have here a telegram from Mr. Tweed, directing me to present you with the keys to the city—and to the U.S. Mint, if possible," said Congressman Wood.

He was a cool, debonair man with a narrow, sharp-nosed face behind a precisely curled black mustache. He carried himself with the ramrod posture of a colonel of the British Guards. There were touches of gray in his hair, but he nonetheless emanated an intense, astringent vitality.

"Is this the Fenian girl?" he said, smiling down at me.

"None other," said Colonel Roberts.

"Those newspaper sketchers should be shot for treason to Ireland," he said. "They haven't even come close to doing you justice."

I found myself blushing beneath his direct, steady stare.

"I envy your passionate dedication to your cause," he said. "Although I'm convinced that passion and politics don't mix."

"Perhaps there are some causes that demand passion," I said.

"I think not," he said. "I fear there are people who must have it, to feed a passionate nature. I hope you can profit from the example of our Southern friends and mix some policy with your passion."

"That is precisely what we've come to Washington to do," said William Roberts. "But I wonder what help you can give us, Congressman. I'm surprised that Bill Tweed could not have found a stronger voice for us. Forgive my frankness, but we have no time for niceties."

"I've long been a friend of political candor," Wood said. "I can give you very little help personally. I'm obnoxious to the president and all the other strutting, crowing victors. But I know what's happening in Washington. That may be one reason Tweed sent me to you. The other may have been to let me know that you're his political property, and I had better keep my distance."

"We're no one's political property," Roberts said.

"In that case I'll display a little candor. You should be wary of aligning the Fenians too closely to Tweed. The time may come when you may want to deliver the Irish vote to a candidate he can't back."

"Who might that be?" Roberts said.

"There's a new political party forming here in Washington. Neither Democrat nor Republican."

"We're ready to talk business with them," Roberts said. "We'll talk business with anyone."

"An admirable philosophy," Wood said. "On that basis, I'm at your service, gentlemen. Good night."

He bowed to me and kissed my hand. "Good night, my dear. I will go home and meditate on the place of passion in politics."

He strolled away. Roberts watched him go with a growl. "There's the smoothest article in the history of New York politics," he said. "He could be useful. But you can't go near him now without getting dirt on you."

"Why?" I asked.

Roberts explained that Fernando Wood had made two fatal miscalculations. He had been mayor of New York when the South seceded in 1861. He had urged the city to join the rebels. This had enabled Bill Tweed and other enemies in Tammany to call him a traitor. In a fierce struggle, they had defeated him in 1863, and Tweed had offered him the seat in Congress as a consolation prize. There Wood had continued to call for a negotiated peace that would have recognized the South's right to secede. With the war won by the North, Fernando Wood was now a political pariah.

"Perhaps one of us could go to him in secret," I said. "He would clearly like to be useful to us—in the hope, no doubt, that we might be useful to him."

"Let's wait and see how we do at the White House on our own," Roberts said.

The next morning, John O'Neil sent his card to the White House with a request to see the president. Before lunch, a messenger arrived, saying that Mr. Johnson would receive us that night, about 9:00 P.M. I spent the morning talking to reporters, under Red Mike Hanrahan's approving eye. Mike had given me another pep talk, stressing the importance of the Washington, D.C., newspapers, and I managed to bring off a satisfactory performance. We had a head start with the best and oldest paper, the *National Intelligencer,* which had a Celt named Johnny Coyle among its executive staff. He came with the reporter and virtually cheered me on. The next paper, the *Star,* took a more blasé point of view. It was like the *New York Herald,* ready to print almost anything if it was a good story.

The third reporter, a bald-headed, snub-nosed man named William Colby, from the *Chronicle,* was openly skeptical. He asked me a number of sharp questions, such as whether I believed the bullet was preferable to the ballot in determining political issues. I was not aware that he was using a quotation from the martyred Lincoln to trap me, and said I thought the bullet was preferable when the ruling tyrants were indifferent to the ballot. The reporter for the fourth paper, the *Republican,* took notes dutifully and then sought out Colonel Roberts and O'Neil, who were conferring with some congressmen in the next room, and demanded a hundred dollars to print the story. We gave it to him.

Mrs. O'Neil and I spent the afternoon touring Washington. As a nurse, she was anxious to see the hospitals. One of the largest was in a vast ramshackle series of sheds to the west of the Capitol. As we approached, a sickening odor of putrefaction surrounded us. I had to seize my handkerchief and muffle my face. Mrs. O'Neil, used to such vapors, scarcely noticed it. A soldier guarding the outer gate readily admitted us. Mrs. O'Neil had had the forethought to provide us with a basket of fresh fruit to give the soldiers.

I thought the war was over, and with it the suffering. Margaret O'Neil knew better. She knew how long it took the body to recover from the terrible violation of a bullet. Unlike me, she was not shocked to discover a hall filled with hundreds of beds, stretching for what must have been three city blocks. On each bed a man lay still or twisted and groaned or sat staring listlessly. Those last were the most dangerous cases, she told me. So often a wound depressed the mind, and in the end infection spread like an evil flower to consume the victim's life.

She met a man in his shirtsleeves, who she correctly guessed was a doctor. "How many in this hospital?" she asked.

"Two thousand."

"How many still in the whole city?"

The doctor, who was scarcely thirty, pulled at his brown beard for a moment. "Over thirty thousand," he said. "But we're sending them home as fast as possible. They'll have a better chance at home than in this overheated pigsty."

The sun beat on the flat roof, making the inside of the shed an oven. Margaret O'Neil asked who would make the best use of her basket of fruit. "The amputees," the doctor said. "They're at the far end. We find they do better when we keep them apart from the others."

We walked the length of the building and found ourselves surrounded by men with missing arms or legs, and some with both. "Is anyone here from Ireland?" I asked as we began handing out the fresh fruit.

A dozen raised their hands. Only one was from Kerry, and one from Limerick, our home counties, and they came from villages neither Margaret O'Neil nor I knew well. We were strangers meeting in this strange place, offering mute testimony not so much to our Irishness as to our common humanity. The more I looked about me, the more I felt ashamed for having asked the question. I think it was there in that hospital, surrounded by the awesome sight of the suffering caused by a war, that I felt the first stab of doubt about the goodness, the wisdom, of our cause.

The feeling passed as quickly as it came, largely because of the reaction Margaret O'Neil tried to force upon me as we left the hospital. "Doesn't that sight make you wonder?" she asked.

"About what?"

"About starting a war to free Ireland."

Without warning she launched a violent denunciation of the Fenians. She would never have left the hospital and her vows if she had known John O'Neil was to become a convert to this cause. Her father had been a disciple of the great Daniel O'Connell, the man who had preached moral force and peaceful persuasion as Ireland's only recourse. Coldly I told her I had heard these arguments from my own father and learned to despise them. What a strange combination I was in those days, cold as the grave inside and fiery anger on the surface.

Margaret O'Neil now viewed me with disapproval and disappointment. She had hoped to make an ally of me from that hospital visit. For my part, I felt sorry for John O'Neil if he had to listen to such sermons in his bedroom.

Partly to change the subject, I suggested a visit to the Capitol. We toiled up the hill and soon found ourselves within the spacious dome. The place was filthy. There were piles of refuse behind the statuary and in the corners. It reeked of unpleasant human odors as well. The walls were covered with scribbles of writing, initials of earlier visitors, some with brief messages for posterity. But the sweep of the dome was grand in its ambitious breadth, and the statues had a heroic Roman nobility to them.

"Ladies, good afternoon. Can I be of service to you?" It was Congressman Fernando Wood, looking as urbane and elegant in a suit of dark blue as he had looked last night.

"We're mere tourists," I said, "ready to be interested by anything you suggest."

"There's no point in gazing at these marble monuments to the dead," he said. "Or at that Italian Renaissance painting up there," he added, gesturing to the panels on the dome. "They can't amuse, and amusement is the only possible reason for visiting Congress."

He led us briskly up a broad marble staircase to the visitors' gallery of the Senate chamber. It was a most impressive room, with a lofty cast-iron ceiling, paneled in stained glass, each pane bearing the arms of the different states. The walls were a glowing gold, the doors a bright emerald green. The senators were supposed to sit in three semicircular rows behind small desks of polished wood, but only a few of these were occupied. Most of the salons were sitting offstage, as it were, in the cloakrooms, their feet up on chairs, smoking. Others strolled the aisles, munching apples, whispering to colleagues. The presiding officer, who sat on an ornately carved dais, was writing a letter. Through all this inattention a senator was speaking. He was a burly man with a huge head and a snarling mouth above a massive stubborn chin.

"Mark him," Fernando Wood said, "he's one of your enemies. Ben Wade of Ohio."

"We know we have a drunkard in the White House," Wade roared. "I'm beginning to think we may also have a traitor. Where does this pseudo-president get the power to pardon rebels in arms, to restore the right to govern to the very men who have forfeited it forever by their treasonous murderous acts?"

"I can see he's the president's enemy," I said. "Why is he Ireland's?"

"Wade is part of the Radical Republican machine," Wood explained. "A minority. They can only stay in power by preventing the Democrats in the Southern states from returning to Congress. They want to make the South a conquered territory, a military district, for the next century, while they rule here and pick things clean. They're Sassenachs, as you call them, and despise Irishmen even more than they hate rebels. If they win the game, you can say good-bye to your hopes of American support."

Wade went on abusing the president in a style I found hard to believe, even though I was hearing it with my own ears. He bid fair to continue for hours, and we finally left him and crossed the great rotunda to the House of Representatives. Here, much the same performance was being enacted by a man speaking while the rest conducted other business. This orator was also from Ohio. His name was James Ashley, and he was, Fernando Wood told us with offhand contempt, a former drugstore keeper. He was a short fat man with a large shock of bushy light hair, which he wore over his forehead in a frowzy bang. He had a rather high-pitched voice, and he was using it to denounce President Johnson shrilly. "From this day forward," he cried, "this house must begin collecting evidence to remove this man. Our one hope of saving the nation lies in our constitutional right to impeach the traitor in the White House."

On and on Ashley ranted. Mrs. O'Neil listened with apparently complete attention. In my right ear I heard Fernando Wood's cool voice. "You must know you're very beautiful. I'm something of a connoisseur of beauty—as well as of political intrigue. Would you come to my room at the National Hotel tonight? We might have some things to exchange over a bottle of champagne."

"We have an appointment to see the president at nine." I said.

"I seldom go to bed before two," he said.

"I'll think about it," I said.

My lack of feeling shocked me. I should not have been surprised at it, but I still wanted to believe I was the same passionately sincere patriot girl I had been when Dan McCaffrey walked through the door of our farmhouse in Ireland. I did not want to admit another very different woman was living in that girl's flesh.

At dinner that night we dined on expectation. We scarcely tasted the food, spread in the usual American profusion. We were in our hired carriage by half past eight and rode through the darkening streets to the White House. There was no letup in the heat, even with the shadows of evening. It surmounted the city in a great smothering blanket.

We waited for the president in the East Room of the White House. The room looked like it had been fought over by opposing armies. The cushions on the chairs were ripped and torn, smeared with the dirt of a hundred boots. Couches sagged; draperies dangled in shreds. Someone—we later learned it was President Johnson's daughter—had tried to disguise the damage of the previous four years by filling the room with fresh flowers. But it was impossible to hide the results of the mansion's war service as the Union's headquarters, crowded with grimy dispatch riders and mud-splattered aides-de-camp from the battlefront, day and night. The place was a wreck.

The president met us with a broad smile. He was a square-shouldered, clean-shaven man of middle height, with a broad brow and ruddy complexion. He embraced his friend O'Neil. "By God, John," he said, in a drawl even broader than Dan's, "seein' your ugly face is almost as good as a visit to Tennessee. How are you, anyway, you miserable Irish possum?"

O'Neil said he was fine, now that he had married his nurse. He introduced his wife and then me, Colonel Roberts, and Dan. As he finished, a husky, dark-bearded young man joined us. The president introduced his son Robert. Behind a stiff, jutting beard, he had the president's rough features but a far smoother manner. He took my hand and murmured something about being charmed to meet a genuine Irish beauty. He had dined with the reporter from the *Star,* who had told him about me.

"I got to warn you about this fellow, Mr. President," Colonel O'Neil said, pointing to Dan. "He's a Tennessee man and one hell of a soldier, but he took the wrong side in our little contention."

"So did most everybody in Tennessee," Johnson said with a grin. "Where did you fight, son?"

"With Stuart's cavalry," Dan said.

"I can respect that," the president said. "I can respect a soldier who stands to his arms with honest conviction and risks his all on a hundred battlefields. It's the bushwhackers and outlaws who ran wild in Tennessee that I wanted to hang—and I did hang my share of them. Now you've lost in a fair fight and you want to rejoin the United States. Is that how you see it?"

"Yes, sir," Dan said.

"Robert," the president said to his son, "put this boy's name at the head of our pardon list tomorrow." He threw his arm around Dan's shoulders in the same affectionate gesture he had used with O'Neil. "You're the kind of rebel we want and need to rebuild this country. But those hungry wolves from Ohio and Massachusetts want to feed on your flesh. To the victor belong the spoils, that's their battle cry, but the skunks ain't honest enough to admit it."

The president stormed away on this theme for a good five minutes, and I began to wonder if we would ever have a chance to mention Ireland. But O'Neil, who knew him well, let him wind down and then introduced the purpose of our visit.

"Although I'm still wearing my Union uniform, Mr.

President," O'Neil said, "I'm about to change it for another color—the green of Ireland. I have the rank of colonel in the Fenian army, and McCaffrey here is a major. Colonel Roberts is a member of the council of advisors. You'll read about this young lady's exploits in the papers tomorrow. We're here to ask America's help, to revenge both America and Ireland for Britain's crimes."

"You'll have all the help this honest heart can give," Johnson said, striking himself dramatically on the chest. "What are your plans?"

Quickly, O'Neil outlined the proposal to conquer Canada and hold it as hostage for Ireland's freedom. "I like it," Johnson said, springing up to stride excitedly back and forth before us. "Those damned royal skunks let the Rebs use Canada to send a thousand spies and bushwhackers across our borders. Secretary of State Seward told me just the other day that for the damage those built-in-England Confederate sea raiders like the *Alabama* did to our merchant fleet, we should get two hundred million from the Bank of England. That's twice what Canada's worth. Just this afternoon I was talking to General Rawlins, Grant's chief of staff, about it. He said we could take Canada with one corps of the Army of the Potomac. Twenty thousand men. But why not let you people take it? Then we offer you membership in the United States, like Polk did with Texas. If Queen Victoria yells, we'll just tell her that we're fair and square now. If she don't like it, come on over and try to take it away from us."

"It's in the great tradition of the state of Tennessee," Robert Johnson said. "It will make you a president as famous as Andrew Jackson."

"Now hold on, son, nobody can equal that man, least of all this old stump speaker," President Johnson said. "But I like what you said about Tennessee. I'd like to redeem the honor of the state. What better way than to point to this man and say: Remember Sam Houston?

Here's the Sam Houston of Canada. Both from Tennessee."

The president pounded John O'Neil on the back and literally roared with excitement. "What do you need, John? Tell me, and by the eternal I'll move the Treasury and the War Department around on my back to get it."

"We need guns, ammuntion, the right to sell bonds to raise the money to buy uniforms, and when we attack—recognition as belligerents."

"The way the English recognized the Confederacy. You'll have it. You'll have the chance to buy guns and ammunition from our armories at cost. You'll have everything you need or want."

We left the White House walking on air. Back at the hotel, it was champagne all around and a toast to Ireland's freedom before the year's end. Red Mike Hanrahan rushed off to prepare a report for the Fenian council and telegraph a story about our warm White House reception (minus the explicit promises) to the *Irish-American*. How easy it is for men with power in their hands to infuse the powerless with dizzy hope. I believed President Andrew Johnson as much as the others.

Suddenly I remembered the whispered invitation of that connoisseur of beauty and politics, Fernando Wood. It was dangerous to go near him, I knew, but it might be equally dangerous to stay away.

I went to my room, pretending the champagne made me sleepy, changed to a light blue evening dress, and descended to the street. In fifteen minutes I was at the National Hotel. I had to nerve myself to ask for Mr. Wood's room, but the clerk did not seem in the least surprised. "Miss Fitzmaurice?" he said. "He's expecting you."

I found him in formal dinner dress, with a silver service for a late supper laid on a tablecloth of crisp Irish linen. A bottle of wine cooled in a silver bucket. It was a champagne more delicious than any I had yet tasted. "I discovered it in Paris," he said. "It comes from a small vineyard near Rheims. They let it age twenty years before selling it. I understand it's Napoleon the Third's favorite."

He showed me around his suite, which he had decorated himself, with furniture from Paris. Paintings by Corot, David, and other masters hung on the walls. The golden-yellow wallpaper, alive with shepherds wooing scantily clad shepherdesses, was copied from a room in Versailles. "You must sit here," he said, placing me on a rose-colored couch. "It matches your dress. Did you choose those colors? You have taste to match your beauty."

"Don't you want to hear about my meeting with the president?"

"No. I simply want to sit here and drink champagne and look at you."

I had never met a man like him, so self-possessed, so calm. I decided that he had to be perfectly empty or perfectly surfeited. I inclined to the latter. He had lived a tumultuous life. He had penetrated and mastered his world, seen it from the inside, and was beyond surprises. I felt a great wish stir in me to do the same thing.

"I looked at you and said, *This is no ordinary girl. She wants to attempt great things.* I was that way once. It's the only way to live."

"Don't you wish to attempt them still?"

"My chance came—I made the attempt—and it ended in failure. I have no regrets, only disappointments. I did everything a reasonable man might expect. But history had other ideas about the future."

"That won't be my way. I'm prepared to die for what I believe."

"Don't say that. I won't hear it. Not tonight. I won't preach you a sermon against fanaticism. Simply believe me when I tell you it's the world's greatest sin. It's the sworn foe of beauty and intelligence, the deadliest enemy of love."

"You may call it fanaticism, but what great thing has ever been accomplished without passion?"

"Well said," he replied. "But the fanatic goes beyond passion. He drives his feelings into an arctic zone where they freeze into weapons of destruction. Passion is human. Fanaticism is its extreme, the attempt to transform the human into the superhuman, the real into the ideal. It always ends in disaster.

"More important," he said, "fanaticism is a passion gone political. I say passion must remain personal, if we are to remain human."

As he said this, he took me by the hand and led me to the table. On plates full of ice were Chesapeake Bay crabs, shrimp, and oysters, the finest in the world, he avowed. At the ring of a bell, a black man emerged from another room to replace the champagne with a cold white wine from Austria.

He asked me to tell him about Ireland, why I loved it enough to die for it, what it meant to me. I told him of my discovery of the proud women of the old sagas, how they had struck a flame in my soul. I tried to make him see how much the land itself still shimmered with the aura of ancient glory. I described the fairy raths, the old kings' tombs, the Bel fires on the mountains. He had heard none of it before. If the American Irish knew such things, they never bothered to share them with him.

"To see such a people, with such a heritage, crushed, degraded. For the first time I understand," he said.

He raised his glass. "I salute your passion, from my American ignorance.

"Where does that leave us?" he said, after a moment of silence. "I feel you've passed me like a pillar of fire, leaving me nothing but the ashes of ignorance and disillusion."

"I don't," I said.

"I spoke of an exchange. I thought I could ask it coolly, calmly, as a connoisseur of beauty. Now I can only ask it as a gift."

"You shall have it," I said. "I want to understand your kind of passion."

He led me into the bedroom and gestured to an open door. "There is a bath already drawn for you. If you want the water warmer, simply call."

I bathed in rose-scented water, rich with shimmering oil. A robe hung on the door. I wrapped it around me and returned to the bedroom. It occurred to me that I was about to do a sinful thing, but it was utterly lacking in the feeling of sin. I had felt a thousand times more guilty when I said to Dan McCaffrey, *You can have me if you want me.* This man toward whom I was walking seemed to exist in a world beyond ordinary right and wrong. He was offering me his wisdom in exchange for my beauty, and the terms seemed perfectly reasonable.

The single gas lamp was turned low. It flickered like an orange eye within its globe. In the semidarkness, he seemed more handsome, more powerful, than any man I had ever imagined. If it was romance, it was of a different order. This was not a hero I was embracing, it was Merlin, a chief druid. "I want you to feel perfectly free," he whispered. "You need have no fear of a child. I've taken the proper precautions."

I was not sure what he meant, but in my adventurer's mood I did not really care. He kissed me softly, then deeply, and his hands roved from my breasts down my body. Slowly he slipped the robe from my shoulders and lifted me, his mouth still on my mouth, and carried me to the bed. His robe fell away and for a moment he stood beside me, naked, a whiteness glowing from his flesh in the wavering lamplight. He took my hand and placed his swelling manhood in it.

"I think I may learn to die for Ireland," he whispered as his hand moved up my thigh.

Slowly, carefully, gently, like dancers to dream music, like swimmers in the depths, we began to make love. It was totally different from the wild taking I had known with Dan. That had been a kind of battle, with the triumph all on his side and the surrender all on mine. This man was teaching me a different kind of pleasure, how to use hands and lips and hair as delicately as a musician drawing deep dark music from a violin or pianoforte. I was discovering sensuality, the secret world that respectable women never entered, the night world through which powerful men roamed in search of pleasure.

Perhaps the most amazing thing about it was the pleasure he took in giving me pleasure. The slow sure drawing out with which he aroused me, the dozen kisses on my neck, my breasts, my thighs, until there gathered within me a surging swirling mass of desire that made me cry out with the sweetness, the terrible tearing power of it, thundering from depths I never dreamt existed in me. I clung to him, laughing, sighing, with each stroke of his flesh, begging him at last for breath, release, until a trembling fire ran through his body and he gave a great delicious "ah" of satisfaction, which echoed like a last treasured note in my throat.

We lay side by side in the shadowed bed for a long time. Then he took my robe and wrapped me in it and carried me back to the sitting room and placed me on the length of the couch like a Roman. He pushed the table, which was on wheels, close to me and drew his own chair to the other side of it. On our plates now were crepes filled with some fragrant fresh jam and small cups of black, bitter coffee of a kind he had discovered in Italy. We ate and drank in silence. The black servant cleared the table and presented us each with a great round globe with a dollop of French brandy in the bottom. Fernando showed me how to breathe as well as drink it.

"Now," he said, "tell me what happened at the White House."

I told him almost word for word. He paused to savor his brandy. "Let me warn you first that you're listening to a disappointed politician. You've offered him the most memorable consolation for his disappointment that he's yet received. But disappointment nevertheless distorts the vision as much as it sharpens it."

He sipped his brandy. "My treasure," he called it. "Laid by monks before the Revolution."

Then he got to the business. "The first thing you must remember is the true nature of the man you're dealing with. He's a backwoods idiot, hopelessly out of his depth, a man whose mind changes every time he talks to someone with a new idea."

"I wonder what my friends Dan McCaffrey and John O'Neil, both from Tennessee, would think of that?" I asked.

"They'd probably shoot me, in the style of most Tennesseans, who prefer that way of settling almost all their arguments. I admit it sounds like New York arrogance. Remember I promised to tell you the truth as I see it. I'm not surprised that you've gotten the president on your side. Your problem will be to keep him there."

"Why?"

"If Johnson told his cabinet what he told you tonight, they would march in a body to Congress and urge his impeachment for insanity. The last thing this country can afford now is a war with England. If the war with the South had lasted another six months, the North would have gone bankrupt. Then there's the problem of Mexico. Are you aware that there's a French army in Mexico?"

"I read it in the paper," I said, "but I haven't had time to comprehend the politics of it."

"Napoleon the Third has put an Austrian archduke named Ferdinand Maximilian on the Mexican throne as part of his dreams of imperial glory. We're determined to kick them out of there, by force if necessary. There's an army of forty-five thousand men on the Mexican border at this very moment. There's another fifty-thousand-man army moving into Indian territory to teach our redskinned brethren a lesson for murdering ten or twenty thousand Americans in the last few years, while we were occupied with killing each other down south. These two projects will cost the government at least seventy million dollars. No sane man would start a war with the British in Canada while facing these expenses."

"You mean President Johnson lied to us?"

"By no means. He made a promise. Which he thoroughly intends to keep, if he can. If he can't, he'll simply throw up his hands and say he was sincere in his good intentions."

"What should we do?"

"Go straight ahead. Act as if the promise is going to be kept. Build up your army. Buy your guns and ammunition. But take steps, very serious steps, to win the backing of the men who count in the cabinet."

"Who are they?"

"Secretary of State William Seward and Secretary of War Edwin Stanton."

"Tell me about them."

"Stanton is Democrat, but that's irrelevant. Basically he's a lawyer. He's never run for office, never dared to live without a client to serve. He looks strong, but he's really an executor of other men's designs, a defender of their acts and policies. He'll go where the power goes almost in spite of himself."

"And Seward?"

"He's a different character. A politician. An honorable term in my lexicon. When he was governor of New York, he tried to work with the Irish, to tempt them out of their slavish allegiance to the Democratic Party. He tried to force through the legislature a bill giving public funds to Catholic schools. It almost cost him his career, but it showed his daring. He knew that prizes are only won by taking risks. But he has a fatal flaw. Instead of consulting his own instincts, and following them to their conclusion in action, he's always trying to hedge his bets."

"You're not filling me with confidence."

"Remember what I said about a disappointed politician. They have a tendency to see the worst. Unless they assiduously seek consolations, they're prey to melancholy."

"Strange, they don't disappoint their women."

"In the end they do, if the women seek affection from them. They no longer have it to give. Only a comradeship in pleasure. That's all they can offer—for a while. Soon they're too old even for that."

I heard the toll of genuine melancholy in his voice. I sensed—and soon confirmed from others—that Fernando Wood had dreamt of sitting in the White House itself, the Democratic mediator between North and South, before the Civil War destroyed the possibility.

"You must learn to think as Seward thinks, anticipate his fears, reassure his hesitations. Does the United States want a Canada ruled by Irishmen on its northern border? I doubt it—any more than they enjoy dealing with the Mexicans to the south. You must realize how strange you are to us, with your Catholic religion and your brogues and your superstititions. You must reorganize your movement, give it a more democratic, American look. No one is going to trust a secret society run by centers and circles. You'll have to make extraordinary efforts to persuade people here in Washington to support you."

"I have little influence in such matters."

"You estimate yourself much too low. You proved to me tonight that you could have more influence than anyone in the Fenian movement, if you choose the right man to persuade here in Washington."

"Who would that be? Mr. Seward?"

"In other circumstances, I would say yes. He likes beautiful women. But he's getting old and he's had a series of physical disasters recently—a fall from a carriage and an attack by one of John Wilkes Booth's friends that have left him rather feeble. I think it would be wiser to outmaneuver him by penetrating the White House itself. Old Andy's son Robert."

"He paid me a good bit of attention tonight."

"I can arrange for him to pay you a lot more."

"How?"

"By telling him you're the best thing I've had in a year."

Now I was deep in it, that world of power and sensuality that I had exulted in penetrating a short half hour ago. I was down where its realities wounded. I think I might have recoiled, fled, except for Fernando Wood's ability to sense my hurt.

"Those who attempt to ride the whirlwind of history must expect some hard falls, some painful moments."

"I understand."

"The trick is not to end as I've seen so many— crucified between two thieves, regret for the past and fear of the future."

I sensed he was one of those men, and he was wishing me, out of the affection and pleasure we had just shared, a better fate.

"Shall I arrange it with Robert Johnson?"

"Yes."

I had come too far to turn back now, even though a voice within me whispered warnings.

"One more thing. I don't trust your friend Roberts. He doesn't keep his word. He regards it as lightly as a Wall Street sharper. That won't do in politics, especially in New York. Promises are a politican's only stock-in-trade. Once he starts to water them, he's for sale to all comers. In New York, we would say that he's honest, but he isn't level. Tweed and I—we're not honest, but we're level. Or try to be."

"What might Roberts do?"

"I'm not sure, but he seems to think that by waving your green Fenian flag he can deliver the Irish vote to the man of his choice. It doesn't work that way. The Irish will stick to the people who've stuck with them and taken their lumps for it. People like me and Tweed."

The clock struck one. My political lesson was over. I said I must go. I rose and kissed him gently on the mouth. "I'll never forget you," I said. "You taught me the truth of an old poem.

"In language beyond learning's touch
Passion can teach.
Speak in that speech beyond reproach
The body's speech."

"Who wrote that?" he asked.

"Donal MacCarthy, the first earl of Clancarty."

"I would have liked to be an earl."

I kissed him once more. "You are one."

In Defense of Ireland's Honor

There was no hackney coach. I walked from the National along Pennsylvania Avenue to the Willard Hotel. The tropic temperature had fallen a little. An occasional breeze stirred the night air. I felt strange, more than human. Was it because I had been loved like a woman or spoken to like a man? Both, I decided. One made me feel free, the other powerful. My pride was in total ascendance. I saw myself as a shaper of nations.

For all its dismal daytime appearance, Washington was as much a city of the night as New York. Coaches crowded with laughing parties of pleasure seekers dashed through the dark at a reckless pace. Drunken men staggered past, baying Negro songs. From a dozen buildings swelled the sounds of reveling voices and music. I found myself longing to join them. I was ready to dance and sing and drink until dawn.

Whom should I see strutting toward me, in one of his wildest checked suits, but Red Mike Hanrahan. "Oho," he said. "Where have you been, you young devil? You've had us turning the Willard upside down looking for you."

"Can you keep a secret?"

"Of course not. It's against me religion. I'm a newspaperman," Mike said.

I told him anyway. It was a confession of sorts, to a combination priest and father, who I knew would forgive me. I told him everything except the part about Robert Johnson. "Wurra wurra," Mike said. "You are a wild one. Anyone with that much nerve has got to have luck. Come in here to Chamberlain's and help me break the bank."

Chamberlain's, only a few doors away, was the premier gambling house of the capital. It was furnished in

the ornate style of the Blossom Club and the Louvre concert saloon. At the bar, Mike bought me champagne and
listened to my summary of Fernando Wood's advice.

"It sounds good to me, but you'll have to convince
Roberts. He's got a very high opinion of himself, like
most self-made men. He seldom takes advice from anyone. Which is too bad, because between you and me,
he's a bit of a fool."

"Dear God, why can't we get better men to lead us?" I
said.

"That's what Lincoln kept asking for the first three
years of the war. Why can't I find a decent general? If
your luck runs bad, you've just got to keep drawing from
the box. It's all luck, you know. I think some evil spirit
back there in the prehistoric mist stacked the deck
against us Irish. Which reminds me. The tiger calls."

The tiger was painted on the box from which the dealer
drew the winning and losing cards in America's favorite
game, faro. There were 164 faro banks flourishing in
Washington at that moment, Mike told me. At Chamberlain's the elite played. Around the table were Union generals in their blue uniforms and congressmen and senators
by the dozen, plus numbers of beautiful women.

Each table was covered by a green cloth on which were
painted the thirteen cards of the spade suit. Everyone bet
against the house, placing money on a certain card, or on
several cards, either to win or lose. The dealer drew the
cards from the tiger-headed box, with winning and losing
cards alternating. The great betting came at the close of a
hand, when only three cards were left in the box. The
dealer's assistant, called the casekeeper, kept a record of
the cards drawn, and the dealer would announce in a dramatic voice the names of the three remaining cards. The
man who predicted the order in which they appeared won
his bet at odds of four to one. This was known as "calling
the turn."

Mike insisted on me selecting the cards and calling each turn. With the instinct of a born gambler, he sensed my luck and exploited it. I hardly missed a card and called four turns in a row. At the end of an hour, Mike was two thousand dollars ahead, whereupon he quit, because he did not want to use up such splendid luck at the faro table.

"Let's reserve a bit of it for Ireland," he said.

We had another glass of champagne and strolled back to the Willard, singing an old song, whose words were not entirely irrelevant.

"I know where I'm going,
And I know who's going with me.
I know who I love—
But the dear knows who I'll marry."

In my room at the Willard waited an unpleasant surprise. Dan McCaffrey rose from the darkness in the corner by the window as I turned on the gas jet. I cried out with fright at first. "What the devil are you doing in here?" I said, anger quickly following my first reaction.

"Waitin' for you. To find out where the hell you went."

"None of your business."

"I can make it my business," he said, seizing my arm. "I'll knock that pretty face of yours out of shape."

"Oh, do that," I said. "You'll be sure to get a medal from the commander-in-chief of the Fenian army for that."

"I got a right to know," he said.

"You forfeited what little right you had when you went wandering the streets of New York to bring that creature back to your bed. Now get out of here."

"If you think about it, that was your fault as much as mine. I'm sorry I did it."

"So was I, for a while. But it doesn't change my mind now. Please go. I'm tired out."

He barred my path to the cabinet where my nightdress was hanging. "I want to know where you went," he said.

"I'm under no obligation to tell you anything. Go or I'll start to scream. You'll end up in jail," I said.

Dan retreated, cursing. The clash spoiled much of the pleasure still throbbing in my body, the way a crude hand flung across a harp's strings creates a ruinous jangle. I slept poorly, my dreams full of a wild Ireland through which I ran like a hunted felon.

In the morning, I was visited by Colonel Roberts and Mike Hanrahan before we descended for breakfast. They had the day's newspapers with them. The *Star*, the *National Intelligencer*, and the *Republican* had lively accounts of the exploits of the Fenian girl, but the *Chronicle*'s reporter, Colby, told a different story. It was my first encounter with the malice of the press in opposition.

The fellow began by describing me as a blowsy slattern, with my hair askew and my dress in dirty disarray. He narrated my story with a dozen sarcastic interspersions of his own. Finally he wrote: "As for her claim to have shot up a company of dragoons, the British ambassador has assured me it's ridiculous. The idea of a woman wielding a pistol with such accuracy is on the face of it absurd. It would not surprise me if the Fenian girl has never seen a pistol in her life, except on the stage. She may well never have seen Ireland, either. Rumor says she is an actress coached for the part by the Fenian leadership to help them swindle money from their gullible countrymen."

"Challenge him," I said.

"To what?" Colonel Roberts said.

"To a contest of marksmanship."

"That may not be wise. Dan McCaffrey tells me that you have trouble handling a gun."

"Dan McCaffrey doesn't know what he's talking about.

I've bought my own gun and I know how to use it." I opened my portmanteau and took my National Revolver from a pouch I had sewn for it.

"It would be a singular triumph if—"

I was scribbling a letter while he hesitated.

To the reporter named Colby from the Chronicle.

The Fenian girl would be happy to challenge him to a duel to defend her own and Ireland's honor. But he would no doubt use the excuse of her sex to disguise his own cowardice. She therefore invites him to a contest of marksmanship at targets of his own choice, as soon as possible. The prize will be the amount the British ambassador bribed him to write his story.

"Take that to the *Star* and have them print it tomorrow."

"If Bess says she can do it, I believe her," Red Mike said.

Roberts yielded to our collective recklessness. He was not so ready to be talked out of the next worry on his mind.

"Last night I gather you left the hotel for some unknown purpose. This town lives on scandal. I must ask you where you went."

"To Fernando Wood."

"My dear. His reputation is the worst in Washington."

"So I understand. But I deemed it worth the risk."

Red Mike rolled his eyes and pretended surprise. "I'm as shocked as you are Bill. But after all, the girl's of age. And didn't you say yourself when you were facin' down O'Mahoney that we couldn't run a war on Sunday school principles?"

"True enough, but—"

I distracted Roberts by plunging into what Fernando Wood had told me about President Johnson, and about Stanton and Seward. Roberts seemed staggered, then angry. "Wood is playing his own game. He'd like to capture us. He hasn't given up his dreams of glory. Everything about him is pretense. Pretense and—and seduction."

"There was no seduction," I said. "I may be young, but I'm not stupid."

"I know, I know," Roberts said. He paced for a moment, deep in thought. "I know your intentions were of the best, my dear. And you may have brought us valuable intelligence. We may yet have a need to do business with Wood."

I saw what Fernando Wood meant by the difference between an honest and a level man. Colonel Roberts was honest; he saw himself as living by a strict moral code. But he was not level.

Roberts decided he disagreed with Fernando's assessment of the situation. "Stanton is the strong man in the government," he said. "Seward is timid. He can be frightened by anything." Roberts discoursed on the halfhearted way Seward had dealt with England during the war. "If we keep Stanton on our side he'll bear Seward down, no matter what he thinks," Roberts said.

I gave up trying to persuade him, and we joined the others for breakfast. It was not a cheerful meal. We quarreled first over my proposal to challenge the *Chronicle* reporter. Dan scoffed and said I couldn't hit any target smaller than the front of the Capitol. I said I was delighted to discover that I was going to surprise him as well as the rest of Washington. Meanwhile Mrs. O'Neil was looking daggers at me.

"Did you find out where she went last night?" she asked.

"It's not important," Colonel Roberts said.

"I heard Fernando Wood inviting you, in the Senate gallery," she said.

"How clever of you," I said.

"You'll disgrace us," Mrs. O'Neil said.

"Only if you spread the word far and wide, as I fear

you will," I said. "Mr. Wood is a man of honor, who would not do such a thing to a lady."

From that moment, Margaret O'Neil became my enemy. She may have left the convent, but she was a nun at heart. She regarded me as a desperate sinner, unworthy of trust and hopeless of redemption. Dan was of a similar opinion, but it troubled his soul in a very different way. He glared at me as if his greatest pleasure would be to clamp his hands around my throat.

A troubled Colonel Roberts told Red Mike to take my challenge to the papers. The rest of us, except Margaret O'Neil, boarded a rented carriage and drove to the War Department building on 17th Street, where the president had arranged an interview with Secretary of War Stanton. Going in we passed a room that brought Dan McCaffrey to a full stop. It was full of tattered, blood-stained Confederate battle flags, captured in the course of the war. He stared at them for a long moment, then said, "They never captured Jeb Stuart's flag."

We waited in an outer office for the better part of an hour. Clerks hurried past us with sheets of paper in their hands. Somewhere nearby we could hear telegraph keys clicking. Colonel Roberts remarked that the place seemed almost as busy as it had been during the war. Suddenly he sprang to his feet, his hand out. "General Grant. Colonel Bill Roberts from the Commissary Department, now with the Irish Republican Army."

"Oh yes," said General Grant. The victorious commander looked unprepossessing at close range. His uniform was rumpled, his shoes unshined, and he had an unlit cigar stuck in the corner of his mouth. Roberts introduced us, and Grant smiled at me. "This is your female marksman. I read about her."

"We're here to see Secretary Stanton," Roberts said. "We saw the president last night, and he's given us full backing for our proposal to conquer Canada. You'll remember I mentioned it to you on the reviewing stand in New York two days ago. I would hope, General, that we might submit our plan of campaign to you for your approval—or criticism."

"I'd be happy to look at it—if the president desires me to," Grant said. "But I have no doubt you can whip the Brits out of their boots, without my help."

A clerk from Stanton's office interrupted us. We said good-bye to General Grant and were ushered into a room that brought us a step closer to the secretary of war's inner sanctum. It was the room in which Mr. Stanton received the public. He was already at work behind a high writing desk, which reached to his shoulders. He had the look of a powerful gnome—a round body and short legs. His complexion was dark and mottled, and his face was screwed into impatience and irascibility above his profuse chin whiskers, which seemed to have been tied like a false beard to his large ears. A motley group formed a line in front of him. There were soldiers on crutches, gaudily dressed women whom I guessed to be prostitutes, mournful women in black, well-dressed older men with the look of politicians. Each came before the secretary and stated his request in a low voice, which was nonetheless audible in the silent room.

Stanton rarely listened for more than a minute, then replied with a harsh, abrupt voice.

"No!"

"Write me a letter."

"See the pension clerk."

"Get out of here or I'll put you in jail."

"No."

It was like a scene in the old court of Versailles, when the absolute monarch held an audience. There was never a word spoken to challenge the secretary's decisions. "You see what I mean?" Roberts whispered to me. "There's the man who rules Washington."

"Quiet over there," growled a redheaded sentry by the door. Colonel Roberts obeyed.

The session ended, leaving a half dozen people still waiting on line. The secretary stamped back into an inner office, and the losers trudged wearily away to return tomorrow. We were left alone for another fifteen minutes. Then the door opened, and the secretary appeared again, looking diminutive beside a tall, straight-backed man in a splendid blue uniform, with the stars of a major general on his shoulders.

"That's Stapleton of New Jersey," Roberts whispered to me. "Old Steady, they called him."

"He doesn't look very old," I said.

"It's a way of speaking in the army. He had the toughest division in the Army of the Potomac."

The general was not handsome, but he was formidable looking in a narrow-faced, frowning way. He looked as if he had not smiled in a decade. He spoke to Stanton in a solemn, intense voice. "I've tried to keep faith with the dead of both sides, Mr. Secretary," he said.

"I understand," Stanton said, pulling on his chin whiskers. "It's something we must all try to do, according to our lights."

"This is the last day I'll wear this uniform," Stapleton said.

"You can doff it with pride, General," Stanton said. "Few have given as much to the cause as you."

"Thank you," Stapleton said.

General Stapleton passed us with long sweeping strides. For a split second our eyes met. Lacking an ability to foretell the future, neither of us found anything portentous in the brief encounter.

Secretary Stanton stood in the doorway of his office, studying us. "Is this the Irish Brigade, or the Army of the Tennessee?" he asked.

"A little of both, Mr. Secretary," Colonel Roberts said,

springing up. "You remember me, Roberts of the Commissary Department?"

"Yes, certainly," Stanton said. "Come along. I can give you only ten minutes. That's scarcely time for an Irishman to get through his first sentence, but our rebel friends are keeping me as busy as they did when the bullets were flying."

As he talked, he led us into a simply furnished office. He gestured to a pile of papers on his desk. "A single morning's telegrams. Officers telling me how the South is responding to the president's benevolence. In Alabama, they're plowing up the graves of Union soldiers. In Georgia, a mob burned the house of a loyal Georgia man who went home after fighting with Sherman. In North Carolina, a state judge dismissed a clear-cut case of assault on a Union officer in full uniform."

Roberts glanced nervously at Dan, obviously wishing he had left him at the hotel with Mrs. O'Neil. He decided to take the plunge and identify him. "Maybe it's not all that bad, Mr. Secretary," he said. "We've got two good men here, O'Neil and McCaffrey, who fought on opposite sides but are standing here with me as comrades in arms in the army of the Fenian Brotherhood."

"I've had reports on them," Stanton said. "No one registers at a hotel in Washington without my knowing a great deal about them within twenty-four hours. And this is our Fenian girl?"

"Miss Fitzmaurice," Roberts said.

"Is she an actress, as the *Chronicle* claims?"

"Not a bit of it. She's exactly what she looks to be, a brave Irish girl who's risked her life for her country's sake."

"She risked more than her life last night," Stanton said, "when she spent four hours with Fernando Wood."

My face was aflame. Roberts was too astonished to say a word. We were finding out one of the prime sources of

Mr. Stanton's power. He controlled the National Detective Police, the army's secret service, which had agents throughout Washington.

"If you people want my cooperation—and the support of other honest men," Stanton said, "you must convince us of your loyalty to the Union. The president says you have a scheme to conquer Canada, the way Sam Houston conquered Texas. I reminded him that the conquest of Texas led to the Mexican War and the conquest of Canada might lead to a war with England, which men like Fernando Wood and his friends in the South would welcome. It would be the perfect excuse to abandon all pretense of correcting once and for all the evils that created the rebellion. I'm not afraid of a war with England. Grant's army alone could take on the entire empire. But I am afraid of what sort of men are behind your combination. I dislike secret societies."

"There's not a Fenian, so help me, Mr. Secretary, not a Fenian who doesn't have the greater good and glory of these United States at his heart's core," Roberts said. "We believe that the conquest of Canada and the freedom of Ireland that must inevitably follow from it will signal the breakup of the British Empire, the destruction of our country's bitterest enemy."

Stanton began nodding impatiently when Roberts was halfway through his oration. "I'm as eager to teach them a lesson as you. Without their encouragement the Confederacy might have collapsed two years ago. There are a hundred thousand Union graves from Arlington to Arkansas that can be blamed on England. But we're not going to risk losing the war we've just won. We must have proof—dramatic proof—of your loyalty to this government. And an end to playing games with people like Mr. Wood. He's a traitor. One of my chief regrets has been our failure to hang him."

It was clear that Stanton was yielding, with extreme

reluctance, to the president's wish to help us. It confirmed everything Fernando Wood had said about the relationship of Mr. Johnson to his cabinet.

"You will have proof, ample proof, of our loyalty," Roberts said. "As for Congressman Wood, he forced himself on us and, I fear, misled this young girl into placing her confidence in him."

And I still do, I thought, far more than in anything I hear from your wordy mouth.

"We have too many women like her in Washington," Stanton said.

I watched Roberts weigh the advisability of defending my virtue once more and decide against it. He went back to promising Stanton that the Fenians would demonstrate their trustworthiness. The secretary of war nodded impatiently. "I'm glad we understand each other," he said. "Just remember I have ways of learning things if you're tempted to be insincere."

We found ourselves out on the street in the scorching sunlight. Gaily dressed women strolled past, twirling bright parasols. "I don't like that man," I said.

"No one does, except perhaps Mrs. Stanton," Colonel Roberts said. "But he's the most powerful man in the United States right now. We must study how to make him like us."

I suspected that would never come to pass. But I said nothing. I was brooding over my designation as a scarlet woman. I did not realize how soon I was to believe it.

Keep the Heart Cold and Private

The next day, the *Star* and the *National Intelligencer* both printed my challenge to Colby, the reporter from the *Chronicle*. Before the end of the day, we heard that Fernando Wood had made a bet of five hundred dollars with Congressman Ashley, the president's chief critic in the House of Representatives, that I would worst the penpusher. Since the *Chronicle* was the creature of the Radical Republicans in Congress, Colby was forced to respond. He announced that he would meet me in the President's Park, south of the White House, at high noon the following day.

Colonel Roberts was in a sweat, intensified by Mrs. O'Neil, over Fernando's espousal of my cause. I sent my patron a note, assuring him that he would not be disappointed in me as a markswoman. I then retired to the woods of Rock Creek with my pistol and a large supply of ammunition to spend the afternoon practicing. I prevailed upon Colonel O'Neil to join me as a mentor. He agreed despite his wife's frowns. He proved to be a good-natured and encouraging instructor. By the end of the afternoon I was striking a twelve-inch paper target eight times out of ten, at twenty paces.

"By God, I think I'll put some money down on you myself," Colonel O'Neil said in his mild, easy way. "Don't mention that to Mrs. O'Neil," he added.

That night in the huge bar of the Willard Hotel, betting for and against the Fenian girl became feverish. Dan McCaffrey emerged from the swirling blue smoke and told me Colby's backers were giving three-to-one odds. "Take them, and make some money for the cause," I said. "Tell everyone who bets on me I expect twenty percent for the Irish Republic."

"I wish I could believe you and O'Neil," Dan said through gritted teeth. Colonel O'Neil had spent the dinner hour boasting about my marksmanship.

"Swallow your pride and bet," I told him.

Swaggering to Dan's side was Robert Johnson, the president's son, not a little drunk. "M'fellow Tennessean says it's a waste of money to bet on you," he said.

"Your fellow Tennessean entertains dark prejudices against me," I said. "He's loath to believe in the possibility that a woman can do anything as well as a man, except cook."

"N'me," said Johnson. "I'm in favor of givin' you the vote. How's that for advanced ideas? Know why? Women are natural Democrats."

"We must talk more of such things," I said.

"Yeah. I was talkin' to my friend Fernando Wood. He said you were real good company."

He was not very subtle. Dan strode back into the bar. I forced a smile and said I must retire early. Under no circumstances, said the forceful Mr. Johnson. Before I knew what was happening, I was dragged into the bar, a champagne glass was shoved into my hand, and a dozen arms thrust bottles at me. I smiled and drank more champagne than was recommended for a clear head and steady hand on the morrow. Still, I stayed well within my margin of sobriety and studied Robert Johnson as he presided over a circle of hard drinkers that included a glowering Dan McCaffrey and a smiling John O'Neil. Robert Johnson was obviously enjoying the role of presidential son. At least a dozen men drew him aside to murmur confidentially in his ear. Sometimes he shook his head; sometimes he assured them that all was well. I saw several slip envelopes into his pocket, to which he paid no attention.

I finally declared I must go. "A woman needs eight hours' sleep to avoid wrinkles," I said.

"You're a long way from them," Robert Johnson said.

Red Mike Hanrahan appeared with a fresh bottle in his hand to fill my glass and offer a final toast. "To the Irish Republic, whether we set it up in Canada, New York's Sixth Ward, or Timbuktu. I just wired Bill Tweed and got him to lay a thousand dollars of the public's money on you."

"Where have you been?" I asked.

"Down at Chamberlain's losing what I won last night."

"If I have anything to say about it," I declared, "there will be no faro banks in the Irish Republic."

"And to think I almost proposed marriage to you last night," Mike said.

Robert Johnson insisted on escorting me to the elevator. "When can I see you again?"

"I don't know," I said. "We're waiting here, day and night, for an appointment with Mr. Seward. He appears to be elusive, or ill."

"I'll take care of that," he said. "Long as I know you'd like to see me again."

"I do," I said. "I'm partial to men with beards. From Tennessee. Who live in the White House."

He laughed uproariously. "You'll hear from me," he said. "Good shootin' tomorrow. I've got five hundred on you, just like Fernando."

I went to bed early and was soon asleep. Some hours later, I awoke with strange sensations. I was bathed in sweat. A nauseous storm gathered in my stomach. I seized my robe, stumbled to the bathroom, and lost my supper. Instead of feeling better, I grew worse. I retched and could bring up nothing. I had a raging thirst. A whine rose in my ears. I staggered to Dan's door and woke him.

"I think I'm dying," I said.

He listened to my symptoms and awoke Colonel Roberts. "It's the hotel disease," Colonel Roberts said. "Someone's slipped it to her."

We did not know what he was talking about. He explained rapidly. Shortly before the Civil War, scores of Democratic politicians had been stricken by these symptoms at the National Hotel. Many people believed it had been an attempt by the Republican Party to poison leading Democrats. The National Hotel had been forced to close for several months and almost went out of business.

Whether there was any truth to that story or whether anyone had slipped something poisonous in my food or drink that night, we were never certain, but our suspicions were heightened by a note slipped under my door in the early hours of the morning. *How are you feeling, Miss Fenian? By our calculations you should be a little* sick *with fear by now. A cold sweat should be springing out on your pale cheeks as you think about the truth of the old saying, she who lives by the sword (or pistol) frequently dies of it.*

I remained horribly ill for the rest of the morning. Dan wanted to postpone the contest, but I refused. I knew that would give our enemies a chance to boast their brains out for days while they dodged another meeting. I dressed and asked Dan what was the best whiskey to steady nerves and stomach. He recommended bourbon, and I drank half a glassful before we set out for the President's Park.

"I heard this fellow Colby has been taking lessons from the best pistol shot in the army," Colonel Roberts said as we rode. He had a talent for the lugubrious.

We arrived to be welcomed by a crowd of several hundred, at least half of whom were women. As I stepped down from the carriage in the blazing sun, a swirl of blackness sent my head spinning. I clutched Dan's arm and whispered, "Hold me up."

He fastened one of his strong hands on my arm above the elbow and held me erect until the spell passed. We advanced to where Colby, with his weasel face, was waiting. He smirked and made an elaborate bow. Colonel O'Neil conferred with Colby's backers and returned to say that they insisted on three rounds of ten shots each. They were obviously hoping to wear me down.

Fernando Wood and Robert Johnson strolled over to me. "You look pale," Fernando said. "Are you nervous?"

"The hotel disease," Roberts said.

"You're dealing with a devious enemy," Wood said.

"Is his name Secretary Stanton?" I asked. "He's certainly your enemy."

Fernando glanced at Robert Johnson and smiled inscrutably. "Anything is possible," Wood said. "Good shooting."

I was asked how I wished to fire, first or second? I chose first, fearing collapse if I stayed too long in the sun. "In fact," I said, "I would prefer to shoot my three targets in succession and let Mr. Colby better my score if he can."

A target was tied to a tree by Dan and one of Colby's party, who examined it carefully and declared it satisfactory. Advancing to a strip of cloth laid on the grass, I peered through the shimmering heat and for a moment saw three or four targets. I waited for them to coalesce, and fired.

Steadily, calmly, following the instructions of my various coaches to release my breath, not to think, simply to aim and fire, I pressed off six shots, then handed the gun to Dan, who rapidly reloaded it and handed it to me. Four more shots and they examined the target. "Ten hits out of ten, three in the bull's-eye," Dan stated.

I fired again, Dan loaded, and the next four shots completed the second ten. "Nine out of ten," Dan said. "Two in the bull's-eye."

The sun beat down. For a moment the swirling blackness gathered behind my eyes. I willed it away. A third
time we repeated the performance. This time the count
was ten out of ten, four in the bull's-eye.

My supporters cheered mightily. A four-man brass
band, which I later learned had been hired by Fernando
Wood, struck up "The Wearing of the Green." I walked
slowly back to the carriage, climbed in, and fell helplessly
against the cushions. Another ten seconds and I would
have collapsed on the grass. Robert Johnson sprang to my
side, showing the most sincere solicitude. He ordered a
black servant to race to the White House for some sal
volatile as a restorative. "No," I said. "Let us chat as if we
were tête-à-tête, and pay no attention to Mr. Colby."

"Good," he said, liking the game.

"Tell me what's happening," I said.

"Colby's grin has faded to a sick smirk," he said.
"He's usin' an army Colt, the best gun we make. I don't
know how you hit anything with that popgun of yours.
He's obviously taken lessons, from the way he stands at
the mark. He begins."

The crack, crack, crack of Colby's pistol sounded ten
times.

"The tellers are consultin' the targets," Robert Johnson continued. "The score is—six out of ten, none in the
bull's-eye! You win. The skunk can't beat you even if he
hit ten out of ten in each of his next two rounds."

A cheering mob engulfed the carriage. They collected
their money while the band played a reprise of "The
Wearing of the Green." Many imitated Fernando Wood's
example and gave me all their winnings. I soon had a
pile of greenbacks in my lap. A good twenty celebrators
joined Robert Johnson in the carriage, and the rest
trooped behind it or clung to the carriages of several of
the ladies who followed us back to the Willard. The men
carried me into the bar and toasted me with the inevitable

champagne. It was the acme of my pride as a woman and as a Fenian.

I finally extricated myself and retreated to my room, where after a nap I awoke feeling weak but largely recovered from the hotel disease. It convinced me that some kind of poison had been administered to me.

Colonel Roberts knocked on the door. He was exultant and not a little drunk. "Seward says he'll see us in half an hour. He wants to meet you. Can you come?"

"Of course."

We drove slowly through the inferno of the late afternoon. All the heat of the day seemed to gather itself and concentrate its force in the still air. The State Department was on 15th Street, next to the huge marble Treasury Department. It occupied a humble brick building, as unprepossessing as the War Department. Inside all was silent and calm. There was none of the bustle of the War Department office. Colonel Roberts and I comprised our party. Our Irish soldiers from Tennessee would make no impression on this diplomat from New York. Besides, Roberts said they were getting drunk in Willard's bar on my winnings.

There was no time spent waiting. We were ushered directly upstairs to the secretary of state's office. A small, smiling man rose from his desk to greet us. He was past middle age, with a balding head and a face that sloped downward from a broad brow past a prominent beaked nose to a diminished chin. His mouth had a play of humor about it, as if he had found the world a fairly amusing place. But the dominant impression made by his face was supplied by a raw ugly scar that ran from below his right eye in a curve down his cheek to join another equally awful scar on his neck. These were wounds inflicted by one of the group of assassins who had murdered President Lincoln and attempted to kill Mr. Seward and other members of the government.

To increase his woes, Mr. Seward had his jaw wired almost shut, the result of a fracture received in a fall from a carriage, some days before the assassination attempt. He had also broken his right arm, which dangled uselessly at his side. In spite of these injuries and the recent death of his wife, he was remarkably cheerful. He congratulated me on my triumph over the *Chronicle*'s reporter. The paper had become overweeningly arrogant since the war had ended in victory, and Colby was one of the most offensive of its reporters. "The newspapers like to give the impression that without their help we never could have won the war," he said. "Politicians fear them. They can ruin a man. So we've let them escape without contradiction. In actuality they're the greatest charlatans in the country."

And you're looking at one of their creations, I thought. We were soon into the inevitable discourse from Colonel Roberts on the plans of the Fenians. Seward listened with none of Stanton's impatience. He was used to being bored. It was one of the requirements of a politician's profession.

"The president has told me a good deal about it," Seward said when Roberts finished. "I told him that there was one overmastering consideration, if we are to support you. Can you deliver the Irish vote to the party we're attempting to form behind the president? It will be neither Republican nor Democrat. The National Union Party is what we called it in the last election, and that's what we shall probably call it in the difficult months to come."

"If the Union Party takes a stand on Ireland's freedom, you'll have every Irish vote in America," Roberts said.

"What if we don't take a stand? Let's be realistic. There are a great many people, Democrats and Republicans, who don't give a tinker's damn for Ireland or her freedom and don't like you Irish very much. In some quarters you're less popular than the Negroes, if that's possible."

"You mean we must stand by you," I said.

"Precisely, my dear," Seward said, eyeing me in his quizzical way. He returned to Roberts. "I've heard from people in New York that you've been consorting with William Marcy Tweed. I doubt if he's interested in doing business with a Union Party or we with him. Can you separate the Irish vote from Tammany?"

"Why do we have to do that? Give them what they want in New York and Tammany will back you heart and soul."

Seward shook his head. "An alliance with Tammany will cost us every moderate Republican vote in upstate New York," he said.

"We can't break Tammany," Roberts said. "I'd be a fool to say we could. But we can take enough votes away from them to make a difference in a close election."

"Fair enough," Seward said. "Now, you want guns, you want ammunition, supplies for an army. You must get those things from Mr. Stanton. What does he think of this scheme?"

"He worries about the kind of government we'll create in Canada—whether it will be loyal to Washington—and whether the British will start a war with America to regain Canada, once we accept the invitation to join the United States."

"I think we need not fear a war," Seward said, "if we could engineer a plebiscite showing a majority of Canadians in favor of joining us. You'd have a million Irish votes as a head start. Everything would depend on how swiftly you could crush armed resistance. Until that happens, we'd be unable to defend you against British retaliation from abroad."

"Give us belligerent status, as the British and Canadians gave the Confederacy—let us buy guns and supplies on credit—and we can deal with anything the British throw at us," Roberts said. "Our plan is to pin down thirty thousand of their troops in Ireland. We have agents in India who'll make trouble for them there. Our generals estimate we can conquer all of Canada that matters, from the Atlantic to the western border of Ontario, in sixty days."

"Then you must rule a restless populace for perhaps another year and possibly fight off a British expeditionary force, while we get the legalities of bringing you into our government through Congress. You'll remember it took ten years of argument to annex Texas. I think we can do it faster, but there could be resistance from Radical Republicans and from Democrats, both of whom might see your votes in Congress as a threat to their parties' chances."

This was said in a musing, speculative tone. It was fascinating to watch this man's cool mind at work, exploring the risks, the problems, the possibilities of our plan. He speculated on the advantage of bringing the various Canadian provinces into the American union as separate states. Their chief value would be their presumed loyalty to the National Union Party. It would give the new party enough strength to counter the Radical Republicans.

"I like this," Seward said. "With all its risks, the more I think of it, the more I like it.

"I like this young lady, too," he added. "There's a reception tonight at the Russian Embassy. Would she deign to let a doddering invalid escort her there?"

"I would be delighted," I said.

"It will be amusing to introduce you to the British ambassador," he said. "I'll call for you at your hotel—is it the Willard?—at seven."

Looking back, I see this now as the first step in a long

series of bitter deceptions. At the time, I was too inexperienced and Colonel Roberts too stupid to see it as anything but another triumph.

We rushed back to the Willard, and I bathed and put on my most splendid gown, a great hoop of pearl-gray silk, flounced and trimmed with silk of a darker hue and point lace.

The secretary arrived in a carriage driven by a black servant. He drove us through the humid twilight to the Russian legation, a handsome building on 12th Street. Inside, servants in blue and gold livery stood stiffly at attention. Baron de Stoeckl, the Russian ambassador, a bulky, gray-haired man with bristling mustaches, stepped forward to greet the American secretary of state.

"Good evening, Mr. Secretary," he said with a heavy accent. "Who is this charming creature? I don't have the honor of knowing her."

"Miss Elizabeth Fitzmaurice, an emissary from the Irish Republican Brotherhood, better known as the Fenians," Mr. Seward said. "I've brought her along to show the British ambassador that the Irish are not uncivilized barbarians, as he claims."

"An admirable project, Mr. Secretary," said the baron with a smile. "I am always interested in ways to instruct the British ambassador. Would that we could instruct his country to adhere to a civilized code of conduct. I fear John Bull understands nothing but the kind of lesson we taught him in the Crimea. Perhaps you will have to teach him a similar lesson."

"You see how many allies you have in your desire to thrash the Sassenach?" Seward said to me.

"The Irish people cheered on Russia's defiance," I said, though I scarcely remembered the Crimean War myself, having been only eight years old when it began.

"A pity so many Irish soldiers saw fit to serve in the British regiments," the baron said.

"That is the result of desperate hunger and want, Your Excellency," I said. "A man who sees his wife and children starving before his eyes will take the king's shilling, though his heart breaks within himself to think of serving his country's enemy."

"Yes, yes," the baron said, "but it discourages those who think of helping your countrymen with guns and ammunition. Your leader, O'Mahoney, came to see me a few months ago. He claimed to have fifty thousand troops in Ireland. Yes, I said, but half of them are in the British army."

"What better place for them to be, when the call to action comes?" I said.

"What do you think, Mr. Seward?" the baron asked.

Seward smiled in his inward, secretly amused way. "The American consul at Dublin assures me that the British are in control of the situation in Ireland. The lord lieutenant told him the secret service has an informer in every Fenian center in the country—and almost as many in America."

"They're the grandest liars in the world," I said, but my heart sank with the possible, even probable, truth of those words. I thought of my sudden sickness last night, and my stomach curled ominously.

"Well, we are not here to settle such matters tonight," de Stoeckl said. "Let me get you some good Russian vodka. Or would you prefer champagne?"

"Vodka," said Seward. I accepted a glass of champagne but was wary about drinking it. The secretary of state tossed off his vodka in a flash and asked me if my abstemiousness was the reason for my triumph over Mr. Colby earlier in the day.

"On the contrary," said Robert Johnson, who we discovered was standing behind us. "She can drink champagne all night and shoot all day. She has the habits of a cavalryman, Mr. Seward."

"But not the looks, thank God," Seward said.

"No, sir," Robert Johnson said, eyeing me approvingly. "Not the looks."

Diplomats from various South American countries, many of them dressed in uniforms dripping with gold braid, came forward to be introduced and to congratulate Secretary Seward on his remarkable recovery from his wounds. He nodded and introduced me and Robert Johnson, then let Robert talk about his father's reconstruction plans while the secretary's eyes circled the room like a hunting animal on the prowl. At length he seized my arm and drew me away from the ambassador from Argentina while he was in midsentence. Trailing me in his wake, he bore down on two men in close conversation. Robert Johnson hastily excused himself and followed us.

"What are the imperial powers conniving at now, in peaceful North America?" Seward said.

Sir Frederick Bruce, the British minister, replied with a smile as warm as the sort one sees on a dead fish sprawled on the ice in a market. His hard blue eyes fastened on me for a moment, and I saw recognition as well as disbelief flare. "I have no idea what you mean, Mr. Secretary," he said.

"Mr. Johnson," he added suavely. "I trust the president is well."

"He's in fine fettle," Robert Johnson said. "As we say in Tennessee, he's ready to skin a live mountain lion with one hand and shoe a jackass with the other."

"Delightful news," murmured Bruce, not quite able to conceal his astonishment at this American hyperbole.

"We connived at nothing more dangerous than an agreement that the summer in Washington is beastly," said the other man, in an accent that made one think his tongue was too wide for his mouth. He was as dark complexioned as Bruce was ruddy. With studied purpose, Mr.

Seward introduced me to M. de Berthemy, the French ambassador. "And this," he said, gesturing to Bruce, "is Your Majesty's representative here in Washington."

"She is not my Majesty, nor ever has been but by the use of violence," I said.

"It seems to me, Mr. Secretary, that one could turn the question of connivance back upon you," Bruce said.

"How so?" Seward said with mocking innocence. "I consider this young woman a refugee. I'm merely doing my duty by her. As George Washington said, America is always ready to open its bosom to refugees from every country."

"If my observations in New York are any guide, many of this young woman's sort feel compelled to return the favor."

"You see the kind of repartee to which diplomacy exposes you?" Seward said to me.

"If what Sir Frederick says is true, I can tell him where Irish women learned their debauchery," I said. "Wasn't it William Blake who wrote: 'The harlot's cry from street to street / Shall weave old England's winding sheet'?"

"Bull's-eye," roared Robert Johnson.

Sir Frederick's eyes glistened with cold fury. I saw the face of the enemy. "I'm having papers prepared for your attention, sir," Bruce said to Seward, "asking you to surrender this girl and her companions as criminals, guilty of barbarous murders."

"You mean you'd put a noose around that lovely neck?" Seward said. "What do you think the president would say to such a demand, Robert?"

"I think it would require the entire Army of the Tennessee to make him comply."

"I would be in substantial agreement," Seward said. "According to our latest dispatches, Judah Benjamin, the secretary of state of the Confederate government, has arrived in England, to be received with cheers and toasts and sympathy by your aristocracy. There's no mention of returning him for the atrocious crimes his government committed against the people of the United States. He is the refugee of a *belligerent* power who had the misfortune to lose its war. Perhaps this young woman should be accorded the same status."

"She resembles Mrs. Greenhow. Almost enough to be her daughter," Berthemy said.

"That," Seward replied with sudden sharpness, "is what we in America call a low blow. In western New York we have an even more vivid phrase to describe it."

"It was intended as a compliment, Mr. Secretary," Berthemy said.

"Tell Louis Napoleon that misplaced compliments can be as dangerous as misplaced confidence," Seward snapped. "Have you informed Paris of the movement of our army of observation to the Mexican border?"

"Most assuredly."

"Has there been a reply?"

"If there had been, you would have learned of it immediately, Mr. Secretary."

"If you think we're going to pay several dozen millions to feed an army on the Rio Grande for very long, you're dreaming," Seward said.

"I have tried in my dispatches to make clear America's strong interest in economy," Berthemy said.

"Good."

I could feel the electric force of Seward's power striking the Frenchman, all but making him buckle in front of our eyes.

"Sir Frederick," Seward said, turning to the Englishman, "did you enjoy that copy of my speech?"

"Very much, except for the passage about the magic

circle of the American union. That had a somewhat druidical flavor to it."

Seward smiled thinly and explained to me and Robert Johnson. "I'm referring to a speech I'm planning to give in Albany next month. In it I express the belief that this whole continent, must sooner or later come within the magic circle of the American union. Does that sound druidical to you?"

"It sounds practical," I said.

"I'm inclined to think the Fenians believe more in rifles and pistols than in druids, wouldn't you say, Miss Fitzmaurice?" Robert Johnson said.

"Yes. We're very American," I said.

Seward nodded and made a small chuckling sound in the back of his throat—the nearest to a laugh I ever heard from him. "She does so well, you'd almost think I rehearsed her. But I'm not that clever. Good night, gentlemen."

We paid our respects to Baron de Stoeckl and departed. Robert Johnson climbed into the carriage and placed me between him and Seward. He was laughing very hard and followed it with a Tennessee whoop.

"I told you, Mr. Seward. This girl is something, ain't she?"

I felt Seward's hand on my knee. "You performed excellently, my dear. Bruce was utterly stunned by that quote from Blake."

"I didn't think of it as performing," I said.

"Forgive me. That's how you think of everything after a lifetime in politics."

"Who is this Mrs. Greenhow that I so much resemble?"

"A woman I fancied almost as much as this young gallant fancies you," Seward said. "She sympathized with the Confederacy. The Secret Service arrested her as a spy and sent her south. She went to England and returned with a shipment of gold. Her blockade runner hit a sandbar. She tried to get ashore in a small boat. It overturned in the surf and she drowned."

He was silent for several moments. "Her maiden name was Rose O'Neal. When she first came to Washington she was the most beautiful woman I ever saw. People called her 'the Wild Rose.' That was when I loved her. By the time the war began it was nostalgia. I knew she was selling herself to a certain senator for military secrets."

He pointed to a small house on the corner of 16th Street. "There's where she lived."

"Goddamn," Robert Johnson said. "You can't trust nobody in this miserable town, can you."

"I wouldn't trust Mr. Stanton very much, if I were you," Seward said. "I hope your chin whiskers are not a compliment to him."

"I admire the old buzzard," Robert Johnson said. "He won the war for us."

"But now we must win the peace. Your father's peace. I'm not sure Stanton really wants peace. It would mean the end of his power."

He looked over his shoulder. "You see that carriage light back there?" We could see it bobbing in the darkness. "I wouldn't be surprised if it belonged to one of Mr. Stanton's National Policemen, watching me, or you, or this girl."

"Let's try him," Robert Johnson said. He gave our driver orders to proceed into the country beyond the settled part of Washington. Within minutes we were in a pitch-black wilderness without a house in sight. The carriage light continued to pursue us. Robert Johnson extinguished our own lamp and told the driver to turn off the road into the first open field. It was a moonless night. We were invisible from the road. The other carriage passed us at a brisk pace, then stopped a few hundred yards up the road, turned, and approached us again.

"Goddamn," snarled Robert Johnson. He sprang from the carriage, raced into the road, and leaped into the other vehicle. In a moment he returned dragging a very frightened-looking man by the scruff of the neck. "Take a good look," he said. "Miss Fitzmaurice and Mr. Seward and Mr. Johnson out for a drive. Now get out of here before I kick your ass in."

More and more, I had the feeling that I had wandered into a play in which the actors spoke a foreign language and drew on passions I did not understand. There was a tremendous struggle for power raging through America, part of the same convulsive tragedy that had created the war that left a half million dead, and millions more scarred and bitter. Was it Ireland's opportunity or another in her long history of misfortunes?

We ordered our driver to return us to Washington. We rode warily up and down various side streets while Mr. Seward and Robert Johnson studied the road behind us. Finally we ventured down a dark street with one or two small houses on it.

"Stop here," Seward called to the coachman. We got down and Seward led us to the first house. He took a key from his pocket and opened the door. Inside, the parlor was done in warm shades of dark blue and gold, with a piece of red gauze dividing the room in half. On one side a table was set with a cold supper of chicken and duck and side dishes of green salad. Wine cooled in a silver bucket. Gas jets flickered a tremulous light, not visible through the thick draperies on the windows.

"Now this envious old invalid must leave you charming youngsters to your pleasure," Seward said. He kissed my hand. "Good night, my dear. You have brought back painful but precious memories."

Robert Johnson grinned and untied his tie. He took off

his coat and shirt and offered me some champagne. I shook my head. My stomach was still uneasy from my ordeal of the previous night. "Come on," he said, swallowing his glass at one gulp. "It's more fun when you're a little drunk."

I swallowed enough champagne to be polite. "Now let's get you out of that goddamn iron fortress," he said. He began fumbling with the buttons on my dress. With little help from him—his fingers were incredibly clumsy—I took it off and lifted the iron hoop over my head and stood before him in my chemise.

"That's more like it," he said.

He kissed me, thrusting his tongue deep into my mouth. "How do you like this place?" he said. "Old Seward's hideaway. He's been lettin' me use it. Private, you got to keep things private. The only way to succeed in Washington politics."

"A wise man, no doubt," I said.

I sat down in a chair. He hovered over me and slipped his hand beneath my chemise to squeeze my breast while kissing me again.

"Don't know whether I rightly should fool around with a woman who can shoot so good." he said. "It's damn near unnatural. But I like Irish girls. Always have. When I'd go to a house in Nashville, I'd always ask the madam if she had any Irish girls. Passionate. I could see you were one when I looked at you. A real passionate girl."

He finished the bottle of champagne and put another one in the ice bucket. "Old Andy, m'father, he didn't think much of me until he got to the White House. My older brother, Charlie, was his boy. He was so goddamn perfect, Charlie was. Son-of-a-bitch wasn't smart enough to stay off his horse when there was ice a foot thick on the roads. Horse fell on him and killed him. Busted his head like an egg. Then old Andy grabs me and starts in. 'Bob, you're all I got left now, you got to stand by me.' Now he's in that White House and can't see nobody but what comes to him. Who's his eyes and ears, who gets around this town and finds out what they're sayin' at the Willard and the National? Old Robert. Old why-can't-you-be-as-smart-as-Charlie Robert."

He opened the second bottle of champagne and drank off a glass and a half. "Jesus," he said. "This stuff ain't hittin' me. How 'bout you?" He went into the next room and came back with a bottle of bourbon. He poured it into a water glass and drank off two fingers. "That's better," he gasped. "Good old bourbon.

"Gives you ideas, whiskey," he said. "I like a woman with ideas. Makes it more—interestin', don't you think? A man with ideas, too? You gonna find me a friend at court, Bess. A friend of Ireland. Now you just take off the rest of them clothes and lie down on the sofa. I got to spill a little water."

I sat there, numb. He rose and passed through a door into the next room. Through the red gauze I could see a large dark blue sofa on the other side of the room. I stepped through the blaze of color and a sudden vision of damnation flickered in my mind. Not the hell of the Catholic catechism but the living hell of the degraded woman. Was that where I was going?

How could I stop, now? I had permitted Fernando Wood to tell this man about me, as if I were a piece of merchandise on the open market. I had naively imagined another rapturous forbidden evening with the dividend of winning a man of power to Ireland's cause. It was hard to expect rapture from this drunken, garrulous man.

But I had come too far to flee, even if I had the means. I took off my chemise and lay down on the couch. In a minute or two Robert Johnson stepped through the curtain.

He was wearing only his shirt. He drew a chair to the edge of the sofa and ran his hand slowly up my thigh. "Fernando was right," he said. "You are some piece."

With no more than that for preparation he fell upon me and thrust his sex into me. The smell of him was noxious. He must not have bathed for days. The stiff beard gouged my neck, and the harsh linen of his shirt and its buttons hurt my breasts. He drew out and plunged in once, twice, and then gasped, "Ohh goddam." I felt his seed gushing within me, and the thought flashed down my flesh like flame: *If I get pregnant by this man I will kill myself.*

He slid off me and fell with a thud onto the floor. "Goddamn," he said. He cupped my breast with his hand, then fastened his mouth on it and sucked the nipple for a moment. "Jesus, Bessie. You are some girl," he said.

He left me, lurching through the red gauze and vanishing into the room beyond the door. I lay there, trying to resist the inrushing word that stormed against the desperate barricade my mind was trying to erect. *WHORE,* howled a voice out there in the darkness. *WHORE.* It was no use trying to resist it, Like a mob that has become one huge maddened beast, it stormed over my denial and rampaged through my ruined heart. *For Ireland,* I whispered. *I have become a whore for Ireland.* What else can I do in this strange land? America began by making me a liar, and now she has made me a whore.

Then I remembered my haughty words this morning to hesitant Colonel Roberts, that stupid, honest, but not level man. That was Bess Fitzmaurice speaking at the acme of her pride. If there was to be blame apportioned for this horror, she must accept her share in it.

Robert Johnson emerged, fully dressed. "Goddamn," he said. "Was it that good? You feel like another round?"

"It was wonderful," I said, rushing to my chemise. "But I need your help in getting into my dress."

"Better'n old Fernando, I'm sure," Robert said as he struggled with the buttons at the back of the dress. "How do old coots like him get girls like you into bed? Money?"

"Sympathy," I said. "But men like you don't need it."

"Yeah," he said. "Let's go have ourselves a time."

He had paid not the slightest attention to the food on the table—a sure sign, I was soon to learn, of a drunkard. Our carriage had been returned by Seward and was waiting at the door. With Robert Johnson urging on the driver, we galloped to John Chamberlain's gambling casino on Pennsylvania Avenue.

We stood at the long bar, and men swarmed around Robert Johnson, asking him about pardons, railroad contracts, army supply contracts, the news from the Mexican border, stock speculations based on the government's plans for the conquered Southern states, rumors of a new transcontinental railroad. He drank hard and talked freely—much too freely, I thought. He was drunk not only with whiskey but with power. The scorned second son had become the crown prince of Washington, D.C.

Several of those who approached him were women, who regarded me with unconcealed hostility. He introduced me to them, obviously savoring their envy. One of the prettiest was Mrs. Cobb, a brunette who pleaded piteously with "dear Robert" for a pardon for a Southern friend. President Johnson had pardoned some Southerners, but there was a large number of so-called leaders of the rebellion—officers of the army, officials of the rebel government—who were not included.

Telling Mrs. Cobb to come to the White House tomorrow, Robert seized a bottle of bourbon from the bar and said, "Let's go buck the ole tiger." He led me into the next room, where faro was being played with grim intensity by several hundred politicians and generals. The men in blue seemed to arouse Robert Johnson's ire.

"Look at them," he said. "Our volunteer Napoleons, bettin' their loot."

A man rushed up to Johnson and said, "Ben Butler just lost ten thousand on a single draw."

"Penny ante play," Robert said. He pushed his way to a place at one of the tables, and began to bet recklessly on a half dozen cards at once, drinking the while. He lost disastrously and failed to call the turn as well. I had gotten the gist of the game from watching Red Mike play the previous night. I had seen him "hedge" by placing his chips between two or three cards, the first to show determining the outcome. Sometimes he had "heeled" his bet by leaning one chip against the other, so that the single bet played one card to win, the other to lose. I began urging similar tactics on Robert, and his luck changed— magically, so he thought. Soon he was ahead by two thousand dollars, then by five thousand. He started calling me his good luck charm. He wanted to bet everything on the call of a single turn, but I stopped him. By the end of the next round we were ten thousand dollars ahead.

Robert's bottle was empty, and he was incoherent. The casekeeper reported the final three cards, and the dealer solemnly announced them. "Ace of clubs, queen of hearts, and queen of diamonds."

Robert Johnson grinned drunkenly up at me and moved the full ten thousand onto the board. "Call it, Bess," he said.

"I'll take the dealer's word," I said.

The dealer, who had a hard Irish face, drew. The ace of clubs. He drew again. This would be the decisive card. The red-faced queen, surrounded by hearts, stared up at us. *"Yow!"* howled Robert Johnson. He leaped up and slobbered kisses on my face and neck. *"Yow!"* he howled again in my ear.

The dealer's assistant deposited forty thousand dollars

in chips before us. Robert Johnson shoved them into his pockets and turned to the crowd around the table. "The other day, Gen'l Butler came to the W'House and tried to tell m'father how to run the guvment. Let this remind him that the Johnsons play to win. Like ev'body from the great state of Tensee."

His arm around me for support, Robert staggered back to the bar. There we were confronted by a bulky man in a general's uniform. He had the face of a pirate—strong, unscrupulous, cruel, with a low wide head, crossed eyes, a hatchety Roman nose, and thin lips.

"Did I hear you taking my name in vain in there, you contemptible pisswink?" he roared.

Robert Johnson swayed before him. "Ms. Fitzmaurice," he said. "May I 'troduce you to General Benjamin Butler, known as Beast for short to the people of the South."

"We're going to run you and your whores out of here. We're going to send you back to your shanties in Tennessee where you belong," Butler roared.

"Tell it to the marines, General," Robert sneered. "'Cept you don't even command them anymore. You're mustered out. But they ain't mustered out Andy Johnson."

"We'll muster him out before we're through," Butler snarled. "We'll muster out every traitor and traitor-lover in this country by the point of the bayonet if necessary."

It was a frightening glimpse of the savage hatred of the men opposing Andrew Johnson. Robert Johnson answered it with a reckless arrogance. He pulled chips worth several hundred dollars from his pocket and threw them at General Butler's feet. "There's the only thing you care about," he said.

Butler kicked the chips aside and strode back into the gaming room. Robert Johnson reeled to the bar for more bourbon. He ranted to the circle of sycophants who gathered around him about the way he and his father were going to destroy the Radical Republicans in Congress. "We got tricks up our sleeves like you never seen," he said. "You see this li'l piece of Ireland here? She's from the Fenians. They're gonna take Canada and turn it into states that vote solid for Andy Johnson. Then we're gonna bring the South back to Congress, the loyal South, and the Dem'crats'll be back inna saddle. How you like that?"

I did not like it at all. It was madness to reveal your plans so nakedly to your enemies. I was sure there were enemies or friends ready to sell themselves to enemies in that circle of greedy grinning faces. "Let's go," I said. "I'm very tired."

In the carriage, Robert became amorous again. "Hey, listen," he said, fondling my breasts. "How 'bout a li'l more of that Irish pussy, huh? One good turn deserves another, huh?"

"Remember what Mr. Seward said about privacy."

"Ah, t'hell with Seward 'n rest of'm. No one's gonna touch ole Bob Johnson now."

"Tomorrow," I said. "When you're not so drunk."

"Okay. T'morra and next day and next day. I like pass'nate—Irish—girls."

He passed out on my shoulder. By the time we reached the Willard Hotel he was snoring. I told the driver to take him to the White House.

I spent the rest of the night in my bed, staring into the darkness while images of lust swirled before me to be consumed by gusts of mocking laughter to be in turn devoured by anguished remorse. For the first time I understood the fatality that tormented Dan McCaffrey as he looked at his life. He, too, had tried to ride—and had been ridden down by—Fernando Wood's whirlwind of history. He, too, experienced the double dread, regret for the past and fear of the future.

Dan had emerged from the cyclone of war with nothing but his courage. Another kind of wind was rising now, a political storm, that threatened to wreck me and him and many others in new but no less deadly ways. What could a woman do to survive the upheaval? I remembered the image of my sister Annie's benefactor, Mrs. Ronalds, contemptuous in her white lace and diamonds. I vowed to abide by her dangerous maxim: Keep the heart cold and private.

In Darkest America

Three weeks later, I stood on a street corner in Charleston, South Carolina, and watched a drunken Union sergeant cut the silver buttons off the uniform of a Confederate brigadier general while a crowd of laughing Negroes watched. Beside me Dan McCaffrey growled and started for the sergeant. I stayed his arm. "Do you want to get us both killed?" I hissed. The sergeant reeled across the street and stopped, recognizing me. He handed me the buttons. "Three cheers for Ireland," he said in a thick brogue. "A wee souvenir for the Fenian girl."

"Thank you," I said. "Now get along with you and sleep off that head."

He reeled past us into the nearest saloon. I gave the buttons back to the brigadier. "I'm very sorry," I said. "Please forgive him."

The brigadier, a short, slim gray-haired man, nodded. "It's all right, young lady. It gave me a little practice. We're goin' to have to get used to forgivin' a lot of things."

Around us spread a city of ruins, of houses and churches with gaping holes in roofs and walls, of hundreds more houses vacant, of rotting wharves, of miles of grass-grown streets in which pigs rooted and army mules grazed. Southerners like the brigadier wandered these streets with crushed faces, vacant stares. The few women who ventured from their houses wore dresses made of crude homespun fabrics, dyed with vegetable juices. The spirits of both men and women seemed utterly broken, beyond anything I had seen in Ireland.

But the most astonishing sight to my eyes was not the defeated natives, nor the thousands of victorious blue-clad Union soldiers strolling about or marching briskly along the street in squads. It was the Negroes. They were more numerous than the soldiers, wandering in aimless swarms, congregating in crowds on corners and in vacant fields, playing banjos and singing or gambling at dice or dancing on improvised platforms. They formed huge mobs in front of the Freedmen's Bureau offices, where civilian employees of the federal government distributed rice and cornmeal to them. This black presence filled the ferocious summer heat with a special darkness. It dazed the eye and staggered the mind.

The whirlwind of history was sweeping me in a new direction. We had arrived in Charleston by boat two days earlier. It was our second stop (our first had been Wilmington, North Carolina) on our tour to recruit volunteers for the Fenian army and sell bonds of the Irish Republic. Shortly before we left Washington, D.C., the head center and council of the Fenian Brotherhood had announced the "final call," the signal for an all-out campaign to raise an army and strike a blow to liberate Ireland. They refrained from saying where the blow would be struck, preferring to keep their plans to invade Canada secret.

In spite of the shattered condition of the region, it made good sense to go south. Thousands of the Irish soldiers in the armies occupying the conquered states were soon to

be discharged and were ripe for our appeal. They had their
pockets full of greenbacks and little on which to spend
them. We had a letter signed by President Johnson, urging
Union army officers to show us "every courtesy"—
meaning give us an opportunity to address their troops.

Dan McCaffrey was with us as proof of our readiness
to recruit Southern as well as Northern soldiers. I was
there to win publicity in the newspapers and report on
the woes of bleeding Ireland. John O'Neil was our
speechmaker. He had sent Mrs. O'Neil back to Nashville
(to my vast relief). Red Mike Hanrahan was our speech-
writer, shepherd, and sachem.

The day after we arrived in Charleston, we arranged
to speak to Union troops at their camp outside the city.
There were about two thousand Irishmen in the garrison,
and they flocked to the platform we made from some
planks and two borrowed wagons. I spoke first. I talked
of evicted tenants, brutal landlords, and greedy gombeen
men, then narrated my adventure with Dan McCaffrey. I
ended my vaudeville with a display of marksmanship,
for which Dan called out the scores. The soldiers seemed
to love it, though I suspect they enjoyed the display of
my shape as I aimed the gun far more than my score.

Then came John O'Neil. He positioned himself between the green Fenian flag on his left and the Stars and
Stripes on his right and exalted the courage of the Irish
soldier in the war just ended, especially the exploits of
the famed Irish Brigade. He described the charge of
these men up Marye's Heights at the battle of Fredericksburg. They had been mowed down in swaths by Confederate fire, and one of the regiments left its green flag
on the field, clutched in the cold hands of its dead color
bearer.

A young Irishman in the Southern ranks crept out that
night after the battle, cut the flag from its staff, and

swam across the Rappahannock River to return it to the commander of the brigade, General Thomas Francis Meagher. He discovered the lad had been wounded in the leg by Union sentries who had fired on him when he did not know the password. Meagher called his own doctor to dress the wound and offered the lad the chance to go north as a free man. He refused and swam back across the river, wounded leg and all, to rejoin General Lee's army.

"Will any man here doubt," John O'Neil cried, "that with such men united under Ireland's green flag, we cannot defeat the Sassenach's mercenaries?"

The speech produced storms of applause and over five hundred volunteers. We sold ten thousand dollars in Irish bonds. It was encouragement when we needed it most. Everything else about the trip thus far had been disheartening and disillusioning. If it had not been for Red Mike, with his perpetual fooling, we would have been at each other's throats. Dan and John O'Neil found it hard to agree on any aspect of the war. With me, Dan spent his time glowering and examining my mail for letters from Washington, D.C. I had spent a wild week in the capital as Robert Johnson's passionate girl. I had mastered my distaste for him to play the courtesan, pretending a fervor that I utterly lacked. Dan had watched, appalled and disgusted. I was tempted to tell him that no one could equal my own disgust. But I was still at war with Dan in my heart—and Robert Johnson promised to be a powerful ally in the larger war with England.

His enthusiasm for our Canadian adventure was boundless, and his letters assured me that he was doing everything in his power to keep the president's support strong. I replied with burning epistles of endearment, interlarded with the ease with which we were selling bonds and recruiting men for our Canadian expedition.

I also told Robert that I could see no evidence of a dis-

position to further rebellion in the South. This was almost as important as our recruiting activity. I had no illusion, of course, that Robert or the president was relying
on my information. Robert had told me that they had a
number of confidential correspondents, in particular
Benjamin Truman of the *New York Times,* sending them
reports on the South. If the region remained pacified, and
their delegates were readmitted to Congress quickly, the
president's ability to support our Canadian expedition
would be immensely strengthened. Friends like Fernando Wood, at present part of a weak Democratic minority in Congress, would rise to power.

One might think I was riding high, playing at such
grand strategy, but there were terrible doubts about the
great stakes and frequent bouts of remorse for the part I
played. I wondered how long Robert Johnson could retain
any influence unless he got better control of his drinking
and his egotism. I found myself remembering his crass
hand on my breast or thigh, the crude way in which he
took me, with no interest whatsoever in my pleasure.
Though I struggled against it and vowed my heart was un-
violated, I felt a wound in my spirit that I knew not how to
heal.

I tried and to some extent succeeded in forgetting it
through my fascination with the amazing range of new
sights and experiences our journey south opened to me.
Thanks to my stay in Washington, D.C., I knew the inside story of the struggle that was raging north and south
between men who wanted to follow the forgiving policy
of the murdered Lincoln and those who favored the
vengeful policy of the Radical Republicans. For a personal barometer of Southern feelings, I had Dan McCaffrey. Everything he saw in Wilmington and now in
Charleston filled him with saturnine gloom.

The day we watched the brigadier lose his buttons, we
were on our way to a meeting with one of Dan's wartime

commanders, Wade Hampton. He received us in the parlor of a once opulent house not far from Charleston's fashionable waterside promenade. With him was another Carolinian, Benjamin Franklin Perry, whom President Johnson had recently appointed the provisional governor of the conquered state.

The house was a kind of image of the ruined South. Nothing had been repaired for years. Chairs with missing legs tilted crazily; ripped couches sagged; stopped clocks stared silently. Carpets were in tatters; the windows were bare, their curtains long since used for clothes. Broken panes were covered by boards.

Wade Hampton was a tall, muscular man with a remarkably handsome leonine head. Dan regarded him with much of the same awe he had felt for his original commander, Jeb Stuart. Hampton had succeeded Stuart as chief of the Confederate cavalry. Before the war, Hampton had been the richest man in South Carolina, with thousands of slaves and vast estates. He had not favored secession, but he had loyally followed the majority will of his countrymen, sacrificing his fortune to support the Confederacy.

Hampton was still wearing his uniform. He shook Dan's hand with great warmth and expressed his pleasure at meeting me. He introduced us to Governor Perry, a small, dark, rather volatile man, with impatience and considerable bitterness on his face.

"I wish I could welcome you to my own home," Hampton said, "but it's in ashes. I don't have a suit of clothes to my name, nor scarcely a dollar of ready money. Most of my friends are in the same condition."

Dan nodded, swallowing hard. "General," he said, "if you knew it was goin' to be like this, would you still have surrendered?"

"Yes, I think so," Hampton said.

"I just saw a Union sergeant cut the buttons off the coat of a brigadier general of the infantry."

"Such things will happen for a while."

"If I knew things like that were comin', I would have kept fightin'. So would every man I commanded."

"Then you'd be dead and unable to do anyone a service," Hampton said in his sad, soft voice. "No, General Lee made the right decision. The South needs every man it has left if it's to salvage anything from the wreckage."

He hesitated, embarrassed by the contradiction between that thought and the purpose of our visit. "I gather from your letter that you're serving another embattled cause."

"Yes, sir," Dan said. "The Fenian army of the Republic of Ireland. We ain't got a country and we ain't got an army, but we're gonna have one soon enough. I'd like to see some regiments of southern Irishmen in it." He told him of the plan to attack Canada. "General," he said, "if you'd make a statement recommendin' us, I think we'd get every Irish soldier in this state who still had two legs and two arms, plus a few with stumps."

"I'm flattered, Major McCaffrey," Hampton said, "but I doubt if such a statement would be good policy for either you or me. It would be regarded with suspicion by our conquerors. I'm still an unpardoned rebel. We've been whipped, Major, and we must walk low for a while."

"Why don't you recruit the niggers?" Governor Perry said. "We'll pay you a dollar a head to get rid of them, and no one would ask any questions if they all froze to death in Canada the first winter."

"I don't agree with you, Governor," Wade Hampton said. "As slaves our blacks were faithful. Could we have left our women and children in their power and spent four years fighting in Virginia and Tennessee if we didn't trust them? We need their labor as free men. If we deal with them fairly, we can make them useful citizens."

"You favor giving them the vote?" Perry said.

"Those who can read and write. It will disarm our enemies to the north."

"No nigger will ever vote in South Carolina while I'm governor," Perry said.

Hampton sighed. "These young people aren't interested in our differences. They're in pursuit of other dreams, other glories. Let us wish them better fortune than we've had."

We thanked him and departed. Only dimly did I realize then that I had heard the argument that was tormenting the South and would soon trouble America—how to deal with the four million freed slaves. I only knew—and knew I disliked—the savage hatred of the blacks that I heard in Governor Perry's voice. I was dismayed to hear it echoed by Dan.

"General Hampton's crazy," he muttered as we walked past the crowds of blacks in the hot streets. "Give one nigger a vote and they'll all want it. Next thing we'll be sittin' down to dinner with them."

"You sound like an Englishman talking of Irishmen," I said.

"What the hell do you mean?" he growled.

"Where else in the world are people despised in the mass, but Irish by English?"

"Niggers are different," he said. "Can't you see that by lookin' at them? They won't work if they ain't driven to it."

"Exactly what the English say about us."

"Are you tellin' me an Irishman's the same as a nigger?" he snarled.

"I'm telling you not to slander any people or race wholesale. It's an ignoramus's way of thinking."

In a rage, Dan seized a fat black man who was strolling past us with a slim coffee-colored young woman on his arm. "Hey, boy," he said. "What do you think of the Jubilee? You like bein' a free man?"

"Sure do," he said.

"What sort of work you goin' to do?"

"I don't rightly know. Not much work to be done around here. When Uncle Sam gets me my forty acres and my mule, reckon it'll be time to work."

"How you eatin' now?"

"Why, at the Bureau. They tell us not to worry, Uncle's goin' to take good care of us."

"Don't they tell you to work?"

"They say I's a free man now. Work when I want."

Dan glared triumphantly at me. I refused to be impressed. "Sure why shouldn't he celebrate his freedom? Wouldn't you? I can tell you, if we free Ireland, the whole country'll be drunk for a week. He's ready to work when he gets his land and mule."

Back at the Planters Hotel, we found ourselves at lunch with a group of new appointees to the Freedmen's Bureau, just arrived by ship from Boston. They were two men and four women, all in their twenties or thirties. Red Mike Hanrahan held forth on what he had been hearing from his fellow reporters and from interviews about the pitiable state of the beaten Southerners. A Sister of Mercy at the hospital had told him stories of widowed women and children half starved in their fine houses, accepting charity with eyes swimming in tears. In the countryside the situation was no better. The Union Army had left the region a desert. Numerous great folk found themselves cooking and learning how to milk cows for the first time in their lives. Many people were living on cornbread and sassafras tea. Some were eating cowpeas—cattle food. Bands of Negroes were roaming the roads, casually stealing what they pleased, heading for Charleston, where they had heard they would be apportioned their forty acres and their mules.

"That's exactly what these people deserve," said the oldest man in the Boston group. He had a narrow, supercilious face and a thin, fragile body. "They must expiate every drop of blood that was spilled by Northern men on the battlefields, and every blow of the lashes they inflicted on their helpless blacks."

"Did you fight on any of these battlefields?" Red Mike Hanrahan asked.

"No," he said. "I wasn't healthy enough. But I assisted where I could. On the Sanitary Commission. Buying bonds. Praying for victory."

"I think I can speak for a good many of the men who fought," Red Mike said. "Most of them learned to respect the sincerity of the Rebs, even if we didn't agree with them. We have no desire to grind them into the dust."

"I don't think you Irish have the right to speak for anyone but yourselves," the Bostonian said. There were sniffs and nods of agreement from his five companions. "Most of you were in favor of slavery from the start. You fought for the Union only because the pay was good."

Red Mike lunged across the table and seized the Bostonian by the throat. "You lily-livered Protestant son of a bitch," he said. "You can't insult the men I saw go up Marye's Heights at Fredericksburg."

John O'Neil pried Mike's hand from the Bostonian's quivering esophagus, and the Yankee brigade withdrew from the table in shrill fury, vowing to charge Mike before the military commander of the district. "Go on," Mike roared, "try it. But get the first boat out of here if you do."

They were typical of the employees of the Freedmen's Bureau, Mike said, from what he had learned from his fellow reporters. The Bureau was doing noble work, feeding hungry blacks and some Southern whites as well, but its staff were all Southern-hating abolitionists from New England and the Midwest who were preaching race hatred and giving the blacks impossible dreams.

There was no chance of them each getting forty acres and a mule. It was all wild Radical Republican talk.

Over coffee, Mike and John O'Neil listened to our report of our visit to General Hampton. Combined with the news Mike had gathered, it convinced us that it was futile to recruit Southern Irishmen here. The few Mike and John had encountered were loath to consider leaving their homes and families while the country was in such chaos. So we boarded another steamboat and sailed on to Savannah. This was largely a repetition of Charleston, the city filled with Union troops and idle Negroes being fed by the government, the whites dazed in their splendid mansions fronting the palm-lined squares. The difference was our reception by the Union commander. He waved a telegram from Secretary of War Stanton forbidding him to let us address Union troops on "government property." The commander extended this order to the vicinity of the camp and warned us that he would arrest us if we were caught persuading any of his men to desert. In vain we tried to explain to him that our appeal was directed to men whose enlistments would soon expire.

Unable to distribute handbills in the camp, we had to work with Irish-American soldiers in the ranks to organize a meeting in the city's Forsyth Park. It was successful enough. We got as many promised volunteers as we had won in Charleston and sold more bonds. But a Union officer sat in the front row and wrote down everything that we said. Red Mike Hanrahan assured us that it was on the telegraph to Stanton the next day. I wrote a furious letter to Robert Johnson, accusing Stanton of trying to sabotage us.

We boarded ship and sailed on to New Orleans. In material damage, this city had suffered less than Charleston and other cities of the Confederacy, but its demoralization was much more appalling. Its life was dominated by Federal soldiers and hundreds of Northern cotton jobbers.

They filled the great rotunda of the once fashionable St. Charles Hotel, where the "princes of the Mississippi," the wealthy planters from fine houses up the river, used to assemble. A few crestfallen ex-Confederate soldiers wandered among them, trying to sell cotton or—more often the case—their lands.

Never before I had seen such exotic women—Spanish, Creole, quadroons, mulattos—as in New Orleans. They looked like creatures out of *The Arabian Nights* or *The Travels of Marco Polo*. Unlike the ragged women of Charleston and Savannah, these women wore the latest, most elaborate styles in all their silken and brocaded extravagance. New Orleans had been captured by the Union Army and Navy long before the war ended, and a fabulous trade in contraband cotton had been thriving for a year when the South surrendered. The influx of cash produced a city where gambling houses flourished and elegant brothels glittered on every third corner.

We had high hopes in New Orleans. The Union garrison was commanded by General Philip Sheridan, the highest-ranking Irish-American in the Union Army and a friend of John O'Neil, who had served under him in Kentucky and Tennessee. I found the appearance of this famous soldier disappointing—he was small and squat with a massive chest and long, drooping arms—but there was a primitive, bristling energy about him as he sprang up from his desk to give O'Neil a cordial welcome.

He was polite enough to me and Red Mike, but when O'Neil introduced Dan as a fellow cavalryman, Sheridan growled, "I don't ordinarily welcome rebels to this office. But I'll make an exception this once."

He turned away from Dan as it dawned on us that those cutting words were not spoken in jest. "Now what the devil are you up to, John?" he asked. Sheridan obviously had received a warning telegram about us from Stanton.

O'Neil described our purpose and plans. Sheridan shook his head. "No, no, it's all wrong, John. Can't you see the danger? All this talk of Ireland and Canada. It takes Irishmen in the wrong direction. It makes us look like disturbers of the peace—or worse, like fools. We need to stop dreaming wild dreams and settle down to becoming Americans. Work hard and forget about Ireland. That's what we should do."

"I must disagree, General," O'Neil said. "As long as Ireland remains a place of slavery, we'll never get the respect we deserve in this country."

Again I was hearing the fundamental argument that would break thousands of hearts, including my own. Sheridan was adamant in his opinion. He refused to let us address his troops, and he suggested that we leave New Orleans as soon as possible. He was unmoved by President Johnson's letter. He obviously considered his telegram from Stanton more significant. We refused to be intimidated and told the general we would make our own plans and abide by our stated purpose.

"I have the power to put you on a steamboat in one hour, at the point of a bayonet," Sheridan said. "I know what I'm talking about, goddamn it. I was the only Irishman in my class at West Point. I took insults all day long. Why? Because a lot of mangy louts with Irish names were brawling in the streets of Boston and New York. Their reputation made my life miserable. You'll set us back fifty years with this damn nonsense."

Sheridan was typical of many Irish-Americans who had succeeded in America. He was ashamed of his slower countrymen and baffled by them. Essentially he wanted them to keep quiet and invisible, so Phil Sheridan could enjoy his glory undisturbed. I kept this opinion to myself. A mere woman could not contradict a general to his face. Not that John O'Neil or Dan or Red

Mike said much. We went back to our hotel and sent a telegram to New York explaining our predicament.

We received an astonishing reply from Colonel Roberts. OBEY SHERIDAN'S ORDERS. WE HOPE TO PERSUADE HIM TO LEAD THE FENIAN ARMY IN ITS ASSAULT ON CANADA. It was another glimpse of William Roberts's unrealism. Red Mike Hanrahan wired back: YOU'D HAVE A BETTER CHANCE OF PERSUADING THE DUKE OF WELLINGTON.

We had no choice now. We had to abandon New Orleans and board a steamboat for Vicksburg. It was my first glimpse of the mighty Mississippi and the boats that plied her mud-silted waters. I came aboard expecting little in the way of comfort. Hardship was all we had known in the hotels of the South. They were in the same state of disrepair as Wade Hampton's rented house in Charleston. We had eaten off chipped plates and drunk from cracked cups and slept in rooms with threadbare sheets and peeling wallpaper. The coastal steamers in which we had traveled thus far offered little more in the way of comfort or gentility.

Boarding our steamboat, the *Indian Queen,* I thought for a moment I had been transported in a dream to the splendors of the Blossom Club or Chamberlain's in Washington, D.C. Crystal chandeliers glittered in the dining room and main salon. The walls were aglow with blue and gold brocade, the rugs beneath our feet were inches thick. The dining room's snowwhite tablecloths and gold-rimmed dishes and prompt service by smiling Negroes were the equal of the Fifth Avenue Hotel. Our staterooms, though small, were appointed with every luxury.

It was exhilarating to step from this palatial inner world to the deck and find yourself on the mighty Mississippi. Its breadth was not so striking just above New Orleans—only about a mile—but its muddy, implacable current reminded you of the immense journey it had made through the heartland of a continent. More remarkable was its serpentine course. Never have I seen such windings. Particularly at one of innumerable bends the great river was like a living thing, tearing away at the soft banks before our very eyes, an image of nature's blind, furious energy.

That night I discovered that our floating palace had another appurtenance of city luxury—the gambling den. After supper, Red Mike Hanrahan casually suggested to Dan that they go below and "buck the tiger" for a while. John O'Neil said he was tired and went to bed. I stayed on deck and watched the night come down on the great river. A redheaded Union officer found me and when music drifted out of the main salon, suggested a dance. One dance led to a dozen, and I could see he was growing amorous. I chilled his ardor by telling him I wanted to see how my "husband" was doing at cards and went down a deck to the gambling salon.

The rambling salon was not much different from Chamberlain's. Silent greedy-faced men flanked by ebullient women, winning and losing on the cards that emerged from the tiger-headed box. What shocked me was the pile of chips in front of Dan and Red Mike. They were playing very hard, and I did not know where they got the money. Dan was receiving a salary of $160 a month as a major in the Fenian army. Red Mike no doubt had a salary from the *Irish-American,* his newspaper. But there was four or five times Dan's salary on the table in front of him.

"Your luck is running strong," I said.

"Mine is," Dan said. "Mike's in a hole."

"But I'll be out in a flash if that beast smiles at me," Mike said.

All bets were down. The dealer drew the fateful card, and Mike groaned as his cash was raked into the house pot. I watched for an hour, and Mike won very few rounds. He must have been down a thousand dollars by the time he quit in disgust. Dan left counting at least that much in winnings. He also brought along the woman who had been standing behind him, a brunette named Helen Shaughnessy. She had been born in New Orleans, and her father had been killed in the war, fighting for the South. She was going to Chicago "to get a husband," she said.

One look at her told me that she was long past the husband-hunting stage. At the bar in the main salon, she drank champagne as fast as Dan could pour it and whispered enticingly in his ear. As she said good night, she slipped her cabin key into Dan's hand. I felt a jealous fury surge inside me. But how could I object? I went to bed in such a miserable mood, I all but forgot my original anxiety—that Dan and Red Mike were gambling with the money we had collected for the Fenian Brotherhood.

The next morning, Miss Shaughnessy and Dan exchanged smiles and soft words at the breakfast table. She gushed about the generous reward Dan had given her for being his "luck." If Chicago proved unpromising, she vowed to look him up in New York. I could only bite my nasty tongue and hope she fell overboard before the *Indian Queen* was a mile past Vicksburg.

We debarked at that city in the early afternoon. It was a spectacular sight on its lofty bluff above the junction of the Mississippi and Yazoo rivers, but on closer inspection it was a battered wreck. Houses and churches and other public buildings were riddled by the Union bombardment during the bitter siege that preceded its capture in 1863.

We hired a wagon driven by a ragged white man and pulled by a half-starved horse to get us up the steep hill to the town. After a miserable lunch of some thin soup and gray undeterminable meat at our hotel, we sallied forth to find the Union commander and see the sights. The heat was brutal August at its worst. We had scarcely set foot into Main Street when around a corner came four blue-clad Union soldiers. Hardly a surprising sight, until we focused our eyes on their faces. They were various shades of African—my first glimpse of the thousands of black soldiers in the Union Army.

Four abreast, they bore down on us with unbroken strides. We trimmed to one side of the walk, as people do on crowded streets in New York, but this was not good enough for our oncoming friends. They continued to occupy the whole sidewalk and barged into Red Mike, sending him staggering into the dusty street.

"What the hell?" growled Mike.

Out of a store and across the street charged two white men dressed in darker blue uniforms with hard rounded hats—policemen. One of them, a squat, broad-shouldered fellow built on the style of General Sheridan, shook his club at the black soldiers. "Do that once more and you'll be the sorriest nagur in Mississippi," he said in a brogue as thick as any I ever heard in Ireland.

"Blow it out you ass, Mike," said the biggest of the black soldiers, a mountain of a man with sergeant's stripes on his sleeve.

The blacks continued down the street, resuming their four-abreast progress, forcing two or three other whites into the gutter. The two policemen looked after them, muttering. We introduced ourselves and explained our mission. "Devil an Irish soldier you'll find about here," said the squat policeman, whose name was O'Connor. "They're mostly as black as those that just shoved you into the dust. But there's a hundred of us hired to police the town, and scarcely a one's not Irish."

"There's one or two Welshmen, I think," said O'Connor's smaller partner. "They're just as crazy as an

Irishman. You've got to be mad as moonshine to take this job."

They were all ex-Union soldiers, hired by the military government. The Federals had done the same thing at Memphis and other river towns, including New Orleans. The white Southerners disliked this Gaelic constabulary at first, but the policemen were beginning to win them over by showing they had no prejudice against them.

"All would be dandy, if it wasn't for the nigger soldiers," O'Connor said. "Sure the government made the greatest mistake of its life putting them buggers into the uniform of the Union."

"Why shouldn't they fight in a war for their freedom?" I said.

O'Connor gaped at me in astonishment. "Is she Irish, or one of them nigger-lovin' Freedmen's Bureau Republicans?"

"I'm as Irish as you'll ever hope to be, you lummox," I said. "Two months out from County Limerick."

"Well, someone better explain America to you, me darlin'. You'll find damn few Irish who'll be cheerin' on the Fenians if you come at them with this muck about glorious fightin' niggers."

He strode off, leaving me almost breathless with anger. I was hardly soothed when John O'Neil said, "He's right, Bess," and Red Mike and Dan agreed with him.

"Are we to be laboring to free the Irish so they can hold their heads up before the world while we cast aspersions on another race, barely free of the chains of slavery?" I said.

"I'll cast aspersions on anyone who shoves me off the sidewalk into the dust," Red Mike said.

Dan just stood there, shaking his head. I saw how futile it was to argue with them. We visited the military commander of the town, a regular army colonel from

New Jersey. He confirmed that the Irish in the garrison were few but said he had no objection to our staging a Fenian rally and even suggested the theater on Main Street. We managed to muster a crowd of four hundred, many of them policemen and their wives, and we sold five thousand dollars' worth of bonds. The policemen were well paid and had money to spare.

While I was speaking, there was a disturbance in the rear of the theater. Someone started singing a Negro song, "Shoo Fly Don't Bother Me," and there were cries of "Throw the bugger out." As our rally ended we heard the same voice roaring out another song. People were leaving the theater when two shots rang out. There was a rush to the street. There we found Officer O'Connor standing pistol in hand over the sprawled body of a blue-coated black soldier.

"I told him to shut his mouth," O'Connor said. "I told him ten times."

The black man was dead. His limbs sprawled loosely; his head lolled. Blood oozed down his blue coat, dark red in the flickering gas lamps. I gazed at the Irish faces surrounding this corpse in the hot Mississippi night and felt nightmare engulfing me again. What were we doing, shooting black men in the American south? For the first time I sensed, truly sensed, the power of history's whirlwind and doubted my power—indeed, the power of us all combined—to control it.

Some Shall Wake to Weep

We left Vicksburg the next day with an armed escort of a dozen policemen. The black soldiers blamed us for the death of their comrade and were talking wildly about shooting a Fenian to even the score. I was plunged into gloom by the episode, but my three soldier companions, having seen thousands of similar corpses in their years of war, hardly gave it a passing thought. In fact, as we churned up the Mississippi, I noticed a distinct (and to me incomprehensible) shift toward cheerfulness in Dan McCaffrey. For most of the trip, especially when I was in range of his eyes, he had maintained a sullen, surly exterior. Now, twice in an hour I saw him smile. In the next hour he laughed three or four times at Red Mike Hanrahan's jokes. I did not understand what was happening until the boat docked at Memphis.

The moment the gangplank was laid, Dan was down it. He gave a piercing rebel yell, kissed the soil, and roared, "Here I am in the greatest state God ever made. I'm a whole team with two bulldogs under the wagon and a tar-bucket, yes I am. I'm ready to outholler the thunder, drink the Mississippi, and walk through a fence like a fallin' tree through a cobweb. One squint of mine at a bull's heel would blister it. I'm the genuine article, and anyone who don't think so had better register at the cemetery before tellin' me!"

"Damned if it ain't Davy Crockett hisself come home to rescue us," said one of the grizzled old rivermen who had just finished tying up the boat. "Give us the victory speech, Davy."

Dan sprang up on a box and obliged. "Fellow citizens and humans," he cried. "These is times that come upon us like a whirlwind and an airthquake. They are come like a catamount on the full jump: We are called upon to show our grit like chain lightnin' agin a pine log, to exterminate, mollify, and calumniate the foe.

"Pierce the heart of the enemy as you would a feller that spit in your face, knocked down your wife, burnt up your house, and called your dog a skunk! Cram his pesky carcass full of thunder and lightnin' like a stuffed sausage and turtle him off with a red hot poker, so that there won't be a piece of him left big enough to give a crow a breakfast, and bite his nose off into the bargain!

"Hosses, I am with you! Where is the craven low-lived chicken-bred toad-hoppin' red-mounted bristle-headed mother's son of you who will not raise the beacon light of triumph, smouse the citadel of the aggressor, and squeeze ahead for Liberty and Glory!"

Before he ended there was a crowd of a hundred Tennesseeans around him listening and laughing, as people elsewhere might gather for a song. Riding up the steep hill to Memphis, which sat on a bluff above the river, like Vicksburg, I asked someone to tell me who Davy Crockett was. I learned that he was a famous Tennesseean who had gotten killed in Texas fighting Mexicans in 1836. When I looked confused, Dan explained further. "For twenty or so years before the war, a fellow published *Crockett Almanacs* that had Davy's speeches in them. They were my old man's favorite readin'. He used to make me memorize them and recite them to his friends."

The picture saddened me, somehow. The wandering Irishman requiring his son to learn this new language instead of the beautiful poems and stories of his homeland. I was still in Ireland's grip, unable to accept how quickly and totally people became Americans.

Our steamboat brought the news of the Negro soldier shot at Vicksburg. It sent a shiver of anticipation through Memphis. Here, too, there was the same combination of

Negro troops in the garrison, an Irish police force, and resentful Southern whites. An added ingredient was the fierce antagonisms the Civil War had bred in Tennessee. Few other states had been so violently divided.

The day after we arrived the *Memphis Advance* published a curious poem, entitled "Death's Brigade."

The wolf is in the desert
  And the panther in the brake
The fox is on his rambles
  And the owl is wide awake
For now 'tis noon of darkness
  And the world is all asleep
And some shall wake to glory
  And some shall wake to weep.
  Ku Klux.
The misty gray is hanging
  On the tresses of the East
And morn shall tell the story
  Of the revel and the feast
The ghostly troop shall vanish
  Like the light in constant cloud
But where they rode shall gather
  The coffin and the shroud.
  Ku Klux.

I showed it to Dan and asked him what it meant. He said he had no idea but would try to find out. While we went to the Union commandant's headquarters on Court Square for the usual permission to address his troops, Dan visited his numerous friends in Memphis. The Union general, named Stoneman, was an old friend of John O'Neil. He showed us the telegram he had received from Stanton advising (not ordering) him to forbid us to approach his men. O'Neil showed him our letter from Andrew Johnson, and Stoneman said he thought that carried more weight in Tennessee. Obviously everyone, including army generals, was playing politics, waiting to see where the power in Washington would finally lie. General Stoneman cautioned us to say nothing that would inflame the tension between the Irish policemen and the blacks in Memphis and questioned us nervously about the soldier shot in Vicksburg. We satisfied him on our neutrality and departed.

Returning along Main Street to the Gayoso Hotel, we saw an ominous sign of trouble to come. Four Irish policemen, striding down the sidewalk, confronted four blue-clad Negro soldiers. The policemen shouldered them aside, knocking one of the soldiers onto his back in the street. The Negroes called them insulting names and vowed revenge.

At the hotel we found Dan having a drink of bourbon with an old friend, Captain John C. Kennedy. A fellow native of Pulaski, he had spent the war in a regiment of Confederate cavalry that mostly fought in Tennessee. I disliked him on sight. He was one of those handsome men who loved himself with more enthusiasm than anyone else could ever hope to muster. When we mentioned the altercation we had just seen between the black soldiers and the Irish policemen, Kennedy laughed nastily. "Those niggers are givin' us a great opportunity to teach them a lesson they'll never forget," he said.

"Just sound the call," Dan said. "We'll be there to join you."

"I hope not," I said. "If we can have any influence, which I doubt, we should try our utmost to prevent trouble. Can't you see the effect it will have in the North if we Irish are associated with attacking Negroes?"

"Little bit of a nigger lover, ain't she," Kennedy said.

"Oh, you know how it is," Dan said. "Females tend to fret more over lovin' your neighbor. My ma was that way."

"I don't believe the Bible limited that teaching by sex," I said.

"Like to see what you think of it after one of them big buck niggers in the colored artillery regiment got off you," Kennedy said.

"Say another word like that to Miss Fitzmaurice," John O'Neil said, "and I'll lay you out on the floor."

"I apologize to the lady," Kennedy said, with a sneer that belied his words. "If you mean to stay out of trouble, keep off the streets for the rest of the day—and especially tonight." He stood up and smiled at Dan. "Ku Klux," he said.

He strode into the blazing sunlight on Main Street. Watching him go, I remembered the words from the poem. "What does that mean, that last thing?"

"Nothin' much," Dan said. "It's some kind of crazy secret society they invented one night in Pulaski a coupla months back."

"What is its purpose?" I asked.

"Search me," Dan said. I had a feeling he was not telling the truth.

We decided to disregard Captain Kennedy's warning to stay in our hotel. Only Dan took it seriously. He said Kennedy had told him that there were "organized plans" to teach the black soldiers a lesson. We had grown so used to seeing Southerners crushed and dazed in defeat, it was impossible to believe. "Gwan," Red Mike Hanrahan said. "There isn't enough spirit left in the South to organize a tea party."

"This ain't the South. This is Tennessee," Dan said. But we paid no attention to him.

We should have changed our minds when the chief of police strongly urged us not to try to hold a meeting tonight. He had information that there was trouble brewing, and he did not want most of his men in a theater, cheering for Ireland, when he needed them. We thought the chief was just playing politics with us and coolly insisted on our rights. We reserved the theater, got handbills printed, and hired a few young men to distribute them in the Union soldiers' camp. Red Mike attended to most of this business, and John O'Neil and I wandered off to inspect Memphis. I thanked him for defending me with Kennedy. He dismissed it in his casual way.

"Do you agree with me, that we Irish should look kindly on the blacks, John?" I asked. "Or am I a hopeless idealist, for which you can read female fool?"

"To be honest, Bess, I haven't given it much thought," he said. "Before I was old enough to think, I was in a war fighting for my life and my head was filled with tactics, supplies, morale, from dawn until dusk seven days a week. 'Tis high politics, and I've never thought of myself as more than a soldier."

"Here's a good place to start," I said. "Let's go talk to some blacks and see what they think of it all."

We wandered along Beale Street into the Negro section of town. It was a tumbledown mess, with worse shacks than I'd ever seen in Ireland. "They don't live high, that's for sure," I said.

By now it was close to four o'clock. We saw twenty or thirty little black children coming out of a ramshackle building. They were greeted by women in peasant costumes, many with turbans on their heads, obviously their mothers. They seized the little ones' hands and led them away. In the doorway appeared a tall, handsome white girl, not much older than I was. She smiled down at the children, called to them by name, and patted them on the head as they streamed past her.

She was obviously a Sassenach, but she had a cheerful face. I introduced myself and John and asked her what brought her to Memphis. Her name was Hannah Simpson, she replied, and her father had been killed in the war. She had accepted this job as a teacher in the South

to fulfill the mission of her father's life. He had been a
foe of slavery for ten years before the war and had helped
to raise a regiment in Maine to fight the Confederates. I
was touched, even intimidated, by the intensity of her
idealism. She was like a radiant power there in the doorway of her battered schoolroom, looking out on the lit-
tered street of the Negro slum.

"I know I'm doing what Father would have wanted me
to do," she said.

I asked her where she was living. "With a Negro family down the road," she said. "I don't think we can teach
the children without understanding the parents. You can't
believe how passionate they are to see their children educated. Some of those women walk five miles from the
country to bring their children to this school. I've had to
turn away a hundred pupils. So far there are only four of
us in Memphis."

John O'Neil was listening to all this with the greatest
interest. "You mean they can be taught to read and write?"
he said.

"Of course," said Miss Simpson. "As well as you or I."

John was only speaking out of the prejudice he had
imbibed from his youthful years in Nashville, where he
grew up.

"Believe me," Miss Simpson said. "They're going to
become useful citizens, if we give them a chance."

We left Miss Simpson planning her next day's lessons.
John O'Neil and I strolled back to Main Street and proceeded up it toward our hotel. Down the street toward us
came a half dozen black soldiers, another phalanx pushing whites into the street. They were drunk, to make matters worse. Before they reached us, four policemen sprang
from a store and blocked their path. The policemen raised
their clubs. The black soldiers drew gleaming knives from
holsters at their waists. A shot rang out, and one of the

black soldiers toppled into the street. Another shot and one of the policemen tumbled backward, clutching his throat, to writhe on the sidewalk.

A great roar arose behind us. A squad of black soldiers with drawn bayonets came racing down the street. They were met by a hundred policemen rushing from the other direction. Both sides had obviously been waiting for the signal to begin the battle. They met in roaring, cursing clamor in the middle of the street. John O'Neil drew a gun from beneath his coat. With that in one hand and his other arm about me, he fought his way past the melee and hustled me up the street to the Gayoso Hotel.

For the rest of the afternoon, I watched from the window as the blacks and the police fought up and down Main Street and along the side streets. There were at least a dozen killed on either side from the looks of them as they sprawled in the street before they were dragged away. I could not understand why the white soldiers in the garrison were not called to restore order. It was obviously beyond the power of the Irish police, who were outnumbered by the blacks.

As the sun sank, there came a lull in the battle. I lay down for a nap, sickened by what I had seen and the knowledge that Irishmen had been the chief combatants. I could practically read the headlines in the North. Little did I know that the worst was to come. The battle between the police and the Negro soldiers at least had the makings of a fair fight. They fought mostly with clubs and bayonets and limited their assaults to each other. But when night fell, a different army entered the fray.

We had just finished a very poor dinner. Most of the Negro help had not dared to venture up Main Street to the hotel. We had to make do with cold meat and tired vegetables. Dan McCaffrey and Mike Hanrahan had been out on the street watching the fray and possibly participating in it, if I was any judge of the bruise that Dan had on his cheek. He claimed to have gotten it from a chip of wood torn from a house wall by a bullet.

Suddenly we heard the pounding of hooves on Main Street. Dan seized my arm, and we rushed to the front door. Half a hundred horses were prancing past, their riders each wearing a white hood over his head, with two eyes and a mouth cut in it. "Ku Klux," one of them cried when he saw me and Dan. I was sure it was John Kennedy.

The hooded horsemen swung east at the foot of Main Street and galloped toward the Negro quarter of Memphis. Within minutes there came a volley of shots, followed by the ringing of church bells and a glimpse of flames flickering against the darkened sky. Screams and shouts and rebel yells echoed faintly in the night-shrouded streets. From the opposite end of town, where the black soldiers were camped, came cries of alarm. Soon the blacks appeared on Main Street, rushing furiously past the hotel, guns in hand. A tremendous crash of rifles broke their charge. From buildings on both sides of the street, hidden marksmen poured bullets into them. It was a well-laid ambush. Some tried to return the fire, but it was a lost cause. Dozens toppled before the devastating volleys. The survivors broke and ran in terror. Their enemies emerged to pursue them, whooping like Indians. I was dismayed to see that they were mostly policemen in uniform.

For the rest of the night, Memphis was a city in chaos. White and black men fought from rooftops and storefronts, while flaming terror reigned in the Negro quarter. Screams of pain and fear, shouts of anger and defiance, and bursts of gunfire shattered the darkness.

Not until dawn did General Stoneman send white troops into the city to restore order. We stared from our hotel at a sight that made Vicksburg's single dead Negro seem trivial. At least twenty black soldiers sprawled on

Main Street in various postures of agony. Among them lay one or two whites. When army wagons took away the dead, I ventured down to the Negro quarter with Red Mike Hanrahan, who was gathering facts for a report to the *Irish-American.* There lay more Negro dead, and one or two whites, their hoods still on their heads. The blacks had fought here, too, but equally in vain. Their shanties and tumbledown houses had been put to the torch. Almost the entire quarter was in ruins, including Miss Simpson's schoolhouse. We found her weeping in the wreckage, smeared with dirt and ashes, trying to salvage a few charred books and writing slates.

"We'll build a better school," she said, when she saw me. "We'll build a better school. Wait and see."

"Are you all right yourself? Did they—insult you?" I asked.

"Only with words," she said. "They did far worse to at least five colored women, including the daughter of my—my friends. Where I was staying."

She began to weep uncontrollably. "We'll make them pay for this," she said, raising her clenched fist. "I'm going to write to the president, to every man in Congress. I'm going to tell them what happened in Memphis. We'll make these people pay."

She glared with wild eyes up the hill toward the white section of the town. All traces of angelic innocence were gone from her face. She looked capable of murder.

I felt capable of it myself when Red Mike and I returned to the hotel. Who should I encounter strutting across the lobby but Captain Kennedy. "I see you took my advice and stayed out of harm's way," he said.

"I did because I had no choice," I said. "I have no training as a soldier. But if I had, I know where I would have gone."

"Where is that?" he said with his complacent smile.

"Down to the Negro quarter to shoot a few more of

you hooded heroes out of your saddles," I said. "I have strong opinions about men who attack defenseless women and children."

"You *are* a little nigger lover, aren't you," Kennedy said. "People like you will be much safer out of Tennessee. Out of the whole South, in fact. This is only the beginning. We're going to teach Sambo and Sambo lovers like you that the white race has no intention of letting niggers into our courts or legislatures or schoolrooms."

By now I was too furious to think about caution. "You're a swine and deserve nothing but slaughter," I said.

"If you were a man, I'd ask you to answer that insult with a pistol," Kennedy said.

"I would do so gladly, in the name of those black women you abused last night."

"All right, all right," Mike Hanrahan said, drawing me away. "She's overwrought. No sleep."

"Of course," Kennedy said.

Red Mike escorted me to my room, lecturing all the way. "These fellows are dangerous," he said. "Do y'want to get us all killed? Dan tells me that this Ku Klux thing is racing across the state like a flame up a fuse."

At lunch Mike reported on what we had seen in the Negro quarter and added a picturesque account of my collision with Captain Kennedy, in which he had us drawing pistols at ten paces. John O'Neil decided that there was no hope of staging a Fenian rally in Memphis now—nor was it advisable. Northern reporters were no doubt rushing to the city. Our best move was an immediate departure for Nashville, where things were hopefully quieter. I opined that it might be a good idea to abandon Tennessee entirely, but O'Neil said that he had promised his wife to stop at Nashville. From there we would have no difficulty proceeding west to Kentucky, Ohio, and Illinois.

That afternoon we boarded a train for Nashville. It had none of the comforts of the parlor car we had ridden to Washington. We sat on hard wooden seats with straight backs. The flimsy coach was not much more than a wooden crate on iron wheels. The interior was like an oven. When we opened the windows, soot blew in our faces. The railroad had carried only freight and troops during the war years, when there was little cause for amenities.

Adding to my displeasure was the discovery that Captain Kennedy was on the train. He was drunk and went up and down the cars offering people a swig from the bottle of bourbon he was carrying. It had something to do with celebrating last night's victory in Memphis, from snatches of conversation I overheard. He pretended to be surprised when he encountered us.

"Join me in a toast?" he said, proffering the bottle. "The South will rise again."

John O'Neil shook his head. "I wish you well, but I can't drink to that. Nor can my friend here," he said, gesturing to Mike. "He was in the Irish Brigade."

"I won't bother to ask Harriet O'Beecher McStowe here." Kennedy said. "How 'bout you, Dan?"

"Not thirsty, Jack," Dan said. "And I wouldn't call this lady here any more names. She just might rename your creek for you."

"What does that mean?" I asked.

Dan pointed out the window at a meandering stream. "'Bout a hundred years ago, a settler family camped by that creek. The old man was a mean cuss, and he beat his wife somethin' awful. He gave a big cocka-doodle-do and decided that to celebrate his victory he'd call it 'Daddy's Creek.' Next night the old lady got together with some of her half-grown sons, and they laid into the old varmint till he was beggin' for mercy. To make sure he remembered, they changed the name to Mammy's Creek—and that's what it's still called."

"Those days are gone forever," Kennedy said. "In modern Tennessee we have ways of dealin' with uppity women same as with uppity niggers."

I heard menace in his voice, but if Dan heard it, he chose to ignore it. "Stay away from her, Jack," he said, lighting a cigar. "She's got a little nickel-plated gun that could put more holes in you than this train's got windows."

"Sounds like you agree with her sentiments, old friend," Kennedy said.

Dan examined the cigar for a moment. "Don't go much for the kind of cavalry fightin' you Kluxers did at Memphis. Down in Virginia, General Stuart and General Hampton kind of drew the line on women and children, no matter what their color."

"That kind of thinkin' could make you real unpopular in Tennessee these days."

"My dad didn't worry much about popularity when he stood with the Confederacy," Dan said. "I don't reckon I should change my ways without changin' my name, do you?"

"No, I guess not," Kennedy said. He swigged from his bottle and departed.

It was growing dark when we reached Jackson, which was about halfway to Nashville. There the conductor informed us that we were going no further. Earlier in the day some robbers—bushwhackers, he called them—had waylaid a train in the mountains, and General Stoneman had telegraphed orders to make no more trips without an armed guard, which would not arrive from Memphis until tomorrow morning.

Groaning with impatience, we debarked and hustled

into the town to find beds for the night. Happily we had no trouble. Jackson was a junction for five railroads, and there were several taverns for travelers who had to wait overnight for trains. We lost track of Captain Kennedy in the midst of our transfer, and I thought no more about him. After a poor supper of scorched beef and rancid coffee, I pronounced myself exhausted, having gotten scarce two hours' sleep the previous night in Memphis, and went to bed. The others said they would soon imitate my example.

I fell asleep instantly and dreamt of Ireland, a habit that was beginning to distress me. I saw dozens of familiar faces, Old Malloy and Patrick Dolan, my ex-suitor, looking sad, and Mother and Father, also in some great distress, for reasons I could not understand. If I were with you, how happy I would be, thought the watcher-dreamer in Tennessee.

Suddenly I was staring awake in the darkness, struggling to breathe. A dirty, tobacco-smelling hand was over my mouth and nose. "I got her," whispered a voice. Someone struck a match. A half dozen men in white hoods confronted me. The hand was abruptly replaced by an equally dirty rag, which was shoved into my mouth, all but choking me. Another dirty rag was tied over it to prevent me from spitting the first one out. I was rolled over on my face and my hands tied behind my back, while someone else tied my ankles. A big fellow slung me over his shoulder like a sack of meal and carried me along the upper hall and down a back stairs. Outside waited two more men with horses. I was tied over the back of a saddle, head down one side, feet down the other, and they rode away.

I lost track of how long we rode. I was in constant pain from the horse's haunches pounding into my stomach. Occasionally stones flew up and struck me in the face. Dust blinded and almost choked me. Finally we slowed and picked our way up a trail in some woods. In a moment we were in a clearing, where pine-knot torches blazed. They cut me off the horse and loosed the ropes on my hands and feet. They also removed my foul gag. I gazed at a dozen hooded figures, grouped around a ruler who sat on a crude throne. He wore not only a hood but a long white robe.

"Kneel before the Grand Cyclops of the Ku Klux Klan of Jackson, Tennessee," I was told.

I knelt. I was thoroughly frightened.

"Do you know why you have been brought here?" asked the Cyclops.

"No."

"You have been accused on good grounds of defamin' the noble order of the Ku Klux and maintainin' the dangerous lie that the black man is equal to the white man. Is that true?"

"I insist on being returned to my inn immediately," I said.

"We consider a refusal to defend yourself the same as a plea of guilty. In our benevolence, we are goin' to give you a chance to repent of your ways, and learn a lesson in the bargain. Bring out the other prisoner."

A husky Negro was shoved into the circle of torch-light. He wore city clothes, which were much the worse for wear, and his shoes were missing. "This nigger ran away from a man around here in '58," the Cyclops said. "Went to Ohio and got himself an education at Oberlin College. Now he's come back down here to teach equality to other niggers. Before we're through with him, he's goin' to be teachin' on his knees, and it won't be equality. First we're goin' to give you a chance to find out just how lovable niggers is. Kiss him."

"What?" I said dazedly.

"Kiss him," said the Cyclops.

I shook my head. I heard a hiss, and a terrible stroke of fire raced across my back. Someone had laid a whip to me. I whirled, and another stroke came from the opposite direction. I cried out in agony.

"Kiss him," said the ruler.

I walked slowly toward the black man. Rivulets of perspiration ran down his square, craggy face. His squashed nose and his thick reddish lips loomed gigantically before me. His skin was as grimy and grainy as a piece of old shoe leather. I could smell him, a peculiar, smoky odor, like a drying coat after a rain. At the last moment I turned my face away. The lash struck me, and I fell to my knees, weeping.

Gently, calmly, the black man reached down and lifted me to my feet. "It's all right, Miss. It won't hurt you."

I could not tell him my real torment, or rather, my shame: My revulsion against his blackness. Trembling, I closed my eyes and kissed him gingerly on the lips. I stepped back, and the whip struck me across the shoulders, driving me into his arms.

"Shit," said the Cyclops. "You call that a kiss? That didn't even tickle his pecker. I mean a real kiss. Wrap your arms around him. Shove that little ole cunt of yours into him."

"Let's take off that there nightgown," someone else said. "That'll get things goin'."

"Let it be done," said the Cyclops.

Two of them stepped to my side and ripped the nightgown over my head. I stood naked before them. The whip came out of the night to strike my bare back. I screamed in anguish.

"You better kiss him real quick before these boys get too excited," the Cyclops said.

"Hey, wait. Let's take off the nigger's clothes, too."

"Let it be done," the Cyclops said.

In seconds the black man was naked, too. He had a muscular squarish torso, thick chested and slim waisted, a workingman's body.

"Now kiss him good," the ruler said.

I hesitated. The whip struck me again. With a cry I flung myself against the black man and kissed him with a desperate mixture of fervor and loathing and fear. I stepped back, my head bowed, my eyes closed. They could beat me to death, I vowed. I would do no more.

"Look at that nigger's thing," someone said. "Shows what he'd like to do to every white woman in Jackson County."

"Only one way to make sure that don't happen," said the Cyclops.

I stood there, refusing to look, half mad with terror and shame. How could such men exist? What could drive men here in the center of America to such acts of loathsome cruelty?

"Hey, the Irish beauty ain't lookin'."

"Got her eyes closed."

"Open your eyes, Ireland," said the Cyclops.

The whip struck me. I opened my eyes and looked at my fellow prisoner. His sexual organ was half erect. "It's all right," he said. "It's only nature."

I looked him in the face; amazed by his calmness. I saw an indomitable pride there, which was prepared to survive every kind of humiliation and defeat, even death. My revulsion for him vanished. I felt a great bond with him and his people. I felt capable of loving him in a better time. Did he see any of this on my face? I will never know.

"We got the proof we need," the ruler said. "We have seen this nigger lustin' after a white woman. He's got to be made an example to his kind. Take him away."

Two of them dragged the black man into the darkness. "Give Ireland her nightdress," the ruler said. "And take her back to her bed. If she knows what's good for herself and her friends, she won't say a word about this little lesson she's learned tonight."

They threw my nightdress at me. I put it on, and two of them tied my hands and feet and inserted the foul gag in my mouth again. I was tied over the haunches of a horse and carted back to Jackson. At the tavern, the two cut me loose and carried me up the back stairs to my bedroom. They threw me unceremoniously on the bed and paused. I instantly knew what they were thinking.

"Seems a shame to just say good night, don't it," one of them whispered.

"The Cyclops said . . ."

"What he don't know won't hurt him. We'll take turns. You watch the door."

He cut away the ropes tying my feet and pulled my nightdress up to my waist. I could just make out his shadowy bulk in the darkened room as he fumbled with his pants. Then he loomed over me, his hand groping along my thigh. I drew both my legs together almost to my breasts and drove my feet into his face. He went crashing out of the bed on his back. "You goddamn bitch," he snarled. He lunged back into the bed, but I was no longer there. I had rolled out of it and across the floor to the wall on the other side of the room. My hands were still tied, my mouth gagged, but I was able to pound with my head. Dan McCaffrey and Mike Hanrahan were sleeping next door. My one hope was to wake them.

The Kluxer came after me. I rolled away from him into the night table on which sat a pitcher and bowl. All went over with a crash. "Jesus Christ, let's get outta here," called the man at the door. At that moment his friend managed to get one hand on me. He swung at me with his other hand, cuffing me cruelly on the side of the face. With that farewell the hero followed his friend out the door.

"Bess. Are you all right?" came Dan McCaffrey's voice a moment later. He found me slumped against the wall still bound and gagged, tears streaming down my face. I looked up at him by the glow of the single candle he was carrying and thought of the tender love I had felt for him not so long ago and the bestiality I had just confronted. I began to weep uncontrollably.

Dan rushed back to his room and returned with a knife that freed my hands and the gag from my mouth. "What happened?" he said.

"Ku Klux," I sobbed.

"What did they do?"

"They warned me to tell no one. They said it could be the death of all of us."

"You let me worry about that. Tell me."

I told him. He cursed savagely for a full minute. "Let me see your back," he said.

I turned and let him pull up my nightdress. "Jesus," he said. "You've got welts a quarter inch deep. Only one thing for them. Bear grease."

He went downstairs and woke the tavern owner, who had a supply of this sovereign Tennessee remedy on hand. By the time he returned I was aware of my wounds. They gripped my back in a web of pain. He rubbed the grease gently, tenderly, across them, and their ache diminished somewhat. Perhaps it was simply the sense of his concern that helped. "They won't be so stiff in the mornin'. Heal a lot faster, too," he said.

"Thank you," I said.

"Can't do nothin' for that blue and black mouse on your face."

"You could hold me in your arms for a minute."

He put his arms around me with alacrity. "Seein' as we got to fight the whole world, maybe we should stop fightin' with each other," he said.

"Yes," I said.

He kissed me gently and pressed me back on the pillow. "Get some sleep," he said. "If you can."

I slept poorly and awoke in the dawn, thinking of the

black man. When the sun was well up I rose and examined myself. I was appalled. My nightdress was a grimy mess. I smelled like a stable. My back was striped by a half dozen ugly welts, and my right cheek was bluish and puffy where my would-be rapist had struck me. But the bear grease did make my welts more limber. I was able to bathe and dress myself with only moderate discomfort.

At breakfast, I was greeted with solemn looks by John O'Neil and Mike Hanrahan. Dan had told them of my night. Mike was mortified that he had slept through it all. He agreed with Dan and John that the instigator of my ordeal had to be Captain Kennedy.

"Can't we have him arrested?" I asked.

"What evidence have we to offer a court?" John O'Neil said. "You can't name a single one of your abductors."

"This is Tennessee," Dan said. "We don't settle this sort of thing in a court of law."

"What are you going to do?" I asked nervously.

"We'll let you find out when it happens," Dan said.

"I don't want us killed on my account. I brought some of the trouble on myself with my bold tongue," I said.

"Just go upstairs, get packed, and come on down to the train with us," Dan said.

I did as I was told. Mike Hanrahan carried my bag and his own to the station, telling me funny stories of army days, like the time his friend Tim O'Toole asked the captain for a leave to see his wife. The captain told Tim that his wife had written him a letter, telling him not to let Tim come home because all he did was get drunk. "Sure the two biggest liars in the army are face-to-face here," said Tim. "I've never been married in me life."

"What is Dan planning to do, Mike?" I asked, refusing to be distracted by such blather.

"He's going for him. Kennedy. The worst gouger in Tennessee."

"What's a gouger?"

"He's got a fingernail on his thumb like the blade of a Bowie knife. It can cut a man's eye out of his head with a flick."

"I won't let him."

Dan was striding ahead of us with John O'Neil. I started for him and Red Mike caught my arm. "It would be a waste of breath," he said, "and might distract him."

At the station our fellow passengers—about twenty in number—were milling about, waiting for the train to start. Snuffling steam, the engine and the four wooden coaches were before the depot. We learned that the detachment of Union soldiers had not arrived from Memphis. They were expected within the hour.

"Hello, Kennedy," Dan said.

The captain stepped out of the crowd, looking fresh and self-satisfied. "Greetings, Danny-boy," he said. "How is the Fenian band this morning? Did Miss Harriet McBeecher O'Stowe have a pleasant night in Jackson?" His sneering smile was a tribute to his gall. He apparently expected me to have been terrorized into silence.

I never had to answer him. Without a word of warning, Dan smashed him in the jaw. The punch knocked Kennedy twenty feet into the cinders beside the track. "Get up, you Ku Klux son of a bitch," Dan said. "We know you're good at fightin' women and niggers in the dark. Let's see how you do against a white man in daylight."

Kennedy scrambled to his feet. I glanced to right and left and saw John O'Neil and Mike Hanrahan had drawn guns. "This is a private fight between two men from Tennessee," O'Neil said. "It will be settled according to the usual rules. The loser will be the man who can't get up or is too maimed to continue. If Captain Kennedy wishes to use Bowie knives, Major McCaffrey is agreeable. Otherwise, Major McCaffrey agrees to open rules, including gouging and kicking. He is determined to give Captain Kennedy a beating he will never forget."

"Open rules," Kennedy said. "I don't want to kill him. Just cripple him for life."

I knew nothing of how men fought in Tennessee. I was about to find out. Kennedy stripped off his coat and shirt. Dan did likewise. Kennedy's physique was formidable. Beneath his fine clothes he was a bruiser. "Say some prayers," Mike muttered to me.

At first Dan depended on his fists. He drove a swift succession of blows into Kennedy's face. Kennedy staggered back, then lunged low for Dan's waist, clung there for a moment, then reared up and butted him in the chin. Dan staggered back, and Kennedy was after him with a terrific kick that sent Dan flying into the crowd. Kennedy dove after him, and for a moment I could see nothing. Out of the crowd hurtled Kennedy with Dan after him, pounding him in the belly, the face, the belly, the face, followed by a tremendous kick in the belly that lifted Kennedy high in the air and slammed him down on his back. Dan aimed another kick at his ribs that would surely have ended the fight, but Kennedy seized the foot in midflight and sank his teeth into Dan's ankle. Dan roared with pain, and Kennedy twisted his leg, flinging Dan down on his back. In a flash Kennedy was on top of him thrusting his thumb down at Dan's right eye. Dan caught his wrist inches before the stroke drove home. For the first time I saw the long, murderously sharp nail on Kennedy's thumb.

It was a desperate contest of strength. Kennedy's whole weight was flung forward on the cruel weapon he had fashioned from his own body. Inch by inch it moved closer to Dan's eye. A stroke! Dan turned his head and took it on his cheek. It opened a wicked gash. Still Kennedy had him, pressing down, down. The crowd gave a long, low growl of savage anticipation.

Dan sank his teeth into Kennedy's hand. He screamed like a woman. In the same instant Dan gave a tremendous heave and threw Kennedy off him. He rolled frantically away, but Dan was after him. One, two, three times he lashed his foot into Kennedy's ribs. Even with the crowd roaring we could hear the bones crack. Dan dragged him to his feet and pounded him down with a roundhouse swing. He did it again and again and then went back to kicking him.

"Stop him," I said to John O'Neil. "He'll kill him. We'll all end in jail."

"No, no," O'Neil said. "He can take a good deal more. You're just not used to fighting in Tennessee."

Dan was merciless. Kennedy kept trying to crawl away. Each time he moved, Dan kicked him in the belly. He lifted up his head and spit in his face. He flung him over his shoulder full length into the dirt. Finally I could bear no more. I stepped between them and said, "He's had enough, Dan."

"That's for him to say, not you," Dan said, wiping the blood and sweat off his face.

On his hands and knees, Kennedy glared up at us. His eyes were half closed, his teeth broken and bloody. "The—South—will—rise—again—" he gasped.

Dan kicked him in the face. "Maybe," he said, "but I don't want no part of it."

Kennedy lay still. I looked at the crowd and did not like the menacing expressions on several faces. Before anyone could speak, much less act, we were jolted by a shrill whistle. Steaming into the depot was the train from Memphis with our armed escort of Union soldiers. They boarded the last car of our train, and we hastily got into our seats in the first car. Mike Hanrahan washed Dan's battered face at the water cooler while John O'Neil sat at the window, a pistol in either hand. As we pulled out of the station, two men lifted Kennedy to his feet and carried him into the wooden depot.

A half mile out of town, just as we began picking up speed, the train came to a jolting halt that almost flung us to the floor. John O'Neil peered out the window. The conductor rushed past us, and in a moment Union soldiers were running alongside the track. "What is it?" I said, trying to look past O'Neil.

"It might be better if you didn't see it," John said.

"What in the world are you talking about?" I said. I jumped up and hurried the length of the car to the door. Dan and Mike had preceded me. They stood in the cinders staring ahead at something that was higher than the train's roof.

"It's your nigger friend," Dan said as I joined them.

Dangling from a telegraph pole, a rope around his neck, was the black man I had kissed last night. The Union soldiers were in the process of cutting him down. We walked up to them as he reached the ground. Pinned to the dead man's white shirt was a note.

Deliver this nigger to Oberlin College in Ohio, where they taught him to kiss white women.

"Now I wish you'd killed Kennedy," I said.

"The quicker we get out of the South, the happier I'll be," Red Mike Hanrahan said.

I began to wonder if any of us could escape the South, any more than we could escape Ireland.

America's Crown Prince

"Is it not fair to suppose that the Irish Republican government will find as liberal friends among the Americans, not to mention the Irish-Americans, as the South found in Canada and England? I think the Navy Bureau will have its hands full in equipping cruisers like the *Alabama*. The names will be different; we will have the *Robert Emmet,* the *Wolfe Tone.* Of course I expect that our practical commonsense President Andy Johnson will follow the example of Her Most Ungracious Majesty Queen Victoria and declare the Irish Republic a belligerent."

Colonel William Roberts thundered these words from a crowded platform in Jones's Wood, a picnic grounds on the East River just south of the district called Yorkville. Twenty thousand New York Irish-Americans roared their approval. Behind Roberts sat Head Center John O'Mahoney and the council of the Fenian Brotherhood. The listeners did not know that behind our seeming unity lay murderous division. Nor did they have the slightest idea what their cheers now meant to the troubled heart of the Fenian girl.

It was mid-September of 1865. We had just returned from our six weeks' tour of the South and West. It had been a financial success. We had sold over three hundred thousand dollars in bonds of the Republic of Ireland. But it had complicated my personal life. Soon after the encounter with the Ku Klux Klan and the fight with Captain Kennedy, Dan and I became lovers again. John O'Neil and Mike Hanrahan managed to accept our unsanctified match without cavil. Far from flaunting it, we were as discreet as humanly possible, rarely exchanging a word or gesture of endearment in public. We traversed

Ohio, Indiana, Illinois, and Kentucky without a breath of scandal.

The reunion was made not without grave doubts on my part. Touched as I was by Dan's concern for me and the warrior revenge he exacted in my name, I no longer had any illusions about love magically transforming him or me. We remained strong and not always harmonious personalities, seldom inclined to yield in argument or change our very different ideas about life. He was still determined to acquire money and power as quickly as possible, and persisted in seeing our plan to conquer Canada as a route to this dubious goal. I insisted we should think more of politics and statesmanship than of personal gain. The nakedness of Dan's self-interest troubled me, though I respected the honesty with which he told me of it. But his acknowledgement was like a secret glimpse of the real motives of too many Irish-Americans.

Now that we were back in New York, the city where money seemed to be the only God, my doubts had become more acute. Some of this could be blamed on my brother, Michael, who preached this nasty accusation day and night. In our absence, he had entered deep into Fenian politics and was now one of John O'Mahoney's closest advisers. I found myself suspended between the two groups, attracted by Dan's cold-eyed realism yet repelled by his motives lured by Michael's idealism and repelled by his impracticality. My brother seemed to think that by guarding the purity of every Fenian word and deed and motive, we would achieve the liberation of Ireland by some sort of spiritual magic.

The rally at Jones's Wood had been called to put Fenian bond sales over the first million dollars and send them bounding on to the second million. The titans of Tammany were all on the platform in silk-hatted array. Bill Tweed leaped up to pledge five thousand dollars. Dick Connolly and Peter Sweeny topped him with seven thousand each, and John Morrissey beat them all with ten. But the cash of these powergods no longer meant so much to me. I had come to value far more the money of the thousands of humbler Irish. Whether they lived in Chicago's Kilgubbin or New York's Sixth Ward, their wrinkled greenbacks had come from the bottom of a jar in a tenement kitchen or from beneath a mattress in a fetid bedroom. The money represented a fragile barrier between them and want, yet they gave it to us for Ireland.

They were the only true idealists in the Fenian Brotherhood. Often they placed the bills in my hands with words of simple praise and hope. I heard them that day in Jones's Wood, after the speeches, as I had heard them in St. Louis and Cincinnati. Two homely servant girls, who could never hope to compete with the beauties of Broadway, each gave me forty dollars—a year's savings at least. " 'Tis part of my dowry," said the older of the two, "but I'll wait a year if it helps to free Ireland."

"I was goin' to send it home to my da, to make sure he don't end up beggin' on the road," said the other girl. "But he won't have to do that in a free Ireland, will he now?"

"No," I said. "There will be no beggars in a free Ireland."

I found myself envying their chastity, their simplicity, their trust. I vowed to remain true to their sacrifices, no matter what it cost me in physical pain or spiritual loss. This morning I had had a letter from Robert Johnson— the crown prince, as I thought of him—telling me that he was coming to New York soon and could not wait to see me. *I will even do that for you*, I thought behind my confident smile. *I will sell my body and my soul for you. Can anyone do more?*

"I will take two thousand dollars' worth, Miss Fenian," said a soft, familiar voice on my right hand. I looked up at the smiling face of my sister Annie.

We kissed enthusiastically. "Two thousand," I said.

"That's a thundering lot of money. Dick Connolly just gave seven. Isn't that enough for the both of you?"

"This is my own," Annie said. "Don't mention it to Dick. I sold one or two of his presents to raise it. I want to do what I can, when you're doing so much."

I gave her twenty hundred-dollar bonds. "If all goes well, it will only be a loan at that. You'll get it back with six percent interest."

"Dick's been very thick with Bill Roberts," Annie said. "He told us of the great thing you've done in Washington. The president's son. A mighty catch, Bess."

"Yes," I said, simultaneously proud and wishing Annie didn't know of it—wishing no one knew. I smiled away and sold more bonds to poor and middling Irish while Annie watched me.

"Is he a charmer?" Annie said.

"Anything but," I said.

"I had a few like that before I met Dick," Annie said. " 'Tis not easy, I know."

"Yes," I said, seeing I could never share with her my true feelings on the affair.

"Does the Holy Terror know about it?" Annie asked. She gave a nod in the direction of our brother Michael, who sat at a nearby table, selling bonds.

"No," I said.

"I haven't spoken to him since that night he insulted me," Annie said. "Nor do I think I ever will. Dick says he's causing us nothing but trouble."

"How is Dick?" I said. "He looked well on the platform." I could see Connolly off in the distance, deep in conversation with Roberts.

"He's fine," Annie said. "Things are looking glorious for the election. They have a very good candidate, John Hoffman, from one of the oldest families in New York. They should win in a walk, as the saying goes."

This was not the news of Dick Connolly I wanted to

hear. I wanted him to make Annie an honest woman. She had given too much of her heart to him. I could not say this to her. In part I feared to frighten her. In part I sought to avoid the fear that I had committed the same mistake with Dan McCaffrey.

By the time the last picnicker staggered from Jones's Wood bawling "The Wearing of the Green," we had mountains of money on every table. That night we met at Moffat House for a celebration. Colonel Roberts rose to announce that we had collected $250,000 and were well past the million mark in bond sales. "We're now in a position to buy the sinews of war for the army and navy of the Irish Republic," he said.

Amid cheers and congratulations, the champagne corks popped and a band began to play Irish airs. Michael sat with John O'Mahoney and one or two other members of the council, stonily disapproving the gaiety. They continued to oppose the "final call" and the campaign to conquer Canada, but they were helpless to prevent both from going forward now.

I appointed myself a committee of one and drew Michael into a corner to change his mind. I told him that he ought to be persuading O'Mahoney to join the majority, rather than pushing him into stubborn opposition. I gave him a candid report of what I had seen in the South and why there were good grounds for fearing that blind hatred between blacks and whites would ruin the president's policy down there and deprive him of the power to help us. It was important to strike hard and soon. We lacked the power to do either of these things in Ireland. Canada was therefore the logical target.

Michael shook his head, his mind unchanged. "I still say it's an American scheme. A land-grabbing operation got up by the American Irish and their friends."

"Michael," I said, "division will destroy us quicker than anything the English can do."

"'Tis not division, 'tis divorce toward which we're heading," Michael said. "The separation of the true Irish Fenians from the corrupt Irish-Americans."

Red Mike Hanrahan sat down with us. "What's this?" he said. "Is he tryin' to take you away from us?"

"No," I said. "The other way around. I'm trying to talk sense to him, but I'm getting nowhere."

"Look around you, at the furnishings of this place," Michael said. "Those mirrors, these rugs. Look at them all, pigging and guzzling at the people's expense. We should be living no better than the poor in the Sixth Ward slums, or the peasants in their cabins in Connemara."

"If the riches of America are behind us, what harm is there to a bit of celebration?" Red Mike said.

"What harm," Michael said, in a passion. "Those two words will ruin us in the end. "What harm to wasting money, what harm to selling $300,000 in bonds and bringing back only $250,000 to the treasury. The most expensive sightseeing tour of America in the history of travel."

"Is that true?" I asked Mike with not a little sharpness. I suddenly remembered him and Dan gambling on the Mississippi, and some rueful talk of bucking the tiger one night in Chicago.

"The confusion was in the number of bonds we sold," Mike said. "We miscounted the denominations. Instead of $300,000 it was closer to $260,000. Sure you can testify to how frugally we lived, Bess. Especially in the South. There were colored livin' better."

"Yes," I said, thinking that this explanation was what Americans called double-talk.

"Come on now, have some champagne," Red Mike said, grabbing a bottle from the tray of a passing waiter. He filled two glasses and handed them to us. "We respect your opinion, Michael, but you've got to go along with the majority. That's the American way, you know. We don't want to lose you or the head center."

There was a threat in those words, which I am sure Michael heard as clearly as I. Roberts was head center in all but name already. But Michael's negative politics persuaded him that it was really a confession of weakness. "You need the head center far more than he needs you," he said. "He's made himself the symbol of Fenianism. Without him you're nothing but a pack of pirates."

"Goddamn you," Red Mike said. "You'd rather see us shipwreck and sink than yield an inch of your power. You've wormed your way into the old man's confidence, and you're goin' to hang on no matter what it costs us."

"I'm not impressed by your threats nor your ability to call names," Michael said. "You may be able to dazzle impressionable girls with your spendthrift ways and piratical plans, but the old man and I shall remain true to the cause."

"And the South shall rise again," Mike said. "Jesus God, you sound just like them. Brainless heroes in love with defeat. Don't you know that the American way is to win, and to love a winner? Americans don't waste time on lost causes."

Michael stalked away without even bothering to answer him. "Mike," I said. "Tell me the truth. Did you and Dan lose that bond money bucking the tiger?"

"We may have lost a little of it," Mike said. "I'm a terrible bookkeeper. We had a bad night in Chicago. Both of us."

"I'll say nothing this time. But if I ever see or hear of it again, I'll tell the whole world."

"We'll make it up with your help," Mike said. "When we go on the road again. In the meantime, with a million in the treasury, what harm?"

What harm indeed. It was painful to hear Mike repeating the very words that Michael had denounced. What could I do about it? With desperate recklessness I shoved fears and doubts and premonitions from my mind and hurled myself into the celebration. I tossed off a glass of champagne and sought out Dan for a dance. We whirled about the floor to the beat of a lively reel, and I felt the movement of his muscular body against me, reveled in the daredevil smile he gave me, and laughed at the antic moments of our travels around America.

Whether we or the party grew wilder, it was hard to tell. I remember Annie coming in with Dick Connolly and him dancing about with me. Compared to Dan it was like waltzing with an arthritic. Mrs. Roberts of the ample bosom drifted by laughing giddily in the arms of Colonel Roberts. There was fat Mrs. McGlinchy and her equally fat husband who had stolen a half million from the Croton Reservoir, and pretty Mrs. Meehan with a man not her husband because her husband was still in Ireland on his secret mission, and Dan again, letting me teach him a true Irish jig while everyone gathered about to clap and cheer. When Dan showed two left feet, Annie jumped in for him, and soon there was a demand for me and Annie to teach all the Irish-Americans who had forgotten Irish dancing or never learned it. A table was shoved into the center of the ballroom, and we were lifted up on it, laughing.

Away we stepped, in those lovely intricate patterns that had come down through the generations while the fiddler sawed and the Fenians around us cheered and clapped. Gazing into Annie's flashing eyes and luminous lovely face, I slipped away from New York and America and was back in the parish hall at Ballinaclash and past that, too, in the roll of time and distance to some ancient Gaelic feast where the beauties of the tribe in their silks and golden jewelry danced before assembled warriors. Dancing in spite of history and possible defeat, heads high and proud, with wine and whiskey a sweet fire in the blood, smiles a flash of white promise in the firelight.

Suddenly there was Michael's harsh voice cutting through the music and clapping and cheering. "My God, look at the news. The news from Ireland."

He was holding up a late extra of the *Herald*. The black headline leaped at us like a blow. BRITISH SMASH FENIANS. HUNDREDS ARRESTED.

Reality, history, returned. I looked about me. I was standing on a table in the center of the rented mansion of a patent medicine tycoon. I was in New York City dancing with my sister, who was much too drunk for her own good. The same could be said of me. I jumped down from the table and said to Michael, "Climb up here and read it to us."

He readily accepted. "Shortly after midnight on Sunday the British government suspended the habeas corpus act in Ireland and began a series of raids on Fenian circles from Belfast to Cork. Hundreds have been arrested and are being held without bail. In Dublin the Fenian newspaper, *The Irish People*, has been suppressed and the members of its staff arrested. British authorities say they obtained evidence of a dangerous conspiracy between native Irish and Irish from America from the papers of two prominent Fenians who have been traveling in Ireland for the past three months. They were under close surveillance by detectives, and when they carelessly left behind them certain documents in a Cork hotel, the detectives obtained the evidence they needed to attack the conspiracy, which has been gathering strength in Ireland for the past year."

"The Americans, Michael Meehan and George Dunne, were also arrested in Dublin and deported from Ireland. They are en route to America aboard the steamship *Queenstown*."

"Oh, thank God, thank God," said Mrs. Meehan, tears on her cheeks. She was grateful that her husband was at least safe.

"This is your doing," Michael shouted, pointing his finger at William Roberts and several of his circle of councilors. "You ordered Meehan to betray the Irish to prosecute your land-grabbing scheme in Canada."

"That is as foul a lie as has ever been told," Roberts cried.

Chaos erupted. Red Mike Hanrahan dragged Michael off the table before he could say more. The party became a melee of shouting, cursing arguments between native-born and American-born Irish. The British prime minister himself could not have invented a better apple of discord. Our glorious celebration ended in a barrage of name-calling and mutual disgust between the two sides of our rapidly dividing movement.

Who should arrive in New York the very next day but Robert Johnson, panting to see his Fenian girl. Colonel Roberts sent Mike Hanrahan with a note, warning me of his presence.

He brings us the best possible news, Roberts wrote. *Authorization from President Johnson to buy muskets and ammunition at cost from the federal arsenals. Whether you wish to see him, to express your personal appreciation, is something only you can decide.*

Like Pilate, washing his hands, I thought. I showed the note to Dan, who flung it back at me. "You ain't goin' near that son of a bitch," he said.

"I would love you none the less, no matter what happens," I said. "Can't you do the same?"

"No," he said.

"If I'm any judge," Mike Hanrahan said, "our friend will be very, very disappointed if he goes back to Washington without seein' you."

Dan grabbed him by the throat. "How would you like to spend a year in the hospital?"

Mike dangled off the floor, gasping. "'Tis only—the truth—I'm tryin' to tell. For—the good—of the brotherhood."

Dan threw him into a chair with an obscene comment on the brotherhood.

"I must see him," I said. "If I can stand it, surely you can. We never needed a friend at the seat of power more. This division is sure to get into the papers."

"I say no," Dan snarled.

"I say yes," I replied. I turned to Mike. "Find yourself a girl and prepare to do the town with us. I'll need help if he gets too drunk."

I was privately hoping the crown prince would drink himself into imbecility and I could somehow convince him that we had made glorious love but he had forgotten it. There was no hope of explaining this to Dan. He stalked out with a titanic slam of the door.

"That fellow's a killer," Red Mike said, looking after him. "I hope this isn't a mistake for both of us."

"Never fear. I'll protect you," I said sarcastically. "No doubt Roberts told you to talk me into it no matter what."

Mike grimaced like a boy swallowing medicine. "He did."

"Go find yourself a lady for the evening," I said.

Robert Johnson was drunk when he arrived at Sweeney's Hotel with Mike and his lady friend, a pretty redhead named Peg O'Connell, who looked younger than I but wore the sophisticated smile of Broadway. Robert seized me with a smack of a kiss that almost asphyxiated me while his hands went wandering, practically pulling my dress off.

"How's my Irish girl?" he said.

"She's fine," I said.

"We couldn't keep his mind on politics over at Moffat House at all," Mike said.

"Not true," said Robert. "On to Canada. That's all the politics we need."

We began with dinner at Delmonico's. Naturally the crown prince rated one of the better tables. Across from us sat Bill Tweed and Jim Fisk with two spectacular beauties. Fisk was just beginning his rise as the profligate railroad tycoon. He was a huge glob of a man with long waxed mustaches. Robert Johnson regarded him with awe. "Two years ago he was runnin' contraband cotton up from Mississippi through Tennessee," he said. "Now he's a millionaire."

Money had a truly hypnotic effect on Americans. To this day I cannot understand why so many of them are impressed with mere wealth, no matter how the man made it. Robert began talking about his father, the president. He was too honest, he said. "Too damn proud—or too dumb—to take advantage of his opportunities. You know he ain't got scarcely a dime of money outside his salary?

"But I ain't dumb," Robert said. "I want it understood that li'l ole Robert Johnson has his pick of Canada land. That's what I told them at Moffat House."

He was saying this loud enough for half the restaurant to hear it. Red Mike assured him that the bargain was sealed and there was no need to say another word about it. I found myself remembering what Michael had called our Canada campaign—an American land-grabbing scheme. Could we hope for success when we permitted such corruption to permeate our methods? Once more I struggled with Michael's rage for purity and the contrary knowledge that corruption seemed to have no effect on the power of England—or America, for that matter.

I watched Robert Johnson gorge himself on roast pheasant and beef Wellington at our expense. The French wine flowed and after it the brandy. I found myself losing the fine edge of bravado with which I had begun the evening. The liquor and rich food seemed to depress me, although I drank and ate only enough to be polite. No doubt it was the knowledge of what awaited me at the end of the night. Nor were my spirits raised by

Peg O'Connell, who breathed envy of my "thundering catch" when we were in the ladies' powder room.

Delmonico's was only our first stop, of course. Robert had to see the other sights of New York after dark. We wended our way to Harry Hill's dance hall, where Robert manhandled me about the floor for an hour. We were joined at our table by Dick Connolly and Annie and Peter Barr Sweeny and his Kate. The meeting was probably prearranged by Mike. The Tammany men attempted to talk politics with Robert, but he was too drunk.

"Is he always so soused?" Annie asked me.

"At this time of night," I said.

"A strange emissary for the president to send, if he hopes for Tammany's support," Annie said.

I kept my already grave doubts about Robert to myself. About 1:00 A.M. he announced a desire to buck the tiger. We headed for John Morrissey's opulent gambling house near the Fifth Avenue Hotel. Dick and Annie came along, and Annie wanted to play. Dick gave her a hundred dollars, which she lost in five minutes. She held out her hand for more, and he sternly shook his head and insisted on leaving early. "He's mad at me," Annie said with a pout as they departed. "I lost two thousand in here last week. He says it would have been easier to give the money to Morrissey direct."

I had begun to accumulate small signs that all was not well with Annie and Dick, but that night I was too preoccupied with my own worries to think about it. Robert Johnson stationed me behind him, as he had at Chamberlain's in Washington. "No faro bank in the world can beat the luck of my Fenian girl," he said. Mighty John Morrissey, resplendent in evening dress, took a personal interest in the contest. The best champagne was placed at Robert's right hand, and the play began.

A kind of premonition had stabbed me when Robert made that boast. It is always a mistake to predict good luck in a game of chance. Luck runs by opposites. Sure enough, my luck was miserable. I could not call a card. Robert lost a thousand dollars before he won a single play. He began making his own calls and did no better. Another thousand, at least, drained through his hands. A third thousand vanished almost as swiftly, and he played on credit for another hour, grim and humorless as every gambler becomes when bad luck is on his back.

By the time we quit at 3:00 A.M. Robert was at least five thousand dollars behind. We retired to the bar, where John Morrissey insisted on us tasting some rare French brandy. Robert drank morosely, saying nothing. A clerk arrived with a statement of what Robert owed. I heard Mike Hanrahan mutter to Morrissey, "Rip that up, y'big lug, if you give a damn for Ireland."

Morrissey looked blank for a moment but quickly understood. "Mr. Johnson," he said, "I liked the way you stood up to that tiger, even though it was eatin' your head off tonight. You took it like a man. I can see you're a fighter, and that's what an old pug like me appreciates."

Morrissey ripped up the paper loss and stuffed it into the pocket of Robert's coat. This cheered him very little, though he managed to stammer some thanks to the ex-heavyweight champion. The crown prince had expected to win, and nothing could console him for his failure. Out on the street, Red Mike suggested a nightcap at the Blossom Club. I think he was trying to fulfill my hope of getting Robert so drunk he would be harmless, but my prince declined to cooperate. He said he was tired and the Fifth Avenue Hotel, where he was staying, was just across the park. He seized my arm and said good night. I glanced over my shoulder at Mike. He raised his hands helplessly.

At the hotel, Robert ordered a bottle of champagne sent up to the room. My hope of escape rose, but the wine had little effect on him, except to deepen his dark mood. "So much for the luck of the Irish," he said.

"Surely you can't blame me for your bad run," I said. "Your own calls were no better than mine."

"I lost three thousand at Chamberlain's last night," he snarled. "I came up here thinkin' you'd change my luck. Instead you made it worse."

"Perhaps it's time to think of moderating both your drinking and your gambling," I said. "You may be risking your place in your father's affections—and his councils."

"That son of a bitch don't give a damn for me and never has. I got to make my own deals, find my own luck. Ah!" With a curse he flung his champagne glass across the room. "Take off them clothes and get in bed."

"It would help if you spoke in a more loving way."

"Who the hell's talkin' about *love*?" he said. "Just do what I told you."

He retired to the private bathroom. I took off my clothes and slipped under the bedcovers. A moment later Robert emerged from the bathroom wearing his shirt. He pulled down the covers and gazed truculently at my nakedness for a moment. Then he pulled up his shirt and said, "Suck it."

"What?" I said.

"Suck it. Get me goin'."

"I won't do such a thing. I'm not a whore," I said.

He laughed in an ugly way. "You ain't?" he said. He dragged me out of the bed and thrust his finger deep into me. "Now tell me you ain't a whore."

"I—I'm not."

He moved his finger up and down, clutching my breast so hard with his other hand that I cried out with pain. Withdrawing his finger, he flung me face down on the bed, and entered me from behind. "You—owe—me—three—thousand—dollars'—worth," he growled, punctuating each word with a savage stroke.

I felt the gush of his release. I lay there like one of the

ambushed black soldiers on Main Street in Memphis, wishing for a moment I were like them, dead, unfeeling dirt and mud. It was preferable to the shame and loathing that were engulfing me.

Without speaking another word to Robert, I dressed and left. I could not tell whether he was ashamed or still blamed me for his ruined evening. He did not speak to me. When I turned to give him a farewell glare, I saw that he had sat down in a chair beneath the gas lamp and was reading a newspaper.

A single hack waited in front of the Fifth Avenue Hotel. I rode down Broadway staring numbly at the shops and theaters of the great city. I felt bereft, betrayed by its stolid immensity. How many other women in how many other hotel rooms had been violated like me tonight? Most of them had submitted for money, a few in hopes of something more profound or lasting, offering themselves as sacrificial pledges of their faith in a dubious promise. I could tell myself that I had done it for the nameless poor from whom I had taken money and to whom I pledged fidelity in Chicago and Cincinnati and New York. But nothing could alter what had happened to me. I had been treated like a thing, a receptacle.

At Sweeney's, I trudged up the silent stairs and down the hall to our suite like a forlorn ghost. I opened the door with my key and found myself face-to-face with Dan McCaffrey. My heart leapt with joy at the sight of him. My first thought was that he had waited for me, to take me in his arms and restore my womanhood. Then I got a better look at his face in the dim gaslight. I saw the bottle on the floor beside him.

"Well well well," he said. "Here comes Little Red Ridin' Hood. Back from visitin' the big bad wolf."

"Dan," I said, "please don't be cruel to me. I—I never felt a greater need of you."

"Why?"

"He—abused me, Dan. He made me—" I flung myself at his feet. "Hold me, please. I want to prove to myself— to you—that it hasn't changed me. That I still can love you. Do love you."

With a curse he shoved me aside.

"What makes you think I want Bobby Johnson's left-overs?"

"I'm not a dish of food. I'm a person. A woman," I cried.

"You're a whore," he said. "A goddamn whore. That's what I stayed up to tell you."

"Am I any worse than you, with your greedy dreams of making a million in Canada?" I said. "You'll go up there and kill for it, telling yourself you're doing it for Ireland, but all the time the real reason will be to put cash in Dan McCaffrey's pocket, so he can go out and buy any women he likes. Well, let me tell you something. You may have a million or ten million, but you'll never buy me."

My words blundered against his American passion to become a millionaire, which was not in the least shame-ful to him. He missed the comparison.

"When I have a million, I won't have to buy whores," he snarled.

"Oh, Dan," I said, "don't call me that again. I'll die if you do. I thought I could let him have me without feeling any shame. I thought I could come back to you and laugh it off. But I can't. Don't make it worse for me."

It wounded my pride to beg that way, but I was trying to heal a deeper, more dangerous wound. In my despera-tion I forgot my fears of his hungry ambition for riches, the knowledge that he had gambled away Fenian money. He was my Donal Ogue, and I was clinging desperately to the memory of the girl who had given her love to him on that stormy Irish night, which seemed a century back now, though it was little more than four months ago.

"Don't it mean nothin' to you, what I did in Tennessee? Fought that gougin' son of a bitch. If you were a whore, would I care if he made you kiss one nigger or a thousand?"

"Didn't I show you what it meant to me, the next night in Nashville?" I said.

"Sure. But when I see you act like this, I ask myself, Is that how she pays back everybody? Me and maybe Red Mike and Colonel Roberts and O'Mahoney and Christ knows who else."

I found myself backing away from him, shaking my head, weeping. "Do you really believe that? Or are you just trying to hurt me?"

"I don't know what the hell to believe about you. I don't know what to believe about anything. You think it's wrong to own a nigger, and I spent four years of my life fightin' for the right to own a few. You want to blow the British to hell, but you think it's wrong to try to make money doin' it. You think a man's goin' to love you while you get into and out of bed with every nitwit son of a politician that comes along?"

"Do you know something? That's the first time you've ever said you loved me."

"What the hell do you mean?"

"The only other time you used the word, you told me not to love you because you had no money, no future."

"I'll tell you how much I love you," he said. "Enough to beat hell out of you, right now."

"I deserve it," I said. I pressed myself against him. "O Donal Ogue," I said, "I swear to you that I will never never make this mistake again."

I was scarcely aware of it, but I really meant the mistake of telling him the truth. My private heart was on its way to becoming as inaccessible to me as it was to everyone else.

Ireland's Agony, Recapitulated

"Oh," sighed Annie with a sympathetic sniffle. "The poor devils. Condemned for life."

We were in her new apartment at the Fifth Avenue Hotel, reading the newspaper reports of the trials of the Fenians in Ireland. Outside, rain drizzled down from a gray November sky.

"There's little we can do for them. We must look to our own strength here in America, and do with it what we can by way of revenge," I said.

I was becoming very American in my blithe disregard for our suffering brethren in Ireland. So was Annie, in spite of her sentimental sniffles. Annie enjoyed nothing so much as a good cry. She loved songs about dying birds and faithful dogs who laid down their lives for their masters. She never failed to search out the daily diet of misfortunes in the newspapers—men crushed beneath the wheels of Broadway omnibuses, children trampled by runaway horses.

From all reports in the newspapers and from our confidential agents in Ireland, the British had smashed the Irish Fenians in almost every county. The Dublin leaders were tried, and a dozen were sentenced to servitude for life in the penal colony on the island of Tasmania. Many of the convicted men gave magnificent speeches from the dock, condemning their accusers and calling on their brethren beyond the ocean to carry on the fight.

So far as we could see—which was, alas, not very far—these Irish misfortunes strengthened us. The Irish in America were universally angry, and the sales of Irish Republic bonds boomed. So did recruiting for the Fenian army. On the political front all was going smoothly enough. Robert Johnson remained a supporter of our cause in spite of my personal rift with him, and so apparently did Secretary Seward. At the annual Fenian convention in Philadelphia in mid-October, we had heeded Seward's advice to reassure America about our patriotism. By an overwhelming vote, the convention accepted a plan proposed by William Roberts and his followers to abandon the secret-society structure of the movement and transform it into an imitation of the American government. Elections were held for a president, a vice president, a senate, and a house of representatives. For unity's sake, John O'Mahoney was elected president, but all the other positions of power went to Roberts and his adherents, among whom I continued to number myself.

In New York, the Celts also prospered. Tammany put its man, John T. Hoffman, in the mayor's office, and Dick Connolly in as city comptroller. They were busy naming their friends to dozens of other offices and laying plans to elect Hoffman governor next year, giving them control of New York state.

The Fenians had contributed not a little to Tammany's victory. We sent representatives to rallies in the Irish wards and made statements in the newspapers urging the Irish to back men who were prepared to oppose imperial England wherever they had influence in the American government. Now Tammany was returning the favor, passing the word to its ward leaders and district captains to urge young Irishmen to enlist in the Fenian army. The green flag flew as boldly from Tammany's headquarters as it did from Moffat House.

"Have you heard from Dan?" Annie asked.

"I had a letter yesterday," I said. "He's well, was all I could gather from it, and affairs are fine in Chicago. He writes an awful scrawl."

Because of his military experience, Dan had been appointed to the staff of the Fenian army's inspector general and was traveling about the country, arranging for our regiments to buy weapons from nearby federal arsenals and making sure that they were drilling in the most modern manner.

"I haven't heard from Dick in a good week," Annie said. "I had to write him a letter today. Isn't that the silliest thing? He's overwhelmed with politics day and night."

She spoke lightly, as if it were nothing more than an oddity. Immediately after the election, she had gotten her way and moved to the Fifth Avenue Hotel. Dick had given her an emerald brooch set in diamonds that must have been worth five thousand dollars. Dan and I had been with them the night he gave it to her at the Blossom Club. It had made Dan morose for a week, to think of a man with that much money to spare.

"I hope Dick writes a better hand than Dan," I said. "Otherwise you'll never know what's going on."

Annie burst into tears. "What will become of me, Bess, if he gives me the gate? It's not that I couldn't find another man. I still have my looks. But—I haven't the heart for it. I love him."

"And he loves you. Isn't the proof of it where we are at this moment? You must bear with his new importance without nagging at him, Annie."

"You're right, surely," she said. "But I live in dread of him dropping me. You can take them or leave them, Bess, but I don't have your spirit. I never did."

"Mother always said you're a MacNamara and I'm a Fitzmaurice."

Annie nodded, her good humor returning. "I wrote to her, you know, telling her that we were all together here and doing beautifully."

"Good," I said. "I haven't written a line. I was afraid to bring trouble on their heads by saying anything endearing in a letter the British would be likely to open. Michael felt the same way."

"I heard not a word back from her. I hope they're all right."

"I'm sure no harm will come to them, as long as old Lord Gort lives," I said. "He thinks Father is the best farmer in County Limerick."

"But he died. Didn't you know that?" Annie said.

"When? You never mentioned it to me."

"It must have happened while you were on your bond-selling tour. By the time you came back I forgot it."

There was a knock on the door. "Who is it?" Annie called.

"Michael," said a somber voice.

I jumped up and opened it. "I thought you'd be here," he said. Behind him was another man, whom at first I did not recognize, so haggard and thin did he look. Also, my brain refused to admit the possibility of him being there in the hall of the Fifth Avenue Hotel.

"Patrick Dolan," I said. "Is it really you?"

"Yes," he said. "It's me, to be sure."

"Well, come in," Annie said, from behind me. "What a nice surprise to see a face from home. You must be bursting with news, and we're as eager to hear it. I'll bite my tongue and say not a single hard word to my sainted brother even if it kills me."

"I'm afraid he has news aplenty, Annie," Michael said. "But not the sort we'd like to hear."

My heart sank. I saw that Michael's eyes were swimming with tears. Even fearing the worst brought me an infinity short of what I soon heard from Patrick Dolan's lips. He sat down in Annie's chair and pointed to the headlines about the Fenians in the paper. "You know what's been happening in Ireland," he said.

"Yes," I said.

"There was no rising or anything like one in Limerick. They didn't even arrest anyone. They had pretty much broken the circle when they sent Michael here on the run, and you with him, Bess."

"Curse the day," Michael said.

"But that didn't stop young Lord Gort. He'd been preparin' for harsh measures ever since he came down to us for his father's funeral. No sooner was the old lord buried when I was summoned to the mansion and told that henceforth I was to deal only with certain merchants in Dublin, who were trusted as loyal men. Nor would there be any lending of money in the district by anyone but him. I soon found his men in Dublin charged double prices. I saw that he was determined to put me out of business and get what little power and influence I had into his own hands."

"But you never spoke or thought a rebellious word," I said.

"That meant little to his lordship," Patrick said. "He called himself 'the new breed' and said he and his friends had determined to rip rebellion out of Ireland's heart before it took root. The mere fact that there had been a Fenian circle in the district was enough to convict every influential man."

"And he turned on Father next," I said.

"Yes. He had it in for him worst of all because of you and Michael. He called for his books and swore he'd been cheating his father, for twenty years past. He went to court and asked a summary judgment to cancel your father's lease though it had ten more years to run."

"And he won?" Annie said.

"There was no way he could lose," Patrick said. "Wasn't the judge his brother-in-law? But your father spent a fortune fighting him. He said he wanted to prove an honest man could resist injustice in Ireland by peaceful, lawful means. He couldn't bear the thought of leaving the farm, that was all. It altered his mind, I think."

Sean ait aboo, I thought, remembering our family cry. *Hurrah for the old place.*

"Lord Gort evicted them? Put Mary and Mother and Da out on the road like peasants?" I said.

"He came with his bailiff McCarthy and ten constables. He said he'd heard talk of your father's tenants mobbing him. 'Twasn't a word of truth to it; he wanted to make a show of menace to justify what he was doin'."

I noticed that Patrick Dolan had stopped looking at me. He spoke those last words into his derby hat, which he still held in his hands.

"And where are they now? Mother and Da and Mary?" I asked.

"Well—" Patrick looked to my brother. "God in heaven, Michael, it was hard enough to tell you."

"Tell them," Michael said. "Exactly as you told me."

"The constables stood in the road with nothin' to do. The servant girls and the farmhands were loadin' the furniture on the wagon. The girls were cryin', and so were your mother and sister. Your father left them to go round to the barn to get the horses, we thought. But when he didn't come back Mute Mick, the son of Conn the plowman, went for him. There's a great cry, and Mick came racin' toward us as if he'd just seen the devil. 'Uh, uh, uh,' he goes. 'Twas all he could say, and pointin' to the barn. We went runnin' there and found your father. He'd—he'd cut his throat."

I stood up, shaking my head, and walked slowly around the room. Annie began to sob. From the window I looked down at the horsecars coming up Broadway, the New Yorkers in dark coats, umbrellas raised, hurrying across Madison Square. They neither knew nor cared about the news we had just heard. It had happened three thousand miles away in a bothersome country that meant little to most of them. It was not worth a line in a newspaper, except perhaps the *Irish-American,* and even there it could hardly be reported with enthusiasm. The father of their bold Fenian girl had cut his throat by way of resisting eviction.

"Cut—his—throat," I said. "Da. Father." I pressed my forehead against the cold windowpane.

"I hope you won't think of me only as the bearer of this news, Bess," Patrick said. "I went to Michael because I thought it would be better if—"

"I wanted them to hear it as I heard it," Michael said. "So they'd know my feelings as well as their own."

I didn't know what he was talking about. I was barely listening. I was remembering what I saw on Father's face that last night. His fear of the Ireland beyond our little village world. We had brought it home to him, in all its cruelty and force.

"He must not have died in vain," Michael was saying. "We must make sure of that. We must use all our influence to make sure of that. Annie must help as well."

"What the devil are you saying?" I snapped. "Annie had nothing to do with this. Leave her out of it."

"She must get Connolly to throw his influence against the Canada scheme. Now if ever we must be true to Ireland. Every man, every dollar we raise, must be used in Ireland."

"You're dreaming," I said. "There's no way you can change the direction of that policy now. Nor should you. This is a private quarrel. Between us and that bastard Gort."

"It's not. It's Ireland's agony, summed up, recapitulated," Michael said. "I should have been there to fight for him instead of sitting in restaurants over here, eating the best beef."

"If you were over there you'd be on your way to Tasmania in a prison ship," I said. "You would have been in the dock in Dublin with your friends."

"Goddamn you, Bess," Michael cried. "Don't you feel the shame of it?"

"I feel nothing but hate," I said. "Such hate I never thought it possible for my soul to bear. I won't sleep a whole night through until Lord Rodney Gort is under the ground."

I did not listen to Michael, nor Michael to me. He was tormented by guilt for having begun our involvement with the Fenians—which struck me as foolish. It was like feeling guilty over being born in Ireland, the way I saw it. To be a rebel had come as naturally to me as breathing. For Michael, much more under Father's influence, it had been an intellectual and spiritual struggle. Now he began to dread the thought that he had made the wrong choice.

I was moving in an opposite direction. Before I had only been playing at hatred. My antagonism to the British had been more poetic than real. Even my dramatic thoughts about the price I paid to ride history's whirlwind seemed trivial now, mere posturings of an adolescent in love with adventure. No more would there be such egotistic self-pitying views. History's whirlwind was a fact of my life, and the only thought worth thinking now was how to make my enemies pay the highest possible price. There was nothing I would not do now. I would go to bed with Robert Johnson again, I would even try to delight decrepit old Seward himself if it served the cause. There was no disgust I would not swallow, no crime I would not commit to feed my revenge.

Michael continued to rant about the necessity of throwing the strength of the American Fenians into Ireland, somehow. He vapored on about the loss of our "high purpose" here in America. There was nothing so different in what he said, except for the passion—but that was a very important difference, to which no one paid any attention, until it was too late.

"Mother and Mary," Annie said, demonstrating that a nonrevolutionary had more practical common sense than Michael and me together. "What's become of them?"

"They went to Limerick, to her sister's house," Patrick Dolan said, "but they didn't get along. So the last I heard, just before I left, they removed to a cottage in Killarney, where they're in hopes Mary can find work in the hotels."

"Killarney," I said. "They don't know a soul down there."

"That was Mary's idea, I think," Patrick said. "She wanted to go someplace where she wasn't known. There wasn't a hope of her gettin' married in the old district. There's such a terror of losin' Lord Gort's favor."

"I'll lay that man in his grave if it's the last thing I do on this earth," I said.

"How—how can you hope to do it, Bess?" Annie sobbed. She was still weeping terribly. I had a sudden premonition that she might find it harder to live with this news than either Michael or I would, but I brushed it aside. Hatred was already beginning to obliterate sympathy and every other human feeling from my mind.

"I know the man who will do it for me," I said.

I meant Dan McCaffrey. I know I could depend on my Donal Ogue when it came to murder.

Reach Me Down That Rifle Gun

Riding downtown in a hackney cab, I discovered that
Patrick Dolan was staying at Sweeney's Hotel. Michael
debarked at Union Square and headed for Moffat House.
Patrick continued down Broadway with me. I managed
to avoid personal conversation by pointing out City Hall,
Stewart's department store, and every other sight worth
mentioning. Patrick was stunned by New York's size and
bustle. He was amazed by the pace of the crowd rushing
along Broadway and shrewd enough to observe the contradiction between the rushers on the sidewalk and the
clogged traffic in the street.

"If everyone's in such a hurry, why does it take so
long to get someplace by horse, no less?"

"New York doesn't claim to make sense. It just exists,"
I said. "You have to take it or leave it."

"I think I'll leave it," he said.

He asked me to join him for a bite to eat. Instead I invited him up to our suite, where I brewed some tea for
him on a little gas stove we had installed in a corner of
the room. "You're looking worn out," I said. "Was it a
hard voyage?"

"Oh, no," he said. "I came on the Bristol steamship. It
scarcely took ten days. It's for you that I'm worn down,
Bess. I'm afraid I took your leaving harder than anyone,
even your poor mother. I couldn't sleep and barely ate
for a good month, thinkin' of you. I knew you were runnin' away from me as much as anything."

"No, you're wrong," I lied. If I had heard him say this
the previous day, without the terrible news about my father on his lips, I would have felt sorry for him. Now I
merely observed him as a phenomenon who might teach

me something that would help me consummate my hatred. There was some pleasure and possible profit in being reminded that Bess Fitzmaurice had this much power over a man. The hold I had on Dan, which I had demonstrated perilously but undeniably on the night I had spent with Robert Johnson, was a tenuous thing compared to the thrall in which I held Patrick Dolan. Not even my flight of three thousand miles had shaken it.

"My first intent was simply to guide Michael and the American—Dan McCaffrey—to the coast," I said. "By the time we reached it, I was partner to a half dozen serious crimes and had no choice but to flee."

Patrick seized my hand like a desperate man, up to his waist in a sucking bog. "I was hopin' and prayin' you'd say that, Bess. Hopin' against hope that you'd give fresh thought to my suit."

For a moment I was shaken to my depths by that perfectly ordinary Irish expression, "suit." It sounded so old-fashioned, it was a cruel reminder of how far I had traveled, mentally and spiritually, in the last six months. It reminded me that for all my publicity and notoriety, no man had so much as hinted at asking me to be his wife. That reflection led to an even sadder one—the difference between the woman who sat here letting Patrick Dolan hold her hand and the girl who had sat beside him on Knockadoon Island near the ruins of Lord Desmond's castle on May Eve. Was she the one who was worn and woebegone beneath her bright makeup? The innocence of that May Eve girl, even some of the pride, was lost beyond recall.

I had not yet learned to hold tight to my hatred, to grasp it to my heart until by a slow deadly process it turned that organ to icy metal. It slipped away from me, and I heard my sad voice saying, "Patrick, I'm not the wife for you now if I ever was. I'm a revolutionary. I've done things that would make me ashamed, if I didn't have a cause to justify them. You want a good honest girl like my sister Mary. I can't be that now."

"Bess, what the devil are you talkin' about?" he said. "I'm sittin' here face-to-face with you seein' with my own two eyes that you're twice as beautiful as when I last saw you. Anything you've done is between you and the priest in confession and can be cleared up in five minutes. There's no ring on your finger. That's all that I feared to see."

The word "priest" restored my hatred to me with magical violence. "How can you talk of love with the news you brought?" I said. "If you were a true man, you'd offer me your good right hand and say, 'It is at your service, Bess, to pull the trigger or wield the knife that puts Lord Rodney Gort in the ground.'"

Patrick Dolan thought for a minute in that calm, steady way I found so infuriating. "What would we gain from that, Bess? I'd probably die on the gallows for it. Even if I got away, I'd have a murder on my soul. Lord Gort's done me an injury, to be sure, and done you a worse one. But is anything to be gained from doin' the worst of all to him?"

"*Revenge* is what's to be gained, the dearest thing in the world to me," I said. I had my hatred now, gripped to my heart like a mother clutches a diseased babe, careless of the infection's menace. "I have a man who'll do it for me, and that man will have my love, as long as there's breath in my body."

"I hear no love in your voice, Bess," Patrick said with that calm unflinching stare.

"He'll think it's love," I said. "'Tis the same thing, in this world."

"Not to those that truly love Bess Fitzmaurice, who watched her grow from a wild skinny thing to a proud comely woman. I'll wait for that woman to come back to me. This Fenian girl is a stranger."

"You'll have a long wait," I said. "That Bess Fitzmaurice is as dead as Red Hugh O'Donnell."

"I don't believe that," he said, standing up.

"What will you do?" I said in my icy voice, refusing even to look at him. In a strange way I feared this man, I felt he had some power over me that I did not understand. I thought of Archbishop McCloskey, entering this same room to confront me with those sad eyes. I told myself it was the power of the past, on which I had turned my back. They wanted to chain me as they had chained Ireland to the humiliations of piety and obedience. America proved the futility of those ideas. Violence, blood, was the only test of power, and power was the only gateway to pride and pleasure.

"Do?" Patrick said sadly. "I've brought my little capital with me, what I could get my hands on quickly. About five thousand pounds. Mayhap I can go into business with it somewhere. Not in New York, but in some neighboring city, some smaller place, where a man can get a footing without fear of being washed away in the torrent."

"Good luck to you," I said, and let him go without another word. Even while he spoke of his sober hopes, my hatred was forming my plan of revenge. I lay awake most of the night elaborating it to the utmost detail. The next morning I rose with the dawn and was on my way to Moffat House by eight o'clock. I paid no attention to Michael. His door was closed, and I supposed him to be in his room.

Because I wrote a good hand, I had been working in Moffat House as the secretary of the cabinet, handling the correspondence with the bond-selling committee in the various cities. Occasionally I made a brief tour to New England or Baltimore or some other place that had not yet heard the Fenian girl, but Mike Hanrahan, who had the instincts of an impresario, had warned me against wearing out my welcome with the public and had persuaded Colonel Roberts to let me retire to the wings for a time.

It was as secretary that I stumbled into the scene that tore the Fenian movement to shreds. I journeyed up Broadway, feeling more like a corpse than a girl of twenty. Because I often worked late, I had a key with which I let myself in the big oak door, with its brass knocker in the shape of a harp. In the office where I usually worked, I discovered Michael, John O'Mahoney, and two others poring over books and ledgers, their eyes bloodshot from lack of sleep. There were papers strewn over the tables and on the floor.

"What in God's name is happening here?" I said.

"We've launched a final call—for the truth," Michael said. "I've at last convinced the president that we're surrounded by the greatest bunch of thieves since Judas betrayed Jesus, and we're gathering the evidence to convict them."

"Why do this now, when all is going so well?" I said.

"The news from Ireland—Michael told me about your father—should be the best answer to that," O'Mahoney said.

"You know what you are?" I said to him. "A damned old fool. And you're another," I said to Michael. I stalked to the door.

"Where are you going?" Michael said, following me.

"To tell the men you're trying to ruin. Good God, Michael, does it matter if they stole a few thousand? It wouldn't surprise me in the least. Others are stealing ten times that much every day down at City Hall, and no one is putting them on the block. In Washington, I saw generals and politicians gambling and whoring, and no one says a word against the virtue of the United States of America. Expose us to this disgrace and you'll ruin us."

"On the contrary," Michael said. "We'll rescue two

million dollars in the treasury, to be spent in Ireland, on Ireland, for Ireland."

"If you were more of a hero and less of a politician, you'd only want to spend one thing in Ireland—a bullet in the black heart of Lord Gort."

"We'll see what you think of heroes before we're through with this investigation," Michael said. "Your Donal Ogue is one of the biggest thieves, from what we've found so far. There may be a few even bigger, like Roberts and Hanrahan."

I started for the front door, Michael pushed me away and threw an inside bolt. "We need a few more hours," he said. "You'll stay here by order of the president."

I tried to wrestle past him to the door. He dragged me down the hall and locked me in a sitting room. He was so hurried that he did not notice the windows faced the street. Soon there was a great commotion, as other members of the staff tried to get in. They banged the knocker and pounded on the door. I flung up a window and shouted the news to them. Two of them went scampering downtown to tell William Roberts. Red Mike Hanrahan appeared next, and I gave him a summary. His face went white. I knew then that there was something to hide, which made things all the worse.

Within the hour, Roberts, Red Mike, and a dozen Fenian senators arrived, with a small army of police. They battered the lock off the front door and marched into the mansion. I was released from my prison room in time to see Roberts serve papers on O'Mahoney informing him that a meeting of the Fenian senate had found him guilty of dereliction of duty and had deposed him as president. A Tammany judge had issued an injunction forbidding the old man access to the mansion. He and his cohorts were barred under pain of imprisonment from taking any documents with them from the files.

Michael acted like a madman. Shouting denunciations, he tried to stuff papers in his pockets and under his shirt. The policemen seized him and solemnly extracted every document. They marched him and O'Mahoney and their helpers to the door of Moffat House and warned them not to return. Michael went straight to the *New York Times*, a paper that was slavish in its admiration of England and inveterate in its hostility to the Irish.

The next morning, we were treated to a juicy story on the front page, describing the Fenians as swindlers who had cajoled millions from the Irish poor. Our accuser was, of all people, John O'Mahoney himself. He claimed to have only just recently discovered the extravagance, misappropriation of funds, and misdirection of the movement that had supposedly been raging for years. The *Times* pointed out with nice sarcasm that this did not speak well for O'Mahoney's perspicacity, but it praised his "sensitive conscience" and agreed with his condemnation of the Canada invasion not only as a land-grabbing scheme but also as a plot to embroil America in a war with England.

John O'Neil, who was heading our operations in the Midwest, reported consternation when this story was reprinted in newspapers there. Dan McCaffrey, who was spending much of his time in that part of the country, sent similar alarms. We shuddered to think of what our lukewarm supporters in Washington, D.C., were saying.

A meeting of the cabinet and senate leaders was convened. Connolly and Peter Barr Sweeny attended, to offer Tammany's support and testify to their solidarity with our side of the quarrel. These two veteran politicians were less troubled by the imbroglio than the Fenians. Tammany Hall had a long history of splits and feuds. There was only one way to settle them—by beating hell out of the other side. They offered their battery of orators to talk the spoilers down in New York and urged us to recruit similar support elsewhere.

The Celtic temperament is naturally pugnacious, and this advice was accepted as wisdom. We launched a furious counterattack on O'Mahoney and Michael. We called them would-be dictators, hungry for power, guilty of the very extravagance and peculation of which they were accusing us. We vowed we had nothing to hide; our books and our plans were open to the whole world. They wanted to return the Fenians to the narrow path of the secret society. We had opened our ranks to the onward march of a whole people. The American government was endorsing our plan to conquer Canada and letting us buy guns from its arsenals. Our regiments were drilling openly in the streets of Chicago and Nashville and New York.

O'Mahoney and Michael and their circle replied in kind. They draped themselves in the mantle of O'Mahoney's purity and declared they alone were the true Fenians. They began raising their own funds and recruiting their own army. To counter Michael, who was making most of the speeches, I was often dispatched to address the same audience and call him a madman—which was not far from wrong. I was made the subject of a cartoon in *Harper's Weekly* for my efforts. I was pictured as the Fenian Joan of Arc, with a whiskey bottle on my head for a crown and a shattered broom in my hand. My face was that of a monkey, a favorite trick of the anti-Irish cartoonists in England and America. They regularly drew on Darwin's theory of evolution to portray the Irish as closer to simians than humans. Another issue of that same English-worshipping magazine portrayed the two factions as a pair of drunken Irish apes, fighting over a battered harp.

It was a ruinous melee, but it did serve one good purpose—or so we thought at the time. Beyond question, our plan to conquer British Canada in Ireland's name became as public as the knowledge that Andrew Johnson sat in the White House and Victoria on the throne of

England. The relative lack of public opposition, beyond snipes from pro-English publications like the *New York Times* and *Harper's Weekly*, and the studied silence from the American government encouraged us to think that we had support in both these vital quarters. In fact, powerful newspapers such as the *New York Herald* and the *New York Tribune* repeatedly cheered us on and helped us belabor O'Mahoney and Michael and their friends into relative insignificance.

My part in the quarrel was as exhausting as it was heartsickening. It was not easy to heap scorn and opprobrium and even a little slander on the head of a brother whom I once worshipped and in my heart still loved. I could never have done it without my hatred. It was easy to include Michael within its icy circle, to sacrifice him to its inexorable necessity. His stupid idealism was interfering with my consummation, and he had to be destroyed.

Mike Hanrahan, who traveled with me to many of my performances, was amazed and puzzled by my transformation when I stepped upon a stage or speaker's platform. "You're not the same person, so help me God," he said. "'Tis like an avenging angel possessed you."

"He has, Mike," I'd say. "I hope one soon possesses you, so there'll be an end to bucking the tiger."

"Ah, Bess, a man needs a bit of pleasure in this life," Mike would say with his crooked grin.

There were times when I lost hold of my avenging angel, or he lost me. One snowy December night, I was in Wilkes-Barre, Pennsylvania, speaking to a hall full of Irish coal miners and their wives. Michael had been there the previous day to ask for their money and their sons to invade Ireland in the Fenian fleet. I began by ridiculing my brother the admiral, telling how seasick he was when we crossed the Atlantic. Then I discussed my brother the coward, telling how Dan McCaffrey and I had had to carry him like a whimpering baby across half of Ireland with the police after us. "Sure he wet his pants so often," I said, "I put diapers on him."

Then I told them of the marching men in the other cities, the American government's sure support of our conquest of Canada, the great chance it represented to carve off one of the main limbs of the British hydra. I held up to them the hope of a home on the St. Lawrence or the western prairie instead of a hovel beside a mineshaft. Finally I reminded them of the fate of the convicted Fenians, in the prison camps of Tasmania. I ended with a poem that Mike had written for me. Someone, I think it was the *New York Herald*, called it the "Fenian Marseillaise."

> *"Away with speech, and brother, reach me down*
> *   that rifle gun.*
> *By her sweet voice and hers alone, the rights*
> *   of man are won.*
> *Fling down the pen; when heroic men pine sad in*
> *   dungeons lone,*
> *'Tis bayonets bright, with good red blood, should*
> *   plead before the throne."*

As the applause thundered to the roof, I glimpsed Michael's face in the back of the hall. Defeat and humiliation were written upon it in such scarifying terms, my hating heart faltered. I was destroying him, my own brother, the one who taught me to love Ireland with passion and pride. For a moment I almost cried out begging words of contrition and forgiveness. But long before I could get off the stage, he had turned away and vanished into the night.

Through all this turmoil, I seldom saw Dan McCaffrey. When he was in New York, I was usually en route to some distant town like Wilkes-Barre, and when I stumbled off a train in Jersey City and trudged to the ferry with Mike, it was to discover that Dan had just departed for Boston or Pittsburgh. When I did encounter him I had to struggle to produce a loving smile. But I managed it, just as I managed to write him words of passionate endearment in my letters. Not because I loved him. Except for stray moments, like that episode on the stage, I loved nothing but my hatred—and my Donal Ogue remained an important part of my dream of murderous revenge.

With the cruel humor that fate seems to prefer, Michael's going berserk and plunging us into an Ireland-first versus Canada-first quarrel played neatly into my hand. Toward the end of January in the new year 1866, when we had him and O'Mahoney well on the run, I went to William Roberts with my plan.

"It's not enough to go about making speeches about rifle guns," I said. "We must show we can use them."

"We will, as soon as the snow melts in Canada," he said.

I shook my head. "We must also show we can use them in Ireland."

He glanced up in alarm from the latest bond-sale reports, wondering if I was about to change sides on him. Like most men, he saw a female as fickle, swayed by every contrary wind.

"We must concentrate our strength, not scatter it," he said, giving one of the standard military answers we had devised to counter the Ireland-firsters.

"Of course," I said, "but surely we can spare three people, two men and a woman, to strike a blow that will reverberate through Ireland and America. A blow that will prove no one can abuse Ireland and live in safety."

Roberts stopped reading and started listening.

"Lord Gort of Limerick has become head of the landlords' association in Ireland. You know what he did to my father," I said. "He's bent on terrorizing and humiliating everyone within his reach—and if the association gains strength, it will reach everywhere in Ireland. I want to go there and kill him. On the orders of the Irish Republic. As an act of war."

And revenge, I added silently, my true love, dear sweet savage revenge.

"Can it be done?" he asked.

I had him hooked. He saw it would be the perfect answer to the Ireland-firsters. Tell us what *you* have done in Ireland, we could sneer, and point to Gort's corpse.

"It can," I said. "With the help of Dan McCaffrey and Mike Hanrahan." I told him of my plan.

"It's dangerous," he said. "Can we ask the men to do it?"

"Make it worth their while," I said. "Pay them for it. A thousand dollars each."

This was the most painful part. Admitting my Donal Ogue had the soul of a mercenary. Letting go, perhaps for good, that dream I had in Ireland of teaching him the nobility of sacrifice. But my hatred consoled me. It was a small price to pay.

I did not know what a liar hatred was.

The Sassenach Was Human

A telegram summoned Dan from his training duties. Red Mike Hanrahan, busy with staging Fenian rallies, was similarly recalled. We met in President Roberts's office. "Gentlemen," he said, "we have an assignment for you. A very dangerous assignment, but one that will bring you imperishable glory in the history of Ireland."

Dear God, I thought, watching frowns grow on the foreheads of both these veteran soldiers. They had seen too many bullets fired at them to put much stock in glory. Roberts went on to describe the proposal "he and the cabinet" had devised to strike a blow in Ireland and solidify the movement. I had persuaded him without much difficulty to take credit for the idea. I knew Dan and Mike would look askance at a plan drawn by a woman.

"Because of the danger of the assignment, I'm authorized to offer you a thousand dollars each to undertake it."

That was more like it. Dan accepted on the spot. Red Mike was less enthused. He said he had spent most of his courage in the charge up Marye's Heights at Fredericksburg. "But I'll do it if we can buck the tiger for a few nights in London on the way back."

"It can't be done without you, Mike. You must be the stage director of the whole business," I said.

"I wouldn't be surprised," Mike said, "if I'm lookin' at the real director."

Dan glowered at me. "Is that true?"

"Of course not," I said.

"Henceforth," William Roberts continued in his oratorical style, "you shall consider yourselves under the orders of the government of the Republic of Ireland. You, Major Daniel McCaffrey, and you, Captain Michael Hanrahan, are to choose one other volunteer and proceed to Ireland. We will obtain the necessary false identities and provide you with the money and weapons for the expedition. In Ireland you are to make your way by the safest route to Limerick, and thence to the village of Ballinaclash, where you are to execute Lord Rodney Gort, landlord, for atrocious crimes against the Irish people. I wish you well."

He handed us our orders. I was, of course, the other volunteer. We immediately set to work on our plan. Mike obtained the services of one of the best actors in New York, Charles Everett, and he spent the next two weeks teaching me and Dan how to impersonate old age. Next, he showed us how to apply the makeup that made our speech and our mannerisms supremely realistic. With powdered hair, a gray mustache, crow's-feet around the eyes, and a raddled neck, Dan grew old before my eyes. I did the same, with the aid of the same powder, a pair of eyeglasses, and expertly added wrinkles. I cut my hair short, the way older women wore it in America. Under Everett's tutelage, Mike Hanrahan became our makeup man. Again and again, while Everett timed us with his watch, Mike took us from youth to age in fifteen minutes. Furious effort and concentration finally enabled him to do it in ten—five minutes for each. We were ready.

Meanwhile, Secretary of State Seward was asked to prepare two passports for Mr. and Mrs. Clayton Stowecroft, aged sixty-five and sixty-six, who were leaving on an extended tour of Ireland, England, and Scotland. The secretary had been providing us with false passports for almost a year now, so there was no difficulty about obtaining them. Mr. and Mrs. Stowecroft, who were supposedly from Pittsburgh, Pennsylvania, booked their passage on the Cunard line steamer *Servia*. Their tour was arranged by the New York office of Thomas Cook, and their meeting with the agent, Mr. Soames, was (unknown to him) a dress rehearsal that was thoroughly successful. Mr. Soames, a balding little bulldog of a man, said he was delighted to discover two Americans in the evening of their lives with such a penchant for visiting the mother country, if he might call it that. Mrs. Stowecroft (me) assured him in her tremulous old voice that she thought of England as the mother of our arts and sciences, our very speech. Mr. Stowecroft (aka Dan), who was a "railroad man," said he was looking forward to riding every mile of track in the United Kingdom. Mrs. Stowecroft fluttered and said he could do what he pleased, she was sick of railroads and was going to enjoy herself in London, Dublin, and Edinburgh. Mr. Soames assured them that they would enjoy themselves immensely no matter what they did.

So we embarked from Jersey City in Cunard's big, dowdy steamer, which was brand-new but looked, with typical English bad taste, as though it had been built twenty years ago. A decade later, I read a paean of praise to the *Servia* by that hopeless Anglophile Henry James. He canted on about how she was "spacious and comfortable, and there was a kind of motherly decency in her long nursing rock and her rustling old-fashioned gait." Almost certainly, Mr. James sailed in the spring or summer. On the North Atlantic in February, the long nursing rock was closer to the careen of a hopeless drunkard. The decks were awash morning and night; the ship resounded with the crash of crockery, the clang of falling ornaments, and the screams of nervous passengers. The stench of seasickness drifted from every corridor into the ornate grand salon. The food, normally poor in the great tradition of British cooking, was atrocious. But the ordeal suited us well. It enabled us to remain in our cabin most of the time. When we did emerge, everyone was much too frightened and disconsolate to pay much attention to us. On every hand we heard "Cunard has never lost a life," repeated like a pleading litany. We recited it along with everyone else, but never for a moment did I doubt that the good ship *Servia* would carry me safely to Ireland and my revenge.

To guarantee my moment of consummation, I made sure Dan McCaffrey thought of little else. Day after day, I gave myself to him until he was all but drunk with the love of me. He thought it was my worship of his daring, his cunning, his deadly aim with a gun. He did not know he held a woman of ice in his arms, a woman who lied her love to him, who worshipped nothing but her hatred. I began to think I did not know what I thought or felt about him, or anyone.

It was necessary to mesmerize him, narcotize him with my body, because when he thought of our plan he was afraid. He tried to hide it from me, but my hatred gave me a preternatural ability to scent his fear. He lacked my fierce faith in my hatred's predestined consummation. As a veteran soldier who had seen the best of plans go wrong and men die in writhing agony, he weighed our chances and knew they teetered on a knife edge. If even one thing went wrong, we were doomed. Every so often he would look at me as if he were seeing his death. That was when I crooned my lying love to him, opened myself with a high exultant lust that I imagined Emer offered her warrior hero on the eve of battle, and promised him unimagined delights if he fulfilled my wish. Simultaneously I was proving my passion to myself. I took no precautions against pregnancy nor asked Dan to take any. I was ready to sacrifice my reputation, even my life, on the altar of my dark god.

Below us, in a narrow third-class compartment, Mike Hanrahan no doubt sweated the same fear. I could do nothing for him. Mike's risks were slight compared to ours. He carried a passport that identified him as one Peter Kinkaid, going home to Limerick to visit his aged mother. He, too, had a patter, well rehearsed, which he talked night and day about his career as a brakeman on the Erie Railroad.

At last, toward dusk on the fifteenth day, the *Servia* lumbered into the calm waters of Cork's great harbor. We stayed aboard until the next morning, listening to the bells of Shandon drift out to us on the chill evening air. The nearness of Ireland tempted me to drop my disguise a little. "There's a lovely poem that goes with those bells," I said. I began to whisper it to Dan.

He cut me short with an impatient wave of his hand. "Remember what Red Mike told you? Even when we're alone, we should think and talk like old, rich Americans. You go Irish on me and I'll take the first boat home."

We strolled to the stern and watched the third class passengers emerging like moles into the fresh air. A fiddle began to play. Someone started singing a Come All Ye.

My love Nell
Was an Irish girl
From the Cove of Cork came she.
I left her weeping and awailing
And the big ship sailing
For the shores of Amerikay.

Perhaps he was coming home to claim his Nell, with American dollars in his pocket. I entertained myself with these sentimental thoughts until the singer pranced out of the crowd and tipped his hat to us. It was Red Mike Hanrahan.

The next day we went ashore in smaller vessels that carried us to quays on the River Lee. The approach to Cork in the morning sunlight was grand. Superb gardens, parks, and villas covered the shore on each bank. The city closed the view, rising with its roofs and church steeples on two hills on either side of the Lee.

The illusion of splendor and beauty ended abruptly at the dock. We were set upon by the most ragged, noisy swarm of beggars, hackmen, and baggage boys I have ever encountered. The boys fought and cursed over our luggage, and the losers beseeched pennies of us for consolation. The hackmen were ready to commit murder, until Dan sternly chose one suppliant and banished the others. We could not resist the female beggars, who ranged in age from tots of five and six to girls as old and as large as I. We were sprinkling coins into their hands when a stern voice interrupted us. "Here now. If you take my advice you'll stop that."

A ruddy-faced little Englishman in a bowler hat and long tan raincoat confronted us, his brush mustache quivering. "Noticed you on the boat. The captain told me you were Americans. Beastly weather made sociability impossible. Name's Quackey, as in the duck. Feel I should tell you there's no point whatsoever in dispensing charity to these lazy curs. All for helping the worthy poor, but if you can find one of these in Ireland, I'll give you a fiver. These are the laziest people God ever made. Drain you dry if you give them half a chance. Professional beggars, every one of them."

"Why, thankee, friend Quackey," said Dan, tipping his hat. "You've saved us a power of money. Wouldn't you say so, dear?"

"My stars, yes," I trilled.

I looked around me, staggered and ashamed by the way the beggars, the baggage boys, and even the hackmen, most of them twice the Englishman's size, shrank back and accepted this abuse. If an Englishman said such things to Irish-Americans, he would have been beaten black and blue on the spot. I realized my disguise was going to be much more difficult to maintain than I had thought it would be. No wonder Red Mike, no slouch at judging human nature, had urged me to think and act like an American as much as possible.

Friend Quackey was delighted that we were staying at the Royal Hotel. So was he. Would we have dinner with him? We could hardly say no. At the hotel, he laid about him with his lash of a tongue and quickly scattered another swarm of beggars and baggage boys. The cabman asked for a shilling. Quackey advised us to give him twopence and tell him he was lucky to get it. While John Bull was snorting at the beggars I took a shilling from my purse and slipped it into the fellow's hand. He was wasted to a skeleton. "God bless you, ma'am," he murmured.

We endured Quackey for dinner. Here was a good chance to test our performances as aged but still sturdy Americans from Pittsburgh. Quackey was so interested in dispensing his own opinions, he gave us little time to talk. He discoursed on the hopelessness of civilizing the Irish. They were incurably lazy, dishonest, dirty. He could not understand how God, whom he sometimes called "the Great Engineer," could have permitted such awful people to inhabit such a beautiful country. "Ireland would be the jewel of the empire, if we could just get rid of the Irish," he said. "But they breed like rabbits, if you'll excuse me, Mrs. Stowecroft. Like rabbits."

Quackey was a railroad engineer. He had been to America making a survey of the nation's railroads, with a view to advising some British capitalists who were thinking of investing huge sums there. He thought the prospects were good. America was ready for a great burst of railroad building, now that they had settled the Civil War. "But I intend to advise my clients not to invest a red cent," he said, "until the American government does something about the Fenians in America. The beggars are forming regiments and talking of invading Canada. The Americans had damn well better smash them, as we did here, if they want to see any British capital in their railroads."

"Oh, it's all talk," I said. "You know how the Irish are. I have an Irish servant girl at home in Pittsburgh. You should hear the moonshine she serves up about the Irish conquering England someday."

"Damndest people I've ever seen," Dan (as Mr. Stowecroft) said.

"Lower on the evolutionary scale, that's the only answer," Quackey said. "Study the faces as you go. You'll see amazing numbers that belong in a zoo."

"Yes," I said, thinking how pleasant it would be to shoot him between the eyes.

The next day we began our stint as tourists. We had at least a week to wait, while Red Mike Hanrahan journeyed to Dublin and bought a closed touring coach and returned with it to Limerick. We jogged about Cork on our first day, taking in the sights of the town. It was an unnerving experience. Everything looked so shabby, so dismal, to my eyes. I could not believe it was the same city I had visited more than once with my mother and father, admiring it as if it were imperial Rome in its glory. Compared to New York and other American cities, the shops were drab and empty of attractive goods. In several places, the merchants did not have change on hand for a one-pound note. Patrick Street, the chief thoroughfare, had less bustle than the main street of battered Vicksburg. The greatest shock was the market on the outskirts of the poor section of the town. I winced at the ragged women and boys gazing hungrily at dirty apple pie stalls; at fish frying and fish raw and stinking; at clothes booths, where you might buy a wardrobe for scarecrows; at battered old furniture that had been sold against starvation. In the streets roundabout, in the thin March sunshine, squatted women with bare breasts nursing babies. Idle men, as dirty and desperate looking as any in New York's Sixth Ward, lounged in the mouldy doorways or stared from the black, gaping windows.

Gradually, I realized that my American identity was not a complete lie. It was part of me, and I was seeing Ireland with American eyes. I stood in the Cork library and stared disapprovingly at the years' worth of dust and dirt on plaster ceilings and walls. I gazed at the still uncompleted Catholic cathedral and listened impatiently to a priest explain that they were waiting for more money to arrive from America to finish it. I fumed when Dan informed me that the post office did not have money on hand to cash a five-pound order. I writhed when I overheard clerks in the stores fawning over English tourists, telling them how they went to London for their holidays. Everywhere I was dismayed or distressed by the lack of pride, energy, or enterprise among the people, both high and low.

The following day we hired a guide and rode out to Blarney Castle. The fellow must have kissed the stone every time he visited it. He never ceased talking, one story after another about this ruin and that house, all a jumble of historical events and names from a half dozen centuries, scrambled together. He was an ignoramus who depended on the ignorance of his visitors to escape challenge. He had St. Patrick fighting the Vikings and Brian Boru battling Queen Elizabeth and Red Hugh O'Donnell of the sixteenth century a friend of Wolfe Tone, Ireland's hero of the 1798. He was a monological example of a man who had lost touch with all but the scraps and tatters of his heritage, which he wore as lackadaisically as his patched coat and drooping trousers. Eventually he led us to the tower of Blarney Castle to enjoy the view and then to the turret where the small blue boulder lies embedded. I kissed it with more than ordinary emotion, hoping it would give me and Dan the powers of deceptive speech we needed to complete our mission. I was more and more shaken by my sight of Ireland with American eyes. I needed to draw fresh strength from something like this mystic stone.

The next day in a cold drizzle whipped by gusty March winds, we left Cork for Killarney in a battered old coach with the paint rubbed off. Our only companions were a morose British naval officer and a commercial traveler from a British hardware company. At least forty men in long ragged coats and battered steeple hats stood around, watching us depart as if it were some great event. The two Englishmen made no attempt to introduce themselves and spent their time damning the fate that had driven them to Ireland, which they agreed was the worst assignment in the empire. The steaming jungles of West Africa, the miseries of the Punjab, were nothing compared to the vexations of Irish indolence and stupidity.

The commercial traveler told of ordering some coals brought to his room to start a fire against the chill of the late afternoon. The servant girl arrived with the coals, not in a scuttle, but upon a plate. The naval officer told of a well-to-do Protestant Irishman who had fought a duel over some trifling political disagreement with a neighbor who lived in a house across the road. He lost and received a bad wound. In revenge, he tore down his house and built a castle, to "plague" his neighbor's house. In the process he went bankrupt, and the castle was now sliding into ruin.

At the village of Millstreet we stopped for lunch. A loaf of bread, a half cheese, and a huge piece of cold baked beef were set upon the table in the dirty barroom of the inn. Each went and cut for himself, filling mouth, hands, and pockets, if he chose. The Englishmen crammed all they could manage into these receptacles, as did Dan. As we returned to the coach, we were set upon by a band of beggars, who literally pleaded the food from Dan's hands.

"There's been a reign of terror hereabout," the coachman told us. "One of the new breed of landlords, as they call themselves, has been evicting all who won't sign new leases, at double the rent."

Leaving the town, we mounted a hill at a slow pace. As we approached the crest, about twenty or thirty people emerged from an old lime-kiln, where they had been sheltering themselves from the wind and rain. They were mere skeletons, wrapped in the coarsest rags. There was not a pair of shoes among them. They stretched out their lean hands, fastened upon arms of skin and bone, and turned their wan ghastly faces and sunken lifeless eyes imploringly up to us, with feeble words of entreaty. The Englishmen made some cold remarks about their indolence and worthlessness and gave them nothing. I flung them some coins, almost weeping with shame and vexation at the sight of them. Why did they accept their very deaths with such resignation? If they had to die, why didn't they at least go down striking a blow? Their passivity and hopelessness shrank the significance of my revenge to a small, selfish, possibly meaningless gesture.

We approached Killarney along a road that commanded a view of the famous lakes. In the evening light, the surrounding mountains were clothed in purple like kings in mourning; great heavy clouds were gathered round their heads. The main lake lay beneath us on the right, dark and blue, with mist-shrouded islands toward the center. We were met at Kenmare House by servants with blazing torches and by the usual swarm of beggars, urchins, and idlers. My thoughts had little to do with the scenery or the creature comforts of the hotel. I was obsessed with how to find my sister Mary and my mother, without exposing our true identities to them.

The next day I inquired at the desk if a girl named Mary Fitzmaurice was employed here, or at any neighboring hotel. I told the pompous little clerk she was the sister of a girl I had in my employ in America, and I had gifts for her. He said he knew no one by that name, and inquiries at other hotels produced no results. So we had to proceed to play the interested tourists for the next two days, while gazing in vain at every passing face for a glimpse of my mother or sister. Our guide, said to be the finest in Killarney, was Sir Richard Courtenay, a small, lean man of sixty, descended from the earls of Desmond. The bitter history of Ireland had deprived his family of lands and wealth, leaving him only his title. He was an educated man, spoke Gaelic fluently, and always had an appropriate bit of poetry on his lips, but there was a vein of sadness in everything he said and did. No wonder.

Sir Richard led us about the lakes in boats, telling us legends that swarmed on every hill and crag and island. The next day we ascended Mount Mangerton, riding surefooted little ponies that picked their way along the perilous path to the summit and the finest view in Ireland. Halfway up, we were assailed by a squad of girls in their teens and early twenties, seeking to sell goat's milk and poteen—Irish whiskey—to quench our thirst. It was clear from their deference to him that they were in Sir Richard's employ. With a desperation that may have been accentuated by the time of the year—a month or two before the start of the usual tourist season—they begged us to take a drink.

Each was uglier than the next, peasant types, with streaming hair and dirty skirts. I hesitated, glancing over the lot of them, and gasped with shock. At the rear of the squad, looking as forlorn as a creature in a fairy spell, was my sister Mary. The sadness on her face was enough to destroy me on the spot. I let the rest pursue the half dozen other tourists with us. Bridling my pony, I dropped back until I was abreast of Mary.

"Land's sakes, child," I said in my American accent. "You don't look like you are enjoying this outing."

"I'm feeling a bit weak, ma'am," Mary said. "I've had nothing to eat since yesterday breakfast."

"Why in the world not?" I asked.

"My ma is sick, and I'm giving as much of the little we've got to eat to her, to keep up her strength."

"Have you taken her to a doctor?" I asked.

"We haven't the money. It's the weather. She caught cold when the warm winds left us, and we hadn't a penny for a bit of turf."

"Oh, did you hear that, Mr. Stowecroft?" I said to

Dan. "This poor girl—what's your name, dear?—hasn't a cent for a sick mother. Surely we can spare her something."

"I'd be eternally grateful," Mary said. "I'd pray for you for the rest of my life. My name is Mary Fitzmaurice, and I've two sisters and a brother in America."

"Isn't that nice," I said.

"Here," Dan said, and handed her a five-pound note.

"Oh, dear God," said Mary. "You can have all my whiskey and milk for that, twice over. I'll go down the mountain and get another serving."

"Never mind," I said. "What you have will do us nicely. Have you thought of going to America yourself?"

"I have. But now I'm not sure. I had a letter from my brother, Michael, just the other day, telling me the sad tale of what's become of my sisters."

"I can't imagine," I said.

"They're ruined women, ma'am, if you'll excuse such language," Mary said. "Michael says America will do it to everyone who goes out. It's either that or working as a slavey for some rich family. 'Tis a better life by far in Ireland, he claims."

"It's none of my business," I said, "but your brother sounds like a fool."

"With all due respect, ma'am," Mary said, "I must resent that. He's fine and true. He went to America to rally the Irish there for Ireland. But he says there's no hope of it. They think of nothing but making money."

I was in torment. I longed to fling aside my disguise and speak in my natural voice. Dan was glaring at me, already fearful that I had said too much. "Come on, Mother," he said. "We're goin' to lose the view. Sir Richard's already there and talkin' a blue streak."

He seized my pony's bridle and fairly dragged me up the path to the summit, where we admired the vistas in all directions, following Sir Richard Courtenay's gesticulating arm. To the west glittered Dingle Bay and the Bay of Ken-mare; to the east, wild mountains and desolate glens, bro-ken by numerous little lakes bespangling the landscape like stars in the firmament of heaven. Resting, we partook of Mary's milk and poteen, which she served and then stood at a respectful distance until we drank it.

"Don't say another word to her, Mother," Dan mut-tered to me in his true voice.

"Go to hell, Father," I said.

But what else could I say, without risking everything? Even if it were worth the risk, what would it accom-plish? Would Mary take advice from her ruined sister, whom she had reason to envy and suspect, even before she heard the worst from Michael? What could I tell her, anyway? Come to America and marry Patrick Dolan? I had no such power to dispose of her or him.

Though it almost strangled me, I could do nothing but return the cup to her, express more sympathy for her plight, and descend the mountain, mute in my American identity. I did manage to inquire about her mother's ill-ness and was dismayed to hear that she was coughing blood. I expressed some alarm, and Mary sighed hope-lessly. "I suppose it's a charge against us, for the sins my sisters have committed," she said. "God help them, is all I can say. When my mother goes, I hope to enter the con-vent in Limerick and give my life over to praying for them and the souls of her and my poor father."

"How—noble of you," I said in my American voice, while shame scalded my cold hating heart.

Back in our room overlooking the lake, Dan cursed and threw things. "I told you to stay away from her," he said. "To look right past her if you saw her. She was eyein' you pretty strange by the time we got down that mountain. Why didn't you shut up when I told you?"

It was his fear speaking. I knew it, but I had lost my will to control it. "If you want to quit this, do it now,"

I said. "I'll undertake it alone. Go back to New York and tell them why you ran out. Don't waste your breath on me."

He glared at me with something close to hatred in his eyes. Gone was the lovely camaraderie of shipboard. Ireland was destroying my ability to play the passionate girl. "I made a deal," he said. "I don't walk out on my promises."

Except to women, I thought bitterly, remembering the ragged woman on Priest's Leap. I suddenly saw her demonic face, screaming that curse at us in the wind. With a shudder I turned the memory aside. We made no attempt to console each other that night. I lay beside my "husband" in the big double bed and wept bitter silent tears.

We spent another day in Killarney, traveling through the Gap of Dunloe in jaunting carts, admiring the wild view and enduring a sudden hailstorm. The next day, harried by the usual swarm of beggars, we boarded another coach and headed for Limerick. Our hotel was in the new town—Newtown Pery, as it was called, after the man who owned the land. It fronted the handsome main street, which was a mile long and considered one of the most fashionable thoroughfares in Ireland. The houses were all bright red, and the street was full of carriages and chaises containing numerous well-dressed women. Along the sidewalk strutted dozens of young British officers, with tight waists and absurd brass shell epaulets on their absurd little frock coats. They stared at all the women, even one as old as I was supposed to be, with cold, nasty eyes.

The sight of the enemy uniform and the knowledge that Limerick was a major military base inspired me and Dan McCaffrey to forget our differences and concentrate on our roles. We leaned hard on our canes and tottered to our rooms croaking of our weariness.

The next day, still complaining of exhaustion, we con-
fined ourselves to wandering about Limerick. At dinner
we met two upstate New Yorkers, William Balch and
Frederick Havemeyer, retired merchants on a tour similar to our own. Balch was small and exciteable, Havemeyer heavy and stolid. They were from Buffalo, a city
with a large Irish population, and several Celtic friends
had urged them to visit Ireland after touring England,
Scotland, and Wales.

In the morning we all strolled from the new town into
old Limerick, which is divided into Irish and English
sections. In the Irish part Balch and Havemeyer gazed
aghast down St. Giles, St. Mary's Gate, and other narrow
streets. There were hundreds of people sprawled against
the grimy buildings, or lying in the gutters, or staggering
about bawling songs. Every second house was a gin,
beer, or slop shop. On the faces was everything from
smutty childhood to bloated dissipation to ruined old
age.

"There's nothing in Buffalo or even New York to
match it," gasped Mr. Balch, and his friend Havemeyer
solemnly agreed.

"We have the better class, who had the strength to emigrate," Havemeyer said.

I was stunned speechless, which was just as well. Limerick was a city I had visited a hundred times, but my
aunts lived on a comfortable street in the new town, and
my convent school was on the outskirts of this same section. I had never ventured into old Limerick. All I knew
of it was some vague words of disapproval spoken by
my parents or my aunts.

The English town was not much of an improvement
on the Irish town. It, too, swarmed with poor Irish. The
major difference was the presence of hundreds of prostitutes in the streets around the English barracks. They

stood in the doorways of their houses or leaned from the windows, combing their hair. Many of them were young, and some were as beautiful as any Broadway demimondaine. Mr. Balch and Mr. Havemeyer were embarrassed by the sight of them and spluttered about the "inevitable depravity" of army life.

Returning to our hotel, I began to wonder if I might die of shame, or of undischarged hatred. What should I see lounging on the hotel steps but the most welcome sight I could imagine: Red Mike Hanrahan. He was wearing rough countryman's clothes, chatting away with the hackmen. He tugged on his right ear and began talking loudly about the weather in Dublin. Nothing but rain, he said. It was good to see some sunshine here in Limerick.

It was the agreed-on signal that all was well. Mike had bought a large touring coach and four good horses and was supposedly en route to Cork to meet an American millionaire who was the real buyer. That night after supper, Dan and I announced we needed some fresh air before bed. We strolled into the Irish town, and Mike followed us. We paused on the corner of St. Giles Street, and he tipped his hat and pretended to strike up a conversation with us.

"His lordship is waiting for us," he said. "He's busy evicting tenants in a five-mile swath. Seventy-two families, five hundred and twenty-two souls, in the past month. His fellow landlords have pitched in to bring the total to seventeen hundred. Never was there a better moment to strike a blow."

"Where's the coach?" I asked.

"At the livery stable owned by your hotel," Mike said.

"What have you found out about his lordship's daily routine?"

"Not much. Except that he spends almost all his time upon his estate and seldom comes to Limerick."

"That's good enough. Tomorrow we'll begin our trips into the country. You can do the same, exercising your horses. We'll meet you here tomorrow night."

Limerick was not a tourist center. It was primarily a commercial city, so there was no system of guides. Therefore no one made the slightest objection when we rented a chaise the next day and asked for suggestions of sights to see in the countryside. Lake Fergus and the ruined castle of Lord Desmond, Gort House, and the cairn of the old kings nearby were among those suggested—as I knew they would be. We now had every reason to be in the vicinity of the man we wanted to kill.

Red Mike Hanrahan was meanwhile telling his friends at the livery stable that he had received a telegram from his American employer, informing him that he'd decided to stay in London an extra week, so there was no need to hurry to Cork.

The dutiful groom had decided to remain in Limerick for a few more days, because the roads were infinitely better than those in the hills around Cork. Each day he hitched his team of fine dappled grays and rode out for an hour or two. The livery stable manager was of course delighted to keep a customer who paid hard cash and tipped liberally.

Dan was my chief worry. Each day his doubts multiplied and his questions grew more numerous. He saw a hundred ways for the plan to miscarry. I was finally reduced to crooning to him as if he were a baby, "All will be well, all will be well." Meanwhile, deep within me, other voices whispered the opposite. I was overwhelmed by the hopelessness of rallying people so far gone in degradation. I had already lost faith in the power of my act of hatred, but my will to perform it was still intact. The hatred itself was still alive within me and would swell there like a tumor, I thought, unless it was vented.

The next day, the tenth of March, 1866, we arose from

our sleepless beds and descended to breakfast, took our picnic lunch from the head porter, and trilled our enthusiasm for another day in the country. It was perfect weather, a soft spring breeze and a warm sun in a blue sky. In an hour Lake Fergus was in sight, shining like a blessing below its guardian mountains. We avoided the west side, where Ballinaclash and the Fitzmaurice farm lay, partly because I could not bear the agony of seeing them close, and partly because we feared a familiar eye might, by some quirk, recognize me. Our single horse, a sturdy brown gelding, trotted by the gate of Gort House and along a narrow road to the north where thick stands of trees masked the shores of the lake. A woodman's track ran into this little forest. We followed it into the silent shadows.

We sat there for an hour, saying little. We nibbled a bit of our lunch. Dan took his pistol from the carpetbag at his feet and loaded it. I did the same with the pistol in my purse. Across the lake I could see our old house and the cottages of the laborers. They were the size of toys at this distance. It was all unreal. Was I the same Bess Fitzmaurice who had sat outside Malloy's cottage in the sunshine, listening to her prediction that I would marry a rich man? The same headstrong girl who had refused Patrick Dolan's offer of marriage while knowing, dreading, that eventually she would accept it? It was hard to believe anything was real, once you mounted history's whirlwind.

A clatter of hoofs on the road. We both stiffened. Red Mike was here. The coach came creaking down the woodman's path to where we sat. Mike did not have to assure us that he had paid his livery bill and told his friend the manager that he was off to Cork. Dan glanced at his watch as Mike and the horses became visible in the trees. Eleven o'clock. Time to get busy.

With scarcely more than a nod to Mike, we hauled the

trunk from the back of the coach. Within it were bottles
of cleansing fluid, which quickly enabled Mike to daub
the traces of age from our faces. A black wig was fitted
over my gray head, and a red wig replaced Dan's gray
one. Off came our sedate middle-class clothes. I stepped
into a gorgeous dark green traveling dress and donned a
velvet hat of the same color, with a dark veil. Dan
shrugged into an English tweed suit. A shoulder holster
held his gun. A walking stick was another weapon. Mike
buttoned me up the back, cursing his thick fingers.
"Jesus God," he muttered. "Who'd think that a sergeant
of the Fighting 69th would end up a ladies' maid?"

By eleven-thirty we were ready. In my purse were my
gun and my calling cards, which read MRS. PIERRE LO-
RILLARD RONALDS. I was impersonating Annie's old
benefactor. Dan's card read GEORGE DANGERFIELD. He
would have no trouble playing one of Mrs. Ronalds's
many male friends. We had a firm grasp on these identities, lest his lordship be out and we had to sit and converse with some other member of the family.

By noon we were turning in the gate of Gort House.
Mike Hanrahan, wearing the red and yellow livery of a
well-tailored coachman, boldly announced our arrival
with a call on his bugle. It had taken him the better part of
a week to learn it. We should have had another man on the
box, but rather than worry about a fourth confederate, we
decided it would be easier to explain his absence by a
story about an illness that left him sick in bed in Limerick.

We clattered to a stop in front of the house. A scrawny
gray-haired doorkeeper ran out. I handed him my card
and Dan's. "Is his lordship at home?" I asked.

"Oh, yes, ma'am," he said.

Our first hope was that Lord Gort would come out to
greet us personally. We had no great desire to enter the
house, which could easily become a trap.

Within sixty seconds a husky, fair-haired English butler appeared on the steps. "His lordship has just returned from the fields. He begs you and Mr. Dangerfield to wait for him in the library and hopes you can stay for dinner at the very least."

"I'm afraid that's impossible, at least today," I said.

I allowed the butler to hand me down from the carriage. Dan followed. We were led down a long center hall covered with swords and armor and frowning portraits of earlier Gorts. The library was a large, pleasant room with a fire in the massive fieldstone fireplace. We walked over to it, moving deep into the room, and stood with our backs to the door, gazing up at an oil painting of the mansion by an artist who must have been aboard a boat in the lake. We had plotted every move, studied every alternative, and decided nonchalance was the key to success. It was better by far to lure him into the room rather than lurk by a door, something no lady would do.

Five minutes stretched into ten. I could see Dan's jaw tightening with impatience and the fear drifting like fog into his eyes. "All will be well," I whispered.

Footsteps in the hall. Then a cheerful voice crying, "My dear, why didn't you warn me of this American invasion? What is this about not staying for din—"

I was turning as he spoke. Lord Gort stood about six feet away, incomprehension befuddling him as he saw my face. From the rear in my rich black wig I could easily pass for Mrs. Ronalds. Face-to-face he saw a different woman.

"But you're not—"

"No," I said. "The name is Fitzmaurice. John Fitzmaurice's daughter. The Fenian girl."

I was drawing my gun as I said these deadly words. Terror banished puzzlement from Gort's face. He threw up his hands as I fired, aiming point-blank at his chest. My little gun sounded like an artillery piece in the closed room.

"Oh, my God, I'm shot," Lord Gort screamed in a shrill woman's voice.

He whirled, clutching his chest, and staggered toward the door. I fired two more shots that I know struck home, but still he stayed on his feet. From the beginning Dan had argued that he should use his heavier gun with its far more destructive bullets, but I had insisted on my right to vengeance. Now beside me I heard Dan curse, and an instant later his gun boomed. The impact of the single shot sent Lord Gort hurtling out the door into the hall on his face.

We raced for that same door. As we rushed toward it, a terrified face, then the body of a young girl, no more than ten or eleven, appeared in it. She was wearing a white organdy dress with a blue sash, not unlike ones I had worn at that age. She flung herself on Lord Gort, screaming, "Father, Father!"

Incredibly, Gort was still alive. Blood gushed from his back onto the girl's dress. He flailed at her. He was trying to crawl away. We burst into the hall and confronted Lord Gort's wife and two other daughters, both younger than the girl on her knees, and the butler. The wife and the two other girls were shrinking back, screaming hysterically.

We stood there for a pandemonium-filled second. I was numb with the horror and shock of it. Nothing had happened as I imagined it. I had envisioned Gort toppling, dismay and fear on his face, from a single shot, then swift escape while servants cowered beneath our guns. Somehow I had even avoided noticing that Lord Gort was married and had children, daughters. The Sassenach was human!

If I had been alone, I might have died there. I might have handed my gun to that young girl and whispered, "We are even, now you may kill me." My hatred, which I had imagined was as imperishable and impenetrable as tempered steel, had vanished. I see now that it had been shriveling, withering, from the day I landed in Ireland and began to doubt the cause. This scene of horror and death had been a final ruinating blow.

But Dan McCaffrey had been ordered to kill Lord Gort and paid a thousand dollars to do it. He had seen ten thousand men die in four years of war. No doubt some of them had cried out and tried to run and may even have had a friend if not a daughter plead for them when they fell. But war—which was what we claimed to be fighting here—allowed no place for soft hearts or guilty nerves. Brutal years of experience were Dan's armor against the weakness that was disabling me. With a snarl he shoved the daughter aside and aimed a final shot into the back of the dying man's head. The gun crashed amid the echoing screams.

And crashed again. The butler had seized a sword from the wall and rushed heroically at us, like a man from another century. His reward was death.

"Come on," Dan roared, and seized my arm with a wrench that almost amputated it. The pain was what I needed to restore some semblance of reality. We raced for the front door. Behind us the screams continued, with one voice, a daughter's voice, louder than the rest: *"You've killed my father! Killed my father!"*

Outside, Red Mike was on the coachman's box and the horses were turned to the gate. We sprang in and were instantly on our way. Out the gate we rumbled and down the road to the north. As we expected, there was no pursuit. In ten minutes of furious driving, we were at the turn to our forest track. Into it we crept. There stood our chaise and faithful gelding, still munching a bag of oats we had provided for him. We leaped from the coach and struggled back into our middle-class clothes. Fiercely to work went Hanrahan, our makeup artist. In ten minutes we had recaptured the wrinkles and gray hair of old age. Dan's mustache was in place, and the handsome young couple who had called on Lord Gort had vanished as if they never existed. Red Mike put on countryman's clothes and discarded the black-haired wig he had worn as our coachman. He lay down beneath our feet in our chaise, and we covered him with a blanket. In ten minutes we emerged from the woods and trotted sedately up the north road around that end of Lake Fergus and headed back to Limerick.

About a mile from the city, on a deserted stretch of road, Mike slipped from beneath the blanket and headed for the railway station on foot. By nightfall, if all went well, he would be in Cork. Within another day or two he would be aboard an immigrant ship for America. Mr. and Mrs. Stowecroft would take a train to Dublin and resume their sightseeing.

"What happened to you in there?" Dan said, as we left Mike behind us on the road.

"It was the blood—and the children."

Dan nodded. "I was afraid it was goin' to be messy. Shootin' a man in his own house."

"I'll never get it out of my mind."

"Yes you will. I remember the day I got my first Yank. Split his head with one swing of my saber. I was sick as a skunk for a while. Then they killed some of my friends and I killed a few more of them. It stopped botherin' me."

"How? Why did it stop?"

"It just does. You stop thinkin' about it. You tell yourself to stop and you do."

I wondered if I could ever learn to do that. Or would I hear for the rest of my life that girl's parting scream? "*You've killed my father.*" Desperately I searched within myself for my hatred. I all but prayed for it to return, to armor me once more against thought and feeling. There was nothing within me now but a hollow dread. I stared at Dan's grim warrior face beside me in the chaise. I had neither love nor hate to console me.

Honest but Not Level

Lord Gort's murder caused a tremendous furor in Limerick. The British garrison was placed on full alert. Soldiers patrolled the streets with fixed bayonets. The crime dominated the conversation at our hotel. We listened, appropriately wide-eyed, while our American friends, Messrs. Balch and Havemeyer, told us the gory story at dinner. They had gotten it from an English officer. The next morning, we rode in a hack through the tense city to the railroad station and boarded a train to Dublin. No one gave the elderly American couple more than a passing glance. In Dublin, after two more days of leisurely sightseeing, we took a steamer to London. We had scarcely time to do more than goggle at the immensity of the imperial capital. At our hotel was an expected cable from Pittsburgh informing Mr. and Mrs. Stowecroft that one of their children was seriously ill.

We sailed immediately for New York. It was a lackluster voyage. I let Dan have me when he wanted me, but I could muster neither enthusiasm nor passion. I was still numb from what I had seen and heard at Gort House. I could only wait and hope for my normal feelings to return. My mind seemed detached from the rest of me, circling my body like a moon around a planet. Again and again, it told me that I did not regret killing Lord Rodney Gort. He deserved to die for what he had done to my father, for what he and his class had done to Ireland's poor. But my body, my feelings, refused to cooperate with these assertions. The same was true of my feelings for Dan McCaffrey. I had lied to him and to myself about him in so many ways, I could no longer trick rapture from my flesh. I could only watch, in my

moon-mind, while my earthly body went through the
motions of love.

In New York we disembarked, a solemn, shuffling
pair. One would almost think our elderly disguises had
penetrated our very souls. A familiar face and voice temporarily lifted our doleful countenances. Red Mike Hanrahan came prancing toward us in a brand-new suit of
violent green and white checks, singing a favorite Irish
song, "The General Fox Chase."

> *"They searched the rocks, the gulfs and bays, the*
>   *ships and liners at the quays,*
> *The ferryboats and steamers as they were going to*
>   *sea.*
> *Around the coast they took a steer from Poolbeg*
>   *lighthouse to Cape Clear*
> *Killarney town and sweet Tralee, and then crossed*
>   *into Clare."*

"Mike," I cried, tears starting down my cheeks.
"Thank God you're safe."

"I've lit a candle or two at the side altar for you both,"
he said. "Now come on with me and collect your money.
I lost half mine last night bucking John Morrissey's tiger,
but at least I got this new suit out of it. I've bought everything new, from the inside out, in the hope of getting the
immigrant smell off me. So help me God, I don't think
I've taken so many baths in me life as I have in the past
two weeks. Steerage stink, they call it. Not a woman will
come near me."

He had us laughing halfway to Fenian headquarters.
Then he turned serious and told us that our bloody deed
had caused almost as much of a sensation in New York
as it had in Ireland. "Roberts put out a statement that
Gort had been executed by order of the Fenian Brotherhood. The newspapers have been battling over it ever

since. The Anglos—the *Times* and *Harper's* and their ilk—have been damning us, and the *Herald* saying hurrah, though not very loudly."

"The cowards," I said.

"But it worked wonders among the Irish. O'Mahoney and your brother are thrown into the shade entirely. We've shown we can strike in Ireland while they're talkin' about it."

"So the way is clear for Canada?"

"Yes and no." Mike said as we entered the noise and traffic of Broadway.

The sight of the great buildings, the hurrying pedestrians, the tumult of cartmen and coachmen and omnibus drivers, worked magically on my spirits. I wondered if it was New York, its energy, its excitement that I needed.

"What in hell does that mean?" Dan snapped.

"We've got nothing to worry about from our own dear kind. Nine out of every ten Irish are with us now. But there seem to be signs of trouble in Washington, D.C. They introduced a bill in the House of Representatives authorizing the United States to annex any Canadian province that wanted to join up. Nothing's happened to it. Everyone goes deaf when it's mentioned."

"Why?" I asked, half-knowing the answer.

"The Negro. It's all they talk about in Congress from morning till night. The Negro and the unrepentant rebels, like this bucko. I'll tell you what. Let's teach this one the act of contrition and have him stand on the Capitol steps in his Confederate uniform and recite it ten days running. It might work."

Mike gave us a crooked grin. I knew he was upset. He always blathered when he feared the worst.

"What's to be done?" I asked.

"I don't know. Roberts thinks—if that is the correct word—that there's nothin' to worry about, but I say it's time for another delegation to Washington. The British are spendin' money by the ton down there and every-where. They've speakers goin' around the country tellin' people the newspapers got it all wrong, they didn't back the Confederates in the last war, it's all a dreadful mis-understandin'. And people are listenin' to them. Even Irish people. I went to a talk by that fellow who wrote *Tom Brown's Schooldays*. Half the people were Irish. Not a one but me stood up to call him a liar when he started on about the misunderstandin' of Her Majesty's policy toward America. Our love of English literature will ruin us yet."

At Fenian Headquarters in the Moffat mansion, Presi-dent Roberts greeted us warmly. "I wish I could give you a banquet and write your name large across every news-paper in the land," he said in his oratorical style. "But it's better for your sake and the sake of the cause if your identities remain secret. The mystery will strike added terror into our enemies."

"Suits me," Dan said. "When can I get back to work with the troops?"

"Colonel O'Neil wired only yesterday, requesting your assistance in Nashville."

"I'll take a train out tonight."

"Now, now. You and your lovely partner here deserve a few days' vacation."

"I had my vacation on the boat."

The coldness in Dan's voice saddened me, but I de-served it. I thought mournfully of how I had imagined our trip home, one long orgy of love and triumph. I be-gan to wonder if I was a failure as a revolutionary or as a woman. I neither understood nor foresaw the spiritual crisis I was approaching.

"I told Bess about our troubles in Washington," Red Mike said. "She agrees we ought to go down there in force."

Roberts shook his head. He began spouting about his

"position." As president of the Fenian Brotherhood, he was a head of state, but Washington would not accord him that recognition. He would be subjecting Ireland to needless humiliation if he accepted this refusal, or involving us in needless quarrels if he insisted on recognition.

This attitude struck me as plain silly. It was like the ostrich who tried to hide from his foes by sticking his head in the sand. William Roberts was not qualified to lead a daring political enterprise. How I longed for someone with the coolness, the realism, of Fernando Wood.

I asked after Robert Johnson, from whom I'd heard nothing since our unfortunate meeting in New York. Had Roberts heard from Seward? From anyone in Congress? What was Tammany saying about it all? Roberts gazed at the ceiling. "I've been keeping Tammany at arm's length. Everything I hear about the conduct of Connolly and Tweed since they took over the city fills me with disgust. When we raise our banners high, we want no Tammany mud on them. As for Seward, he equivocates so much it's pointless to see him. Robert Johnson was never an important part of our plans. He was an insurance policy. The important thing is the proof of American backing that we have in the hands of our men—thirty thousand rifles bought from American arsenals, with enough ammunition for a ninety-day campaign, thirteen batteries of artillery of various calibers, with ammunition, a thousand miles of telegraph wire, ten thousand tents—"

He reeled off an array of statistics for a good five minutes—all the "sinews of war" that we had purchased from U.S. government arsenals, with the silent blessing of the president, the secretary of state, and the secretary of war. "How can they deny such cooperation?" Roberts asked in a tone that implied there was only one answer to the question.

"All true, all true," Red Mike said. "But could there be

any harm in me and Bess going to Washington, in an un-
official way? Not to represent the Fenian Brotherhood
but to make a full report on what we see and hear?"

Roberts could hardly say no without convicting himself of inexcusable ignorance. He agreed with the plan
and advanced the money we needed. Dan McCaffrey
watched all this manuvering with sour eyes. He was a
soldier. The politics of our enterprise did not interest
him. The answer Roberts gave to our worries satisfied
Dan. It was proof that a real army, fighting men with
guns in their hands, had been brought into being by the
Fenians. This was his reality, his profession. Beyond
that, he did not at all like the idea of my going to Washington, D.C.

Back at the hotel, with exclamations of relief we
stripped away our disguises. The crow's-feet and the
withered folds of flesh were scraped away. A bath restored the luster of my hair. Dan's gray wig and mustache hurtled into the wastebasket. I confronted my
Donal Ogue, young and handsome once more. I thought
of how he looked that first night in our doorway, his
blond hair wild with the rain and wind, the glow of battle
in his eyes. Now I saw only puzzlement and hurt. With a
gasp of pain I flung my arms around him and pressed my
head against his chest.

"Forgive me for not loving you more," I said. "Tell me
you forgive me."

"What the hell are you talkin' about?"

"You know," I said.

"You're a crazy woman, you know that?"

"I wish I was blind so I saw nothing, felt nothing, but
your hands and lips."

It was the first genuine thing I had said to him or to
anyone since my hatred possessed me. He left on the five
o'clock train for Nashville feeling a little better about his
wild Irish girl, even if she did not feel much better about

herself. Still, that hour of honesty was enough to steady my shaken nerves and restore my sense of purpose, my commitment to the Fenian Brotherhood, no matter how many doubts I had about its leaders and its goals. I told myself I would somehow find my purpose in my wounded love for Dan, in my continuing wish to strike a blow at British arrogance and greed.

I had others close to my heart to think about as well. I took my thousand-dollar payment for our murderous mission in Ireland and bought a postal money order with it. I mailed it to my sister Mary in Killarney, urging her to emigrate and bring Mother with her. I felt uneasy about using blood money this way, but I had no choice. I said nothing about seeing her in Killarney or knowing of Michael's letter. I simply said Michael and I had parted company and he was telling a great many lies about me and Annie.

Next I boarded a horsecar and rode uptown in the evening traffic to the Fifth Avenue Hotel. The room clerk looked owlish when I asked for Anne Fitzmaurice. "No one here by that name," he said after a hasty scan of his register.

"Has she left a forwarding address?"

"Eighteen Christopher Street."

I knew something was very wrong. The address was far west of Broadway in a section of New York called Greenwich Village. I hurried there in a hack. As I suspected, it was a rooming house. The landlady was a round-faced, button-nosed biddy named Mrs. Lynch. I asked for Annie, and she sniffed, "Miss Fancy? You'll find her in her room. Well soused by now, no doubt."

I hurried to the room at the end of the third-floor hall. There was no answer to my knock. At length I pounded and called, "Annie, Annie. It's me, Bess."

A thick voice answered, "Jus' a minute."

A minute turned out to be five. At last the door

opened. Annie stood there looking more dead than alive. She clutched a robe about her. She had tried to pin up her hair and touch up her face for my benefit. "Where in the world you been?" she said with a forced smile. "I went to Fenian headquarters, and they said you were on some secret assignment."

"I went to Ireland with Dan McCaffrey and killed Lord Gort," I said. "Surely you read about him being shot? I thought you'd see in a flash it was I who did it."

"Haven't been reading the papers," Annie said, turning away. "Come into my lovely apartment. Like it?"

The room was about six feet square with a window that looked out on a narrow alley. The furniture consisted of a dresser, a bed, and a single straight chair. "Annie," I said, "tell me what happened."

Annie tossed her head in an attempt to be flip. She went to the dresser and took a bottle of gin from the top drawer. "Want some?" she said.

I shook my head.

"Best thing for the glooms," she said. "That's what I got. A bad case of the glooms."

"What happened between you and Dick?"

She took a hefty swallow of the gin. "He dumped me. Not famous enough for Dick Connolly. He can get anybody now. He's number two man in the city. Actresses, socialites, everybody wants to play around with Dick. Why should he stay with tired old Annie Fitzmaurice? Used to me, Bess. Like a wife. No novelty. I made a mistake, Bess. Did I make a mistake with him."

The gin was taking effect before my very eyes. Half her words were slurred. It was horrible to watch her mouth droop, her eyes close to slits, destroying her beauty.

"Did he give you anything?"

"No. Said I'd gotten plenty. I did, but I spent it. That's why I'm down here in this—pigsty. Till I get over the glooms. Mistake, Bess. Stickin' with one man too long. Forgot what Miz Ronalds said. Keep heart—cold and private."

"You must stop this," I said, and took the gin glass out of her hand.

With an angry exclamation she snatched it back. "Don't give me orders, baby sister. I know what I'm doin'. Curin' the glooms."

"And ruining your looks."

Standing there with the gin glass clutched to her bosom, she started to cry. "Shouldn't say that. Just 'cause you're—younger."

"Annie. You're only twenty-eight."

She sat down on the bed, still weeping. "Old, Bess. That's old in this—business."

I opened the window and poured the rest of the gin bottle into the alley. "You're talking nonsense," I said. "At the very least you should be able to get a handsome sum from Mr. Connolly. Enough to set you up in a business of some sort."

She shook her head. "Dreaming Bess. I—no head for business. I want a *man*—to take care of me—to love me."

"Then go look for him. You still have all your fine clothes, your looks—"

Again, that sad demoralizing shake of the head. "Don't have the heart, Bess."

"How can you let any man do this to you? Stop it, now. Get on your best dress and we'll go have a good dinner at the Fifth Avenue Hotel or Delmonico's or wherever you please. Like as not you'll catch the eye of some handsome man and you'll be on easy street before the week is out."

She shook her head. " 'Twould only waste your money. When I get rid of the glooms I'll take matters into my own hands. I'll set myself up in a house and go it with a different one every night. I'll send Dick Connolly a list of the names at the end of each week."

I was appalled but tried not to show it. I gave up trying to persuade her to come to dinner and resolved to take matters into my own hands. I made her promise to drink no more gin and left her there for the night. The next morning I rose early and was at City Hall by nine o'clock. There was a mass of people, at least two dozen, waiting in a straggling line in the hall outside the comptroller's office. I strode past them to the inner sanctum, which was guarded by a number of clerks and assistants toiling at high writing tables, on which ledgers were spread.

"I'm here to see Mr. Connolly," I said to the nearest clerk, a plump, red-faced, squinty-eyed fellow with slicked-down black hair.

"Do you have an appointment?" he said.

"Yes," I said.

I was wearing my best daytime outfit, a black plush pelisse trimmed with beaver fur over a green silk gown. It intimidated him as much as my bold lie.

"Over there," he said, pointing to a corner office.

The comptroller was in the process of taking off his high black hat and hanging up his French-styled green sack coat with satin-faced lapels. He was surprised to see me, but he did not lose his usual aplomb.

"Well, well," he said. "The Fenian trigger girl. Shot any more lords lately?"

I shook my head. "You know why I'm here."

"To talk about Annie. Sit down."

I sat in the straight chair beside his desk. "You can't leave her this way. She's a wreck. You must know it's for love of you."

"Is it? If that's true, she shows it in strange ways. Like throwing lamps at my head."

"I might do that, but not Annie."

"You haven't seen her drunk. Really drunk. I've tried to get her to stop drinking for a good year, but this news about your father—it was just what she was looking for. A perfect excuse."

"You bastard," I said. "You know the real reason why she drinks. You won't make an honest woman of her. It's been eating away at her. And why shouldn't it? She knew you were getting her cheap because she loved you."

A hard, cruel expression settled over his face. His eyes became hooded. I had struck home, but he would not admit it to me—or perhaps to himself. "There are people waiting to see me about more important things than this."

"There's nothing more important to me. You're a wealthy man, from what I hear. You can take care of her."

"I have no sense of obligation. I bet I've given her ten thousand dollars' worth of jewelry."

"Which is worth two at the pawnbrokers. Write out a check now for twenty thousand dollars."

"Give me one reason."

"If you don't, I will shoot as many holes in you as I shot in Lord Gort. With as much pleasure."

"You've got a gun in that purse?"

"Yes," I said. It was a lie. I had come here to plead for Annie, not to threaten him.

Dick Connolly leaned back in his armchair. "I don't think you'd do it, but why should I take a chance?" He took out a large red checkbook and wrote out the check and handed it to me. It was drawn on the Tenth National Bank. "Don't worry, it won't bounce," he said. "I own the bank."

"You're rising to glory," I said, putting the check in my purse. "But what of your great talk of helping the poor Irish?"

"We have to help ourselves first. We'll help them in the long run. A lot more than you and your Fenian friends with your Canadian dreams."

"'Tis no dream," I said. "I saw the list of regiments last night at Moffat House. They've got the guns, the cannon. They're ready to march."

"Where?" Connolly said. "The whole thing's a swindle. Stanton's unloaded a million bucks' worth of guns and ammunition he doesn't need on you Fenian suckers, and Seward's just waiting for the right moment to scare Johnson into banning the whole thing. Seward thinks this will turn the Irish against Johnson and make it impossible for him to run on a Democratic ticket. Meanwhile he, Seward, washing his hands like Pontius Pilate, gets the Republican nomination and the Irish vote because he tried to help the poor feckless Fenians."

"Where is the proof of this?" I asked.

"You don't need proof if you know anything about American politics," Connolly snapped. "We told Roberts to buy the guns and ammo and lie low, drilling, organizing, until we elect our noble Saxon mayor to the governorship of New York next year. The governor of New York is always the country's prime presidential candidate. If we put John Hoffman in the White House, there's nothing we couldn't do together. Instead, Roberts is fooling around with this half-baked National Union Party and with Republicans. He thinks he can deliver the Irish vote to the party of his choice—after promising to stick with us. Bill Tweed doesn't like people who break promises."

Honest but not level, I thought, recalling Fernando Wood's summation of Roberts. "Thank you for the lecture," I said. "And the check."

"You're welcome for both," he said. "How did you get to shoot Lord Gort? By pretending to have an appointment?"

"That's a state secret."

"Say hello to Annie. Tell her I'm sorry."

In spite of his cold heart and crooked ways, I almost liked Dick Connolly.

"I'll say hello," I said.

Back I went to Annie's lodging house and mounted the stairs to knock and knock once more in vain. At last she opened the door. The room smelled like a distillery. I was furious. "You promised me you'd stop drinking," I said.

"Gin," she said. "I said I'd stop drinking gin. I thought a little Irish whiskey wouldn't hurt. I can't sleep without something, Bess."

"You can't sleep because of the worry. Here's something to banish care."

I gave her Dick Connolly's check. She stared at it blankly for a moment, then glared at me. "Where did this come from?"

"From Dick. I went to him and demanded it."

"Without asking me? Jesus God, what business is it of yours? You've ruined me with your goddamn simple-minded Fenian ways. Now he'll never come back to me. He's gone forever. You've let him write me off."

I was totally bewildered. "Annie, he let you down without a cent. He owed you at least this much. Here's money to live on for years with good management, or keep in a bank as security against hard times."

Annie kept glaring at me, shaking her head. "You're still nothing but a stupid Irish country girl. Don't you see, as long as I didn't take a cent from him, he *has* to come back to me. The guilt will eat at him forever. He loves me, and he won't be able to stand the thought of what he's done to me."

"You're dreaming, Annie," I said. "He loves nothing but the power he has now in his hands and the more power he hopes to get and the millions that will come with it. Men don't love like we do. We must take them as they are."

Slowly, proudly, Annie ripped Dick Connolly's check to shreds. She walked to the window and flung the pieces into the alley. "Get out of here," she said. "You've brought me nothing but bad luck."

I blundered down the three flights of stairs half blind with tears. The next morning I left for Washington with Red Mike Hanrahan. He blarneyed away for a half hour about his acting days, trying to cheer me up. I finally told him Annie's story. He shook his head. "She's playing a long shot. I've seen other women try it. Sometimes it works, but not often."

He took my hand in his rough grasp for a moment. "It's her life, Bess, not yours. You can't live it for her. It's fearfully hard to change grown men or women. I watch you and wonder if your heart won't break before you find that out."

"Are you talking about Dan? You don't think we're a match?"

"Listen to her. Trying to get me to talk down a wild man from Tennessee that could knock me into smithereens with a single punch. If I admit such a meaning, I can just see it coming out the next time you have a spat." He mimicked me deliciously. " 'And what's more, Mike Hanrahan says we're a sorry pair.' 'He did?' says McCaffrey and instantly hunts me up. Whop, one punch and I'm smithereens, and a few Tennessee kicks to make sure I'm well scattered."

By now he had me almost laughing. How I loved that runty Irishman. In Washington we had rooms reserved at the National Hotel. As Mike signed the register, I wrote a note to Fernando Wood and sent it up to his room. *The Fenian girl has returned in search of more wisdom.*

I could see Red Mike did not approve. "If you mention it to Dan, I'll be the one who makes smithereens of you," I said.

"I didn't see or hear a thing," Mike said. "I'm not only blind but I've gone deaf and dumb."

You Irish Aren't Part of This Country

Before I finished unpacking, a note was handed to me by one of the black bellboys. *If you are truly in search of wisdom, you have come to the wrong man and the wrong city. But if you wish to hear the latest pessimisms from a disappointed politician, he is at your service from 10:00 P.M. until you grow weary of his aged maunderings.*

While Mike went off to buck the tiger at Chamberlain's gambling house and learn what he could from the caucus of politicians regularly assembled there, I ascended to Fernando's suite on the sixth floor. He waited for me in the shadowed room, resplendent in a red silk robe with a blue velvet collar. I wore a black lace mantelet over a blue silk gown. Politely, with that ironic detachment that was his safeguard against love, he asked me if our friendship was to be conducted on the same terms as my previous visit. I coolly informed him that I still valued both pleasure and wisdom. So after another delicious late-night supper we performed the sensual ritual of bath, perfume, bed.

Without the dimension of surprise, I was less aroused than the first time. In the very midst of it, even as my breath quickened and my heart beat faster, I found myself thinking of Annie. It was a strange fate that made her so unfitted for this sort of exchange. While I, with my moon-mind watching from above, was far better suited to be a woman of pleasure.

It was a dangerous thought, the beginning of a fatalism that went back to the need to accept the murderous scene in Gort House. Dissembling now, I lay beside Fernando after the consummation and whispered, "I'm glad I don't come here often. I could fall in love with you."

He liked the compliment. He brought me a robe and sat me at the table once more to end our dining with crêpes suzette and champagne. Then he got out his brandy and his cigar and told me I was a girl when I came to him the first time. Now I was a woman. He could see it in my face, feel it in my measured response to him in bed.

"Is it because you've killed your man? Southerners believe that, you know. Of men. Perhaps it's true of women, too."

"How they fascinate you still, the Southerners," I said, preferring not to answer his question.

"They were the only aristocrats we had in this benighted country."

"I'm no lover of aristocracy."

"You mean the earldom you placed on my head the last time was a mere compliment?"

"They had their place in the old days, but these are new times."

"How true. How unfortunately true."

"How sets the political wind for Canada?"

"Foul weather is all I can see. The president and Congress are at each other's throats morning, noon, and night. The Republicans are determined to humble the South for a generation and suck every cent out of it that they and their business friends can get. The Southerners play into their hands by refusing to give any Negro the vote and secretly encouraging night-riding thugs like the Ku Klux. The president still thinks he can rally a third party—the National Union—against the fanatics of both sides, but I begin to doubt it. I can't believe that Seward, who thinks as I do, has a different opinion. As for Stanton, he's already chosen his client. As secretary of war, commander of the army, he has his foot on the South's neck. He's working with the people who want to keep it there—the Republicans."

"Doesn't the president know that?"

"It's amazing what the president doesn't seem to know. He clings to Stanton—and Seward. He doesn't seem to understand that both of them have to ruin him to get what they want. I'm beginning to think they may use the Fenians to do it."

"How?"

"By double-crossing them—and blaming it on the president."

"What would Seward gain from that? Doesn't he see that if he helps the Fenians win Canada, we'll be heroes to every Irishman in America? We can place every Irish vote in the land behind him."

"But the Irish are only ten percent of the vote. They can make a difference in a close election, but Seward no longer thinks it will be a close election. To get the Republican nomination, he has to go along with Stanton and with Congress."

I remembered what Dick Connolly said about the whole thing—selling us the guns, encouraging us to go for Canada—being a swindle. I told Fernando this theory. He laughed sourly and shook his head. "Connolly and Tweed are swindlers, so they think like swindlers. Seward thinks on a different scale. There's another reason for letting you threaten Canada. Seward is claiming that the British owe us two hundred million dollars for the damages the *Alabama* and other raiders did to our commerce. He's letting the Fenians threaten to take Canada to force the British to negotiate a settlement. If they buckle and agree, he'll sit on the Fenians and simultaneously make himself look like a diplomatic genius and a peacemaker."

"Could any man do such a thing?" I said. "Lead us on to make fools of us before the whole world?"

"I'm afraid men who think on this scale—in terms of national destinies and the part they can play in shaping them—don't worry too much about such things."

"You're one of those men, aren't you?"

He sighed and stared into his brandy. "I'm afraid I am."

"Would you do the same thing if you were in his place?"

"Probably. You Irish aren't really part of this country. You're international flotsam. As a piece of national flotsam, I recognize our kinship."

I put my brandy aside. It suddenly tasted like wormwood. "You've poisoned my pleasure this time, I fear."

"Remember you're talking to a disappointed politician. Isn't it wisdom to be prepared for the worst?"

"There's something about being Irish. Just hearing the worst seems tantamount to it happening."

"It's happened so often in the past?"

"Yes."

"There's only one way to avoid it. Wait. Do nothing. You have your guns. Let Seward and Stanton sweat. Maybe Johnson will wake up and throw them out. Maybe Connolly and Tweed will pull off their big play and land their woodenheaded Mayor Hoffman in the White House. Maybe next year this old war dog will be able to help you."

"Here in Washington?"

"In New York. I'm coming back to go another round with Tweed. There are people who think I could take Tammany Hall away from him. He's scaring a lot of people with his sloppy, greedy style."

I suspected this was only a dream. I brought Fernando

back to reality, to Washington, D.C., with a practical question. "Robert Johnson. Is he still worth my time?"

"Less and less. He's become the biggest souse in the city. Falling down drunk in the street. When he's on a real bender the president has to lock him in the White House. It's too bad. He could have been the adviser outside the cabinet that the president needs so badly."

I told Fernando about my encounter with Robert in New York. For a moment the disappointed politician lost his serenity. He sprang up and walked around the table and placed his hand against my cheek. "I feel responsible for that. It makes me ashamed of the whole male sex."

It was time to go. I rose and kissed him softly on the mouth. "Don't talk of shame. You're the only man with whom I've felt none."

Downstairs in my room I bathed again and waited for Red Mike. I heard him open his door and called to him. He reeled into my room clutching a fistful of greenbacks. "Look at that, will you?" he said. "I called the turn four times running. With that kind of luck, how can we fail to conquer the whole blithering world?"

I told him what I had heard from Fernando Wood. It sobered him momentarily. "Ah, Bess, why do you want to think about it now? Let's go get drunk and worry about it in the morning."

"What you heard is just as bad?"

"Worse," he said. "None of the congressmen or the generals take us seriously. They think it's all Irish moonshine."

"Which gives Stanton and Seward a completely free hand."

"The crown prince was there, losing a fortune. Before he got too drunk to make sense, he swore the president was still behind us. He begins to think now the Fenians are his best hope to steal a march on the Republicans and distract the country from the South and the Negroes."

"Jesus," I swore. "When I think of how often they call drink the curse of the Irish."

Everything we heard in the next few days confirmed our original gloomy information. In Congress there was nothing but rant and more rant about Southern perfidy and the rights of the Negro. The newspapers printed shocking stories about President Johnson, calling him as big a drunkard as his son, accusing him of taking bribes from Southerners, of being a traitor to his oath of office, the Union dead, the martyred Lincoln.

Johnny Coyle, head of the *National Intelligencer,* the one true friend we had among the capital's newspapermen, was inclined to agree with almost everything Fernando Wood said and added a few pessimisms of his own. "They'll risk no war with England till they've got the South well in hand. There are some of them in Congress who'd like to grab Canada, but they've small enthusiasm for letting the Irish do it. You can be sure they'll be against tryin' it while the South remains defiant. They've gone too far with their rage for punishment to get a man from the South to fight England. It might well be the other way around."

"So we must wait," I said, thinking of what Fernando Wood called the Irish in America, international flotsam. There was a bitter truth to it. We and our rage and our woes were not in step with America's history. We marched to our own grim drumbeat, and it was easy to see why the clashing rhythms could cause disaster.

"Wait," Coyle agreed. "You must lie low, and maybe Stanton and Seward will hang themselves with the rope they're trying to loop around the president's neck."

My impatience, my hunger for victory, vengeance, would not permit me to accept this advice. Fighting against it, I decided to overcome my repugnance and risk another meeting with Robert Johnson. I could think of no one else. There was no hope of getting to see the president, nor much point to it. A twenty-year-old Irish girl could hardly convince the ruler of a great nation that his two most trusted advisers were ready to betray him and ruin his chance of winning four million devoted Irish followers.

Each Monday night, Johnny Coyle had parties of friends in for supper, drinks, and cards. Most of them were congressmen. Because the *Intelligencer* supported President Johnson, Robert Johnson had been a guest in the past, before his drinking became unmanageable. Coyle agreed to risk ruining his party by inviting him again. I was to be the surprise guest of honor.

The party began well. The congressmen were all from states where the Irish vote bulked large—Illinois, Maryland, New Jersey, Pennsylvania. They toasted me and vowed they were ready to do brave things on Ireland's behalf. It was political hot air but pleasant listening. The party was well along, and supper was about to be served, when Robert Johnson appeared. He was thoroughly oiled and made straight for the sofa where I sat chatting with Coyle and a congressman from New Jersey. With the skill of a born host, Johnny instantly drew the congressman away and let me deal with the crown prince alone.

"Bess," he said. "How's my old girl?"

"If you think I'm old, you need glasses," I said. "If you think I'm your girl, you need a doctor, because you're on the verge of lunacy."

"What in hell are you talkin' about, Bess?" he gasped.

No one had treated him this way since his father became president. He had enjoyed a full year of uninterrupted adulation.

"I'm talking about you. It's the last time I'll talk about you, or to you, until you convince me that you're a gentleman. Now please go away."

All this was said in a quiet voice that attracted no attention from anyone else in the general babble of two dozen voices.

"I was a little rough with you, I guess, but I was sorta sore at the world, that night, Bess. You know what happened."

"Yes," I said. "I know what happened. I learned to despise a man about whom I had cared a great deal. I learned to loathe a touch that had once aroused me as few other men have done. Now leave me before I begin speaking in a voice loud enough for the world to hear."

He reeled off in total disarray from these thundering lies. He stayed at the party only a few more minutes, conversing abstractly with one or two congressmen, glaring across the room at me the while. The next day he appeared at my table while I was having lunch at the hotel with Mike Hanrahan. Robert was hopelessly drunk, but he babbled his devotion to me and swore he would never again abuse me.

"Love you, Bess. Love Irish girls," he said.

"I will believe you only if you prove it by escorting me in public like a gentleman and acting in private like a man of sensibility," I said. "You can't do either when you're drunk."

"I ain't drunk," he mumbled.

"You're stupidly drunk," I said. "Come back when you're sober and we'll talk."

He crept away like a chastened child. "By God," Mike Hanrahan said. "You'll make me swear off if you keep it up, Bess."

"It's the faro table that you must swear off," I said, like a true termagant.

Two days later, Robert Johnson reappeared at the hotel, his hands trembling, his lips twitching, to vow he had not had a drink in twenty-four hours. We went for a ride along Rock Creek in his chaise. It was a lovely day in late April. The trees were leafing; the wisteria and Spanish bluebells were in bloom. Robert breathed deeply and said he felt like a new man. I deserved all the credit. "I'll tell you the truth, Bess," he said. "I never thought anyone cared that much about me. I mean, I could have gotten sore, could have turned into an enemy. You cared enough about me to take a risk like that. It means a lot to me. It really does."

I was touched and a little guilty. It was sad to see how vulnerable this man was to genuine feeling. He was not vicious. He was merely a stranger to true affection. The inner life of President Johnson's family must have been a very strange affair. Robert talked about the trouble he had been causing his father, the worry and grief. Sober now, he regretted it. A kind of madness had come over him when he found he was only one among many presidential advisers. Now he thought he was ready to accept that condition. He would not forget who was responsible for bringing him back to sanity.

We discussed the Fenians, and he reiterated his support of them. He declared that he now saw them as the one hope of his father's embattled administration. The president was losing the struggle with Congress, step by inexorable step. Only some dramatic change of front, a counterassault from a new quarter, could break the momentum of events.

We paused beside the rushing waters of Rock Creek, with a field of deep blue hyacinths nearby. "I hope you'll stay in Washington and let me court you like you deserve," he said. "Give me a month. I think you'll see a Robert Johnson you might consider for a husband."

"Let me say only this," I replied. "I'll never marry until my country's freedom is won. That accomplished, I would be ready to love you forever."

Of the many lies I told in politics' name, this was the worst. But I thought I was close to a tremendous political victory. I could envision the gratitude of a president who saw his drunkard son miraculously reformed. I could imagine the energy with which this son's love could beseech his father's aid for a downtrodden people. For a week I saw Robert Johnson every day. He remained sober. The news of his reformation spread throughout Washington. Mike Hanrahan and Johnny Coyle reported the amazement of the White House watchers, the sense that something important was happening.

On the tenth day—which happened to be the last day of April—came a reaction from one of the most important of these White House watchers. A note was delivered to my room. *Mr. Seward hopes that the Fenian girl will give him the honor of escorting her to supper tonight. If agreeable, his carriage will await her at the hotel at 8:00 P.M.*

I signified my acceptance to the black coachman. It was May Eve. Exactly a year ago I had mounted history's whirlwind and begun my ride. I was imbued with a sense of destiny. My pride was in the ascendance as I stepped into Mr. Seward's carriage and began my journey through Washington's dark streets.

After thirty minutes of circuitous driving, designed to confuse me, we arrived at the house I expected—the one to which the secretary of state had brought me and Robert Johnson last summer. William Seward was waiting alone among the red gauze draperies. He rose to greet me with a bow and a quizzical smile. He had recovered completely from his injuries and wounds. There were only faint traces of the gashes left by the assassin's knife on his face and neck. The wires were gone from his jaw. His helpless arm had been restored, as he demonstrated when he drew out a chair for me. Without such distractions, I was able to better study his smooth-shaven face. In spite of his smile, I did not like it. There was a calculating quality to the small, thin-lipped mouth. The high-crowned beaked nose gave him a bird-of-prey look.

"A beautiful dress, my dear," he said as he poured me a glass of champagne. "The Fenians are obviously prosperous."

I was wearing a faille silk gown with white taffeta drapery and pearl embroidery, the latest Paris fashion, bought just before I left New York.

I laughed and said he looked ten years younger without his wounds. We dined lightly on cold chicken and ham. He talked carelessly about the pleasure of seeing me again. It had to be done this way, in private, because the British ambassador had begun to take the Fenians seriously.

"But you don't?" I said.

He paused to sip his champagne. "We Americans know you Irish far better than the British, I think. We enjoy your love of words, your fondness for vast imaginary deeds. Your enthusiasm."

I struggled to keep my temper in the face of such condescension. "Mr. Secretary," I said. "Two months ago I went to Ireland on a forged passport from your State Department. I stood before a man at about the same distance I am now from you and shot him dead. Do you think that is serious?"

He sighed and shook his head. "Fanaticism. It does not go with—it should be forbidden—beauty. Beautiful women."

He took me by the hand and led me through the red gauze curtains to the couch on the other side of the room. He sat me down on it and said, "Lean back, to the left. Drape your arm so." He showed me. Then he slowly sat down in an easy chair and gazed at me with shining eyes.

"It is uncanny," he said. "It's like returning through

the mists of time. When you sit that way, you're Rose O'Neal. I told you about her. The woman I loved until fanaticism turned her mouth sour and drew the crow's-feet of hatred around her eyes."

He went back and got us more champagne. "It's for her sake—your sake—I'm here, as much as affairs of state. I dread what will eventually happen to you. The thought of a rope around your lovely neck—or a bullet between those young breasts. It's too horrible."

"I know the risks I'm taking," I said, struggling to remain calm in spite of those awful images, trying at the same time to divine his purpose.

"You've made a notable conquest in the last two weeks. The president is tremendously relieved and grateful. For some time I've been advising him to get Robert out of Washington. I had arranged with the secretary of the navy to send him on a cruise aboard a warship, but now his miraculous reformation makes us think he might be better off in California. Providing that you went with him, as his wife. A private friend of the president is ready to contribute fifty thousand dollars to purchase a cattle ranch near Sonoma."

"Who is the private friend? Sir Frederick Bruce?"

"How clever you are, my dear," he said, with a fleeting smile. "In fact he's an American, a railroad magnate."

"Who hopes to borrow fifty or a hundred million from the British."

"My dear, we politicians are only sailors who must trim our sails to shifting winds and waves. Winds that blow millions are difficult to resist. Why should we resist them? America needs the money. It will create thousands of jobs for Irish laborers. Let me advise you, from pure affection, from nostalgia for the love of the woman I tried in vain to save. Be a little stubborn, and another fifty thousand will be placed in a private account in a

New York bank in your name. So if life in California
with Robert becomes unpleasant, you have a refuge."

"I will not be bribed—"

"My dear, we go through life bribing and being
bribed. Sometimes the medium of exchange is money,
sometimes it's power, sometimes it's love. Think for a
moment, think seriously. Who are you now? A somewhat
notorious Irish adventuress. I'm putting it in the light in
which respectable folks see you. In one stroke you're the
wife of the son of a president of the United States. Let us
hope for the best and assume that Robert conquers his
weakness, with your help. There's nothing to which he
could not aspire, in California, in the nation. With you at
his side."

I thought of my sister Annie, drinking gin in her dingy
room in Greenwich Village. Of my sister Mary, selling
milk and whiskey to tourists in Killarney. It was true. I
was nothing. William Seward was offering me—telling
me—that I had in my grasp all that a woman supposedly
wanted in life. But to take it was to betray those homely
servant girls who spent a year's savings on Irish bonds,
to turn my back on those defeated, starving beggars who
tottered beside the carriage on the road to Limerick; it
was to abandon the men on the quay at Cork to endless
years of sneers from the likes of Quackey; above all, it
was to deny I ever loved or hoped to love a man named
Dan McCaffrey, to let him and John O'Neil and the others march blindly to their deaths in Canada.

> *Donal Ogue, when you cross the water*
> *Take me with you to be your partner.*

"I'm sorry," I said. "I can't do it."

The secretary of state shook his head. "Is there something in the Irish blood that loves defeat? I sat in this

chair ten years ago and told your double why the South couldn't win the war. Her answer was 'You make me love them all the more.'"

"Perhaps our hearts are not for sale."

He made a mocking sound. "Some of your hearts, perhaps. The true ones. But a lot of others are for sale. You're honeycombed with informers. The British know your plans. They've spent at least a million to make sure you have no friends in Congress. The only friend you have left is in the White House."

"Perhaps that's the only one we need to have," I said.

Slowly, without taking his eyes from my face, he shook his head. There was such certainty, such knowledge, in the motion, my breath caught in spite of all I could do to prevent it. "Mr. Secretary," I said, "if we had a friend in the Department of State—"

"The secretary of state is only a servant of the people. Which means he's the servant of the representatives of the people, assembled in Congress."

"So we must all take our chances," I said.

"It will cause everyone needless pain. You, Robert, the president. He's a decent man but utterly out of his depth."

"I'm touched by your humanity, but I also wonder if you would expend this much time and attention on me if there were not some advantage in it for you. Perhaps a chance to try once more to become president?"

He shook his head again a bit curtly. "Good night, my dear," he said. "The coach will call for you in half an hour."

I waited, wondering what he meant by needless pain. I found out soon enough. The coach did not return in a half hour. Or in an hour. I grew more and more apprehensive, but I hesitated to plunge into Washington's unlighted, unknown streets in the middle of the night. At last I heard the clop of horse's hoofs. A key turned in the lock. Robert Johnson stared stonily at me.

"So it's true," he said. "You're in cahoots with them. Stanton and Seward. A friend told me that yesterday. I laughed at him. Tonight he sent me a note, telling me I'd find you here."

"No, Robert," I said, hearing the feebleness of my denial even as I spoke it. "Seward asked me here to try to bribe me away, but I refused. I said my love for you was not for sale."

"He could have offered you that—and you could have refused him—in the dining room of the National Hotel. Or in his office at the State Department. Why here? There's only one explanation. What you sell can only be delivered here."

He whirled away and started for the door. Passing the table, he saw a half-empty champagne bottle. He put it to his lips and drained it. He wiped his mouth and looked at me one more time. "Whore," he said, and strode into the night.

I pleaded for a chance to explain. He mounted his horse and rode away as if I did not exist. I followed him to the end of the block and then wandered aimlessly for the better part of an hour until I found a main street. Another half hour of trudging with my high-heeled shoes in hand finally led me to a cabstand before a second-rate hotel. It was 2:00 A.M. by the time I reached the National Hotel.

Red Mike Hanrahan was not in his room. I went to John Chamberlain's and dragged him away from the faro table. "Just in time," he said. "I was about to go a thousand in the hole."

I told him what had happened. "Wurra, wurra," he said. "Let's go look for the crown prince."

As we hurried to the door, the sound of angry voices carried over the usual hubbub. Robert Johnson swayed in the entrance hall, arguing loudly with the burly Irishman in evening clothes who guarded the door. "I'm sorry, Mr.

Johnson," he said. "Mr. Chamberlain left strict orders not to let you in when you're drunk."

. For a reply he got a stream of obscenities and insults. "I ain't drunk. It takes two days to get a man from Tennessee drunk. I only just started."

"Robert," I said, stepping forward. "Will you listen to me?"

He squinted at me. "Jesus," he said. "I didn't know they let Irish whores in here."

Beside me Red Mike muttered, "Let me hit him. Let me hit him just once."

I shook my head and hurried him into the night. "There's only one recourse now," I said. "We must convince Roberts to give up Canada for a year."

"Not a chance," Red Mike said.

A Good Little Army

Three weeks later, obeying orders with a heart that scarcely beat, it was so heavy in my breast, I sent a coded telegram to John O'Neil in Nashville: YOU ARE HEREWITH ORDERED TO HAVE YOUR REGIMENT IN BUFFALO N.Y. NO LATER THAN 6:00 A.M. JUNE 1. I sent similar telegrams to colonels in Indiana and Ohio, Maryland and Pennsylvania. A final telegram went to the commander of the Fenian regiment raised in Buffalo itself. In spite of my prophecies of doom and pleas of dissuasion, the Fenian Brotherhood was invading Canada.

I had not been ignored. Our president, William Roberts, and his cabinet had listened politely to my report from Washington. In their minds they had disqualified me in advance. I was a woman, hence emotionally unstable in their masculine eyes. Worse, I was the sister of the hated Michael Fitzmaurice, their most savage critic. No matter that Red Mike Hanrahan confirmed everything I said about our lack of support in Congress, the opposition of Stanton and Seward. They suspected Mike, too, because of his connection with me. Some of them may have half-wondered if I had not seduced him. Others hinted that I had become Michael's secret ally and was trying to subvert the men of action.

The decisive vote belonged to William Roberts. If he had suspicions he did not voice them. He seized instead on the undeniable fact that we still had President Johnson's support. "That's all we need," he said. "That will give us the week we need to reach Toronto." We could not be stopped, he said, without an order from the president, embodied in a proclamation of neutrality. This the president would not issue until we secured Toronto, the capital of the province of Ontario, which guaranteed us mastery of the rest of British America.

It was Roberts's optimism that carried the day. The cabinet voted unanimously to proceed with our plan. So the telegrams went out, and a few days later Red Mike Hanrahan and I took a ferry to Jersey City, where we boarded an Erie train for Buffalo. We carried with us a proclamation to the people of Canada, which we were to issue when our troops crossed the border. The two of us were to preside over a Fenian press office to procure, as far as possible, kind words in the newspapers.

All day the train rattled and clanked along the Pennsylvania border and then swung west through Oneonta and Binghamton, into the vast distances of upstate New York. Previously, in traveling across Ohio and Indiana to Chicago, I had found American vistas exhilarating. Now the very size of this vast country—three Irelands could be tucked into this single state of New York—intimidated and discouraged me. I continued to fear the worst.

Red Mike had changed his mind. Roberts had convinced him we might succeed in spite of our enemies in Washington. "There aren't five thousand British regulars in all Canada," he pointed out, "while we've got thirty thousand veteran troops. A good third of the regulars are Irishmen, which would scare the bejesus out of me if I was the British commander." The British had raised some four thousand Canadian volunteers, but these could be discounted almost entirely. They only had one squadron of cavalry and no engineers or supply or signal units. They were "show soldiers," fit only for parades.

Mike told me more about our battle plan. Our main army would gather in Buffalo and launch the invasion by seizing the village of Fort Erie, just across the Niagara River. Fort Erie was the terminus of several railroad lines, which would enable us to move swiftly into the heart of Ontario. Meanwhile, detachments would make demonstrations at a half dozen other points along the border in Vermont and in eastern New York, opposite the province of Quebec. They would force the enemy to further divide his small force of British regulars and Canadian volunteers.

By the time we reached Buffalo at midnight, I was half hopeful. I slept away the weariness of the long ride and emerged to bright sunshine and a grand welcome from the Fenians of that thriving city. I was taken to lunch by a half dozen women who were leaders of the local Fenian Sisterhood. I was especially charmed by Ellen Bailey, the pretty red-haired wife of Michael Bailey, the lieutenant colonel of the Buffalo regiment. She and her friends told me that they had raised over a hundred thousand dollars for the cause and showed me a flag they were about to present to their local regiment. It was a beautiful green silk banner, with a gold harp and sunburst in its center, and beneath it the words "7th Regiment, Irish Army of Liberation." Their fresh faces, their sweet brogues, the high expectation with which they regarded me, were in painful contrast to my fears and doubts. I masked my dark thoughts behind smiles and was soon talking as enthusiastically as William Roberts himself.

As we emerged from the Continental Hotel, I was aghast to see a newsboy waving a paper and shouting, "Hey, read about d'Fenian army in Buffalo." Beneath a black headline the paper, the *Buffalo Express*, gave an alarmingly accurate account of our plans. "Oh, don't worry about it," smiled Ellen Bailey. "The paper is owned by an Englishman. He's been writing that kind of tale every other week for months. It's the old story of wolf, wolf. No one will listen to him."

"Anyway," said another woman, "we have friends on this paper." She handed me a copy of the *Commercial Advertiser*, which had a story ridiculing the very idea of the Irish invading Canada. From the hotel we rode to the Pearl Street auction rooms of Patrick O'Day, a leading Fenian. Along the way Ellen Bailey pointed out to me the opulent houses and business offices of Buffalo's numerous wealthy Irish. At the auction rooms, Patrick O'Day, handsome and gray-haired, walked me through rooms filled with unopened chests. He raised the lid of one, and I gazed at a nest of gleaming U.S. Army rifles.

"How many have you got here?" I asked.

"Twenty thousand," said O'Day with a grin. "We've been advertising a tremendous sale of military stores on the first of June. The federal district attorney was down here pokin' about. But what could he say? He'll find out too late that the sale's goin' to be in Toronto."

Everyone was so confident, it was agony to remember the slow, certain shake of William Seward's head. Could so much hope, effort, and expense end in failure? Did we not have some credit with the fates, for our seven centuries of suffering?

Patrick O'Day began gleefully rubbing his hands and talking about the fortune he expected to make in Canada. There were bound to be some die-hard Canadians who resisted our conquest. Their property would be confiscated, as the North had done with the rebels in the South. He expected to have and enjoy the business of selling the goods and chattels of these "royalty lovers." There would be a really tremendous sale! I thought of Michael's maledictions on Irish-American greed and grew anxious again.

I spent the latter part of the afternoon going down to see the chief attraction of the region, Niagara Falls. It was worth the trip, although my mind was hardly relaxed enough to play the carefree tourist. I pondered the great cataract while Mrs. Bailey, with typically American enthusiasm, recited to me the staggering statistics of the number of gallons that went over the precipice hourly, daily, weekly. My anxiety found it a somehow menacing symbol, a fit companion to the image of history as a whirlwind that Fernando Wood had fastened on my mind. Was I, were all of us, likely to be swept away by this American torrent we were trying to leap? Would we end here, shattered flotsam, at the bottom of this cataract?

That night there was a Fenian rally in St. James Hall. The place was packed. At least six thousand men and women cheered wildly when I was introduced and roared their enthusiasm when Patrick O'Day, the chief speaker of the evening, boldly predicted that Canada would be ours in a week's time. Behind him, assistants drew back a curtain displaying a large map of the British provinces. "You may come up here while refreshments are being served," O'Day said, "and pick out your farms now."

"Mr. Chairman," called a voice from the rear. "Mr. Chairman."

I knew who it was, even before he stood up. My brother, Michael.

"Mr. Chairman," he said. "I, too, am a member of the Fenian Brotherhood. I have in my pocket telegrams from ten Fenian circles in Canada, begging you to abandon this criminal scheme to invade their country. They testify, with an ardor which anyone must respect, that Canada is their adopted homeland, just as yours is the United States. They fear that you will bring ruin and shame on themselves and their children."

I had no doubt that Michael had the telegrams. Among his many faults, lying was never claimed against him by anyone.

Cries of rage erupted from all quarters of the hall.

"Throw him out."

"Shove his head up his ass where it belongs."

"He's a British spy."

Bruisers from the Buffalo 7th Regiment came racing down the aisles and climbed over shrieking women to get at Michael, who was already struggling with two or three men near him in the seats. They dragged him out, still shouting, "Irish men and women, listen to me, Ireland's honor is the question here—"

I rushed from the stage and up a side aisle, remembering the black soldier in Vicksburg. Would I step into the night and find my brother sprawled dead beneath the gas lamps? I doubt if Michael would have met such a fate then, but I undoubtedly saved him from a very bad beating. I reached the street just as a fellow twice his size stretched him on the ground with a terrific punch in his face.

"Stop," I said. "He's my brother. I give you my word, he'll leave Buffalo on the first train out tonight."

They dragged Michael to his feet and all but threw him at me. "He's yours," growled the fellow that struck him. "If he's still here in the morning, it's over the falls with him."

Michael teetered away from me. Blood streamed from his nose over his chin onto his white shirt. "I don't want

any help from *you*," he snarled. "You billingsgate harri-
dan. Underneath your painted face I see the whorehouses
of New York and Washington."

"You must accept my help or take something much
worse," I said in a low voice. I hailed a cab and ordered the
driver to take us to the railroad station. All the way there,
Michael ranted against me and the attack on Canada. He
said he had just spent a month there. The Irish were happy
and contented. They were more respected and prosperous
than in the United States. There were no Sixth Ward slums
in Toronto or Montreal.

At the station, I learned there was a train leaving in an
hour. I sat with him, letting him talk. He spouted his defiance of the men who had beaten him up. He was not
afraid of them. He was half inclined to stay in Buffalo in
spite of them.

"Those men are going over the river tomorrow or the
next day to risk their lives for Ireland," I said. "Only a
fool would ignore their threats."

As we blazed at each other, a familiar voice with the
accents of Tennessee interrupted us. "What the hell is
goin' on here?"

Boldly, with a mind to deliberately insulting
Michael, Dan McCaffrey drew me to my feet and kissed
me. "What's he doin' here?" he growled, his arm still
around me.

Dan looked tired and gaunt. It was clear that he was
tense with worry and the expectation of battle. I tried to
describe Michael's intrusion in neutral tones. Dan
grabbed him by his blood-spattered shirt. "You son of a
bitch," he said. "I've been wantin' to put a bullet between
your eyes for a good six months. Don't give me another
excuse."

The stationmaster began calling the New York train.
We escorted Michael to it and saw him aboard without
further argument. Watching the red lantern on the rear

car sway into the night, Dan growled, "You should've let them send him over the falls."

"Are the regiments coming in?"

"They got off the train at the Union Iron Works, about a mile down the line," he said. "They're comin' into town in groups of forty or fifty so as not to attract too much attention."

"How many are with you?"

"About two thousand. There'll be another four thousand tomorrow night, and four more the night after. The railroads can't handle more'n that at a time."

We got in a hack. I told the driver to take us to my hotel. "No," Dan said. "I got to spend the night with the men."

"You look like you could use a little rest and supper," I said.

I felt a wish, probably more a need, to love him with our old emotion.

He looked without interest at Buffalo's wide, dark streets. "They're good men," he said. "We got a good little army."

"Not too little, I hope," I said.

"Little by General Lee's standards. Thirty thousand men. Probably twenty thousand will show up here. Can't expect more than that. A man has to quit his job, maybe sell his business." He was silent for a while. "A lot of people are doin' things like that, Bess. We're askin' a lot of people to tear up their lives for this thing. It's got to work."

"Yes," I said. "It's got to."

My hopes, borne on my wounded wishing love for him, temporarily banished my doubts and fears. I decided not to mention these to him.

At the hotel, he bathed while I had a cold supper sent up to the room. He asked for whiskey with it and drank a glass, with no visible effect. As he drew back his chair from the table, I sat down in his lap and kissed him. "As

I said once before," I whispered, "if you want me you can have me."

He smiled and shook his head. "Too tired, Bess," he said. "I've been goin' eighteen hours a day. Drillin', recruitin', travelin' all over Tennessee, Kentucky, Indiana, Ohio, Illinois."

He kissed me briefly on the neck. "We'll make a date. The best room in the biggest hotel in Toronto or Montreal."

I suddenly wanted him, not with the vague blind romance of the virgin but with the explicit desire of the mature woman. "I didn't know war did such things to men," I said.

"What the hell does that mean?" he said.

"Nothing," I said. "I was only joking."

"Hell of a joke," he said.

He drank off another half glass of whiskey and put on his sooty coat and dirty shirt. "I'm gonna have to wear this when we go over. Others are wearin' their Union uniforms. Rebel gray wouldn't mix too good."

"I wish I could go with you."

"Margaret O'Neil's the only woman we're takin'. A nurse."

"I'll go with her."

"You? The sight of blood turns your legs to jelly."

"I'll go with her. You'll see."

"Now wait a minute. If the British grab you, they'll find out pretty quick you're wanted for murder."

"The same applies to you."

"They'll never take me alive."

"Oh, God."

I clung to him shaking, all my fear and dread and doubt beating in me.

"Who was it in Washington this time? Old Seward himself?"

I stepped back as if he had struck me. "No one," I said. "I didn't let a man touch me."

I didn't realize I was telling a lie until the words were spoken. Somehow my visits to Fernando Wood had no relation to my real life, our troubled love.

"Okay," he said. "We've really got a date in Toronto."

He kissed me and went to his men, leaving me alone with my tears.

God Be on the Road with You

The next morning, I had breakfast with Red Mike Hanrahan and John and Margaret O'Neil. Mrs. O'Neil greeted me with the coolest possible smile, while her husband leaped to his feet to give me a warm embrace. Margaret began talking down the expedition. She was sure it was going to fail and the result would be nothing but slaughter. O'Neil tried to make a jest of her pessimism, calling her "Mrs. General" and reminding her that she took the same gloomy view of Sherman's march to the sea in the Civil War.

"She was sure I was never going to come back from that alive," O'Neil said. "She was all but sending packages to the Sisters of Mercy in Charleston to smuggle into the prison camp at Andersonville for me."

"When will you attack, Colonel?" I asked.

"In two nights, if all goes well."

A ragged lad came through the hotel dining room selling copies of the *Buffalo Express*. Red Mike Hanrahan bought one and growled when he took a look at the front page.

"The first play by our friends in Washington," he said.

He pointed to an advertisement by the collector of customs for the port of Buffalo. It announced that no ship or boat would be permitted to clear the port without special inspection and prohibited the departure of all vessels from the harbor between 4:00 P.M. and 9:00 A.M.

"How do you know it's from Washington?" asked John O'Neil. "It may be just some federal busybody here in Buffalo. We'll call a council of war and work out alternate plans."

"Let's get to it," said Mike, and the two men instantly left me at the table with Mrs. O'Neil.

"I understand you're going to go with the army as a nurse," I said. "May I assist you?"

"Have you had any hospital experience?"

"None," I said, "but I would be happy to serve as cook and bottlewasher. Whatever duties you assign me. I've given a year of my life to this great effort, and I'd like to be part of it now, whether we march to defeat or victory."

She shook her head. "You'd probably faint or do something equally foolish."

I left her nibbling smugly on a roll, wondering once more how a man as fine as John O'Neil had fallen into the clutches of such a woman. As I stormed through the lobby, I heard a voice calling my name. "Bess Fitzmaurice?" Rising from a leather armchair was my reporter friend George Pickens. He was as cocky and debonair as he was the day he stepped aboard the *Manhattan*.

"Is it Pickens of the *Herald?*" I asked sarcastically.

"Now of the *Tribune,*" he said.

"They don't lie as assiduously as the *Herald,* as far as I can judge. Won't that cause you problems?"

"What's your bark?" he said. "I made you famous. What's happening up here?"

"The Fenians are invading Canada," I said.

He laughed heartily. "Come on, give me the corner. Everyone knows the Fenians would have trouble invading Staten Island."

"I see you're well informed. Why bother to ask me anything?"

"I need the corner. Are you running low on money? Are the Republicans sending you up here to put the screws to the president?"

"Do you want the God's honest truth?"

"Sure."

"We've come up here to fish in Lake Erie."

I left him spluttering and went down to the docks, where Dan had told me the men were being quartered in warehouses and hiring halls. There were hundreds of them lounging about in the spring sunshine. I asked them if they knew Major McCaffrey. Several of them laughed. One red-haired lad said: "Everybody knows Major Mc-Caffrey. There isn't a man here who wasn't cussed out by him at least once."

"So you hate him cordially?"

"The devil you say. He's the best officer we've got. The men would follow him anywhere."

A short, swarthy, scowling man in a business suit interrupted us. "Where are you fellows from?" he said.

"What business is it of yours, my friend?" asked the red-haired lad.

"My name is Dart. I'm the federal district attorney for northern New York. They tell me you crazy Irishmen are going to invade Canada. Is that true?"

"Some of us are thinking of going over the border to look for work. Isn't that right, lads?"

There were nods of assent from those around him. Dart sniffed skeptically. "There's a law against it, you know. The Neutrality Act. It's a crime to wage war against a friendly nation from the soil of the United States."

"Since when is the British tyrant a friendly nation?" said the red-haired lad, getting to his feet. He towered over the federal district attorney. His companions rose, too, their Irish tempers rising with them.

"Mr. District Attorney," I said, "it's a bit early in the season for a swim. If you don't want to take one, I think you'd be wise to go back to your office and shuffle your papers."

"Who are you?"

"A close friend of President Johnson," I said. "I saw him but three days ago in Washington. He told me there was nothing he wanted more than to see Canada conquered and the wrongs the British worked on this country during the war avenged."

The district attorney's eyes bulged. I could see his mediocre brain sifting the possibility that this well-dressed young woman was telling the truth. Doubt and the threatening scowls of the red-haired lad and his friends persuaded him to retreat, muttering.

"Is that the truth?" asked the red-haired lad.

"Close to it," I said. .

His name was Hennessy. He was a Fenian captain. From Indiana, he had fought as a cavalry sergeant in the last two years of the Civil War, marching with Sherman to the sea. His father owned a tavern in Terre Haute. He had borrowed ten thousand dollars on it and put the money into Fenian bonds, so great was his enthusiasm for the cause. If we failed, the Hennessys, father and son, would be bankrupt. Captain Hennessy pointed to other men who had quit good jobs on street railways, in stores and mills, one who had sold his farm to join the expedition. All believed that the government of the United States was behind us.

John O'Neil, Dan, and Lieutenant Colonel Michael Bailey arrived in a carriage. They wore confident smiles, which did not diminish when Hennessy told them about the retreat of District Attorney Dart. "We've been to see the collector of the port. He told us to be easy, he's only trying to protect his skin," Colonel Bailey said. "The same goes for Dart. He's a mean little weasel."

Hennessy told them how my reference to President

Johnson had discomfited Dart. The chunky, dark-haired Bailey nodded cheerfully. "That's all he needs to make him run for cover."

Hoping he was right, I left the officers with their men and returned to the hotel. There I found Red Mike Hanrahan deep in conversation with George Pickens. "This fellow says you wouldn't even give him the pinky when he asked you a straight question."

I was in no mood to struggle with American slang. I was feeling very Irish. (I later found out "giving the pinky" means making a promise to tell the truth.) "I gave him the back of my hand," I snapped. "He said the Fenians couldn't invade Staten Island."

"I was only kidding, sweetheart," Pickens said. "Mike here's changed my tune. I'm going to burn up the wires. Thanks, Mike."

He rushed away to the telegraph office. "You've got to control that temper of yours," Mike said. "He's the kind of reporter we need on our side."

"How much did you pay him?" I said.

"Not necessary," Mike said. "His paper's behind us. He says they want us to teach the British a lesson about neutral rights."

"Hurrah."

"Still fearing the worst?"

I told him about District Attorney Dart. Mike nodded glumly. "He's been telegraphing Washington every hour," he said.

"How do you know?" I asked.

"The telegraph office is staffed entirely by Irishmen. We get a copy of everything that goes out of Buffalo."

At that moment, a boy of about fourteen came panting in the door. He handed Mike an envelope, which he promptly opened. "Holy Toledo," he said as he read its contents.

He handed it to me. It was a copy of a telegram.

> *Gen. Barry is here and in command from Buffalo to*
> *the mouth of the Niagara River. The State authorities*
> *should call out the militia on the frontier to prevent*
> *hostile expeditions from the U.S. and to save private*
> *property from destruction by mobs.*
>
> U. S. Grant

Ulysses Grant, commander-in-chief of the United
States army, the man whom the Fenians had gone out of
their way to fete and fuss over in New York and Washington, D.C. "What's he doing in Buffalo?" I asked.

I answered my own question. "Stanton sent him. It
shows how serious they are. Who's General Barry?"

"He was commander of the artillery in the Army of
the Potomac, one of Grant's right-hand men. A West
Pointer."

"What can they do? Do they have troops here?"

"Scarcely a company. That's why he wants New York
state to call out the militia. We must wire Roberts. We
have men in Albany who can deal with the governor,
even if he is a Republican."

"Will the governor refuse General Grant himself?"

"He won't hear from Grant," Mike said. "The general's thinking of running for the presidency. He won't
show his face in this thing and lose himself the Irish
vote." He thought for a moment, fingering Grant's telegram. "I'll give this to Pickens for a beat in tomorrow's
paper. He'll find out where Grant's going. He'll go
straight to Barry and ask him."

"I thought Grant was all for us taking Canada."

"No doubt he was until he talked to Stanton and Seward. The man's a political child. Spent his whole life in
the army."

We were playing a game of continental chess, with
thousands of lives, the future of nations, in the balance. I

rushed to the telegraph office to wire Roberts, ordered the hack to wait, and then raced to the docks to find John O'Neil and Dan. I told them what was happening. They were stunned.

"I thought they were with us," O'Neil said. "The president promised me. You were there. Dan was there."

"Obviously the president is not in control of his government," I said.

"Can't we send him a telegram?" Dan asked. "Tell him what's happenin'?"

John O'Neil shook his head. "All the telegrams go through Stanton. The War Department. That's the way it was during the war. I doubt it's changed."

"Stanton has made sure it hasn't changed," I said. "You can depend on it."

"There's only one thing to do," O'Neil said. "We must cross the river with the men we've got here. Tonight."

"That will barely make us equal to the Canadians. And none of our artillery has arrived," Dan said.

"No matter," O'Neil said. "If we begin the game and show them that we mean business, they won't dare stop us. The country will rise to cheer us on. You've seen how many people have come down here to wish us well. Not all Irish, by a long ways."

Faith, I thought, the whole thing was being run on faith and love, and I had none, or very little of both. I thought of the young, smiling, believing faces I had seen this morning. I flinched at the sight of Dan's saturnine countenance. He did not have much of these two spiritual virtues either. Defeat and death had withered them in his soul. We were well matched, for once.

"What the hell," Dan said. "We've come this far."

That was the gambler speaking. The hard, empty voice made me shudder. I preferred John O'Neil's faith. "You may be right, John," I said to him.

Back at the hotel, Mike was in the lobby, talking with Pickens again. They waved me over to them. "I told you this newshound would sniff out the truth. Grant stayed only long enough to send that telegram and give Barry his orders. He's already left for the West."

"What's Barry doing?" I asked.

"He's trying to get two companies of New York militia to report for duty, but he's having a hell of a time," Pickens said. "They're all with the Fenians. Or afraid to be against them."

"We've arranged with our friends in Buffalo to send out a few warnings," Mike said dourly.

I decided to reward Pickens for his help with Grant. I told the news of the decision to cross the river tonight.

"Where?" Pickens asked.

"I don't know. Someplace outside the port, no doubt."

"We'll take you there," Mike promised.

I spent the rest of the day setting up the press office in the hotel room next to mine. I unpacked printed copies of our proclamation and newspaper stories about the Fenians. I hung flattering portraits of President Roberts and heroic Irish leaders of earlier eras on the walls, hoping to suggest that our man was the equal of Wolfe Tone and Robert Emmet.

About 6:00 P.M., I descended to the lobby to find reporters from a half dozen New York papers milling about comparing notes. Several recognized me and rushed to surround me, shouting questions. "The press office will be open for business tomorrow," I said. "Until then I can tell you nothing."

"Are you invading Canada with your boyos, Miss Fenian?"

I turned to confront William Colby's sneering face. "I only wish I could," I said.

"I think you'll find your little popgun no match for British breech-loading cannon," he said. "But if your conduct in Washington is any indication, maybe you plan to use other tactics to distract the British. There are only five thousand regulars in Canada. You should be able to exhaust them in a night."

I saw smirks on several faces. They were eager to believe the whole affair was a joke, with a little smut thrown in to make it more entertaining. "There's only one thing you need to show your true colors, Mr. Colby," I said. "A red coat with a yellow stripe down the back."

That night, as darkness fell, I slipped from my room and descended a back stairs to the alley behind the hotel. I found Pickens and Mike Hanrahan waiting in a chaise. We went briskly through the twilight to the docks. As we arrived, we saw the Fenians in column formation heading toward the water. There, to the shouted orders of Dan McCaffrey, they performed various evolutions and drills. Beside me, I heard Pickens mutter, "By God, they're real soldiers."

Dan dismissed them with a stentorian bellow. They split into groups of fifty and vanished into the side streets to the north. We followed them at a discreet distance for two miles and reached the suburb of Buffalo known as Black Rock. There were more docks along the swift-flowing Niagara. Puffing quietly at one wharf were two steam tugs. Behind them were four long, narrow Erie Canal boats. The men formed in ranks once more, and John O'Neil stood on a box to give them a brief talk.

"We will soon be in enemy territory. We must remember that it is peopled largely by our friends, and by people whom we hope to make our friends. The man who steals from a civilian or abuses a woman will be shot on the spot. Our only enemies are men wearing the uniform of the tyrant who has despoiled our homeland."

Dan McCaffrey now took charge. He called out a half dozen companies by their captain's names—"Hennessy of the 17th, Murphy of the 13th"—and they moved swiftly down the wharf to the lead canal boats. Other companies were ordered to unload seven or eight wagons of ammunition and carry it aboard one of the canal boats. The tug at the head of the wharf, towing the canal boat with the picked troops, moved into the darkness. It took an hour for the working parties to load the other canal boats. Dan came over to our carriage as the task neared completion. "We're takin' an extra thousand rifles with us," he said to Mike Hanrahan. "It'll make it easier for the reinforcements to reach us tomorrow."

"You expect more than a thousand tomorrow, do you not?" Mike asked.

Dan nodded. "Send over the ones who seem most rested. They should all have a day's rest after ridin' those trains."

I sprang from the cab and flung my arms around him. "All will be well," I said. "We'll celebrate in Toronto."

"Sure," he said, and kissed me perfunctorily.

"Good luck, soldier," Mike called.

The tug was getting up steam as Dan walked slowly down the wharf. He stepped aboard the last canal boat as they untied it from the piling. I thought he raised his arm in farewell. Then he was swallowed by the darkness on the river. *God be on the road with you*, I prayed.

The Great American Betrayal

We waited there beside the black rushing river for another two hours. There was not a single sound of war from the Canadian shore, not a gunshot or a battle cry. We thought it was strange. There was supposed to be a detachment of Canadian volunteers on guard in the village of Fort Erie. At last the tugs chugged out of the night. We rushed down the wharf to greet them. The captains and deckhands were all Irish, with thick Connemara brogues. They told us Fort Erie was ours. The Canadian volunteers had been totally surprised and surrendered without a shot.

"Sure there wasn't a peep from a soul," one captain told us. "Except some lads fishin'. They sprang from the bank like the very devil was after them and leaped into their wagons. We could hear them yellin' and drummin' on their wagon boxes goin' up the road. No doubt they're arousin' the countryside."

"That's not good news," Mike growled. "We're depending on getting enough horses to mount half the men."

"I doubt they'll get it now. 'Twon't be a farmer that hasn't got his best horses into the woods before morning."

"The railyard. Did they alarm them, too?"

"I don't know," said the tug captain, lighting his pipe. "The whole thing's daft, if you want my opinion. When we come down from the harbor this evenin', the word was out that the Englishman, the new captain of the *Michigan*, and that Federal general was tryin' to hire tugs to close the river. What do we do then?"

"What new captain of what *Michigan*?" Mike asked.

"The revenue cutter *Michigan*. Come down from Erie last night. They took the captain off her last week. A good Irish-American named Malone. Put an Englishman in command. Captain Bryson. Should hear the bugger talk. Straight from St. James, so help me."

We rode back to the hotel in a state of shock. "An Englishman," I said. "Why didn't someone tell us?"

"The Buffalonians think all can be managed by local politics. They don't know the stakes," Mike said.

"I'll put it in my dispatch," said Pickens. "It may help if they print it."

There was no sleep that night. The next morning, feeling more dead than alive, I opened the press office and released to the newspapers the proclamation to the Canadian people. It was written by William Roberts in his most oratorical style. The main points of our policy were clear enough within the soaring rhetoric. We tried to assure the Canadians that we were not trying to steal their country. "Our work for Ireland accomplished, we leave to your own free ballots to determine your natural and political standing." But we intimated strongly that we were anxious to "make these limitless colonies spring from the foot of a foreign throne, independent and as proud as New York, Massachusetts, and Illinois."

The heart of the proclamation and the heart of our hopes was the appeal to the Irish within Canada.

> *To Irishmen throughout these provinces we appeal in the name of seven centuries of British iniquity and Irish misery and suffering, in the name of our murdered sires, our desolate homes, our desecrated altars, our millions of famine graves, our insulted name and race, to stretch forth the hand of brotherhood in the holy cause of fatherland and smite the tyrant where we can in his work of murdering our nation and exterminating our people. I conjure you, our countrymen who from misfortunes inflicted by the very tyranny you are serving or for any other reason have been forced to enter the ranks of the enemy, not to be an instrument of your country's death or degradation. If Ireland still speaks to you in the truest impulses of your hearts, Irishmen, obey her voice. No uniform, surely not the blood-dyed coat of England, can emancipate you from the natural law that binds you to Ireland, to liberty, to right, to justice. Friends of Ireland, of humanity, we offer you the olive branch of peace, the grasp of*

friendship. Take it, Irishmen, Frenchmen, Americans,
take it and trust it.

The thought that those noble words, all that passion
and hope, might be wasted made me heartsick. It could
not happen! By pure force, I willed myself to believe in
victory. That made it no easier to endure the press office,
the stupid questions of smirking reporters like Colby.

"How many leprechauns did you bring with you?"

"What will the boyos do for whiskey over there?

"When was the last time the Irish won a battle—the
year 1200?"

"Go to hell, the lot of you," I said, and left them there
drinking our whiskey. I rushed to my room, put on an old
worn traveling dress, and took a hack to Black Rock.
There I found Red Mike Hanrahan, Patrick O'Day, and
other Buffalo Fenians before the wharf from which the
army had departed the night before. It was, I saw by daylight, the dock for a steam ferry, which ran from the village of Black Rock to the village of Fort Erie, directly
opposite it on the Canadian shore. The ferry was at the
dock as I joined Mike. Just offshore, at anchor, was another vessel, flying the American flag. It was a small,
squat craft with a single smokestack and sidewheels.
Ugly black cannon peered from gunports on the side. It
was close enough to read its name on the bow: U.S.S.
Michigan.

All but knowing the worst before I asked the question,
I rushed to Mike. "Have they cut us off?"

"From here," he said grimly. "But we have hopes of
getting something across from other points. They can't
cover the whole river with that pipsqueak boat. There's a
lower ferry where people cross by rowboat. We've sent
over a good hundred men that way."

"When you need two thousand. Where are our tugs?"

He pointed down the river. "At Pratt's Wharf. Watch now. We'll see what our lime-juicer captain does."

Following his finger; I saw the tugs, with wisps of steam coming from their stacks, beside this wharf, a half mile down the river. The four canal boats were beside them. Suddenly one of the tugs swung into the river and men appeared on the lead canal boat to heave a fat tow-line to seamen on the stern of the tug. Two canal boats left the dock and followed the tug toward the Canadian side.

A tremendous shriek burst from the *Michigan*'s stack. Seamen raced along its decks to haul in the anchor. The Fenian tug ignored the warning and continued to plow straight for the opposite shore. "Are there men aboard them?" I asked.

"No. Just ammunition and food. The farmers have stripped the countryside of their cattle for miles around," Mike said.

"Where are the reinforcements?"

"In the fields behind the village," Mike said, gesturing to the houses of Black Rock.

Premonitions of disaster began to grow strong in me again. "Has Margaret O'Neil gone over there yet?"

"No. John sent word forbidding it. But there's two doctors going on this ferry."

"I'm going with them," I said.

"Why, for God's sake?"

"If they're going to die over there, I want to die with them. With Dan."

"Jesus God." Mike turned away from me and walked ten steps and back again. "Do you want to break my heart entirely?" he said, wiping his eyes.

The *Michigan*'s anchor was up. Its sidewheels thrashed the river furiously as it headed downstream after the Fenian tug and her two barges. It was clear that the tug would be more than halfway over before the *Michigan* got close to her. Bells clanged aboard the revenue cutter, and her forward progress came to an abrupt halt. The captain had changed his mind.

"There's some tricky shoals on that side of the river," Mike said. "He doesn't have a pilot on board. Couldn't hire one in the whole damned harbor. The Buffalonians have done what they could to help us. The ferry captain, for instance. Not a drop of Irish blood in him, but he said he'll take as many of us over without guns as he can manage with them looking down his throat. Says he wants to teach the Canadians a lesson in patriotism."

The *Michigan* drifted with the swift current for a few minutes as the captain thought things over. Then he gave two hoots of his whistle and headed up the river toward Buffalo. In a moment we saw why. Forging toward him were three tugs, each flying the American flag. In a few minutes they clustered around the *Michigan* in the center of the river, and we could see sailors from the cutter boarding the tugs. Next, gleaming brass cannon were set up on the bow of each tug. In ten minutes the tugs were ready to operate as men-of-war. The U.S. government now had a flotilla to patrol the river.

The steam ferry at the dock gave a warning hoot. Blind fatality consumed me. I ran for it. I had sent Dan, I had sent them all, into this monstrous trap. I would fight and die beside them. Behind me I heard Mike cry, "Bess—don't." I stepped aboard the ferry as it left the dock.

In the cabin I found four or five reporters and two serious-looking men carrying black bags. "You must be the doctors," I said, and introduced myself to them. The older of the two, a tall, dignified man with a short black beard, was Edward Donnelly. The shorter man, who had dark red hair and a rakish, reckless smile, was Thomas Gallaher.

"I hope I might be of some help as a nurse," I said.

"A girl as pretty as you? said Dr. Gallaher. "I'll be sawing off the wrong leg half the time."

"We may need all the help we can find," said Dr. Donnelly, who I saw was as solemn as Dr. Gallaher was wild.

"My fellow sawbones here was in the war. The heroes in his regiment let him get captured, and he did a tour in Richmond's Libby Prison," Dr. Gallaher said. "I was too busy making money in Brooklyn. I didn't have that much enthusiasm for sewing up abolitionists, anyway."

"What attracted you to the Fenians?" I asked. "It can't be making money."

"Pure impulse. I went to headquarters and volunteered when I heard about the invasion. Every man must do something idealistic at least once in his life. It's good for the digestion. My father starved to death in the famine of '47, but that has nothing to do with why I'm here."

"Of course," I said.

"Hungering for revenge is bad for the digestion. Taking it when it comes your way is best, I assure you."

He began discoursing on his philosophy of life. He did not believe in God, Jesus, the Virgin, or the Blessed Trinity. He was a man of science. He had his own blessed trinity—pain, pleasure, and digestion. It was necessary for a thinking man to maintain a proper balance between pain and pleasure and do nothing that might disturb his digestion. Once that was disturbed, he became morbid and lost his ability to balance pain and pleasure in nice proportion.

"At least the weather is in our favor," Dr. Donnelly said, looking out at the sunny river. "This reminds me of the day before Antietam."

"Wasn't that the bloodiest battle of the war?" I asked.

"Oh, some say so," Dr. Gallaher said. "There were more killed at Gettysburg but more engaged. More wounded at Chickamauga and fewer killed. It's the sort of thing people love to argue about. The world's mad, don't you know that?"

"I'm beginning to think so," I said.

"It's got to be. Here I am, sailing into the cannon's mouth, talking to a pretty woman about the statistics of death, on my way to saw off mangled legs and arms, which she's volunteered to dispose—"

"Please," I said, and bolted away from him, out on the open deck. I was trembling and half sick at the images and thoughts he had thrust in my face. Dr. Gallaher followed me.

"Never been a nurse before, have you?"

I shook my head.

"There's someone over there you love."

I nodded.

"Damnation. I always meet a girl like you five minutes after she's gone head and heels in love with someone else."

"Get on with you," I said. "You're just trying to make me feel better."

"And what's wrong with that? Isn't it a doctor's job?"

I gazed out at the Canadian shore, which was fast approaching. It looked utterly peaceful. Well-tilled fields and white farmhouses and groves of trees filled the landscape west of the village of Fort Erie. The village consisted of about a hundred frame houses, most of them facing the river on the west side of the road that paralleled the shore. A half dozen streets ran down at right angles to the main street. Behind the village rose a clay bluff about forty feet in height with a fine brick house on it. On the north side of the village, a railway embankment extended along the river for about a half mile. Railyards and a roundhouse lay nearby. At the water's edge was a dock, where a huge ferry, capable of carrying twenty railroad cars at a time, was moored.

"We were supposed to have the use of that," said Dr.

Donnelly, joining us at the rail and pointing to the rail-road ferry. "It could have put the whole army over in two trips. But they tied it up and shut down the boilers yester-day at sundown. Someone over there knew something."

I began to wonder if we had been teased into a trap, like so many mice. What better way to ruin the Fenians than to lure a detachment of them to Canada, slaughter them, and then laugh the rest of them out of existence?

The ferry thumped against the wharf, and we de-barked. The first man I saw was my young red-headed friend, Captain Hennessy. He was in command of a de-tachment of men guarding the riverfront. "General" O'Neil, as Hennessy called him, and the rest of the army were at a farm west of the village. "When are the rest of the lads coming over?" he asked.

"Soon," I said, and left them hastily before they could ask more questions.

Twenty minutes of hard walking carried us to the farm, which was owned by a justice of the peace named Newbigging. The men were camped in the fields around the neat white house. Inside we found Dan and John O'Neil and the colonels of the other regiments studying maps spread on the dining room table.

Dan was aghast at the sight of me. "What in hell are you doin' here?" he growled.

"I came with the doctors, to be of some service."

"You're goin' right back," he said.

"That will take some doing," I said. "It's a long walk to that ferry, and you'll have to carry me every inch."

"As a physician, I would advise against such strenuous exercise on a hot day in June," Tom Gallaher said.

"Didn't you know I forbade Margaret to come?" John O'Neil said.

"No," I said. "I'm also here to tell you the bad news. The river is shut tight."

I described the tugs being manned by seamen from

the *Michigan*. Their faces fell. They forgot about sending me back. Dan strode up and down, cursing under his breath for a full minute. The colonels looked equally undone.

"We must do something with the men we have," John O'Neil said. "Let's consider our best move."

He called them back to a study of the map. "There's one enemy column moving up from Port Colborne," he said, pointing to that city on the shore of Lake Erie. "And another moving up from Chippewa on our other flank. The maxim for us is to fight them separately before they can meet and overwhelm us with sheer numbers."

"Colborne is the lighter column, and they don't have artillery," Dan said.

"Let that be our first opponent," O'Neil said.

In that moment, I glimpsed the inner secret of the art of war, the steady calm of a born soldier. Panic and hysteria ebbed from me, and from everyone else in the room. No matter what else happened, with John O'Neil in command our expedition would not end in shameful surrender.

He turned to the doctors and me. "Where will you set up your hospital?" he asked.

"I would prefer to use a building in town, near the ferry," Dr. Donnelly said. "Perhaps the post office. I paid a visit to Fort Erie last week and made a pretty careful survey of the place."

"Fine," O'Neil said. He scribbled an order to Captain Hennessy, instructing him to detach a dozen men to help Donnelly set up an operating room and commandeer cots and mattresses from nearby houses.

"Have any of our medical supplies gotten over?" Dr. Donnelly asked.

O'Neil sent for another officer, Major John Canty, a fat, perspiring man. Canty shook his head. "Not so much as a swallow of opium," he said.

"We'll imitate your example, General," Dr. Donnelly said, "and do the best with what we have."

"Good. Say nothing about the river being closed. It might panic the men."

We nodded our acquiescence and returned to town, where Captain Hennessy quickly obeyed O'Neil's order. We soon had a half dozen strapping fellows clearing counters and tables from the post office. Another set went with me along the main street in search of bedding and sheets for bandages. The items were usually surrendered without opposition, although glares of enmity often accompanied the process. The size of my escorts and the guns in their hands were very conducive to cooperation. Only at one house—where I least expected it—did I get backtalk.

Fat, red-faced Teresa O'Brien, wife of James O'Brien, according to the name on the door, exploded when I asked her to surrender her mattresses and sheets. "Isn't it enough that you've taken me husband prisoner to hunt up food for yez, now y'want me furniture?" she bawled.

"It's for the cause of Ireland and to ease the suffering of wounded men," I said.

"You're daft, the whole lot of you," she yelled. "Ireland's three thousand miles away across the ocean. We've left the whole bloody mess behind us with the help of God, and now you've brought it to our very door. You'll ruin us all. When the regulars are finished thrashin' yez they'll hang poor Jimmy, and him the father of two babes."

She slammed the door in our faces. The men were for smashing in and taking what we pleased, but I decided to let her go unpunished. Though I said nothing to the men, and scarcely admitted it to myself then, there was truth in her bawling.

The doctors and I dined that night in the house of the mayor of Fort Erie, Dr. Kempson. He and Dr. Donnelly were well acquainted. They discussed the pros and cons of our expedition with the polite demeanor of professional men. Dr. Kempson maintained that our foray made no sense, because Canada was only nominally part of England. It was as much a separate country as America; British rule was more theoretical than actual. Because men had been wronged in their own country by a powerful enemy, it gave them no right in invade a third country, which had had nothing to do with inflicting the wrongs. Dr. Donnelly maintained that Canada was as much a part of England as Scotland and Wales, and we had every right to be where we were.

After supper, I walked out to Newbigging's farm to see Dan. I wanted to put my arms around him at least, before tomorrow's day of battle dawned. But I was dismayed to discover that the fields where the Fenians had been so numerous were empty. The army had already begun its march toward Port Colborne. John O'Neil had decided it was wiser to go part of the way in the coolness of the night, rather than in the morning heat. Only Lieutenant Colonel Bailey of the Buffalo regiment and about fifty men were still there. They were engaged in a sad business. They were taking the surplus rifles—a thousand of them—from wagons and smashing them against the trees. The men had deadly faces. They knew what it meant—there was no hope of reinforcements. John O'Neil had ordered them to do the destruction after the army left, to keep the secret.

I watched, heartsick, until the last gun was flung to the ground, its stock splintered, its barrel bent. Bailey took a letter from his inner pocket. "I was going to leave this with Mr. Newbigging, but he's no friend of our cause. It has some sentiments in it that might be misinterpreted. Give it to my wife, if it comes to the worst for me."

I promised him it was in safe hands. He mounted his horse and rode off into the deepening twilight. Back at

Dr. Kempson's house, Dr. Tom Gallaher was waiting on the dark porch for me.

"I'm leaving tomorrow at 4:00 A.M. with a medical wagon to join the army. Can you handle a two-horse team?

"Of course. I grew up on a farm."

"It could be dangerous. But I think you're like me. You enjoy danger."

"Not really," I said, "but I'll come."

He knocked softly on my bedroom door at 4:00 A.M. It was already dawn. The June nights are surprisingly short in northern New York and Canada. The wagon was waiting beside the house; in it were some medical supplies, mostly opium, procured from Dr. Kempson and the Fort Erie pharmacy. We rode along the river road for some four miles and met no fewer than fifty or sixty Fenians. They shambled past, declining to look us in the face.

"Stragglers," Tom Gallaher said. "Donnelly told me to expect them. There's some before every battle."

"But we need every man," I said, glaring at them.

"Better they run now than when the shooting starts. They might panic everyone," Gallaher said.

We swung west as the sun began to rise and jounced for several more miles through open, thinly wooded country. At length we struck a rail line and followed it on a parallel road that ran along a ridge. Rounding a bend, we caught sight of our army on the road a half mile ahead of us. We persuaded our two tired horses to go a little faster and soon reached the rear of the column. Up ahead we could see O'Neil and the other colonels, all in Union blue, on horseback. As we watched, Dan and two other horsemen came racing up to them. Dan waving his wide tan hat to whip his horse. They reined up and reported urgent news to O'Neil, pointing to the west.

O'Neil turned and shouted an order to the column, which quickened its pace. Dan rode down the line of march to us. He glared at me. "I knew you'd get out here," he said through clenched teeth.

"Why did you bring her?" he said to Gallaher. "Don't you have any brains at all?"

Dan wheeled and galloped away. "I knew love was blind," Gallaher said. "Now I see it is also deaf and dumb."

"Have you ever been in love?" I asked.

He shook his head. "Bad for the digestion."

The Fenians had been marching parallel to the river as well as the railroad. Ahead lay a crossroad that ran into their route at right angles. In the southeast corner of the intersection stood a fine brick farmhouse with a barn and other outbuildings. From the crossroad, pastureland sloped gradually for a half mile, broken by several fences. On the left as we faced this open ground was a lower road also roughly parallel to the river. The crossroad was really the crest of a ridge, and under John O'Neil's direction the Fenians moved along it to form a battle line. Several companies took up positions around the farm and in a grove of trees beyond it. There was a ditch running along the road, fringed with trees and shrubs. The men pulled down a fence on the opposite side of the road and made A-shaped rifle pits with the rails, jamming loose stones between them.

As they worked, we heard the sound of a train engine to the west, then a clear, unmistakable bugle call. The enemy were on the scene. They had come by rail from Port Colborne to the nearby village of Ridgeway. Several dozen of our men emerged from a grove of maple trees on the far left of our battle line and ran swiftly across the fields in that direction to vanish into a thicket of pines. Dan rode up to us and ordered Gallaher to get the medical wagon and me behind the brick house.

"Where are they going?" I asked, pointing to the running men. I wondered if they were more deserters.

"Skirmishers," Dan said. "We're goin' to try to tease them into a nice little trap here."

Even my unmilitary eyes could see the position was well chosen. We were largely invisible to the enemy, who would have to advance across open fields to reach us. For another minute, all remained perfectly still. There were only the sounds of summer, birds twittering, a faint breeze stirring the topmost branches of the tress. The day was growing very hot.

Then came the crack of a gun, followed by another, and another. In an instant it was followed by the rolling crash of a dozen guns, joined by the staccato cracks of so many more that they became a continuous thunder. Still there was not a sign of a man in the fields between us and the pine trees, or on the road that ran along the edge of the fields about three hundred yards below us on the sloping ridge. Dan sat quietly on his horse, the battle glow gleaming darkly on his somber face. "Heavy skirmishin'," he said.

I thought of how many other times he had heard the sound of those guns and seen his friends falling before their murderous mouths. If he thought about it, he gave no sign.

For twenty minutes the heavy firing continued. Then the first of our skirmishers appeared, running in and out among the trees by the lower road. Others burst from the pine trees and raced across the pastures to crouch behind fences and single trees for another shot. Suddenly the enemy was there, an explosion of brilliant red against the green and brown and yellow landscape. From the lower road to the edge of the pasture directly opposite us they formed a long swaying yelling line. They advanced erratically, pausing to fire, then whooping and running forward again. Our skirmishers waited until they were climbing over a fence to return their fire and retreat once more. Twice I saw a Redcoat clutch his chest and fall.

A tremendous crash of riflery erupted from the grove of maple trees at the far left of our line. The red line opposite them wavered, recoiled; two or three men dropped, but they rallied, and squads of them went racing to the right to get around the flank of that position.

"I don't like this," Dan said. "They're fightin' like veterans."

He rode to the center of our line to confer with John O'Neil, then rode back, waved a junior officer to his side, and in a moment detached a half dozen men from the battle line. They followed Dan across the road to where the horses belonging to colonels and lieutenant colonels were tied in a grove of trees. Dan's men mounted these and rode rapidly off to the north.

Before I could wonder where they were going, much less ask, the men all around us opened fire. I thought my head would split and my eyes spring from my head, the noise was so tremendous. An acrid haze of gunsmoke swirled over the field, in some places so thick the Canadians appeared like ghosts through it. Up and down the whole battle line, the firing became universal. The Canadians returned it with a vengeance and came on, cheering and shouting. Bullets hummed all around us, but most of them were high, clipping twigs and leaves from the trees above us. A few whizzed close enough to make me crouch behind a brick wall, but Dr. Gallaher stood calmly in the open, taking his own pulse. He later explained that he was trying to determine scientifically whether he was a hero or a coward.

Suddenly the red line halted, and there was a loud bugle call. Men pointed to the north, and we heard someone shout, "Cavalry." They scampered back a few hundred feet and began trying to form squares, the standard formation for infantry attacked by horsemen. Now I knew where Dan had gone and what was about to happen.

"Soldiers of Ireland," John O'Neil roared. "Charge."

Out of the rifle pits and from behind the trees and fences the Fenians sprang. At their head raced a lad carrying a great green flag. Bayonets flashed in the sun. They stopped, fired a volley into the Canadian squares, and resumed the charge, roaring and yelling like men possessed. The howl of the Union veterans mingled with the shrill *yi-yi-yi* of the Confederate yell. Redcoats toppled right and left. Everywhere the squares buckled. Dan and his half dozen horsemen appeared on their northern flank firing pistols and rifles into them. A wild bugle call and the squares dissolved. But their last volley brought down the lad carrying the green flag when he was within ten yards of them. Behind them came his roaring fellows. A few Canadians tried to make a stand and were swiftly dispatched. The rest ran.

What a glorious sight that was, the backs of those red coats. They scampered pell-mell, flinging away guns and packs, screaming like frightened children. It was hard to believe they were the same confident, cheering soldiers who had advanced so bravely only minutes before. They had thought the contemptible Irish would run at the first volley. Their bravery was born of prejudice and ignorance.

I found myself cheering like a madwoman. "We beat them, we beat them!" I screamed. I sprang up on the stone wall and leaped off into Tom Gallaher's arms. Battle lust, battle madness, I was drunk with it.

Heavy firing continued for a few more minutes on the left. Some of the companies that had made the charge let the rest continue the pursuit of the Canadian center and swung to cut off the Redcoats who had attempted to outflank our position in the maple trees. This they did handily, turning that branch of the Canadian army into frantic fugitives like the rest, while a half dozen threw down their guns and surrendered.

Five more minutes and it was over. Not a sound but an

occasional triumphant yell and a random shot from far down the road. "Now we must go to work," Tom Gallaher said.

"What?" I said blankly. In my frenzy I had forgotten he was a doctor, why we were here.

"Go to work," he said. He took off his coat, rolled up his sleeves, and took a white apron from the rear of the wagon. He gave it to me and tied another around his waist. He handed me a box containing opium pills and bandages. We walked slowly down the line of the rifle pits. We heard a groan. In the ditch lay my red-haired friend, Captain Hennessy. He had been shot through the face. His dead eyes stared at me in a sort of ghastly surprise. Beside him writhed another man, clutching his belly. Blood trickled through his fingers.

"Oh, my God," I gasped and turned away. I lurched past Tom Gallaher, the ground heaving beneath me, the blue sky turning black and purple. He grabbed my arm and cuffed me in the face. He was a muscular man. Except for the Ku Klux whip, I never felt such pain.

"If you can cheer for them, you can bandage them," he said.

I clutched my aching cheek, too stunned to be angry.

"I can't help it, I—"

"You can help it," he said, and struck me again.

"You—you bastard," I cried.

"Precisely," he said, with a cold smile. "That is precisely what you must be in this business. Now cut away his shirt and trousers and hold him while I probe for the bullet."

He handed me a scissors. With a hand so steady I could not believe it, I cut away the bloody cloth and confronted the torn red ugliness of the wound. Dr. Gallaher knelt down, the steel scalpel in his hand. "If I can get the bullet out before it works too far into him, it will be all to the good. Give him an opium pill."

I popped one into the man's mouth, and Dr. Bastard went to work. The man clung to me, groaning in agony. He was about thirty, a thickset fellow. I asked him his name. He said it was Doyle. He had been in the Civil War from Bull Run to Appomattox with never a scratch. He had a wife and child in New York. "Oh, Jaysus, I know the belly's bad, is it bad, Doctor?" he gasped.

"You'll be fine," Dr. Gallaher said with his empty smile. He called to some men from Doyle's company and ordered them to carry him into the brick house.

"He'll be dead before morning," Gallaher said as soon as Doyle was out of earshot.

So we proceeded across the battlefield in the blazing heat of Sunday, the third of June, closing the eyes of the dead like poor Hennessy and probing wounds, bandaging them. We treated friend and foe alike as we came to them. Around the maple grove there were a half dozen Canadians either dead or badly wounded. I was shocked by their youth. I asked one of the least wounded, a blond red-cheeked boy so pretty he could have passed for a woman if he wore skirts, how old he was. "Seventeen," he said.

"Good God," I said, "what are you doing here?"

He glared at me. "Defending my country," he said.

By the time we reached the field where the Canadians had tried to form their squares against Dan's cavalry feint, my artificial calm, created by the shock of Tom Gallaher's slaps, was beginning to crumble. He saw it and began another shock treatment. He told me how he had sat on the porch last night and imagined himself in bed with me, slowly seducing me, touch by kiss by touch. It was described with cold intensity, with no detail left unimagined. Yet it did not seem in the least obscene.

"*And then I took the nipple of your left breast and placed it in my mouth and rotated my tongue against it,*" he whispered and simultaneously felt for the bullet in the breast of a half-conscious young Canadian.

We gazed down at the crumpled figure of our color bearer, wrapped in the folds of his green flag. *"Your mons veneris was as warm and soft as the inside of a rose,"* he said as he took the pulse, found nothing, and closed the sightless eyes.

A few feet away, two Fenians were tugging loose a Union Jack from beneath the body of a young Canadian, about the same age as the Irish color sergeant. We performed the same sad service for him, while my mad doctor said, *"You cried out when I entered you. Never had you known such pleasure was possible."*

He began to infect me with his madness. I suppose it was preferable, anything was preferable, to thinking about what we were doing.

"You make it sound so interesting, I might let you try it," I said. "If he didn't object."

Dan strode across the field toward us, stepping over the dead bodies as if they were stones or stumps. There was no victorious exultation on his face. Nor was there any on or within any part of me, now.

"We're goin' to fall back to Fort Erie," he said. "Those boys won't stop runnin' till they get to Port Colborne. But the other column is a different story. Twice as big and with cavalry and artillery. We've got to get some reinforcements. Maybe you can get back across the river and tell about this fight. It might change some minds."

"Yes," I said dully, without the slightest hope.

"We'll go ahead with the wounded—the ones worth moving," Tom Gallaher said. "The rest we'll leave in the farmhouse."

We loaded a dozen wounded into the wagon, gave them more opium pills, and set out for Fort Erie. It was late afternoon by the time we came down the river road into the center of town. We noticed a tug tied up at the wharf. Our hopes rose wildly. Had the river been opened? Not until we got much closer did we realize the tug was flying the Union Jack. It was impossible to flee. A ride in a runaway wagon would have destroyed the wounded men. So we continued steadily to the door of the post office. There we were confronted by a big man in a red coat. On the side street lounged half a hundred men wearing the enemy's colors. "What's this?" the big man boomed.

"Wounded men," Tom Gallaher answered.

"And who might you be?"

"Dr. Thomas Gallaher, volunteer surgeon with the Irish Republican Army."

"I am Colonel J. S. Dennis, brigade major of Her Majesty's loyal militia in this district, and you are under arrest. So are those criminals and your wagon and that woman, whoever she is."

"She's a nurse. Her name is Fitzmaurice."

"She's under arrest, too. Get off that wagon. Where is Colonel Booker?"

"Was he the commander of the column that marched from Port Colborne?" I asked.

"Of course," snapped Dennis, who had a short Prince Albert beard below a huge pendulous nose. He was the very picture of British pomposity.

"I imagine he may have reached Port Colborne by now," Tom Gallaher said. "He was running well ahead of his men the last time I saw him."

"This is not the time or the place for jokes, sir," huffed Colonel Dennis.

"I'm not joking, and I would like to get my patients out of the sun and into the expert hands of my colleague, Dr. Donnelly."

Colonel Dennis mouthed a few words and then rushed down the wharf to confer with the captain of the tug. We helped our wounded down from the wagon and half-walked, half-carried them to the mattresses Dr. Donnelly had stretched on the floor inside. While we worked, Donnelly told us that Dennis had arrived from Port Colborne with two companies of Canadian volunteers aboard the tug and arrested about sixty of the stragglers we had seen that morning on the river road. They were imprisoned belowdecks in the tug.

We heard shouts in the street. We rushed out to discover an old man on horseback, anxiously pointing to the bluff above the town. "They're comin', the whole dang bunch of them," he yelled.

"Form, form," bellowed Colonel Dennis, and his men scrambled into ranks in the street before the ferry wharf. They stood there in parade formation, with Colonel Dennis on the wharf facing them. "Remember, men," he said, "you are fighting for Canada and the queen. Duty—"

He was stopped in midsentence by the appearance of the Fenians on the bluff above the town. They were led by Lieutenant Colonel Bailey on a white horse. As they spread out along the ridge, it was obvious that they numbered in the hundreds. The old man had told the truth. Colonel Dennis remained paralyzed, speechless, like a man struck by a spell. Terror had numbed his brain.

A sensible officer would have rushed his fifty men aboard the tug and fled. A pugnacious one might have thrown his men into nearby houses for shelter, and tried to make a fight of it. Dennis did neither. He let his men stand there in the street. The Fenians on the bluff fired a volley over their heads, hoping to drive them off without bloodshed. A Redcoat in the first rank, with as Irish a face as I've ever seen, dropped to his knee, aimed his rifle and replied. Lieutenant Colonel Michael Bailey clutched his chest and toppled from his horse. The men on the ridge fell back, amazed by such deadly aim.

Still Colonel Dennis stared, gape-jawed, his men drawn up in the street. The Fenians started firing back at them in earnest. The Canadians opened their ranks a bit and began returning their fire. We stood in the door of the post office, watching in disbelief. When the first shot was fired, there were ten or fifteen civilians in the street, some of them women and children. They huddled against the houses, in terror of the bullets. "Get in here," I called to the nearest of them, and they scampered to the safety of the post office's stout wooden walls.

On the road to the south, down which we had come in our wagon, there was the sound of hoofbeats. Into view came at least half the Fenian army, Dan and John O'Neil on horseback at their head, all on the dead run for Colonel Dennis and his paralyzed command. The infantry yell stormed from their throats. Heroic Colonel Dennis took one look and squawked, "Save yourselves, men!" Followed by about twenty-five of his best sprinters, he legged it down the river road; Fenian bullets whistled all around them. Five or six Canadians dived behind piles of cordwood on the wharf and fired at the oncoming Fenians. Another twenty or so tried to form a line in the street. The captain of the tug, no more a hero than Colonel Dennis, cut his lines and drifted off with the current, abandoning those who were trying to make a stand. It was a paradigm of the madness, the heroism and the cowardice of war, all in one wild minute.

The Fenians fired a volley at the men in the street and came on with the bayonet. By this time the doctors and I were inside the post office with all the civilians who could get to it. Four or five Canadians went down in the street, and the man who had shot Colonel Bailey legged it into the post office, followed by a half dozen of his friends. The rest threw down their guns and surrendered, many of them falling to their knees and begging for mercy. The men on the wharf were swept away in another minute, a few surrendering, one, an officer, emptying his pistol and flinging himself into the river as the Fenians rushed him.

A crash of glass was followed by the thunder of guns

within the post office. The deadly marksman and his friends began firing into the Fenians in the street. It was pure folly. They cut down at least three or four men before the Fenians realized what was happening. All became madness and fury. The Fenians had already had at least a dozen men wounded or killed in this senseless skirmish, and they turned on these last tormentors with every gun in their army.

"Down on the floor," yelled Tom Gallaher as bullets hurtled into the room through every window. Women and children—half-grown boys, most of them—lay face down, whimpering and screaming. I saw one of the Fenian wounded, weak as he was, drag down and hold a boy who began running about insane with terror. A tremendous crash shook the front door. They were battering it down. But the first Fenian into the room was met by two Canadians with bayonets. As he raised his rifle to fire, one of them plunged his bayonet into his throat. The Irishman gave a terrible cry and toppled back against those who were rushing after him, throwing them into confusion. They retreated to the street, leaving the wounded man bleeding to death on the steps. He died in terrible agony within a few minutes.

Now the Fenian rage was all-consuming. Volley after volley crashed into the building. Prone on the floor, I noticed the Canadians were no longer firing back. They crouched beside the windows, looking as miserable and frightened as everyone else. "They're out of ammunition," I said to Tom Gallaher.

"Who's going to stick his head up to tell the boys outside?" he said.

I seized a sheet we had confiscated for bandages and crept on my hands and knees, and more often squirmed on my belly, to the stairway to the second floor. There were no Canadians up there, so the Fenian fire was all coming into the first floor. I crawled up the stairs as rapidly as possible. I could see the walls shuddering with the impact of the bullets. If one had come through I would have been a dead woman. By the time I reached the second floor I was too weak with fear to do anything but lie there for a full minute, face down. I did not want to die in this stupid, meaningless fight.

Looking up, I almost said a prayer of thanks. There was a window open, just above my head. I sprang up and flung the white sheet out it. "They're ready to surrender!" I shouted. The gunfire ceased almost instantly.

I went downstairs. The Canadian who had bayoneted the Fenian clutched his empty gun. "They'll kill us," he said. "Colonel Dennis said you were giving no quarter."

"Haven't you learned by now that Colonel Dennis is a fool as well as a coward?" I said. "You'll be treated as a prisoner of war. Like your friends captured in the street just now and at Ridgeway."

Walking to the door, I called to the Fenians to parade their prisoners. They shoved them into the street in front of the post office. The Canadians were convinced. They walked out with their hands up. The deadly marksman was the last to leave.

"What's your name?" I asked.

"Daniel Sullivan," he said.

I didn't bother to ask him why he was fighting for the queen. He had stupidity writ large on his slack mouth and in his glazed eyes. Perhaps that explained why he was such a deadly shot. No brain, no nerves.

Outside, the once peaceful village of Fort Erie was a charnel house. There were dead and wounded Canadians and Fenians lying in the street. The post office was a shattered wreck. Many other houses had their windows smashed by bullets. For the next few hours, I worked with the doctors on the wounded while the officers conferred. Lieutenant Colonel Bailey was our most serious case. He had been shot through the lungs. A bloody froth rose to his mouth with every breath. I thought of his pretty, laughing wife showing me Niagara Falls and fought back tears.

It was almost dark when John O'Neil, Dan, and the colonels came into our little hospital. "We've been in touch with the other shore. There's no hope of reinforcements. We're going to set up a defense line around the railroad car ferry dock. If by some miracle they can get men and guns to us, this would be the best place to land. The enemy column from Chippewa is only three miles away. They'll almost certainly attack us in the morning."

"Do you mean to fight to the last man?" Dr. Donnelly asked.

"Yes," John O'Neil said. "There will be no surrender."

Dan caught me by the arm. "We've got some rowboats. We'll take you back tonight, as soon as it's dark."

"I'm staying here," I said. "The wounded need care."

"They'll hang you for what we did in Ireland," Dan said. "Do you think that will make me feel any better when I get my bullet—knowin' they've got you, too?"

I bent to wipe the bloody froth from Michael Bailey's lips. "Is there no hope?"

"We're thinkin' of a night attack, but the men are beat. They only got about three hours' sleep last night. Not much food today. This stupid fight here in the village was sort of the last straw. And they know we're cut off. No reinforcements."

"Maybe you can surrender. If you get decent terms."

"I surrendered once," Dan said. "I ain't never gonna do it again. Besides, you can't trust an Englishman. You should know that. An Irish deserter from their 47th Regiment came in about a half hour ago. He says the officers are talkin' about givin' us no quarter."

"I'm sick from seeing men die to no purpose," I said.

"We all got to die sometime," Dan said.

There it was, the code of the soldier. Even so, in his bitter twisted heart, he found room to love me in his way. Again he insisted that I go back by small boat. Again I refused.

"You're my fate," I said. "I chose you. I'm with you to the end. Remember the poem I spoke to you on our first night together?

"Donal Ogue, when you cross the water
Take me with you to be your partner."

He left me there with the hurt and dying men. It was glorious and tragic. For a long time I thought it would have been better if it had ended that way, in a crash of gunfire and an eruption of battle smoke. They would never have captured me for hanging. I would have joined Dan in the ranks when the battle began and died beside him. But it was not to be. I spent the evening with the wounded, especially Michael Bailey. He drifted in and out of consciousness. Three or four times he told me to be sure to give the letter to his wife.

"I had a feeling my luck was out," he said.

Other men needed comforting, too. Doctors can do little with wounded men, but a woman has a power I do not completely understand. When a man is wounded, he often becomes a little boy again. He finds comfort, hope, memories of love in a woman's touch, in the sound of her voice. I prayed with many of them. Without faith myself, I recited the words of our ancient litany. *Holy Mary mother of God pray for us sinners now and at the hour of our death Amen*. We had no priest with us, which was hard for many of them.

I can still remember the silence of that night, broken only by an occasional groan of pain, and the crunch of shattered glass as I or the doctors walked from man to man, giving opium pills, changing blood-soaked bandages. Once, there was a single gunshot. We all tensed, thinking the night attack had begun, but it must have been a sentry firing at a shadow. About midnight, Tom Gallaher persuaded me to lie down on a spare mattress and get some rest. The moment my head touched the pillow, I fell into exhausted slumber, like a stone dropped into a well.

The crash of a door and the stamp of booted feet awoke me. I sat up, dazed. Dan McCaffrey towered over me. "We're gettin' out," he said in a low voice. "There'll be a tug at the dock in fifteen minutes. Come on."

Still half asleep, I stumbled to the door. Dr. Tom Gallaher was on the steps outside, holding Dan's horse. "Go with him," he said. "I'll stay with the men."

Before I could think, much less protest, Dan all but threw me into the saddle, sprang up behind me, and galloped for the car ferry dock. We passed Dr. Donnelly running in the same direction and arrived just as the bulky shape of a tug loomed out of the night. Behind it was an even larger vessel. What was left of the Fenian army of liberation crowded down the dock to the second craft, a garbage scow. John O'Neil walked up to us. It was too dark to see his face, but his voice was forlorn. "There was no hope of an attack. The enemy outnumbered us three to one. They had sentries every ten feet."

"Where did the ships come from?" I asked.

"From Buffalo harbor. Where they least expected us. Did you warn our sentries, Dan boy?"

"As many as I could reach, General."

"Good. Maybe we'll have better luck another time, Dan."

"Sure, General. You better get aboard."

O'Neil moved away, toward the tug. It was strange to hear Dan giving him orders.

"I didn't warn no sentries," Dan said. "I went and got you."

"You mean we're leaving men out there in the dark, not knowing—with no way to get back—"

"That's war, honey. They don't have a goddamn price on their heads, like you. Let's get on this tug before it goes."

He led me to the edge of the wharf and lifted me onto the tug's deck. A moment later the engine pounded. We surged away from the dock onto the dark river. I clung to the rail with Dan silent beside me. A cold night wind beat in my face. I welcomed its punishment. The betrayed become betrayers, I thought, envisioning the shock and horror when those lonely men on sentry duty discovered in the dawn that we had abandoned them to the enemy.

"Did you know this was gonna happen?" Dan asked.

"I had been warned in Washington, but they wouldn't listen. Roberts and the others in the cabinet wouldn't listen."

"But you wouldn't tell me? You'd let me go over there and get myself killed? Go make another martyr for Ireland?"

"No. Nothing was that clear or certain. It never is, in politics."

"Politics."

He spat past me into the river.

I said nothing. He was too bitter. His ruthless distinction between himself and the cause disheartened me. Why had he bothered to save me? So he could abuse me? I let the night wind tear at my dress. I thought of consoling things to say to him. At least it had not ended in slaughter or humiliation. We had won two victories. We could offer some pride to Ireland's despairing poor. We might even be able to use our victories as political arguments to cow Stanton and Seward and return to Canada. We had proven beyond question that it was in our power to conquer the country, if the Americans let us.

Before I could say any of this, I was all but deafened

by the blast of a steam whistle, dead astern. A moment later a tug, its engines running full, appeared alongside us. A voice bellowed, "Heave to."

We kept running straight ahead. "Heave to or I'll fire into you," roared the voice.

Our tug's engine died away, and we drifted with the current. "Now follow these instructions," the voice bellowed. "Run beside us at a speed of three knots. If you try to escape or resist in any way, you will be treated as outlaws."

In the darkness we could not tell whether he was British or American. There was no flag visible. "If he's a Brit, let's fight it out," I heard Dan growl. "One volley will wipe every man off those decks."

"Under whose orders are you acting?" John O'Neil called.

"The president of the United States."

Our humiliation had begun.

In Deeper than Ever

Dawn found us four miles down the river on the American side, tied up beside the U.S.S. *Michigan* at Pratt's Wharf. Reporters swarmed on the dock. Several came out in rowboats to shout questions, which we ignored. About 6:00 A.M. a ladder was lowered to the deck of the tug. We mounted it to the deck of the *Michigan*. A short, arrogant-looking man in a blue naval officer's uniform regarded us with evident distaste as we came aboard. We were surely a dirty, rumpled lot after two days and two nights of marching and fighting and sleeping in the same clothes. Dan, John O'Neil, and many others had dark growths of beard on their faces. I realized I was still wearing my bloodstained white apron. I hastily removed it as the officer began a speech.

"I am Captain Bryson, commander of this ship. You are under arrest for violating the neutrality laws of the United States. Until I receive further orders from Washington, you will remain aboard. Your men will also remain in custody. You will be allowed the freedom of this ship if you give your promise as gentlemen not to attempt to escape or communicate with anyone ashore."

"Just a moment, Captain," John O'Neil said. "Has the president issued a proclamation?"

"I'm not a lawyer. I'm acting under orders from Mr. Dart, the federal district attorney."

"We demand an interview with Mr. Dart," O'Neil said.

"I hardly think that's necessary," Bryson said. There was a distinct echo of an English accent in his voice. "Here's a copy of a telegram he received last night from the attorney general."

He handed us the piece of paper.

> *By direction of the president you are hereby instructed to cause the arrest of all prominent leading or conspicuous persons called "Fenians" who you may have possible cause to believe have been or may be guilty of violations of the neutrality laws of the United States.*
>
> *James Speed*
> *U.S. Attorney General*

We were utterly stunned by the obnoxious, hostile wording. By order of the president! By order of the man who had cheered us on and told us we were the hope of his administration! John O'Neil was especially devastated. The president was his personal friend.

"We'll give our paroles as you request, Captain," he

said in a pale, spiritless voice. "I'll vouch for every man here. As for this young woman, she served with us as a nurse. I'm sure you have no facilities aboard this ship for her."

"If she participated in your expedition, she's as guilty as the rest of you," Bryson said. "She'll stay."

Dr. Donnelly stepped forward and introduced himself. I was glad to see that he had reached the tug last night. Tom Gallaher had decided to stay with the wounded because he had no official connection with the Fenian army. Dr. Donnelly was on the rolls as the chief physician.

"I'm concerned about the men in the scow, Captain," he said. "Surely they can be allowed onto the dock or taken to an armory or warehouse ashore."

"I think not," Bryson said. "You have too many friends in Buffalo, and we have too few men to guard them."

For the next two days, we wandered the decks of the cutter *Michigan* or slumped in berths belowdecks and ate disgusting cold pork and ship's bread. Behind us, over five hundred men were crammed into the garbage scow. It had been the only craft the desperate Fenians in Buffalo could commandeer. The floor of the hold was covered with slime, and the deck around it could not hold more than thirty men. There were no facilities for relieving calls of nature and no roof or awning to protect the men from sun or rain. On Monday and Tuesday it was brutally hot, and on both days afternoon thunderstorms soaked the huddled, bedraggled men. Fevers began breaking out, and diarrhea became rampant. The odors that rose from the scow caused anyone who came close to it to choke. In desperation, Dr. Donnelly wrote a letter to William Roberts and smuggled it off the ship with the help of a cooperative Irish sailor. He said that conditions on the scow were worse than he had seen in the notorious Libby Prison in Richmond. He could not believe that brave men, most of whom had fought and bled "beneath the starry banner of freedom" in the late war, could be treated this way by the government of the United States.

Finally, on the third day, Captain Bryson, who remained coldly aloof from us (except for condescending to allow me the use of his private toilet) announced we should prepare to depart. The men were ordered out of the scow, and we joined them on the dock. Reporters stood about laughing at our filthy, stinking condition. The men, of course, were far worse. I heard one reporter ask a particularly dirty man, "Have you seen enough of the Canadian volunteers, Pat?"

"Sure we haven't seen anything of them but their backs," the man answered angrily.

The reporter laughed in his face. "Are you sure you didn't go poop in your pants, Pat, and start running before you got a good look at them?"

"We beat them," the man cried. "We beat them fair and square."

His friends hurried him away. The reporter shook his head, still laughing. We were dirty comical Irishmen and had to play our part for them, no matter what we said. My heart began turning to stone within me as I saw the impression we were making. How could the reporters believe this smelly rabble from the bottom of a garbage scow had defeated the Queen's Own and other crack units of the Canadian volunteers?

We trudged to the Erie County courthouse, where a nervous judge set bail of six thousand dollars each for John O'Neil and the regimental commanders. The rest, including me, were released on our own recognizance, simply by promising to appear for trial when called. The courtroom was packed with Buffalo Irish, and we were well represented by skillful attorneys, who assured the judge that the bail for the officers would be paid within the hour. Someone among the spectators called out, "Three cheers for General O'Neil." Instantly there were three tremendous shouts, which fairly rocked the court house to its foundation. The judge, who looked like he feared a lynching, hastily rapped for order and informed all the prisoners that they were discharged and free to go wherever they pleased.

The crowd within joined an even larger crowd of Irish outside the courthouse to escort John O'Neil and the other colonels to the Mansion House, the city's best hotel. I could no longer bear to see or hear any more wasted fervor. I trudged forlornly back to my own more modest hotel, the Continental. I was almost there when an agitated Mike Hanrahan overtook me in a hack.

"I was lookin' high and low for you in that mob," he said.

"Where are they now? In front of the Mansion House, still cheering the O'Neil?" I said.

"Yes."

"They're fools, Mike. We're all fools. Stupid Irish fools."

"If you think you feel bad now, wait till you see the papers."

He was right. I had only begun to drink the bitter brew of our humiliation. Mike had all the New York and Washington papers in the press room. There was scarcely one that had a line of truth in it. The *Tribune* was typical. It described the battle at Ridgeway in the lead paragraph as follows:

The Fenians were hiding in a bush. The British column at once attacked, the Queen's Own firing the first shot. The fight now became general, the Volunteers driving the Fenians. There were a number killed on both sides. The Canadians behaved splendidly, rushing at the Fenians

*with the utmost gallantry. There were eight hundred
Canadian Volunteers and one thousand Fenians. Sixty
were taken prisoner and carried to Fort Erie.*

"Did that bastard Pickens write that?" I cried.

Mike shook his head and pointed to a paragraph deep
in the column, where few would notice it.

*Another account: The Volunteers took a strong posi-
tion but were destroyed by a Fenian feint. They were
turned upon and driven from the field. The Volunteers
retreated to Port Colborne with the Fenians pursuing.*

"The paper preferred to copy the lead elsewhere and
ignored its own reporter," he said. "Look at this summary on the editorial page."

He pointed to a column that began: "The Fenians have
not only been defeated in their attempted invasion, but
the force that was recently engaged has fallen into the
custody of the United States." From the next day's paper,
Mike showed me a column that told some of the inner
truth. With the aid of "sundry leakages," it reported on a
presidential cabinet session on the Fenian question. Seward was described as desiring the president to sign a
proclamation, but others argued against "drawing the
Fenian fire" in the president's direction. The Fenian was
"an ugly animal to seize by the horns." Instead it was decided to send a circular order to federal district attorneys
and marshals to suppress the Fenians. But the attorney
general, who worded the "delicate circular" with Mr. Seward's help, "inadvertently" added "by direction of the
president" to the order.

A clearer statement of Seward's policy could not have
been made, for those who knew the inner story. Not only
had he destroyed us, he had alienated the Irish from
Johnson, making a mockery of any hope of the presi-

dent's reelection on either the Democratic or National Union ticket.

Nearby, in the same edition, was a report of our forlorn hope in Congress. A representative named Clarke from Ohio had risen to ask for belligerent rights for the Fenians. Congressman Rogers of New Jersey had supported him. The majority dismissed it without even voting on it.

"Fools, we look like fools," I said, crumpling the papers to a ball and flinging them to the floor. "The whole country's laughing at us."

"When they should be crying. Or roaring with rage," said a voice from the door of the press room.

It was Dr. Tom Gallaher. He looked almost as bedraggled as the Fenians from the garbage scow. There was a great black-and-blue bruise on his cheek. The British had held him in jail for two days trying to disprove his story that he had come to Canada as a tourist and had been forced into doctoring the Fenians. He had gotten the bruise in the post office when he tried to stop a British officer from kicking one of our wounded men and a regular had clubbed him with the stock of his musket. The rest of his story was a continuation of this initial horror. The British had treated the wounded men abominably, forcing them to stagger out to wagons and climb into them. The officers kept telling them they had their choice of dying quietly or hanging.

"Even Michael Bailey?" I asked, remembering the letter he had given me for his wife.

"No, he died before morning."

Tom was also privy to the fate of the sentries that Dan had abandoned. Most had fled up the river, found boats, and gotten safely across to the American shore, but a half dozen had thrown away their guns and retreated into the woods in back of Fort Erie. The British and Canadians had hunted them down.

"They made a sport out of it," Tom said. They sent men into the woods to flush them out like deer, then shot them while they were trying to surrender. I saw one man, his arms up, yelling for mercy. They riddled him."

He slumped in a chair. "Give me a drink of whiskey," he said.

Mike poured him a hefty glass. "By this cup," Tom said, raising it in both hands the way a priest lifts a chalice at mass, "I swear revenge. I didn't hate them before. Not personally. Now I swear revenge."

"No, Tom," I said, remembering what hatred does to the mind and heart. He silenced me with a wave. In his strange scientific soul I think he welcomed hatred as an elixir.

If the British were talking of hanging the wounded, they would almost certainly accord the same treatment to the sixty prisoners they carried away from Fort Erie in the tug that had fled the town during the skirmish with Colonel Dennis and his men. "Roberts and all the Fenians in New York must raise a storm of protest," I said.

"We can't get a word to them," Mike Hanrahan said. "The army's taken over the telegraph and banned Fenianism from the wires."

I got rid of Tom Gallaher by asking him to deliver Michael Bailey's letter to his wife. I took a bath and put on a clean dress and went to the Mansion House to find John O'Neil. An enthusiastic Irish bellboy proudly led me to "d'general's" suite. I found the door barred by Margaret O'Neil. "He's exhausted and needs rest," she said.

I knew this was nonsense. He had gotten two days' enforced rest on the U.S.S. *Michigan.* "Is Dan with him?" I asked.

Her nun's conscience would not permit her to tell a lie. "Yes," she said.

"They're both drunk," I said.

"Yes," she said, letting me in. She sat down and picked up a scarf she was knitting. "Maybe when he sobers up he'll realize how wrong, how foolish, this whole thing was. He'll admit I was right all along."

My pity for John O'Neil clashed with my dislike of his wife. "Is that all you have to say to a man with a broken heart?" I snapped.

"If you mean what I think you mean," she replied, "John and I are not the slaves of our physical desires. We have agreed to restrain ourselves until he ends this Fenian business, one way or another, and we settle down to raise a family."

"Where are they?" I said.

She pointed to a closed door. I threw it open and found my two heroes seated at a table, a bottle of Kentucky bourbon between them, getting drunk in the manner prescribed for disappointed Irishmen and gentlemen from Tennessee.

"What is the point of this?" I said.

Dan glared at me. "Go 'way," he said. "I don' wanna look at you. For a' leas' a week."

"I'll be surprised if I want to look at you in a month and maybe a year," I said.

"What else c'n a man do, Bess?" O'Neil muttered. "Ruin by pres'dent, m'friend."

"You can use his so-called friendship to save the lives of your captured men."

I told him of the British threats. He grew half sober. "Wha' can we do?"

"Go to Washington directly and demand the great man's help. Tell him it's his one hope of holding the Irish vote. Even if that's a miserable lie."

"A'right. Get me the tickets. Tell Margaret. Dan boy, you mus' come, too. Need you by my side."

"I'll be there, John," Dan said in a voice that did not sound drunk at all. I suddenly wondered what game he was playing.

We went direct from Buffalo to Washington, a long, wearisome ride that took two nights and a day. We went straight to the White House and asked to see the president. In ten minutes, we were alone with Andrew Johnson in his office. The murdered Lincoln gazed mournfully down at us from the wall. Johnson's great hero, Andrew Jackson, glared from the opposite wall. Between stood the living president looking weary and harassed. The confident glow had faded from his eyes, and the ruddy health from his cheeks.

Andrew Johnson embraced his friend O'Neil as he had on the first night, when he sent our hopes soaring so high. "John," he said. "I'm glad to see you're all right. But what happened to all your bold plans? I waited five days to issue my proclamation. In five days, with the army you had, you should have been able to do anything."

John O'Neil gazed at his old friend with astonishment and grief. "Andy," he said. "They closed the border the night we went over, the first of June. We couldn't get another man or gun across the river."

Now it was the president's turn to look astonished. "The first of June? I'd swear—"

He recovered with remarkable speed and began to lie. He was, after all, a professional politician. "You shouldn't have let a few customs inspectors worry you, old friend. And you surely got enough men over there to do *something*. But—maybe there was some—some mixup. You know Congress has been giving me such a devil of a time I haven't had a chance to sort out my cabinet, get rid of fellows I don't trust."

It was painful to watch him trying to conceal that he had no control of his government. He pounded O'Neil

on the back and begged him not to lose faith in him. "If
things went wrong, we'll put them right next time, John.
I need your help, the votes of your people in the elections
this fall."

With a sigh that was equally painful to hear, John
O'Neil gave him up as hopeless. I had warned him on
the train that recriminations would be a waste of time
and would only lessen our chances of saving our captured men. "We still need your help, Mr. President.
They're threatening to hang sixty of our fellows."

"What?" roared Johnson. He welcomed the plea as a
godsent rescue from the need to make further explana-
tions. He thundered and blew about war with England if
they touched the hair of a Fenian head. He would summon
his secretary of state that very morning and order him to
make the strongest representations to the Canadian officials to pardon the captives and send them home, as the
American government had done with the men they had
taken into "protective custody" on the river. With a wink
and a nudge he assured O'Neil that he need never worry
about the indictment against him in the Erie County court.
It would be quietly quashed in due time.

As we walked to the door, I told the president to give
my regards to his son Robert. I intended it as sarcasm,
but I almost regretted it when I saw the anguish I caused.
"Thank you," he said, his eyes downcast. "Robert—is
out of the country. On a cruise. For his—his health."

Outside, Dan McCaffrey looked back at the White
House. "General Lee," he said. "We should've fought to
the last man. That's all I can say."

He did in fact say little else during our ride back to
New York. In Baltimore he got off the train and bought a
bottle of bourbon. He and John O'Neil drank it steadily
for the next six hours. When we arrived in Jersey City, we
had to help O'Neil off the train. Dan was thick-voiced but
steady.

In New York we met nothing but confusion, ridicule, and clamor. Our president, William Roberts, had voluntarily surrendered to the federal authorities and was in the city prison, appropriately named the Tombs. He was issuing statements calling upon the Irish to revenge themselves upon Andrew Johnson. We learned from his friends at Moffat House that he had decided to make a martyr of himself after he read the obnoxious telegram from the attorney general ordering the arrest of prominent Fenians. But few martyrs are made by voluntary immolation. Roberts was only making himself—and us—more ridiculous.

The newspapers had settled into a systematic pattern of vilification and mockery. They called Roberts "the Carpet Knight." The *Herald*, once our best backer, denounced us as "an armed mob, robbing and abusing women and children." Another paper accused John O'Neil of being in the Southern army during the Civil War and starving Union soldiers at the Confederate prison in Andersonville. *Harper's Weekly* published a long poem, "Feniana," a single stanza of which is sample enough to limn its opinion of us.

> *Sing, Muse of Battles! In tones loud and cheery*
> *The wonders of valor performed at Fort Erie!*
> *How, led by O'Neil, the great Fenian host*
> *Disperses a sentinel guarding the post;*
> *How the custom-house banner is dragged to*
> *   the ground*
> *How the hen-roosts are captured for miles around.*

If there is anything more disheartening, more dispiriting, more demoralizing, than the company of failed revolutionaries, I am unacquainted with it. For days on end we retired within our headquarters and did little but snarl and snap at each other. The vaunted good humor of the

Irish vanished. Even Mike Hanrahan was a stranger to a smile. I scarcely saw Dan. He seemed to spend all his time with John O'Neil, who, as far as I could tell, spent all his time drunk. Dan seemed to have no interest in me. In fact he scarcely seemed able to look at me without loathing.

Another source of distress was Dr. Tom Gallaher. He haunted headquarters, urging everyone to continue the struggle. He was drunk a good deal and had given up his medical practice.

"We must strike back," he told me. "Otherwise everyone will lose heart."

"Yes, of course," I said, which was the answer I gave to almost everything.

He seized me by the arm. "You need the kind of treatment I gave you at Ridgeway."

"I do not," I said, backing away from him, remembering the pain of his slaps.

"Or maybe the other kind of treatment I talked about giving you."

I caught a glint of something very close to madness in his eyes.

"Tom," I said, "you must stop drinking. You must go back to your patients."

"The hell with them. Fat pigs all of them, stuffed with meat and money. Who should I talk to? You're all like a collection of cattle, without brains or tongues. Is there no one with courage? I have a plan."

"Talk to Dan McCaffrey," I said, more to rid myself of him than from any real expectation of results. "If anything is done, he'll have something to say about it. He was the brains of the army."

Beyond the boundaries of my Fenian griefs lay larger personal sorrows. The first awaited me when I returned from Washington. It was a letter from my sister Mary, returning my thousand-dollar money order. She told me that Mother had died with the priest beside her, forgiving me and vowing to pray for me in heaven. Mary thanked me for the money but said she was determined to proceed with her plan to join the Sisters of the Sacred Heart at Limerick. I changed the name on the money order to "Archbishop McCloskey" and mailed it to him that day.

Annie was a more acute cause of anguish. I sought her out within a day or two of returning to New York. Her slattern of a landlady told me that she had departed, leaving no forwarding address. I was forced to go down to City Hall and ask Dick Connolly if he knew where she was.

The city comptroller was himself no longer looking so debonair. Power and its harassments had hollowed his cheeks and put a few gray hairs on his heretofore sleek head. "Here's the address," he said with a bitter smile.

He scribbled it on a piece of paper. He began quizzing me about Fenian affairs, but I professed to know nothing and fled past his busy clerks and the horde of favor seekers in the corridor. The address was on West 25th Street. It was a comfortable-looking four-story brownstone. A Negro maid answered my ring. I asked for Annie. "She still in bed," the maid replied.

At noon? I wondered. "I'm her sister. Could you tell her I called? I'll be back at two."

I was already fearing the worst when I returned from a walk to Madison Park, where I bought some oysters from a cartman for a cheap lunch. This time the Negro maid ushered me into a parlor that was furnished with opulent bad taste. An armless, headless statue of a naked woman, a poor imitation of the Venus de Milo, stood in a corner beside a great white piano. On the walls were paintings of naked gods and goddesses in gold scroll-work frames. The rug on the floor was deep red; matching red velvet draperies enclosed the front windows. The couches and chairs were all upholstered with some kind of white fur.

"Thank *God*—you're back alive," Annie cried, hurtling in the door as she spoke. She was wearing a dressing gown of blue silk trimmed with yards of lace and ribbons. It was the sort of outfit a lady wore in her bedroom, and it seemed particularly inappropriate in this overdone formal living room. She looked unwell, thin and frenetic, but there was so much makeup on her face, no one but a friend or relative would know it.

"How do you like this?" she said, gesturing to the room. "I told you I'd pull myself together. A lot of girls in New York would give a year's rent to be sitting in here. It's the most expensive house in the city. Two hundred dollars at the door. I get half."

"Annie—" I began, almost ready to weep.

"Don't give me any sermons, little sister. I'm having the time of my life and saving money by the ton. Which is more than you're doing with your Irish heroes, I'm sure. Have you a cent in the bank in your own name?"

"No," I said.

"Then let me give you a little sermon. Watch out for number one. That's the American way to success. That's how we make millionaires in America, Miss Fenian."

I saw she was half drunk. The maid appeared with champagne on a tray. Annie seized her glass and held it up to me. "All we ever drink around here. To success."

I put down the glass. "I can't drink to your ruin, Annie," I said.

"Then get the hell out of here," she said. "I'll drink to it myself." She downed her glass and did the same with mine. "I'm having the time of my life," she said. "At the end of each week, I send Dick Connolly a list of the men. Sometimes with a little description of what we did. How's that for high?"

I left her there, glass in hand.

That night, as I brooded disconsolately in my room, there was a knock on the door. "Who is it?" I called, thinking it was probably Tom Gallaher, full of rant about action.

"Patrick," said the voice. "Patrick Dolan."

I opened the door. "I never thought I'd see or hear from you again," I said. He was looking very prosperous in a dark brown sack coat, pinstriped trousers, a brown felt derby, and black patent leather shoes.

"I—read the papers, Bess," he said. "About the fight in Canada. From all else I read, the Fenians are—well—"

"Finished?" I said. "So now you think you can pick me off the street, without argument?"

"Of course not. I'd never think such a thing of you. Could we have a late supper somewhere and talk?"

"I've had my supper," I said.

"'Tis almost six months since I saw you, Bess," he said. "The best and the worst six months of my life. 'Twas lonely, at first, in a strange city without a friendly face, but I went to a priest and told him my hopes. He sent me to an Irishman who'd opened a slaughterhouse and was havin' a hard time of it. I put my money in with him and went partners. We sell to butcher shops in the city and retail to some of the rich folks. I do the selling, and he tells me I'm the best he's found yet. Most of the butchers are German and didn't like Irishmen very much. But I got around them by learnin' a bit of their language. You'd be surprised to hear me *sprech Deutsch*. And would you believe it, I know more now about the politics of Germany than I do of Ireland."

"It sounds grand," I said lifelessly.

"Bess, it's a great country, this America. Where else could a man like me with my little bit of cash be on his way to ownin' half and maybe all a business as big as any in Dublin?"

"Great country," I said dully. "Great country?" The words were like a match to a powder keg. All the fury that had been building up in me exploded in his face. "God, you're just like the rest of them. Money is all you care about. Great country. Yes, a great country at selling the Irish to the highest English bidder. Don't you know what they did to us up there in Canada? Sold us like slaves on the block, while they sit down in Washington mouthing high words about freedom and rights and you go about selling your liver and prime ribs to them. Why don't you buy a few poor Irish and butcher them up, too? They're going cheap, these days, cheap as Paddy's pig, as they say."

I was like a drunken fishwife at a fair, abusing this innocent man who had had nothing to do with my woes. Poor Patrick was stunned. He shook his head, all spirit gone from his face. "Ah, Bess," he said. "You're in deeper than ever with them."

"Yes," I said. "I'm in with them till death."

I did not realize how close I was to the bitter truth in those words.

Some Things a Man Must Not Do for His Country

A few days later, Dan suddenly began smiling at me with unaccustomed warmth. He caught me at the door of Moffat House and complimented me on the dress I was wearing. It was scarcely a dress at all but one of the new jackets and skirts worn by women office workers, without an iota of brocade or frills. The fine dresses the Fenian ladies had bought me a year ago were showing signs of wear, and the clothes I bought on my modest salary as secretary of the cabinet had far less flair and style. Dan himself was looking prosperous in a light blue foulard suit with a white waistcoat and green silk cravat.

I was on my way to lunch. He followed me into the hot sunshine of Broadway and suggested we try a new Irish restaurant that had recently opened on 26th Street, Shanley's. I was agreeable, and we strolled uptown talking about nothing more formidable than the weather. By now it was the month of July and the heat of New York was at its worst. I sometimes felt like a chop on some giant griddle.

Many buildings on Broadway were still decorated with bunting from the recent Fourth of July parade. With an aching angry heart, I had watched the confident ranks of blue-coated veterans swing past Moffat House and had listened to the windy speeches about the founding fathers who had defeated England and established the United States of America. How could their descendants have betrayed the Irish, when they had had to pry England's fingers from their throats less than a hundred years ago? History was indeed a whirlwind, sowing confusion and inconsistency as it raged through time.

Shanley's was an agreeable restaurant, with crisp white tablecloths and excellent food, served by well-trained Irish waiters. The proprietor, Tom Shanley, had learned the restaurant business in Paris. He was a well-set-up, handsome young man, whom Dan seemed to know well. As the food arrived, Dan began lamenting the disarray in the Fenian Brotherhood. Roberts was still in the Tombs, making speeches to reporters that sounded more and more like apostrophes to the Republican Party. In Congress, a set of Republicans, led by a former Union general, Nathaniel Banks, was pressing for a revision of the neutrality laws, which would permit the Irish to make war on England from American soil. It was all wind and rant, as far as I could see, aimed at enticing the Irish vote in the fall elections.

Dan agreed and got close to the purpose of our lunch. "I've been talkin' to some of the people in Tammany. They're sore as hell at Roberts. They're scared he can take a lot of votes away from them in the governorship election. They'd back us pretty hard if we decided to get rid of him."

"Who do we put in his place?"

"John O'Neil."

"Has he drawn a sober breath since Canada?"

"Not many. But he'll be better now. I got him to send that bitch of a wife back to Nashville. She left last night. That woman'd drive any man to drink."

I had to agree with that sentiment. But I had no desire to have anything to do with Tammany. "Is that all we have left to do, broker votes for Dick Connolly and Bill Tweed? If so, the Fenians should disband."

"Disband, hell," Dan said. "There's still a half million bucks in the treasury."

"We should return it to the people who bought bonds."

"The hell you say," Dan said. "We've only just started to fight. This is a war. We lost one battle up there on the Canadian front. But there's other fronts."

"Ireland?" I said. I recalled the defeat on so many faces, the cringing submission before English insults, the fawning on English tourists. "There's no hope there."

"England," Dan said, calmly slicing his sirloin steak. "That's where to attack. Carry the war to them, to their front doors, like the Federals did in the South."

"How?"

"Your friend Gallaher's got quite a brain. I been talkin' a lot to him. He's a scientist. Knows his way around a laboratory. He told me about this new explosive, nitroglycerin. Ever hear of it?"

My interest in science was small. I shook my head.

"The federal government's been experimentin' with it in Washington. It's fifty times more powerful than gunpowder. A glassful of the stuff would kill everyone in this restaurant."

I looked around Shanley's peaceful establishment, crowded with well-dressed noontime diners. I found what Dan was saying incomprehensible.

"You mean you'd set it off in restaurants in London? Kill innocent people?"

"Nothin' like that. We'd go for Parliament, Buckingham Palace. Railroad trains. Factories and warehouses. Bridges. I tell you, ten or fifteen people with a supply of this stuff can wreck the city of London. They'd make it look like Atlanta after Sherman left it."

"How can you be sure you wouldn't kill women and children accidentally?"

"We might kill a few. But that's war, honey. You don't think some women and children died when Sherman burned cities like Atlanta and Columbia? How many Irish women and children died in the famines?"

I felt old hatred and that terrible blind fatalism stirring in me after weeks of private passive grief. He finished me by taking my hands in his and leaning across the table to me.

"It ain't over, Bess. We've been through some hard times together. Hard feelin'. Some of it's been my fault. But what I feel about you down deep, what I remember—from Ireland—ain't never changed and never will change. Don't quit on me, Bess."

Looking back, I should have used the place where I sat, this fine new restaurant run by an Irish-American, as a lesson, a symbol, to escape the web of hatred and revenge into which he was luring me again. But my love for him, wounded and doubting and forlorn as it was, nonetheless still lived within me.

"All right," I said. "What do you want me to do?"

"Call a meeting of the Fenian cabinet and senate while Roberts is still in jail. If I did it, everyone would know we were makin' a political move. This way, you can just say General O'Neil wants to make a report on the campaign in Canada. We'll boot out Roberts in ten seconds. Tammany's already got a good twenty votes lined up."

I should have smelled the corruption; I should have wondered about the sincerity of Dan's sudden affection. But I was still inside the whole experience, still within history's whirlwind. I had no second sight. I was glad to find I still had a part to play, I was pleased to discover that I was still important to Dan.

That night, Dan and I became lovers once more. I was startled by his ardor, to which I found it hard to respond. I needed time to restore my trust and ease, to fend off the doubt that assailed me when I thought of Annie and wondered if I was choosing the wrong man again. I could see clearly what he was getting and what I was giving. For a moment as he crushed me almost angrily against him, I thought of Patrick Dolan, that sad, gentle man, the pain on his face as he turned away from me to avoid those cruel words about money. For a moment I almost tore myself loose, fled the room, the hotel, this city with its blazing heat that seemed to devour my flesh and spirit. But it was too late, he was within me, murmuring wordless passion, I belonged to him again and I gave myself wildly to the sweet soaring pleasure of it, whispering *all will be well all will be well* until I remembered those were the words I used to lie to Dan on the shore of the dark rushing Niagara River. Now was I lying to myself?

The next day, I sent telegrams to the Fenian senators in the various states, summoning them to New York for an emergency meeting to hear General O'Neil's report. Most of the cabinet lived in or near New York, and they were notified by letter. It was impossible to keep the thing a secret. Several of the cabinet members, especially Meehan, the publisher of the newspaper the *Irish-American*, were close to Roberts and told him about the meeting. He immediately summoned his lawyer and tried to obtain his release from jail on a writ of habeas corpus. He was dealing with a city government ruled by Tammany. Not a judge could be found to issue the writ. When one was finally produced, the paper was mysteriously lost in transit to the Tombs and the process had to start all over again. Roberts was still fuming in his cell when the meeting was convened at Moffat House.

A vice president named Gilhooley, a contractor with close ties to Tammany, was named chairman. He promptly recognized Dan McCaffrey, who was wearing a newly bought dark green uniform. He introduced himself as "General O'Neil's adjutant." The general, he said, was not present because he had been told there was some political business to be conducted on the first day of this emergency session. The general was a man without political ambition. This was precisely why his friends felt he should be raised to the presidency of the Fenian Brotherhood. The Fenians had been organized to fight for Ireland. As president we now had a "carpet knight." We needed a soldier. We had one in John O'Neil.

Chaos erupted. Roberts had plenty of friends in the senate and a few in the cabinet, and they had been primed for combat. It was not hard to divine the purpose of this emergency meeting, once they realized it had been convened without consulting the president. After hours of fiery debate and parliamentary maneuvering that would have done credit to the U.S. Senate or the House of Commons, the matter was put to a vote and Roberts was defeated by a two-to-one majority.

Revolutionary movements are not great believers in democratic procedure, except when it benefits them. Roberts's followers hurled curses and denunciations at the winners and walked out, declaring their intention to form their own Fenian Brotherhood. An hour later, I stood beside Dan watching John O'Neil take the oath of office as Fenian president. "Now we go to work," Dan said, all but rubbing his hands with grim satisfaction.

I felt a gust of uneasiness. John O'Neil was sober, but he was not the same man who had led the army into Canada. Drink, the humiliation of defeat, and the doubts introduced into his mind by his wife had subtracted strength and confidence from his visage. I saw not a leader but a weak man. Beside me, I realized with a shock, was the man who controlled him. Dan McCaffrey.

For a while I was too busy to think much about it. We had to fight a propaganda war on several fronts. We slammed Roberts and his "secessionists," as we called them. We continued to heap opprobrium on the heads of O'Mahoney and his followers, who freely criticized our "squabbling factionalism." Our hardest blows, delivered with all the strength Tammany could muster from the dozens of corrupt reporters they had at their beck and call, were reserved for "infamous William Seward" and "despicable Edwin Stanton" and their lying Republican colleagues in Congress, who had betrayed us in Canada and were now trying to cover their tracks with their talk of changing the neutrality laws.

New York newspapers had tremendous authority throughout America. Unquestionably, we destroyed William Seward as a potential presidential nominee. By the time we were through with him, he could not have bought an Irish vote with all the gold in Solomon's Temple. His alliance with the Radical Republicans was thoroughly exposed, costing him the support of the numerous Americans in both parties who disliked these hate-mongering extremists. Dan was the go-between in this propaganda war, shuttling constantly between Moffat House and Tammany

Hall. There were frequent conferences with Bill Tweed and Dick Connolly and Peter B. Sweeny at the Blossom Club, Delmonico's, and other places where they liked to do business. Dan often asked me to go with him, although the sight of Dick Connolly with another woman (or a series of them) almost ruined my digestion.

Returning from one of these dinners a little drunk, Dan and I made love with a fervor that carried me back to our earliest days together. When it was over, he looked about my modest room and said, "Tomorrow you're goin' to move into the Fifth Avenue Hotel."

"Why in the world?" I said.

"Because you're my girl, and that's where my girl ought to live." He took a thick wad of greenbacks out of the pocket of his pants, on the chair beside the bed. "Look at that," he said, lying on his back beside me and rippling them like playing cards. "Real money. We can afford it."

"Where did you get it?"

"Where the hell did you think I got it?"

"It's Fenian money."

"Sure. We're spendin' it the way Roberts spent it, the way O'Mahoney spent it. That last appeal we sent out, with O'Neil's name on it, is bringin' in a couple of thousand bucks a day."

"I will not spend a cent of it," I said. "Nor let you." I was half wild, thinking of the way liquor had led me to enjoy him, as it had led Annie into the grip of Dick Connolly's dubious charms, and now he was moving me to the Fifth Avenue Hotel, like Annie.

"Jesus Christ," he said. "What's the matter with you? Don't we rate it? Who went up there to Canada to duck bullets? Who went to Ireland with you? We risked our goddamn necks and you're tellin' me we can't get paid for it? We can't enjoy ourselves?"

His rage was terrifying. I thought for a moment he might strangle me. I could see not a trace of affection in his eyes. He seemed oblivious that he was snarling these words at me in the very bed where we had professed our love only minutes before.

"I can't tell you what to do. I can only tell you what I must do to keep my self-respect."

"Goddamn it." He sprang from the bed and began dressing. "You're as bad as your loudmouth brother sometimes, you know that? Why don't you trust me? If we pull off this offensive in England, we'll take over this Fenian Brotherhood. We'll be somebody in this city, in this country. O'Neil's gonna drink himself dead some one of these days. They're gonna need another hero. It's gonna be me. Dan McCaffrey. And you—the Fenian girl—my wife."

As he said this, he stepped to the edge of the bed and turned my face to him in an abrupt proprietary way. I was frightened and repelled. "What offensive—in England?" I asked.

"The one I told you about. With nitroglycerin. We'll be leavin' in about a month. When Gallaher finishes his experiments. Meanwhile, I'm gonna enjoy myself. No matter what you say."

He stormed out of the room. The next day, when I saw him at Moffat House, he was still in a surly mood. He had a copy of the *New York Times* in front of him. "Look at this," he said, shoving the paper at me. The headline of one of the lead stories on the front page read: EX-FENIAN LEADER URGES CANADIAN IRISH TO SUPPORT CONFEDERATION, QUIT FENIANISM.

My brother had abandoned the Fenian Brotherhood. In violent rhetoric, Michael denounced all Fenians as fools, poltroons, thieves, and cowards. They were tools of evil men in the United States who hoped to seize Canada. There would be another invasion soon if Canada did not confederate as soon as possible. He urged the Irish in Canada to support this movement to unite the disparate provinces and rhapsodized about the superiority of the lot of the Irish in Canada to the condition of their cousins in the United States. There they were the victim of Protestant bigotry and political corruption. In Canada, under benevolent British law, they were welcomed as equals. The solution to Ireland's woes was the steady improvement of their lot in Canada, by dint of hard work and sober living. Eventually, the presence of so many upright, affluent Irish in Canada would change the minds of Britons at home and make them realize it was their oppressive system and not the deficiencies of the Irish character that was responsible for Ireland's woes.

Father had won his struggle for Michael's soul.

I said this to Dan. He was not interested. "Write him a letter," he said. "Tell him to shut his mouth. If he wants to stay alive."

"What?" I gasped.

"There's a lot of people who consider this treason. In a war, that's a crime punished by death," he said, tapping the paper. "For the time being, it's our policy to say we're goin' to invade Canada again. We've got to say it because the Roberts crowd is sayin' it. This could make it impossible."

"So be it," I said. "I'm beginning to think the whole idea was madness from the start, myself."

"I don't care what you think," he said. "I'm tryin' to protect him, for your sake. Every man who had a brother or a friend die up there will be ready to put a bullet into Michael if he keeps talkin' this way. O'Neil himself is real upset about it. He's convinced we're goin' back to Canada. It's all he talks about."

I wrote Michael the letter. Knowing the Irish hatred of turncoats and informers, I had to admit Dan was right. I might as well have saved the ink and the price of the stamp. All I got for my trouble was a stinging reply from

Michael, urging me to join him in Canada before I ended like Annie. America had become for him a synonym for degradation and corruption. He ranted on this topic for pages of furious, almost illegible scrawling. At the close he informed me that he was not only going to keep making speeches—he was coming to the United States to attack "the Fenian snake in its lair."

I showed the letter to Dan, noting the close. He cursed and crumpled it in his fist. "You may have to go answer him, like you did the last time."

"No," I said. "I haven't the heart."

"Bess," he said, "I'm tryin' to save his life."

"No," I said. "I'd feel like I was mocking the dead. My father. I can't do it."

Michael wisely began his tour far from the Canadian border, where tempers were still volatile. If he had appeared in Buffalo, he might have been torn apart on the spot. We soon heard reports of his progress through the Midwest into Pennsylvania. We not only heard them, we felt them in the decline in contributions from each city after Michael left it. He used wit and ridicule as well as invective to attack the Fenians. There were now three wings, he said, which made the Brotherhood the strangest creature in the world, all wings and no body. But he reserved his strongest language for our association with New York, the Babylon of America. He urged his audiences to "resist with scorn and detestation this billingsgate beldame, this shameless impostor who claims to speak for Ireland, reeling and disheveled from the purlieus of Manhattan, with blasphemy on her lips and all uncleanliness in her breast."

It was easy to see that the dominant image in his mind revolved around me. He had said similar words to me in Buffalo. In every city and town, the local priests and bishop all but gave Michael their blessing, considerably adding to the strength of his assault. By the time he reached New York, the O'Neil wing of the Fenian movement could not mention his name without cursing. He was received like a visiting cardinal by Archbishop McCloskey and given the use of St. Peter's Hall on Barclay Street, one of the largest auditoriums in the city. Michael made no attempt to see me, even though he stayed at the Metropolitan Hotel, only a few blocks up Broadway from Sweeney's.

On the night he was to speak, Dan insisted I go hear him and answer him. I refused, but he badgered me so intensely, I finally agreed to go and promised to reply if Michael said anything outrageous about me personally or about Dan. He ordered Red Mike Hanrahan to go with me, because there was a good chance of a riot. The word was out that Michael also intended to attack Tammany.

In spite of a hot August night, the crowd was large. There was a heavy sprinkling of priests in the seats, making me think that each parish had been ordered to turn out a delegation. Michael was supposed to appear at eight o'clock. At eight-fifteen men began glancing at their watches. At eight-thirty there was a conference among his clerical sponsors and one of them hurriedly left the hall, no doubt heading for the Metropolitan Hotel. I was vaguely worried, thinking it was strange for Michael to be late. Punctuality was always one of his strongest virtues, inculcated by Father with many a thwack while he was growing up.

"Where can he be?" I wondered.

"Maybe he heard there might be a riot and decided to confine his audience to six reporters in his hotel room," Mike said.

"I doubt that," I said.

We sat there until nine o'clock. Finally a discomfited priest announced that Mr. Fitzmaurice was "indisposed" and his lecture was postponed. We rode back to Sweeney's

Hotel in a horsecar to find Dan impatiently pacing my room. "Well, what'd little Jesus have to say?" he snapped.

"Not a blessed thing," Mike said. "He did a disappearing act. He may be walkin' on water to Brooklyn this very moment."

"What in hell do you mean by that?" Dan said with startling truculence.

"Not a thing, me lad, not a thing. Just a manner of speaking," Mike said, backing away.

"I've half a mind to go to the Metropolitan Hotel to see if he's all right," I said.

"The hell with him," Dan said. "Maybe he got one threat too many and it shook his nerve. I heard he's been gettin' a lot of nasty mail. Let's go celebrate. I'd say we just won a victory."

He insisted on Mike joining us for dinner at Delmonico's. Dan had not paid much attention to Mike since John O'Neil became president. Mike had been a Roberts man originally, and he had little influence among the new lineup of leaders under O'Neil. At Delmonico's, Dan lavished the best French champagne on Mike and insisted I match them glass for glass.

A number of politicians, including Peter B. Sweeny and Bill Tweed, stopped to shake Dan's hand. It was obvious that one reason for coming here was to demonstrate Dan's growing power in New York. Everyone knew he was the man who could put words in John O'Neil's mouth, the man who controlled the reputed million in the Fenian treasury. He used this aura of power to persuade Mike to join us in the nitroglycerin offensive in England. He lured him with the promise of new prestige in the Fenian movement. To Mike, half drunk on champagne, it sounded glorious.

"You know why I stuck with you, Dan?" Mike said. "Roberts offered me the moon, but I stuck with you. Because of this colleen, if you want the truth. I've been half in love with her since I first saw her. I know you've got her all in that department, but that still doesn't stop me from enjoyin' the sight of her."

"Be my guest," Dan said. He poured more champagne. "We're a team. We proved it in Ireland. We'll prove it again in England."

I suddenly remembered Lord Gort on his face in the hall, blood oozing from his back, staining his daughter's skirt, and I wondered what we'd prove in England. But I stilled my uneasiness with champagne and wine and brandy. At 1:00 A.M. we went rolling back up Broadway to Sweeney's Hotel, singing an old Irish war song, "O'Donnell Aboo," into which we inserted our own names.

> *"On with the Hanrahan*
> *Fight the old fight again*
> *Sons of McCaffrey, all valiant and true*
> *Make the false Saxon feel*
> *Erin's avenging steel*
> *Strike for your country, Fitzmaurice Aboo."*

Singing away lustily, we marched into the hotel. I kissed Red Mike good night, and Dan, too, and went off to bed, where I had terrible dreams.

I seemed to be in Ireland, and Lord Desmond was on his white horse with the silver shoes riding down upon me and Michael, in the open road beside the lake. Michael thrust me aside, but Lord Desmond caught him on his lance and flung him like a toy into the depths of the lake. I ran wailing to the edge of the water and saw Michael's face turning turning turning in the darkening depths. I knelt and began to keen like a peasant.

"Miss Fitzmaurice?" called a ghostly voice. I sat up, terrified. The voice was out in the hall. It was dawn.

"Yes?"

"It's Detective Grogan of the Ninth Precinct, miss. Could you let me in?"

"One moment." I struggled into my night robe, a hundred awful possibilities racing through my head. Dan and Mike had gone off for more drinking and had been arrested and given my name for bail. Annie was in some sort of trouble.

Detective Grogan was about fifty, a great solemn slab of a man with a brown derby that looked like an iron helmet on his big head. He had a policeman with him, another Irishman named Mulcahey, who was as wide but not quite so big.

"Sorry to come at this hour, miss, but we've got some bad news. They took a body out of the East River about two hours ago that we have reason to believe is your brother, Michael Fitzmaurice."

I sat down on the bed, shaking my head.

"He had a key from the Metropolitan Hotel in his pocket. That gave us the clue to trace him. Once we knew his name, of course we knew who he was. His connection to you."

"What happened to him?" I said.

"As far as we can tell," Detective Grogan said, "he's another one of those young fellas who think they can come to New York and have a wild time. He was last seen drunk and dancing at Billy McGlory's."

"I don't believe you," I cried. "My brother would never go near such a place."

"Now now," Grogan said. "I know a girl likes to think the best of her brother. But we've got a half dozen witnesses. They saw him go off with some woman. She may have had a confederate who put the bullet in the back of his head, then threw him in the river. It happens every night down there, you know, on the East Side."

I was weeping now, shaking my head still.

"We'd like you to come down and make an identification, if you can manage it," Grogan said.

"Would you—wake up a friend who lives here? Dan McCaffrey. He's in Room 315."

"The chief of staff of the Fenian army? I know him," Grogan said. "I had a boy with him in Canada. He's the finest soldier in the army, my boy says."

Dan was there within minutes, tieless, wearing the rumpled foulard suit he had worn to Delmonico's. He held my hand and murmured, "I told you—I was afraid—I had you write that letter—"

I nodded and clung to him, my tears a torrent now. After a patient two or three minutes, he told me to get dressed. We had to go to the morgue to identify Michael's body.

A police department wagon was waiting at the door of the hotel. We rode through the hot empty streets to Bellevue Hospital at 26th Street on the East River. We got out in front of the massive gray stone building and entered the lowest door of several in its front, on the upper side of 26th Street, marked by a single word in gilt letters— MORGUE. Inside it was cool and dim. The big room was about twenty feet square with rough walls and a brick floor. A partition of glass and iron divided the room in half. In back of the glass screen were four stone tables on iron frames. On them lay four naked bodies, their loins covered by sheets. Streams of water from spigots above each corpse fell on their lifeless faces.

"The cold water prevents decay," Grogan whispered.

One corpse was a woman, a beautiful blond young girl who did not look more than seventeen. There was not a mark on her body or face. She had apparently committed suicide by jumping in the river. Michael lay beside her. His face was composed and solemn. There was not a mark on it, or on his body either, but Grogan told me there was an ugly bullet wound in the back of his head. I shuddered at the way the film of water on his face made it resemble the face in my dream.

"You identify this man as your brother, Michael Fitzmaurice?" Grogan asked.

"Yes," I said.

Oh Michael, I wanted to cry. *What cruel dark god has betrayed us to this meeting here in the city of stone beyond the ocean, so far from the green fields where we laughed and dreamed? How could love and pity and hope end in this act of blind meaningless doom? Truly we are an accursed race.*

So went the keen in my heart. Outwardly, I was American, performing the formalities of the great city, signing papers, discussing burial arrangements, thanking Detective Grogan for his considerate treatment, stumbling out with Dan's arm around me into the hot still dawn, in which the city stirred like a huge beast, ready to devour another day of life.

Back at the hotel, I began to weep so violently that Dan became alarmed and called Dr. Tom Gallaher. He gave me some bitter-tasting liquid to calm me and sat beside my bed, holding my hand. "You know what I think?" he said. "Your brother was killed by the British. They do that sort of thing, to sow hatred among us. They hired him to sow discord and then killed him to sow hatred. Perfidious Albion, Bess."

"You could be right," Dan said.

I gazed into Gallaher's wild burning eyes and did not know what I saw—madness or truth. I looked up at Dan, standing behind him. The grim, almost lifeless mask of his face struck terror into me. I writhed like a woman in childbirth, trying to expel something that possessed me both within and without, fear, hatred, love, I did not know what it was, I only knew it was a force that was stronger than my will.

The sedative struck me down into blank dismal sleep. I

awoke in the late afternoon, feeling exhausted. The dim room was empty. I was alone. The August heat gathered around my bed. My mouth was like a piece of flannel. The sheets were soaked with my sweat. I reeled·to the bureau and poured myself a glass of water. Drinking it, I wandered dazedly around the room. Near the door, a rectangle of white on the red carpet caught my eye. Mail. The bellboys often delivered it to me and other long-staying guests.

I drew the curtains and saw it was a letter from Michael. I sat down slowly and ripped it open and read it by the harsh white light of New York's summer sun.

> *My dear sister:*
> *I had hoped to see you before I spoke tonight, to pre-pare you for what I plan to say. I would hope that you at least would not take personally my attack on the Fenians. I do not want to widen the breach between us. I want to do everything I can to close it.*
>
> *I know I am in danger. The New York police have assigned a detective to guard me, a mountain of a man named Grogan. He has a son in the Fenians, and he could not be less friendly! I am sure he is keeping a record of everyone I see, and reporting it to Moffat House. So I am sending you this letter without his knowledge. I don't want to compromise you. For the moment you must depend on them for support. I have not a cent to offer you.*
>
> *I have been compelled to this course by something deep within me, a voice that whispers:* There are some things a man must not do for his country. *I see myself as trying to rescue Ireland's honor from the confusion in which I have helped to mire it. And rescue you, too. Whatever happens to me, I want you to know that the love I felt for you, the love that was misplaced in the turmoil and tumult of our rage, has returned now, with all its old force and sweetness. If I do nothing else with*

my confused life (for I realize the small chance a single man has of stemming a revolutionary torrent) I hope I can redeem you, your purity of heart and nobility of spirit from the madness into which I have led you. Let us write to each other without anger and spleen, with our old affection, and see what comes of it.

Fondly,
Michael

In Search of an American Life

I do not know how long I sat there with that letter in my hand. Occasionally I reread the words *The New York police have assigned a detective to guard me. A mountain of a man named Grogan.* Then it grew too dark to see the words. Thereafter I recited them dully to myself. I knew what they meant, but I could not think about it. My brain was stone. My heart scarcely beat.

A knock. Then a key turning in the lock. Tom Gallaher advanced softly into the room. "Ah. The patient is awake. How do you feel?"

"Where's Dan?" I asked.

"Talking to Tweed and Connolly about elections. I grew bored, and he sent me along to check on you."

"Go away," I said.

He sat down beside me. "Ah, Bess, Bess," he said. "You're full of pain. Now would be the time to let me take you. It would be like nothing you've ever known before. That is the highest ecstasy, you know, equal amounts of pleasure and pain."

I saw the madness and sickness that raged in his soul. "*Get out!*" I screamed.

"You'll feel better in England," he said, standing up. "When you see British blood and brains splashed in the streets. You'll love me *and* Dan. You'll take turns with us."

An hour later Dan arrived. I still sat there by the window, the letter in my hand. "Doc says you're still pretty upset," he said. "Sorry I couldn't get here sooner. What've you got there?"

I handed him the letter.

"I'll—be—damned," he said as he finished reading it.

Carefully, deliberately, he ripped it into little pieces. "We don't want no one to read that," he said.

"You killed him, didn't you?"

He turned away from me, emitting a great sigh. He walked up the room to the door, as if he wanted to get out, then returned to glower down at me. "It had to be done, Bess."

"Oh, God," I cried.

He seized me by the arm. "It had to be done," he snarled. "He was ruinin' us. Someone'd given him a copy of our books. He knew exactly how much money we'd been spendin'. And how. He was goin' to blab it all down there in St. Peter's Hall."

"How do you know?"

"He had his speech written out. Grogan read it."

"Tammany. Grogan's Tammany."

"Sure. They're dependin' on us—on O'Neil—to deliver the votes that can make their guy governor. Then maybe the presidency. You think Bill Tweed's gonna let some pipsqueak like your brother ruin a move like that?"

I could not look at him. All I could see was Michael's face with the drowned look, the film of water on it. "So there'll be no justice," I said. "No one will ever know how he died or why. Tomorrow the Tammany reporters will tell how he got drunk and missed his speech and went off to McGlory's and got killed by a prostitute's pimp."

"Yeah. It's dirty, but it had to be done. The witnesses are all lined up. So's the district attorney for the inquest."

I got up and began to dress. I put on my office outfit, the plain coat and skirt, without hoop or any other trace of fashion.

"Where you goin'?" he said.

"Away."

"Where?"

"Anywhere."

He caught my arm again. "No, you ain't."

"I am," I said. "Don't try and stop me. If you do, I'll go straight to the *New York Times* or *Harper's Weekly* and tell the whole story."

"England," he said. "I need you in England. We're gonna use the same disguise—"

I shook my head. "It's over, Dan. The Fenians are finished. Get away from them now. Soon only the crazy ones, like Gallaher, will be left."

"You don't know what you're talkin' about!" he shouted after me down the hall. "You can't get away from me. You know that. You'll come crawlin' back. Or I'll find you—"

All night I walked and walked through New York's hot August darkness. At least a dozen men thought I was a prostitute and asked me what I charged. I ignored them. Most of the time I did not know where I was. Several times I came to water; whether it was the East River or the Hudson I have no idea. I stood there, hypnotized by the swift current, thinking of the blond girl without a mark on her. What had driven her into the dark filthy flow? A lover's quarrel, a betrayal? Or the loneliness of this huge impersonal city? Another time I found myself on 25th Street staring dully at the curtained windows of Annie's house of pleasure. Why not volunteer? I thought. Why not sell myself for the best price, now that I was done with giving myself to anyone, anything? Toward morning I found myself back on the docks again, looking at one of the big transatlantic steamers getting ready to sail. Her portholes glowed dully, and white steam belched from her stack. Not for me, the return journey. I was an outlaw in Ireland. My mother and father lay in unmarked graves. My sister Mary was meditating on life's vanity in her convent.

I was irremediably in America, whether I liked it or not. I wandered down the river to the Battery and watched the flag rise over the round fort on Governor's Island, while a band played "The Star-Spangled Banner." I had no love for that starry banner now, no loyalty toward it, no faith in it. I was a woman without a country, a soul without moorings.

Around noon, I found myself back on 25th Street again. A plan was taking shape in my petrified brain. I would rescue Annie from this place, and together we would turn our backs on power, glory, profits. We would think no more of history's whirlwind. We would live out our days as quiet, modest working women.

I rang the bell and asked for Annie. I was told by the black maid that she was no longer "in residence." I asked where she had gone. "You have to ask Mrs. Foster," she said.

I was ushered into the garish living room. I sat there in a daze until I heard a husky voice say, "Well, another Fitzmaurice."

I confronted the ugliest woman I have ever seen. She was about four feet nothing and almost black. I first thought she was an African, but from her talk and some contemplation of her wrinkled visage, I realized she was an Indian. She had a wide flat nose and a mouth full of misshapen teeth. She looked for all the world like something straight out of the devil's furnace room.

"I had to let your sister go," she said. "She was drunk all the time. Men don't like it. The kind of men we have here. A little bit drunk—all right. But not stupid drunk. Nasty drunk."

"Where is she?"

"I got her a place in a downtown house. I told her she could come back here anytime. If she gets off the booze."

While she talked, she was looking me over. "You don't have her complexion, but you're not bad looking. Interested in taking her place?"

"No," I said.

"It's the only way you're going to make any real money before you die. Got a job now?"

"No," I said.

"Wait'll you start looking for one. Maybe you'll change your mind."

I asked her for Annie's address. "James Street. Della Varley's house. You won't have any trouble finding it."

I wended my way downtown aboard a horsecar and walked east into the twisting web of streets where New York sought its pleasure by night. In hot summer daylight it was a welter of repulsive sights and sickening odors. Bloated women and ragged men, most of them Irish, sat dully in doorways or stared from windows. I got some curious stares when I asked for Della Varley's place, but there was no hesitation about directing me to it. The building's ugly peeling wood had not seen paint these ten years past. There was no bell or knocker on the door. I rapped with my knuckles until they were sore, then turned the knob and found myself in a dark, narrow hall. An immensely fat woman in a dirty calico gown came out of a room in the front, yawning and scratching herself.

"What the hell do you want?" she said.

"Is Annie Fitzmaurice here?"

"Never heard of her. What's the beef?"

"The what?"

"The charge. Are you a private detective?"

"No. I'm her sister."

"Last door on the right, on the second floor," she said and slammed her door, leaving me in darkness. I groped my way upstairs, where a front window cast enough light to see another long hall, a repetition of the one below. I knocked on the last door on the right. Again it was a long process. Finally a thick voice said, "Who in hell's that?"

"It's Bess."

"Come in. Door's open."

The room was not much different from the one in the Greenwich Village boardinghouse. There was a thin curtain drawn on the single window, but it permitted enough light to see a bureau, a bed, a straight chair, and a night table with a bottle on it. Annie lay on the bed in her nightgown. The bed was covered with a dirty quilt. There were no sheets, no case for the brown pillow.

I started to draw the curtains. "No, no," Annie all but snarled. "The light hurts my eyes." She struggled to a sitting position on the edge of the bed. "Jesus, do I need a drink," she said. She took a long swallow direct from the bottle.

Even in the half-light I could see she was a wreck. Her hair was a tangled streeling mess, her face sagged. She was naked beneath her nightgown.

"Annie," I said, "you must stop this."

"Stop what?" she said, and took another drink. "Earnin' a livin'? You wan' me to starve?"

"Annie, I've left the Fenians. Come away with me to some other city. We'll find work and start anew."

"Fin' work?" she mocked. "Wha' n'hell you talkin' about? I got work. Here. You think this isn't work? Last night"—she paused as if to count—"at leas' twenny." She laughed and took another drink. "Twenny. Tell it to Dick. Twenny a night for his Annie now."

"To hell with Dick. To hell with all of them. Annie, we're our own selves. We must live our own lives."

She laughed briefly, harshly. "How? How, li'l sister? With a scrub brush? Ever scrub a swell's hall—a god-damn hall two hundred feet long? Or a stairs—a hundred and fifty steps? Ever feel how y'back aches after doin' that? Not for me."

Another long pull from the bottle, which had no label on it. The smell of cheap gin crept across the room to me. "I'll be okay. Soon's I get a li'l money together I'll blow this crummy joint. I'll be back inna big time. Y'watch." She giggled. "Twenny last night," she said. "Twenny a night. Maybe thirty. Tell Dick."

Suddenly her face convulsed with rage. She glared at me like a gorgon. "You hear me? Tell Dick. Tell the son of a bitch."

"I'll tell him," I said.

I left Annie there. I left my sister to the death that awaited her as surely as it had awaited Michael in some foul alley on these same streets. America, history, life, call it what you will, was too strong for us; we came into it wounded and went out of it the same way. I walked down the hall past rooms containing other women on Annie's ruinous journey. I counted the doors. Twenty on this floor and as many on the floor below. This was only one house among hundreds.

I stood in the odorous street blinking into the fierce sunlight. A hackney coach came down the street at a clip. A familiar face leaned from it. "Bess," a voice said.

It was Red Mike Hanrahan. "Thank Jesus I found you," he said when the driver obeyed his shout to stop. "I feared the worst. Get in."

"Where are we going?" I said, not stirring an inch.

"No place you don't want to go," he said.

"Who sent you?"

"Dan. He's wild."

"You know what he did?"

"Yes."

"And you still come to fetch me, like his bailiff? Get on, before I fling some filth in your face."

"I was afraid you'd hurt yourself. That's why I went after you. No other reason. Now get in."

I got into the cab's dark interior. We rode back toward Broadway. "How did you trace me here?" I asked.

"From the other place. I figured you'd go to Annie."

I began to weep. "Oh, Mike," I said, "I walked the streets all night trying to think of what to do. Now I want to close my eyes and die, that's all."

"You'll do no such thing. You'll get the hell out of this town. You'll start a new life. A new life, hear? In some other city."

I was amazed to hear Mike speaking with such strength and authority, but it did not impress me.

"What can a woman alone do, an Irish woman, but be a slavey? It's not that I fear hard work, but I dread the loneliness of it. Toiling among strangers."

"You haven't the face or the brain of a slavey. There's no reason for you to be one. Now listen to me. I've got a brother who's as different from me as the ace of hearts from the two of clubs. I usually refer to him, when I mention him at all, as Simon Legree. The name is not misplaced. He runs an agency that puts people to work in the houses of the rich. He's got a very good reputation in New York, New Jersey, and Connecticut. He's goin' to certify your references as an experienced governess, trained in London in the best English manner."

"Why will he do such a thing?"

"Because I'll threaten to blow his miserable miser's brains out if he doesn't."

I could never have thought of such a scheme. In my state of mind, I was not sure I could carry it off. "I don't know, Mike. It may only lead to more grief. Maybe it's better to let me go down into the mass, scrubbrush in hand, and forget me."

He seized my arm, not with anger but with a kind of desperation. "Listen to me," he said. "I've wasted a lot of time and talent in this life. I've never finished anything I've started. I don't know why. Maybe it's me brother, Peter, with his smug sure way of creepin' along, penny by penny, tellin' me I'll die in the gutter. He may be right. But I want to know I've done one thing. I've saved somethin' I *love*. Love, do you hear me? From the general disaster."

In my confusion and misery, I accepted his affection. I saw no other hope on my horizon. To know that one human being still cared about me was enough to make me acquiesce in his scheme. If it failed I was resigned to the scrub brush. There was no pride left in me to drive me to a higher station. Only the wish to please this sad little man.

So we drove to a building on Broadway near 22nd Street. The name of the business was lettered in glass on the door. CUNNINGHAM AND CLAYPOOLE, DOMESTIC SERVANTS. "Claypoole's dead," Mike said, "and Cunningham took to drink years ago. But the English name is good for the business." He led me into an anteroom filled with Irish girls just off the boat. They clutched their straw bonnets and shawls, gasping for breath in the New York heat, and gazed in awe at my modern outfit. I looked at their innocent faces and was tempted to cry, "Go back." Then I remembered the stinking alleys of Cork and Limerick and told myself to let history take its course. Drift passively with the dark stream. Our fate was written out in advance.

From the inner office, whence Mike had disappeared, came the sound of angry voices. For five minutes they raged through the closed door, with only scraps of words reaching me. At last Mike emerged and beckoned me inside. His brother, Peter, sat behind a desk, looking like a mummified version of Mike, propped up to simulate life. He had blankpenny eyes and a mouth like a sore, and his red hair had faded toward gray.

"This thing he wants me to do will ruin me if you're found out," he said.

"I know."

"It can't be done in New York. You'll have to go elsewhere."

"I told him you were prepared to make that sacrifice," Mike said, giving me the wink.

"Yes," I said.

"I've an offer here from New Jersey. Bit of an emergency, it seems. They won't ask too many questions. Their governess just quit. I put her in. She come through here yesterday. Told me the lad is a heller. Needed a week's rest at least before even thinkin' about work. I could put you in fast enough, I think. You parlez French, don't you?"

"Yes," I said, wryly amused by the way Peter Hanrahan affected an English accent. "I haven't spoken a word of it for a good year. But I know it well."

"You know your English literature—Dickens, Shakespeare, Lamb?"

"Yes," I said, sadly remembering Mother reading away the winter evenings to us.

"I'll cook some references for you. As for yourself, you've got to turn Orange, you realize that? Protestant as old Calvin himself?"

"Yes," I said. "My father was one."

"That should make it easier. Americans like the Orangemen, you know. They call them Scotch-Irish, whatever the hell that means."

"Who are these people?"

"Stapleton's the name. Live in North Jersey. Hamilton. I'll telegraph'm tonight. Can you leave tomorrow morning?"

"Yes."

"Good. Read this on your way. I'll have your references ready in the morning."

He handed me a book entitled *The Duties of a Governess*. I had the feeling that Peter Hanrahan had "cooked" a few previous references. There was money in it for him, and perhaps a bit of satisfaction, to put an Irish girl into a job usually reserved for English and Scots. He could not be Mike Hanrahan's brother without having a bit of that sort of devil in him.

All settled, Mike took me to the ferry and aboard it to Taylor's Hotel in Jersey City. He was afraid that when he returned to Dan and told him that he could not find me, Dan would call the police, and with his influence he could soon have them checking every hotel in New York for me.

"Why are you sticking with him, Mike?" I asked. "Why not go west, south, anywhere? Do you really believe in nitroglycerin?"

"You remember what I said about never finishin' things?" Mike said. "When I got in this fight, I told myself it was to the finish, one way or another. Besides, Dan's promisin' the moon this trip. Five thousand dollars each for Gallaher and me. Think how long that will last me at Morrissey's faro palace. A night and a half, at least."

I wept a little and kissed him. "God bless you," I said, "no matter what you do."

An Irish prayer, if there ever was one.

I fell into bed, forgetting supper, and slept the sleep of exhaustion. At nine in the morning, a bellboy knocked on my door. He handed me a thick packet, in which I found my references, a letter of introduction to Mrs. Stapleton, and a railroad ticket to Hamilton, New Jersey.

I did not know it, but my Irish life was almost over. I was about to begin my American life.

The Power of Sympathy

My train did not leave until noon. I spent the morning reading *The Duties of a Governess* and found little that intimidated me. With money Mike had loaned me, I went out and bought a half dozen outfits similar to the business suit I was wearing. To explain my scant wardrobe, I planned to invent to a story about a lost trunk, and buy what else I needed in Hamilton. I dressed my hair as plainly as possible and omitted all trace of makeup from my face. I had never worn much anyway. I studied my letter of introduction to remind myself that I had acquired a new name.

Dear Mrs. Stapleton:

This will introduce Miss Elizabeth Stark, daughter of a good but impoverished Scotch-Irish family. Miss Stark is twenty-five years of age. She attended the convent school of the French Sisters of the Sacred Heart in Limerick where she acquired a perfect knowledge of the French language and other liberal arts. (The sisters teach both Protestant and Catholic young women. I need hardly add that Miss Stark is Protestant, a member of the Church of Ireland.) She was trained in London in the most approved English manner and served three years as sub-governess in the family of Lord Fingall of Killeen. I append references from Lady

*Fingall. Miss Stark has agreed to the same terms as
Miss Hardy, the lady who has left you so abruptly. I
trust you will remit Miss Stark's first month's salary of
fifty dollars to me as my commission, in the usual
manner. Hoping to be of further service, I remain,*

Yours sincerely,
Peter Hanrahan
for Cunningham and Claypoole

The heat on the station platform was explosive. The
sun beat on the tin roof and glinted off engines, steel
girders, and tracks. The train was a dirty little four-car
local, with an engine that spewed soot and cinders into
the face of anyone foolish enough to sit near a window.
After we left Newark, it was practically empty. I gazed
out at the rolling wooded hills and small rivers. The
landscape reminded me of the countryside over which
we had fled to Bantry Bay with Dan. I thought with dull
pain that Michael would be buried without a single person to say a prayer for him except a priest, whose
prayers were discounted in my bitter mind. In agony I re-
lived Michael's warnings against Dan, the times he had
revealed his murderous mercenary's soul to me, the way
I had excused him, clung to him, lied to myself about
him.

"Is this Miss Stark?"

I looked up at a tall man with a very American face—
long and narrow, with thin lips, a strong aquiline nose
and penetrating, intelligent eyes. It was still a young
man's face, though there was a patina of sadness or
weariness that almost made me doubt his age. His hair
was thick and gray—almost white—and swept carelessly back from his head. He had a rather ugly scar on
his right cheek. I would soon learn it was from a Confederate bullet—and the white hair was also a product of the
war's terrible strain. He was dressed in a black suit,

shiny from much wear, and a striped tie. He had a gray
felt top hat in his hand. For some reason I felt intimidated by him. His eyes reminded me of the mournful
unillusioned stare of Archbishop McCloskey. Perhaps it
was my upward view of him, swaying there to the motion of the train, gazing down at me like a kind of god.

"Yes," I said.

"I thought so," he said, "Since there's no one else on
the train. I'm Jonathan Stapleton. I was told you were
coming. I had to go into Newark for an unexpected business meeting that lasted most of the night."

That sounded strange, but I said nothing. "May I sit
down?" he said.

"Certainly," I said, moving over for him. "I have my
letter of introduction here—"

I fished my papers from my purse. He glanced through
them perfunctorily. "Fine, fine," he said. "Let me warn
you in advance, my mother was rather opposed to hiring
you because you were Irish. She seems to think only an
Englishwoman can be a governess. But you Scotch-Irish
are not like the rest of the tribe."

"We try not to be," I said, almost choking on the
words.

"The important thing is, you're young. Miss Hardy
was too old to cope with Rawdon. Mother couldn't see
that."

Mother? By now I was thoroughly confused, but I pretended to be well informed. "I was told Miss Hardy left
in great haste."

"Very," he said in a dry way.

"Perhaps you might tell me more about it, Mr. Stapleton, if it is not too delicate or personal," I said in the formal English manner I had resolved to adopt.

"I dismissed her. She tried to blame me for Rawdon's
behavior. She said I antagonized the boy. I called her a
fool, and we parted."

"How old is Rawdon?"

"Eleven."

"What is there about his behavior that disturbs you?"

He frowned for a moment, his head lowered, as if he were trying to decide exactly what to say. "There are certain ideas that must be eliminated from Rawdon's mind."

As he spoke his voice deepened in intensity and he lost his polite explanatory tone.

"What might they be?" I asked.

He paused for another moment and placed both his large but remarkably fragile hands on the seatback in front of us. "He must stop thinking of me as a murderer."

The train clanked and groaned as we rounded a curve. In the distance a large city sat atop a long narrow hill. A broad river wound along its base. Jonathan Stapleton gazed past me at the city, his face blank and haggard. I saw red streaks of sleeplessness in his eyes, grayish circles beneath them.

"My family—my father, my mother, my wife—didn't believe in the war. They thought we—and the whole state of New Jersey—should have remained neutral. I said that was impossible. The Union was too important—not just to this country but to the whole world. My father died of a broken heart not long after the war began. My younger brother Paul was killed at Nashville, one of the last battles—"

"How—how terrible."

"War is a terrible business," he said. "Rawdon conceives of me as the murderer of my father—and Paul. He was very fond of them."

Jonathan Stapleton. The name roved teasingly through my mind for a moment. I suddenly remembered the major general in Secretary of War Stanton's office in Washington. It was hard to believe that proud, erect warrior and this hunched, brooding man beside me were the same person.

"But has he no pride in you, his father, who came home with the victors? Surely your wife takes your part with him."

"My wife is dead."

He said it flatly, matter-of-factly, as a man might say, "It looks like rain."

"She died two years ago, giving birth to my second son, George. Rawdon must not be allowed to corrupt that boy. He must not be allowed to spread his damnable opinion—"

"Has he actually said this to you?"

"No, but I've overheard him—saying it. He implies it, hints it, in his constant opposition to me, his open dislike of me—"

Something struck me as wrong, profoundly wrong, in this account. Whether he was consciously lying to me or lying to himself I could not tell, but it was clear that he wanted me as an ally. I doubted his story of going to Newark on business. I suspected he had arranged to meet me this way. For my part, I was more than ready to offer my assistance—I could hardly refuse and hope to keep the position. But I could not understand why the previous governess had failed to side with him.

"Surely Miss Hardy must have done her best to dissuade Rawdon."

"She didn't understand the situation. She was a fool. She thought the war was a case of simple black and white, the South wrong, the North right."

I had an inkling of what he meant, but I had to pretend ignorance. "As a newcomer, I know nothing of such matters," I said.

"Precisely why I thought you were the right person for the task. You can acquire a correct understanding of the matter—with my help. Not that I have a wish to control your opinion in any way, of course, but simply with a view to composing the difference, healing the breach be-

tween me and Rawdon—you can see with some degree
of objectivity my side of the quarrel."

"It sounds to me more like a misunderstanding than a
quarrel," I said.

"No," he said with a harshness, a grimness, that filled
me with foreboding, "It's a quarrel."

By now we were crossing the broad river and clanking
to a stop in the station. Beyond it was another glinting
steel world of tracks and locomotives and boxcars. This
city, too, was a terminus. It was also an industrial center.
Factories belched smoke, creating a noxious haze in the
thick, hot summer air. Jonathan Stapleton insisted on
taking my carpetbag and shook his head sympathetically
when I told him about my vanished trunk.

"I'll be glad to advance you money to buy anything
you need in the local stores," he said.

Outside the station, he led me toward a handsome
cream-colored coach drawn by a matched pair of fine
black horses, with a coachman and a man-on-the-box
beside him. The man jumped down and said cheerfully,
"Good afternoon, General. It's a hot day, isn't it now?"
He was a short, husky Irishman. The coachman had a
face that suggested a similar ancestry.

Jonathan Stapleton nodded his assent and assisted me
into the interior of the coach, which was upholstered in
gleaming leather, with polished brass fittings. I was a little surprised by this display of affluence. While I was
sure Jonathan Stapleton was well-off, I thought I read a
very moderate sort of wealth in his worn business suit, a
country-squire level of living, where land might be held
in abundance but cash was often short. This was common in Ireland and England, and I thought a prominent
man in the American provinces would be similar, while
the lords of wealth and power predominated in New
York, like the hereditary lords in London.

We rode through the industrial fumes beside the

railroad track and were soon in some of the worst slums I had seen anywhere. Great pools of stagnant water lay in fields off the road. The ground all about was marshy in the extreme, and a number of rickety three-story tenements tipped at a dangerous angle, their foundations obviously slipping into the muck. Cows and pigs and goats wandered beside the road. There was an incredible profusion of saloons. Nearly all the faces were Irish, and great numbers of them were idle men. They stood outside the saloons, staring glumly at the coach.

"I shudder to think of what we'll be paying this year in poor relief," Jonathan Stapleton said. "Disbanding the armies has produced a glut of laborers like we haven't seen since the panic of 1857. We hired as many as possible on the railroad, but half our cars are idle. The factories are producing at half speed."

"It's far worse in Ireland," I said. "There people are starving by the road."

"These fellows manage to eat, through one thing and another," he said, looking stonily at the idle men. "Poor relief, church aid. Stealing. There's hardly a house that hasn't had a burglary. We've had to triple the size of the police force in the past ten years. How do you deal with them in Ireland?"

"Transportation to the penal colonies."

"That makes no sense. The man leaves his wife and children behind to be a permanent charge on the state."

"No. They starve to death soon enough. Forgive me if I sound extreme," I added hastily, "but there are scenes in Ireland that would move anyone to sympathy, no matter what your religion."

"Perhaps you're ready to join the Fenians. If so, Rawdon will induct you. Our Irish maids have made him a passionate supporter of that forlorn cause." Then, with a delicacy for my possible feelings that stirred me, he added, "Perhaps I shouldn't talk so casually of it. You may take it more seriously."

"You think it's foolish?"

"I've seen what wins wars, Miss Stark. Sheer weight of metal and men. A capacity for slaughter. The British have both."

"Yes," I said, struggling to sound indifferent. "My former employer, Lord Fingall, had the same opinion." I looked down a side street swarming with animals and children playing in pools of stagnant water. "What did you think of the Fenian attack on Canada?"

"The politicians who encouraged them should be driven out of office. It was nothing but the cheapest, crudest sort of vote-chasing. But justice will not be done. Americans have lost interest in justice."

As he said these words in a bitter, dismal voice, we emerged from the Irish riverside slum and began ascending a long, gently curving grade that led to the crest of the city's hill. There was a good view of the river, tumbling over some falls about a mile away, and the country between it, occupied by huge redbrick factories that made locomotives, Jonathan Stapleton told me in response to my question. Eventually we reached the crest and drove down a wide boulevard lined with magnificent elm trees. Streets with similar shade trees slanted down from it to the west, where the city sloped gently to another marsh formed by a branch of the river. These streets were clean and dry. Neatly dressed children rolled hoops and jumped rope. Women sat on broad porches, watching them.

We jogged down the boulevard for a mile or two and turned in a gate that was crowned by gold-tipped spears. A huge shade tree stood in the center of a green lawn. A white gravel drive, oval shaped, perhaps a hundred yards long on both sides, led to an imposing redbrick mansion with white trim on the windows and a wide white front door with a graceful fan above it. "That's Bowood," General Stapleton said. "It's named for the country estate of Lord Shelburne, the man who signed the peace treaty that ended our war for independence. He and my great-grandfather became friends after the war."

A stooped gray-haired Negro in livery opened the door and welcomed us to a wide center hall with a glistening parquet floor. The walls were covered with portraits and paintings of battles, seascapes, and country views. "This is Jackson, our butler," Jonathan Stapleton said. "Miss Stark, our new governess. Is Master Rawdon around?"

"He's in his room, sir, playing with his soldiers," Jackson said, without a trace of a Southern accent. I was relieved that he was not an Englishman, who might have been able to ask me some embarrassing questions. I did not stop to think of the strangeness of a Negro butler in this Northern city.

We passed ample rooms crowded with furniture and mounted a curving staircase to the second floor. Down a wide hall we went to a room at the rear. It was a playroom, full of toys, a small swing, a dollhouse. A boy was sprawled full length in the middle of the room, with hundreds of toy soldiers spread before him. He wore loose linen pantaloons and a gray shirt. He looked over his shoulder at us as we walked into the room. There was a quickness to the movement that reminded me of a forest animal or a hunted man. But he did not rise. He remained prone, gazing at us with a cool self-possession that struck me as remarkable.

"Stand up when a lady comes into the room," his father snarled. His voice was like a lash, and it was clear that it had the impact of a blow on the lad. He stood up slowly and gazed at me as if I were an accomplice in his unjust punishment.

"This is your new governess, Miss Elizabeth Stark," Jonathan Stapleton said. "You're to obey her as if her commands came from me. If I hear of any defiance or disobedience, I'll punish you. Is that clear?"

"Yes, Father," the boy said.

Rawdon had thick wavy black hair and dark green eyes beneath a high forehead remarkably like his father's. But the rest of his face was more conventionally handsome than Jonathan Stapleton's. In fact, Rawdon was one of the handsomest children I have ever seen—so handsome that he did not seem a child. He was tall for his age, and his cool, distant manner added to the impression of maturity. I found it hard to believe he was only eleven. He could easily have passed for fifteen or sixteen.

"What's this you're doing?" Jonathan Stapleton said, walking past Rawdon to look down at the soldiers.

"Nashville," Rawdon said.

"You have it all wrong," Jonathan Stapleton said. His voice trembled slightly. He grew angry, perhaps because he, too, noticed the tremor. "If you're going to play at war, do it right. General Thomas concentrated most of his army on the left flank the first day. Generals don't spread their troops evenly. They mass their guns and men at one point to outnumber the enemy there."

Rawdon followed his father's directing hand as it swung over his little battlefield. "Where did Uncle Paul die?" he asked.

Jonathan Stapleton's agitation was out of all proportion to the mildness of the boy's question. "You've asked me that twice," he snapped. "On the right flank. In the second day's attack."

"Could we go there someday, Father? We would get there by train."

"I don't want to go near the place. There's no point in this—this glorifying the dead. Where's your brother?

"Grandmother took him to the cemetery."

Jonathan Stapleton literally flinched at the words. "Miss Stark," he said, turning to me, "you might as well settle yourself in your room. It's above us here, on the third floor. Jackson and his wife, Bertha, our cook, are the only servants who live in. The rest are local girls. Jackson will introduce you to them."

"Certainly, General," said Jackson, who had been standing in the door of the nursery this while.

"I'll see you at dinner, Miss Stark. We've missed lunch, I'm afraid, but Bertha will be glad to fix you a plate. I'm going to try to get some sleep."

He went down the hall with long, swift strides and vanished into a room at the end of it. Jackson led me to the door of the nursery. It revealed a flight of stairs to the top floor. The heat beneath the roof was stifling, but my room was large and tasefully fuirnished, with a wide brass bed and several bureaus and chests. Jackson opened both windows, and a dull breeze stirred the chintz curtains.

"You won't get much sleep up here," Jackson said. "It's hotter than Mississippi. We should rightly be at the shore. But Madam won't go, and the general ain't got the courage to make her."

"Why won't she?"

"Too many memories of the dead," Jackson said, in a voice that might have come from a sepulchre. He sighed heavily. "You've come to a troubled house. It'll be hard for you to believe, but seven short years ago it was the happiest of places."

His face and his voice were so melancholy, my heart almost ceased beating. What could I bring to such a family but more grief, more melancholy? I was swept by new doubts about the wisdom of this deception, but I lacked the strength of will to end it.

The sound of horse's hooves on the drive drew us to the window. A tall gray-haired woman was being helped from another fine coach, this one dark brown, trimmed with gold, drawn by white horses. She was dressed entirely in black. She had a small blond boy with her, dressed in a sailor's suit.

"Is that Mrs. Stapleton—the general's mother?" I asked.

"Yes," Jackson said with another sigh. "She goes to the cemetery every day. She took Master Rawdon with her till the general came home and put a stop to it. I suppose he thinks it can't do much harm to little George. But I wonder."

Jackson turned his face away from the window, as if he found it hard to look at Mrs. Stapleton. "Dear God, how the general must regret the day he defied his mother and persuaded his father to let him go to war. We should have stayed quiet here and let the murdering madmen on both sides fight it out. We'd be a happy family still."

"You've been with the Stapletons a long time?"

"All my life. My father was born a slave, property of the general's great-grandfather, the congressman. He freed my daddy, and Senator Stapleton, the general's father, decided to train me as a butler when I married the best cook in New Jersey."

"I didn't know people in New Jersey owned slaves. I thought that was a Southern custom."

"All the rich folks hereabouts owned them. There was twelve or thirteen here at Bowood. All dead now or gone away to try other things."

"Didn't you want General Stapleton to fight to free your people in the South?"

Jackson shrugged. "Wasn't any talk of that around here. It was all about the Union, the Union must be saved, and the senator sayin' the Union was gone, gone forever, and the general—Mr. Jonathan he was then—tellin' his father he was a worn-out old man and didn't know what he was talkin' about. Far as I was concerned, I didn't want all them Southern niggers comin' up here to take jobs away from my children and grandchildren."

Jackson led me to the kitchen, where his wife, Bertha, a tall, thin black woman, presided over a fat Irish girl my own age who was washing vegetables for a salad. I was given cold ham and well-buttered bread and a cup of tea. Bertha Jackson was as silent as her husband was talkative, but the Irish girl, Kate Sweeney, more than filled the vacuum.

Kate was as inquisitive as a detective about where I had come from in Ireland and as disappointed as Lucifer on Easter Sunday when I told her. She and almost everyone else in the city were from Connaught, the west of Ireland, and regarded those from the east with suspicion and dislike.

"'Tis the color of the ribbon that counts with you anyway," Kate said, meaning I preferred Protestant orange to Catholic green.

"I'm no politician," I said. "I'd like to see Ireland peaceful and prosperous for all."

"But how is that to be when your kind side with the English and divide and ruin us?" Kate said, tearing apart lettuce as if she wished it were my flesh.

Three more maids, Mary, Ellen, and Hannah, trooped into the kitchen for their afternoon tea, rescuing me from the argument for the moment. But we were back at it within minutes of our introduction when Kate said, "She's fresh from Ireland with her orange garters and says she'd sooner wed the pope than cheer a Fenian."

"I said no such thing," I replied.

"What else do you mean with your peace talk?" Kate said. "We hear the Fenians are ready to rise. They're Ireland's only hope."

"Then God help Ireland," I said, surprised that I could

say something I really meant and make it part of my new identity. "Excuse me now."

My instruction book had made it very clear that a governess never associated with the servants or spoke to them on their level. As an educated woman, a governess was considered part of her employer's family. It pained me to be so aloof to my own people, but I could not help feeling they brought it on themselves with their aggressive hostility.

I went upstairs to the nursery to find Rawdon and his little brother George, in the midst of staging another battle. George squatted, fascinated, while Rawdon narrated the bloody drama. He had squads of soldiers posted on a height he had constructed from a pillow stuffed beneath the green rug. "The rebels were here on the hill, thousands of them," Rawdon said in a low, tense voice. "Father's division was down here in the valley. The order came to charge. Up the hill they went—" He shoved a line of blue-clad soldiers up the slope. "Then blam! The rebels gave them a volley and down the hill they came—"

He tumbled them with a sweep of his hand. George gasped with delight.

"But that didn't stop Father," Rawdon continued. "He rallied his men and led them up the hill again. Blam!" He swept another line of men down the hill. "The same thing happened. You know what they called Father?"

Little George shook his head.

"The butcher. General Butcher."

I was amazed. Was it true, the boy really thought his father was a murderer?

"What a fascinating tale, Rawdon," I said. "Did it really happen?"

"Fredericksburg. Marye's Heights," he said, avoiding my eyes.

"The Irish Brigade made a great charge there, too. Did they call their general a butcher?"

"I don't know," Rawdon said.

"Who said they called your father such a name?"

"It was in the newspaper. A man wrote a letter home. Do you want to see it?"

"Not now," I said. "I must say hello to your brother George."

I sat down in a chair and lifted the little fellow onto my knee. He was very shy. He shoved his thumb into his mouth and would not look at me. Rawdon crouched beside him and whispered, "Georgie porgie puddin' and pie, kissed the girls and made them cry. Kiss her, Georgie. She's pretty."

George refused to do any such thing. For a moment he looked like he was going to cry, but I tickled his ribs until a smile appeared, then had Rawdon pull off his shoe and tickle his toes. George began to laugh. "There, you see," I said. "We can laugh in spite of all. We need not always be thinking of battles and dying."

The words made me think of Michael and Annie and Dan, of the shattered face of young Hennessy in the ditch at Ridgeway. I felt myself an infernal liar. Worse, I sensed or thought I sensed that Rawdon knew it. His fierce eyes fastened on my face. For a moment I thought scorn would curl his lip, but he remained impassive and turned away to stretch out beside his soldiers. He sent another line up the slope and tumbled them down again.

Watching him, seeing his somber young face, I was suddenly swept by the most terrible choking dread. It was as if a presence had entered the nursery and seized me by the throat. I had to struggle for breath. My heart pounded in my breast. I found myself clutching George to me as if he were in danger.

With a terrific effort I mastered this assault of nerves and spent the rest of the afternoon with the boys. I devoted most of my time to George, letting Rawdon immerse himself in his soldiers. I sensed that he was prepared to resist me as an intruder, although I did not know why. So I decided, not unlike a coquette who has studied how to win a standoffish man, to ignore him for the time being.

At about 5:00 P.M. a large motherly woman appeared and announced herself as George's nurse, Mrs. Kent. She was the wife of the head coachman and looked a bit of a slattern to me. Her dress was soiled and damp, and her hair was streeling down the side of her face. But she seemed good-natured, and George ran to her without a qualm until Rawdon called, "George. She's going to put you to bed. Do you want to go to bed so early?"

Immediately George's round little face puckered, and he fled back to me with a howl. Mrs. Kent lost all her apparent good nature and wagged her finger at Rawdon. "You must stop that, young man, or I'll get your father to give you another hiding."

"Try it," Rawdon said. "I'll get you in worse trouble. I'll tell him how much you steal from the smokehouse."

"How dare you talk to me that way?" Mrs. Kent cried. Her agitation suggested that Rawdon had struck home. "You'll have your hands full teaching this one manners and obedience," Mrs. Kent said, turning to me. "Come here now, George."

George clung to me, his little face screwed into defiance. I ran my hand through his hair and said, "Now, George, go along with Mrs. Kent, and take this to play with in the tub." I handed him a block. "When you're in bed, I'll come and tell you a story about a magical dwarf named Fer Fi, who lives within the lake near where I was born in Ireland. I'll tell you of the tricks he plays, the music he sings. We'll be laughing and singing while Rawdon is here playing with his old soldiers."

George stopped crying and said, "You promise to come?"

"On my heart," I said, crossing my breast.

George departed without further protests. Rawdon looked coldly at me. "You won't teach me obedience, except when I want to obey," he said.

"I'm sorry to hear that," I said. "I came here hoping to be your friend."

"I have no friends," he said.

"Why is that?" I asked.

"Because of my father. At school people point me out. They call after me, 'Son of the Butcher.' I had a friend—George Talbot. His father was killed at Chancellorsville. He doesn't speak to me now. He hates me."

I found this hard to believe. How did the North win the war if such feeling prevailed against the men who fought in it? I wondered if the boy's mind was disturbed to the point of madness and illusion. Yet little else in his manner suggested such a thing.

"Why do you find fault with your father for all this? Others say these things."

"You don't understand," he said. "You're a foreigner. Are you really from Ireland? You don't talk like Hannah and Kate and the other girls."

"I have more education," I said, "so my way of speaking is closer to the English."

"You're Protestant. They're Catholic."

"Yes."

"Do you believe in God?"

"Of course. Do you?"

"No."

Here was precocity beyond my imagination. He really meant it.

"Why do you say such a thing?"

"If God is good, why did He kill my Uncle Paul and not my father? He made Paul go to war. He killed thousands of people. He even killed—"

He paused and his face flushed. It was the first time I

had seen him show emotion. "Who? What were you about to say?"

"Nothing."

He rearranged his soldiers for another battle. "What one is this?" I asked.

"Chancellorsville," he said. "There is Stonewall Jackson's men." He pointed to one body of gray-coated soldiers. "They're coming through the woods. The Union Army doesn't know they're so close. They attack! It's a slaughter!" He swept down ranks of blue-clad soldiers. "The whole Union Army is being routed, until they reach Father's division. One regiment breaks, the division starts to panic. The color sergeant starts running with the flag. Father picks up a gun. Blam! He shoots him dead. He catches the flag before it falls and leads them back to the battle line. A bullet hits him in the face. He ignores it. They fight like madmen and Jackson's men are stopped. The Union Army is saved."

Rawdon's eyes were bright like a patient with a fever. He was as violently excited as a soldier in the very battle.

"How do you know so much? Did your father tell you all this?"

"No. I have a scrapbook. But you can't see it. No one can see it. Father would make me burn it."

"Why?"

"You're a foreigner. You wouldn't understand."

"But I want to understand. I'm here to become an American. If you don't let me share such things we shall never be friends. I mean it sincerely when I say I want to be your friend."

He looked away from me, down at his soldiers, for a moment. "No," he said. "You'll show it to him."

"You've hurt my feelings," I said, "to accuse me of having such a low idea of friendship."

He shook his head. I saw it was too soon and did not press him. Jackson came by and told us dinner would be served at seven. Mrs. Kent informed me that George was calling for his promised story. I told Rawdon to dress and filled George's little head with one of the legends of Lake Fergus. I left him humming himself to sleep with *suantraighe*, Fer Fi's magic slumber music.

I had thought Mrs. Stapleton might send for me before dinner, but she seemed content to meet me at the table. What a formidable woman she must have been in her time. Her face was as imposing as her son's, in another way. It was wide and strong-boned, with a full sensual mouth. Were it not for a graceful, very feminine nose, it might have been a man's face. Her large eyes must once have been luminous and striking. Now they were clouded by age and grief.

"How do you do," she said in a rather chilly way when her son introduced me. "Jonathan tells me you have been trained in London."

"Yes," I said.

"Did you enjoy your time there?"

"To tell you the truth, I saw little of it," I said. "The lady who ran the school I attended would not let us go far alone. She said it was unsuitable for young ladies to go about London."

"Yes, I suppose she was right," Mrs. Stapleton said. She sighed. "How I long to ride along Pall Mall again. I sometimes think a single day of it would restore my spirits."

"There's no reason in the world for you not to go and try it, Mother," Jonathan said.

"You may think so, Jonathan," she said, "but I can't allow your sons to grow up with army manners or worse. They need a woman's influence."

"Precisely why I've hired Miss Stark," he replied.

"You said that when you hired Miss Hardy, but she didn't stay long."

That was the end of family conversation for some

time. There was no sound but the click of knives and forks on the gold-rimmed china. The food was all cold, sensible in such hot weather—largely beef, ham, salad, and bread. It was served by one of the maids under Jackson's supervision. The drink was cold cider. I held my tongue, feeling it was hardly my part to lead the conversation. But as the silence deepened with the twilight, I began to realize that none of the Stapletons was going to speak another word. Rawdon busied himself with several helpings. Mrs. Stapleton ate moderately, while her son Jonathan barely touched his food.

"Do you wish me to begin instructing Master Rawdon in French?" I finally asked.

"As soon as possible," the general said. "I also want you to select some good histories of England and France, and some essays and novels—Lamb, Dickens, and the like—for him to read. His mind is full of nothing but rubbish from newspapers."

"I like newspapers," Rawdon said. "They tell you the truth."

"For every inch of truth in a newspaper, there's a yard of lies," Jonathan Stapleton snapped. Turning back to me, he added, "I've hired a young engineer from the city to tutor him three hours a day in mathematics and natural science. In the four years I was away, his mother and grandmother left him at the mercy of the public school. I fear his mind may be too rotten to rescue, but we must make the attempt."

This was a shocking thing to say about an eleven-year-old boy—especially to his face. I thought Jonathan Stapleton's mother would rebuke him. Instead, she sharply informed Rawdon that he was using his dessert fork for his main course. She ordered Jackson to take it away from him and replace it with a fresh one. "I hope you'll concentrate on making this young man a gentleman," she said. "He persists in resisting me. Don't despair. His father and his uncles were the same way when they were his age."

For a moment her face softened. "Those were my happiest years, when the boys were growing up," she said. "Did I tell you I dreamt of Paul last night, Jonathan?"

He was staring blankly past us into some shadows in the corner of the room. His mind was far away from us.

"Jonathan."

"Yes, Mother?"

"I dreamt of Paul last night," she said. "He was about Rawdie's age. At first I was shocked. He held out his hands to me, and they seemed covered with blood. His mouth, his chin, was the same way. Then I realized he'd been out picking raspberries. He smiled and showed me his basket. It was full of berries. He loved to scare me with that kind of joke."

"I wish you'd let me go to the cemetery with Grandmother," Rawdon said. "I'd like to say a prayer for Uncle Charles and Uncle Paul."

"Say it tonight, right here. You can pray anywhere," his father replied.

"Why does Grandmother go every day?"

"She worries about the flowers on their graves."

"Do people in heaven know what we do for them?"

A nerve began twitching in Jonathan Stapleton's bullet-scarred cheek. "Do you believe Uncle Charles and Uncle Paul are in heaven?" Rawdon asked.

Jonathan Stapleton flung the contents of his cider glass in Rawdon's face. "How dare you even ask such a question?" he roared. Whirling to me, he said, "Get him out of here."

"Jonathan," Mrs. Stapleton cried. "You're impossible. How can you ever hope to teach your son manners? I'll no longer eat at the same table with you." She flung down her napkin and stalked from the room.

I sat paralyzed. I saw triumph glittering in Rawdon's

eyes. He made no move to wipe the cider from his face or shirt.

Jonathan glared after his mother, then whirled back to me. "Did you hear what I said? Get him out of here."

"Come, Rawdon," I said, rushing around to his side of the table. I hurriedly wiped at the cider and pulled him toward the door. He stood up, shook his arm free of my hand, and said, "I don't think you believe they're in heaven, Father."

I remembered what Rawdon had said to me earlier about not believing in God. This conversation with his father had been malice from start to finish. I gazed at Jonathan Stapleton's pale, twitching face and saw myself there, as in a mirror, tormented by death's irrevocable power and shorn of consolation. Where a moment before I had been full of outrage and detestation, I felt a rush of sympathy.

Alone in a New Country

That sympathy, the memory of it, was what enabled me to play a part in the war between Rawdon and his father. I suspect that the previous governess had swung from one extreme to the other. She had begun by condemning Rawdon for his seeming hatred of his father and ended by condemning Jonathan Stapleton for the intemperate words and acts that virtually justified Rawdon's attitude. My advantage, if it can be called that, was my sympathy, which became a small flickering light that led me into the darkness of the father's inner life.

At first I welcomed the challenge as an escape from my own troubled past. I saw myself as beginning a new

American life here, within this family with its deep roots
in America's past. I learned all I could about them and
about the city in which they lived. I made the butler,
Jackson, and young Rawdon my teachers. It was an excellent way to draw Rawdon's attention from the troubled present. He took me on long walks to show me the
houses of their numerous relatives along the boulevard,
which was called Hamilton Parkway. He showed me
maps of the family railroad, which spanned the state. He
took me down to the cotton mills on the river, built before the war under the direction of Jonathan Stapleton's
late father, Senator George Stapleton.

I took special interest in what Rawdon had to tell me
about the portraits of previous Stapletons that hung on the
walls of Bowood, in particular his great-great-grandfather,
who had been a member of the Continental Congress and
a leader of the American Revolution in New Jersey. Rawdon's favorite was a younger man, a cousin named Kemble Stapleton, who had died in a charge against an enemy
fort toward the end of the Revolution. Alas, even here
Rawdon found cause to criticize his father. "He was a real
hero," he said, gazing at Kemble's thin, intense face in the
portrait. "He made the charge himself. He didn't order
other men to do it for him."

I soon grasped that the Stapletons were as wealthy as
any New York tycoon and far more powerful. But they preferred to exercise their power largely within the state of
New Jersey. It was a revelation to me, the distinctiveness
of an American state, when seen with an insider's eyes. I
had been in the habit of lumping them generally into the
South and North, or New England and Midwest, with Tennessee, for obvious personal reasons, an anomaly.

What brought this distinctiveness home with special
force to me was Rawdon's scrapbook of the Civil War. A
month to the day after my arrival, he offered to show it to
me. It was, I knew, part of his campaign to win me to his

side of the quarrel with his father, but it was also an acknowledgment that I had made some progress in my efforts to become his friend.

The scrapbook was a collection of stories and articles from the local newspapers. I was staggered to discover how violently people in New Jersey had opposed the Civil War, especially in the city of Hamilton. General Jonathan Stapleton had been repeatedly denounced for his active support of it. He was called a traitor to the Constitution and to the Democratic Party, which his family had long led. When the casualty lists lengthened, someone fastened the name "Butcher" on him.

The scrapbook was both disturbing and pathetic. It was an attempt by a lonely, confused boy to understand the mortal struggle that was tearing his nation and his family apart. It was both a reaching out to a lost father and an indictment of him. I longed to show it to Jonathan Stapleton, but it was impossible given the disordered state of his nerves.

For an entire month I scarcely saw him. He immured himself in his room for days at a time, never seeing anyone but little George, whom he ordered sent to him each day for an hour or so. He issued strict orders, through Jackson, to keep the two boys apart. He seemed to regard Rawdon as infected by some contagious moral disease from which he was determined to save George.

Mrs. Stapleton continued to take George with her on her daily visits to the cemetery. At first I regarded her with pity. She was a woman who had lost her husband and two sons in the space of six horrendous years. But as I got to know her better—she returned to the dining room in spite of her declaration the night Rawdon got cider flung in his face—I began to change my mind. She was a formidable woman, with strong opinions about American politics. She detested New England abolitionists and blamed the war on them and the "gullible" in other states who followed them. This was hardly an endorsement of her older son's politics. She did not lecture Jonathan. It was unnecessary. He was visibly suffering from the aftereffects of four years on the battlefields. Mrs. Stapleton seemed to take a morbid satisfaction in his state of mind. More to the point, she made no attempt to correct Rawdon's opinion of his father.

The Stapleton family's woes were hardly therapeutic for my own personal sorrows. I found myself waking in the middle of the night to stare into the darkness, wondering if there was any hope for me. At other times I awoke from a recurring bad dream. I saw Michael's face with the film of water on it. Sometimes he was in Lake Fergus and I could see our family farm in the distance. At other times he was in the East River. I stood at the end of the pier, with New York looming behind me.

One night toward the end of September, when the summer's heat had abated and nothing prevented me from sleeping but my own brooding mind, I went down to the kitchen to make myself some tea. I was pouring hot water into the pot when I heard a footstep behind me. I turned to find Jonathan Stapleton, his eyes glaring with menace. It was a glimpse of how he must have looked when he led his men against the Southern trenches.

"Ah. It's you, Miss Stark," he said. "I told you—I worry about thieves. We're a likely target."

"I'm sorry if I disturbed you," I said.

"No, no. I'm awake for most of every night. A bad habit I contracted in the war."

My eyes traveled to his hand, which was clutching a huge black pistol. He half smiled and looked down at it. "Don't be alarmed," he said, no doubt thinking I had never seen a gun before. "It's a good friend. I sleep with it beside my bed."

I thought I heard a hidden message in those words. I

asked him if he would like some tea. He nodded. We sat down at the kitchen table, all stiff formality. I tightened my night robe about me. He did the same with his robe, an old tattered silk thing with the sleeves out at the elbows.

"Please excuse these rags," he said. "Moths got at most of my civilian clothes. I've been meaning to go to New York and outfit myself, but I can't seem to organize myself for the trip. How is Rawdon?"

"In good health. But he misses you. I wish you would spend more time with him."

"I doubt if he misses me. When he comes near me he does nothing but antagonize me."

"I fear Rawdon's mind is terribly confused. I'm sure he feels great love and admiration for you. But so many of the people here in the city reviled you during the war. I had no idea such opinions were current in the North."

He brooded over his steaming tea for a moment. "Before it was over, I became a butcher. We were all butchers. Lincoln, Stanton, Grant, Sherman, Lee. But knowing this, and hearing it as an accusation, a condemnation, are two very different things."

He took a swallow of his hot tea, ignoring the pain it must have caused him. "You can imagine how I felt when I came home and found my own son believed this. I heard him telling it to little George. I—I almost went berserk. I beat Rawdon with my belt. I told him he was a traitor to his country. I said stupid foolish things."

At last he was telling me the whole truth. "Could you not apologize—or at least try to make it up with him? Show him you no longer feel that way?"

"No," he said, his voice going cold in the way that had chilled me on the train. "I begin to think that there's something seriously deranged in his character. I suspect he uses his dislike of me as a subterfuge to hide his laziness. His teachers all say he's bright but indolent. Deplorably indolent. Whether he likes me or not is irrelevant. He must learn to like responsibility."

This was the general in him speaking, the man who had steeled himself to bear hatred and suppress compassion. I should have seen this, but I didn't know him well enough then. I tried to alter his mind by direct argument. I told him about Rawdon's scrapbook and tried to explain the meaning I saw in it.

He dismissed my sentiment with a curt wave. "Where is it?" he said. "I'll put it in the fire, tonight."

"I don't know where it is," I said, "but if you search it out and tell him how you learned of it, I'll resign instantly and go my way."

Fury gathered on his haunted face. "I'm giving you an order, woman," he said.

"You may order till doomsday," I said. "I won't obey it. I promised Rawdon the secret of his scrapbook was safe with me. I regret telling you even this much."

We sat there glaring at each other. The nerve twitched in his cheek. "A woman of honor," he said.

"You don't think a woman is capable of honor?"

Anger faltered on his face and retreated to sadness. "They allow other concerns to overcome it."

"That's true," I said. "But once a woman sees the disastrous results of such a weakness, she may become more devoted to honor than a man."

"You're one of those?" He was openly skeptical.

"You're trying to make me ludicrous," I said. "We're talking about a very small piece of honor, here."

"It's all one thing. A seamless garment, my grandfather used to call it. If you could teach that to Rawdon—"

"You must. No one but you can do it."

He shook his head. Sad, slow shakes. "You're looking at a man who miscalculated his strength, misjudged himself, his country. I'm an anachronism, Miss Stark. A left-over from another age. I begin to think there's only one solution for such a creature."

His eyes went to the gun, which he had put on a cabinet a few feet away. I saw with horror where his wounded spirit was veering.

I also saw his isolation, his need to explain himself to someone, even a person as trivial as I was to him then. Like an invisible thread, my sympathy led me into the labyrinth of regret and guilt in which he was thrashing himself to death.

"When we met on the train," I said, "you promised you'd tell me a true history of the war."

"I decided it would be a waste of time. You're too much a stranger. A foreigner. Even though I said the opposite when we met. My mind veers between choices these days. I find it hard to decide anything."

"Tell me now. We have the rest of the night. I sleep no better than you."

He began a rambling, spasmodic discourse. Its central theme was his conviction that the secession of the South was an act of madness and folly that could not be permitted. He narrated his father's role in the numerous compromises that the politicians had constructed in the decades before the war to heal or at least to prevent the breach from widening. He quoted letters and speeches his father had made apostrophizing the federal union as the source of America's greatness and strength and denouncing the extremists, the abolitionists, and the defenders of slavery who were undermining it.

There was a heavy irony in the story. His father had convinced his sons, especially his oldest son, Jonathan, that the Union was a sacred cause. But when the moment of decision came, and the South left the union, the son was ready to fight to preserve it, while the father could not bring himself to shed blood in its name. What had been the shadow world of theater, sentiment, to the older man was living flesh, reality, to the son.

The son had a hidden source of strength. As a boy he had revered the memory of his great-grandfather the Congressman, the leader of the Revolution. He had imbibed from him a vision of America as a colossus, a continental nation in which freedom and honor flourished equally with power. The son had struck down the father in the name of that vision. "I saw the future of the nation hang in the balance in this house, Miss Stark. If I hadn't silenced my father—yes, silenced him—he would have spoken for secession, when the North chose war. My mother urged him to speak. His voice would have carried New Jersey with him. The mayor of New York, that despicable opportunist Fernando Wood, was preaching secession there—"

He poured himself more tea and gulped it scalding hot, as if he welcomed the pain. "It wasn't an easy thing to do. I loved my father. But he'd lived too long. He'd made too many compromises. Of every kind—moral, political. But he was right in his warning that the war would last a long time—and demoralize the winners and the losers. To think I almost laughed at him. I was sure it would be over in three months. And now—"

He was scarcely talking to me. He was facing the ghosts of his dead brothers, the ghostly ranks of his dead soldiers. Listening, I felt my sympathy flower into a kind of love, a nostalgic thing but also new and exalting. I saw in him the purity of purpose, the nobility and courage, that I had seen in my brother and had dreamt of finding in the Fenian cause. More important, for the first time I met a man who believed in America, who saw it not as a place to make his fortune, to win power or fame, but as a purpose, a faith, which he was committed to guard.

Jonathan Stapleton was not like William Seward or

Andrew Johnson or Fernando Wood or Bill Tweed, men who had risen from the mass of the people by an unstable combination of talent and luck, whose link to the inner American faith existed in minds equally absorbed with the main chance. America beat in Jonathan Stapleton's blood as well as in his mind. His great-grandfather had heard George Washington speak. James Madison and Alexander Hamilton had dined at Bowood's table.

With the special sight of one who had made a similar plunge, I saw the poignancy of his choice. I also saw its power and intensity, which leaped like a flame from earth to sky, utterly dwarfing my small spark. I saw the white fierce light of his soul, as vivid and profound as the facade of the Presbyterian church where I took Rawdon each Sunday, and wondered at the father's absence. I understood now where his faith had gone. It had departed that original shrine to enter the vast distances of the American prairie, to surge over Niagara and pulse in the Mississippi. He was borne on the windlike memory of the founding fathers' vision, the toil of a wilderness won, of victory over the primary imperial enemy, England, personifier of old Europe's imperial greed. He could not let the great experiment fail! Yet what it had cost him, what it had cost them all.

"And now."

I saw the sorrow on his face, I watched the pain gather in his eyes. Now the America of 1866 confronted him. America stripped of its visionary gloss by the savage revelation of war.

America was Jonathan Stapleton's faith, but he could not find his justification in the America of 1866. This, and not the personal losses he had suffered as the result of the war, was the real source of his agony. He asked me if I had ever been to Washington, D.C. Of course I lied and said no. He began telling me of the corruption that had raged there during the war, the millions of dollars that contractors and crooked congressmen and generals had mulcted from the government. Secretary of War Stanton had put a stop to much of it. This was why Jonathan Stapleton admired him. Stanton was one of the few honest men in Washington. But he did not have the power or the strength to eliminate other forms of corruption.

With white-lipped fury, Jonathan Stapleton described the thousands of prostitutes and the hundreds of faro banks that flourished in the national capital while men were dying to save the Union on battlefields a few miles away. The close of the war had brought no improvement. Faro still reigned on Pennsylvania Avenue, and even the White House had succumbed to the corruption. He said that he had proof from Stanton that the president's son Robert was selling pardons to Southerners. New York was in the grip of Tweed and his legion of corrupt Irishmen. This city, Hamilton, was not much better. The thought of dealing with these greasy disciples of greed sickened him.

He was far beyond talking to me for Rawdon's benefit now. Nor was I listening with the boy in mind. Perhaps it was that very night that I began my betrayal of Rawdon (I must call things by their right names; betrayal was what it became). My sympathy, my identification with Jonathan Stapleton was almost complete. How I longed to tell him the reason for it, to open my heart to him as he was opening his inner self to me (though really to himself, to his ghosts). I have come to believe that sympathy is a potent spiritual substance, which is communicated without words—at least without words that directly express it. In its root meaning, sympathy means "same-feeling," and it was on this current that I reached out to this tormented man.

"It seems to me," I said, "your country needs you now more than ever. Your country, your family, your state."

He shook his head. "I can't walk the streets of my own

city without seeing a dozen, a hundred, faces of men and women who have lost sons, husbands, brothers, under my command."

"Do they blame you any more than they blame God or the South or history? None of them could foresee the future any more than you could. We all take voyages into the unknown—"

He thought I was talking of my immigration to this country. He smiled sadly. "I fear I'm giving you a poor introduction to America," he said. "Please don't think the picture is as dark as I see it, for someone like yourself. There's room, ample room, for honest men and women to prosper, to be happy. But I'm forced to think, to act, on a different plane, and there the prospect is— sickening."

I said nothing. It was not necessary. He heard his own words as clearly as I heard them, and they confessed that his vision was narrowed, distorted, by his special role, his hard fate. For a moment he hesitated, and puzzlement, doubt, grew in his eyes. I could see him asking himself, *Is it possible I am wrong?*

He stood up, fussing with his robe. "We must try to get some sleep," he said. "Why do you have trouble sleeping?"

"Homesickness, I suppose," I said, clearing away the cups.

"Are your parents still living?"

"No."

"No brothers or sisters?"

I shook my head.

"So you're alone in a new country. I can see—yes, I can see how hard that must be."

The mystery of sympathy flowed between us, the current now reversed. I could only sense it then, but now I understand why. He, too, was alone in a new country, the America created by the cataclysm of the Civil War.

"Good night, Miss Stark," he said. "Maybe we've—accomplished something."

"I think we have," I said, a bit too dryly. He glanced sharply at me for a fraction of a moment and turned to go.

"General," I said. "You're forgetting something."

I handed him his gun. He looked ruefully at it for a moment. "I must put this away somewhere," he said.

The Voice of the Jersey Devil

A few days later, I was finishing Rawdon's French lesson when Hannah, the big, heavy-footed (and -handed) upstairs maid, appeared at the door of his bedroom. "Have y'heard the news, Miss Stark?" she said. "Sure it will make your orange garters pop, it will."

"What news?" I said. "This is not the time to interrupt us."

"The Fenians are blowin' up London," she said. "It's here in the paper."

"Really, now," I said, my mind frozen to the variations on the French verb *aimer* that I was teaching Rawdon. *Aimer à l'idolâtrie,* to idolize, *aimer passionnément,* to be passionately fond of, *aimer mieux,* to prefer. Hannah was waving the newspaper like a flag of triumph. Rawdon ran to get it from her. Together we sat and read the story, which was reprinted from the *New York Tribune.*

At 4:00 P.M. on September 27, a powerful bomb was exploded in Bowling Green Lane beside the wall of Clerkenwell Prison. A hole ten feet wide was blown in the wall. Houses along the block were leveled and win-

dows smashed for a radius of almost a mile. At least three persons, one a girl of six, were killed and forty, including a dozen other children, were seriously injured. Many more bodies may be buried in the debris. In a letter to the London Times, *the Fenian Brotherhood takes credit for the outrage, declaring it to be the opening shot in a war that will destroy London and every other city in England unless Ireland is given immediate unconditional independence. They declare themselves to have unlimited supplies of the new explosive, nitroglycerin, at their disposal and agents throughout England ready to use it.*

"Great!" Rawdon cried. "Don't you think so, Miss Stark?"

I could only shake my head numbly. My mind was clotted with images of the mangled bodies of women and children. Was it possible that Dan McCaffrey, the man to whom I had pledged my love, and Mike Hanrahan, who had sent me to this refuge, were committing these atrocities in Ireland's name? I thought of the words in Michael's last letter to me. *There are some things a man must not do for his country.*

"It's not an honorable way to make war," I said.

"What's honor to England?" Hannah said. "Didn't the Americans kill a million here in this country to free the coloreds? Why not kill a few thousand English to free Ireland?"

"Get out of here, you blatherskite, before I have you dismissed for interfering in my duties," I said.

She pranced out, leaving the newspaper behind her. Rawdon read the story again. It was uncanny, his fascination with newspapers. He enjoyed reading little else. He was a typical American of his age. Few of them read anything but newspapers.

"I'm going to put it in my Fenian scrapbook, anyway," he said.

This was the first that I had heard of a Fenian scrapbook. The American Fenians had been quiescent for months now. I asked to see it, and he produced it from beneath his bed. He had been well supplied by the maids. There were all the stories I knew so well, including a vivid account of the exploits of the Fenian girl, complete with an illustration of her famous gunfight on the cliff's edge at Bantry Bay. There was equally thorough coverage of the murder of Lord Gort and pages of information, little of it correct, on the battle of Ridgeway in Canada.

"I'd like to marry a girl like that," Rawdon said, turning back to the story of the Fenian girl. "Someone who was brave. Not like my mother."

"What do you mean?"

"My mother was a coward. She cried all the time after Father joined the army. She talked about killing people being a sin. She tried to make me think that way. And she didn't stop Father from hurting her when he came home."

"Hurting her?" I was more and more amazed. "Why would your father hurt her?"

"What men do to women," he said. "That hurts them, doesn't it? They cry and say they don't want to do it. Cowardly women like mother. But men like Father—they do it anyway."

"Where did you hear this? You're surely having bad dreams."

"I got up and listened by their door in the middle of the night. Later, after he went back to the army, I heard Mother telling Grandmother that she never should have let him do it. They were downstairs in the library. They didn't know I was in the hall listening."

"That was a very bad thing to do. Dishonorable. It's ungentlemanly to listen at doors."

He had learned too much to be intimidated by my moralizing. I shifted my ground. "You're too young to understand everything about married men and women, but I assure you that they don't hurt each other. They use their bodies to express their love. There's nothing of hurt in it. It's beautiful and exalting."

"How do you know? Has anyone ever done it to you?"

"Of course not," I said, feeling a hot blush redden my face. I didn't like the way Rawdon was looking at me.

"Then how do you know?"

"I've read books on it. I've talked with older women. Married women."

He shook his head. "You don't know. They probably lied to you. Grown-ups lie all the time. I asked Mother why she let Father hurt her. She said she didn't, but when George was born you could hear her screaming all over the house. It hurt her so much she *died*."

"But your father didn't know that would happen. He wanted another son. He wanted to give you a brother. Don't you love George? Isn't he the sweetest little boy?"

"Why won't Father let me near him? Is it because he's afraid I'll tell him the truth about how he was born?"

I was staggered to discover how deep and complex were the roots of the boy's antagonism to his father. Imagine my uneasiness when Jonathan Stapleton, in the best humor I had ever seen him, appeared at the luncheon table and announced he was in the mood for a drive in the country. He invited me and Rawdon to accompany him.

It was a beautiful fall day. The trees were turning red and gold on the hillsides before us as we crossed the marsh of the river's west branch. We rode in a chaise pulled by two powerful trotters, one white, the other black. Jonathan Stapleton made the wheels fairly skim along the plank road, and he scarcely diminished his pace as we entered the hills. The beating hooves made conversation difficult, which I decided was just as well.

At length Rawdon asked if he might take the reins. After some hesitation, his father agreed, but he proceeded to give Rawdon so many orders and admonitions that after a mile the boy quit the task in a rage. Jonathan Stapleton grimly resumed control.

After about a half hour, we turned off the main road and laboriously climbed a narrower winding path to the top of a considerable height, probably tall enough to merit the name of mountain. From the summit there was a marvelous view of the city, the river, and the rolling country southward to the coastal plain. We watched a toy train chug along a track no wider than my thumb.

"This is my favorite spot," Jonathan Stapleton said. "Somehow, it relaxes my mind, just thinking of it. My brothers and I used to picnic here when we were boys."

"Can I go look at the mine?" Rawdon said.

"Yes. But don't go inside," Jonathan Stapleton said.

As Rawdon disappeared around a curve in the road, the father continued his reverie. "My brother Charlie, who tended to be blasphemous, used to reenact the temptation of Jesus with me as the Savior. He used to do it American style. 'Unanimous votes shalt thou have in the legislature, and perpetual control of the congressional delegation. A gold pass for first-class passage on the New York Central.'"

"What grand fun that must have been," I said, delighted to hear him recalling happy memories.

I saw him rub his eyes and detected tears on his cheeks. I quickly turned away and wondered if we should find Rawdon. "What did he mean by a mine?" I asked.

"The family's old copper mine," he said. "It was worked out a year or two before the Revolution. We used to go down in it, against Father's strict orders, of course."

"Let us hope Rawdon is more obedient," I said.

I suspected it was a vain hope even as I said it. Sure enough, there was no sign of Rawdon at the entrance to the mine, a gaunt square aperture in the limestone cliff face. We halooed in vain. Jonathan Stapleton began to look very angry. "It's one thing to disobey a general prohibition," he said. "Boys have done that since time began. But to disobey your father to his face—"

"Rawdon!" he bellowed into the mine.

No answer.

We ventured down the narrow passage, which sloped steeply into the bowels of the mountain. I slipped and fell against Jonathan Stapleton, who caught me with one of his long arms and pressed me close to him. "Rawdon," he said. "I'm getting angry. Come out of here immediately. If you're there, answer me."

Not a sound.

We continued, with the light from above fading and him still holding me in a way highly indelicate for an employer and a governess. He stopped and began lighting matches to guide our way. I saw that the walls around us were oozing moisture and noticed passageways that ran off to right and left.

Suddenly the narrow tunnel was filled with an eerie wail. An oracular voice said, "Greetings, General Stapleton. This is the Jersey Devil."

I felt Jonathan Stapleton's arm tighten around me. The match in his hand went out. He fumbled another match from his pocket and tried to strike it, but the wet walls prevented him.

The voice wailed again, then resumed. "I have come for your soul, General Stapleton. I have lured you down here to collect your soul. We will continue together in our downward journey to join the legions of the dead."

"Stop it, Rawdon," Jonathan Stapleton said. I felt his heart pounding wildly. He was close to mindless panic.

"Yes, stop it, Rawdon," I cried. "I'm here, too, and you're frightening me."

Jonathan Stapleton finally struck another match. An

instant later, a shape sprang from the darkness and scampered past us up the slope. Jonathan Stapleton released me. I gazed into his pale, twitching face. It oozed moisture like the walls. He seized my arm and half dragged, half carried me back up the passage to the surface. There stood Rawdon, smiling like an angel, Jonathan Stapleton stretched him on the ground with a blow to the face.

"I told you not to go in there," he roared.

"I only wanted to play a joke," Rawdon said, clutching his bruised cheek. "Like Uncle Charlie."

"You're not him and you never will be. It was a rotten joke."

At home came more carnage. Mrs. Stapleton had left us to dine with a friend. Since I had come to regard the mother as a subtle irritant, I thought we might have peace, but Rawdon began a whole new argument by asking his father what he thought of the Fenian bombers. Jonathan Stapleton denounced them in the most scorching terms.

"Only cowards make war on women and children," he said.

"We killed a million men to free the Negroes," Rawdon said. "Why can't the Irish kill a few thousand English to free Ireland?"

"I begin to think you're morally degenerate, Rawdon," Jonathan Stapleton said.

"I'm sorry you think so. But I don't intend to change my opinion, General Butcher."

"Rawdon," I said. "Go to your room instantly."

He departed. In a rage Jonathan Stapleton started after him, no doubt to administer another beating. I caught his arm. "Please," I said. "I'd rather have you strike me. I take responsibility for Rawdon's opinion of the Fenians. When the maid gave him the newspaper this morning, I was too mild in my disapproval."

"But you do disapprove?" he said, still half enraged.

"Yes," I said, and began to weep genuine tears. "I'm filled with horror, loathing. It makes me ashamed of my very blood. I find myself wishing I could cease to be Irish."

Appalling words, yet true ones, spoken to this American, words that were both a confession and a plea to this man who had come to personify so much of the America I once hoped to find.

To my amazement his anger vanished. He took my hand. "My dear Miss Stark," he said. "I know how you feel. I felt the same way when I saw some of the things Americans did during the war. I wanted to quit the race, the country."

He realized Jackson and the downstairs maid, Ellen, were watching us and withdrew his hand.

There was no sleep for me that night. I lay in bed, listening to a cold rain beat on the roof. I was haunted by a new sense of fatality, of having cut loose from the few inner moorings that linked me to my old self. I went on like this for several days, dazed from sleeplessness, while more news of the Fenian bombers filled the newspapers. Each blast shattered another piece of my spiritual landscape. I listened numbly to Rawdon defending the Fenians in the face of his father's rage. It was absurd on both their parts. My sleeplessness gave me a strange clarity about the cause of their antagonism. For the first time I saw that people were driven by blind emotion to quarrels and hatreds that had nothing to do with their true feelings. These existed beneath the surface of their lives, grappling them the way an octopus seizes a swimmer and blinds him with a gush of his inky fluid.

One night I heard a clock in the upper hall strike three. I decided to try once more that sovereign remedy for insomnia, a cup of tea. I descended to the kitchen. Within five minutes I was joined by Jonathan Stapleton. This time he did not have his pistol in his hand. Nor did he say he was worried about burglars. He said he was worried about me. And Rawdon.

"I see the toll these Fenian outrages are taking on you, Miss Stark. I gather you have to put up with stupid sallies from the maids. It's obvious that Rawdon agrees with them and disagrees with you and me out of sheer perversity. I've decided it might be best for you—and him—if we separated for a while. We have another house, Kemble Manor, down on the shore in Monmouth County, where we used to spend our summers. I'd like to send you there. You can hire a local cook. We'll discontinue his scientific tutor. You can continue his French and English literature and add some American history, for which I'll give you an outline—

"Of course, you'll visit us from time to time," I said.

"I doubt it. The less I see of Rawdon, the better."

"No," I said. "You must not abandon him. There's good in the boy. I don't agree with your doctrine of moral perversity. I think I know what's troubling him. It has nothing to do with the war or your role in it. All that is as much subterfuge as the Fenians. It's a delicate thing that I almost hesitate to broach to you. Rawdon told it to me in a moment of boyish impulse, without an iota of prurience."

With a good deal of stumbling and blushing, I told him that Rawdon had conceived the notion that his father had caused his mother's death. I carefully omitted all mention of listening at doors. "His mind is confused, one might even say ignorant, about the whole process of—of sexual love. He thinks of it as a hurtful thing. He heard his mother's cries when she was giving birth."

I looked up from my teacup to find Jonathan Stapleton staring at me like a man transfixed. "I'll talk to him," he said.

"No," I said. "It cannot be approached directly. It would only rub the wound raw again. You must somehow find the patience to wait for him to grow out of it—to discover a woman's love for himself. Or better, to see you marry again. Have you not thought of it?"

"No," he said. "I—I made such a botch of it the first time."

"I—I can't believe that," I said.

His two hands were on the table, gripping each other convulsively. "I'm not a lover by nature, Miss Stark. I'm not at ease in women's company. I don't know how to please them. My wife—and my mother—made that very clear to me."

"But—but you can't let the verdict of one or two women condemn you for life. Who—who knows what flaws there were in your wife's feelings for you? For life itself. I want to speak no evil of the dead, but—"

Now I saw the wound within the wound, the pain beneath the pain, in this man's haunted gray eyes. I wondered if it was in my power to heal that wound, soothe that pain. I simultaneously shrank from and welcomed the idea. Perhaps within me I already sensed the possibility of a terrible explosion of love, hope, and desire, that could destroy us both.

"I—I appreciate your kind thoughts of me," he said. "I fear they're wasted. But I'll accept your feminine wisdom about Rawdon. I'll try to be patient. I'll come visit you—often."

House of Happiness

The next morning, Rawdon raced up from the kitchen after breakfast with an Irish-American paper carrying the latest news of the Fenians. I braced myself for more carnage. What I read was something worse.

FENIAN BOMB FACTORY EXPLODES

The Fenian bomb war in England may have received a fatal setback if there is truth to a story carried in the London Times *on October 15. As police surrounded a house in Warrington, outside Liverpool, it exploded with devastating impact, killing several officers. Two bodies found in the wreckage were said to be Dr. Thomas Gallaher and Michael Hanrahan, both American citizens of Irish descent. Fenian spokesmen in New York confirm that these men were part of the "dynamite brigade" led to England by General O'Neil's chief of staff, Colonel Daniel McCaffrey.*

Alas, poor Mike, I thought as tears started from my eyes. *An end to blarney, an end to bucking the tiger. You have finished something at last.*

"Do you know any of them?" Rawdon said, noticing my agitation.

"No," I said. "Besides, we have more important things to talk about. Your father wants us to go away together, to Kemble Manor, and live there for a while."

"That's all right with me," Rawdon said. "Kemble Manor is a nice house. We used to have fun there."

Pleased that he was accepting the transfer so well, I went downstairs in search of Jackson or his wife, Bertha, to learn more about the house and where we could buy food, the sort of cook we might hope to hire, the clothes I might need. I walked into the kitchen and saw a man in a white apron delivering something to Bertha. She stepped over to her cashbox to pay him, and I got a full view of him. It was Patrick Dolan. He stared at me as if I were an apparition. God knows what might have happened if I had not held out my hand and said, "My goodness, is this Mr. Dolan from Limerick? You remember me, Elizabeth Stark? My mother rented a house not far from your parents' house, remember?"

"Oh—oh, yes," he said. "What a start it gave me to see you here, so unexpected."

"I had no idea you were in this city. I've been here for three months as governess, but I've gone out little."

"Yes. Well—would you be going downtown by any chance? I'll be glad to give you a lift in my wagon."

"I was, as a matter of fact," I said. I was desperate to get him out of the kitchen. "Let me get my coat, and I'll meet you at the gate."

He was waiting beside his wagon, which had his name and his partner's name, Delahanty, painted in large letters on the canvas top. As for Patrick himself, he was anything but a good advertisement for the meat he was purveying. He was appallingly thin and until he saw me coming toward him, woebegone. He began telling me how he'd read about Michael's death and gone to New York again in search of me but could only learn that I'd disappeared.

"If there's ever a sign that we're fated, Bess, that my prayers are going to be answered, it's this," he said.

I found myself disliking intensely the Irish sound of that statement. I was nevertheless stirred by the coincidence, almost as much as Patrick. I told him I had quit the Fenians and why.

"I thought I had left you as well, left everything and everyone from the past, even my name. I don't know what my feelings are now," I said.

"Surely you won't object to my coming to see you, asking you to dinner at my partner's house. He has a lovely wife and two children."

I shook my head. "I'm going away for a few months to their other house on the shore. The boy and his father don't get along."

"Few get along with him, the general, I hear. The saying in town is, he got all the brains and none of his father's good nature, while his brother Charles, who died invading Cuba in '59, was the reverse. Does he treat you well?"

"Yes," I said, "but he's a troubled man. The war ruined his nerves."

He persuaded me to let him drive me downtown, explaining the while that he usually did not make deliveries, their wagonman was ill. In the business section, a dozen people called out greetings to him in every block. He had clearly established himself in the city. Once he made a stop to deliver some meat to a butcher and took me into the shop. The owner was a huge fat German who boomed, "*Guten Tag,* Herr Dolan."

"*Guten Tag* to you, Herr Schneider," Patrick replied. "Look at this, now. Here's where I win my argument about which are prettier, German girls or Irish girls. Here's one from the Emerald Isle, just off the boat."

"*Schön, schön,*" said Schneider with a twinkle in his eye. "But can she cook? German girls will put flesh on your bones, Dolan!" Schneider thumped his vast girth. It looked as if a half dozen German girls had been working to put flesh on him. "I tell him he should marry. A bachelor life is pfui. You starve to death."

East of the business section, we entered a series of tree-lined squares fronted by new brownstones. This was where the well-to-do but not rich people lived. Patrick stopped the wagon before one house on a corner lot in Morris Square. The house was empty. "My partner, John Delahanty, put up half the money to build this. He's been deviling me to buy it—and move into it with his sister as my bride. They're all mad to marry me off. Now that I've found you again, Bess, I think I will buy it. All about here are Irish, fine people, Bess. Men like myself, who got together a bit of money and invested it and are working their heads off to see it grow."

I didn't like the sound of any of it. I had no enthusiasm for living with Irish in America. I wanted to *be*

American. Even as Patrick talked, I felt the blind wish swell in me. I was back in Bowood's midnight kitchen traveling with Jonathan Stapleton on our current of sympathy into the ideal heart of America. Beneath it, beyond the reach of my mind, lay the other more dangerous wish that I had glimpsed last night, the wish that sympathy could become love that would transform me into an American beyond the reach of Ireland and its bitter memories.

All Patrick Dolan could see—I could not see much more—was my lack of enthusiasm. "I'm sorry, Bess," he said, taking up the reins again. "I'm letting my mouth run miles ahead of your feelings. I'll buy the house no matter what. A man with a good business needs a decent address."

"Yes," I said. I wanted to say I was sorry, genuinely sorry, for the pain I was causing him, but I was too engulfed in my own pain and my blind hidden wish to escape it. I was already unknowingly the captive of a dream of impossible love.

We rode back to Bowood in silence. I got down from the wagon and looked up at Patrick. He had such a sad expression on his thin face, I climbed back up again and kissed him. "Marry a German girl," I said. "She'll put flesh on your bones!"

The next day Rawdon and his father and I set out for Kemble Manor. It was ten or fifteen miles beyond the main terminus of the family's railroad, the Camden and Amboy, in a place called Middletown. At Perth Amboy, we transferred to a dirty two-car train, pulled by a small huffing red and blue engine. Jonathan Stapleton told us it was one of the oldest engines on the line.

Rawdon spent the trip reading the newspapers. He asked his father numerous questions about Washington politics, which continued to be absorbed in the struggle between Congress and President Johnson over the treatment of the conquered South. Jonathan Stapleton said both sides were wrong. Congress was too hungry for vengeance against the defeated South. Some Southerners were trying to enslave the Negro again, using subterfuge and midnight violence.

"Here's a story that claims the Fenians have quit bombing England," Rawdon said. "General O'Neil says the whole thing was a mistake. He says the man who started it, McCaffrey, has been thrown out of the brotherhood."

"I'm not surprised," Jonathan Stapleton said. "They've won themselves nothing but universal detestation. Even Tammany has condemned them. Their friends in Congress have all deserted them."

So my Donal Ogue had fallen like Lucifer into the hell he dreaded—poverty. If he was still alive. His body may have been in the wreckage of Tom Gallaher's bomb factory.

"Why did the Fenians let McCaffrey start bombing and then throw him out?" Rawdon asked.

"If you must waste your time reading newspapers," his father said, "look for some pleasanter topics. Miss Stark finds those Fenian bombers upsetting. I don't blame her."

The engine emitted a great shriek, and we began to slow down. In a moment we were at a station, which was little more than a shed. We got down with our bags, and Jonathan Stapleton led us inside and over to a wire cage where a man sat.

"Good morning, Fred," Jonathan Stapleton said. "How are you feeling?"

"Why, just fine, General," replied Fred, who had a quizzical drooping face and hair that spilled in a kind of cowlick onto his forehead. "Funny thing, though, in cold weather the wooden leg hurts more than the real leg."

"Others have told me that," Jonathan Stapleton said. "Does the wooden leg work well?"

"Otherwise fine. I'm eternally grateful to you, General. For the job here, and for gettin' me off them crutches."

"Good. Any sign of Abner with our carriage?"

"He should be along any minute. I told him just when you were comin'."

"He may have trouble hitching up a team."

"No, sir, General. He does just fine. I've seen him drivin' down the main street lookin' as smart and sure of them two big horses as the wildest young dust raiser around."

We heard the clump of horses' hooves on a sandy road, then a voice calling "Whoa now." We went out to find a burly, handsome man driving an open carriage. He jumped down to help with our bags, and I saw that his left sleeve was empty. He was introduced to me as Abner Littlepage. "Abner's mother will be cooking for us," Jonathan Stapleton said. "He was the color sergeant of the 6th New Jersey Volunteers."

"Did you shoot him?" Rawdon said, staring at the empty sleeve.

"What?" Jonathan Stapleton said.

"No," Abner said. "That was a feller in the 4th New Jersey. He deserved to get shot. He was runnin' the wrong way. I don't think the old 6th Regiment ever run, did it, General?"

"Only *after* the rebels," Jonathan Stapleton said, with a grim smile.

"Yeah, we chased them, all right," Abner said, climbing into the driver's seat again.

For another flashing moment I had a glimpse of the battle commander Jonathan Stapleton had been. Rawdon saw it, too. I think he was nonplussed to find this man and the stationmaster, who now appeared in the doorway on a cane, showing so much admiration and respect for his father. According to the devil theory that was operating in Rawdon's mind, they should have hated him.

As we went swiftly down a narrow road through the woods, a deep, fresh smell filled the air. I asked what it was. "Jersey pines," Jonathan Stapleton said. "I never smell them without feeling like a boy again. Soon they'll mingle with the smell of the salt air."

"I like it, too," Rawdon said. He wanted to sound defiant, but it came out closer to halfhearted agreement.

Abner was acting as caretaker and man of all work at Kemble Manor, Jonathan Stapleton said. "I've tried to find places—on the railroad, at the mills—for all the men from my division who came home without arms or legs. There are over a thousand of them. The state of New Jersey has done nothing for them, no special aid, not even artificial legs. Some Southern states, bankrupt as they are, are spending more for their crippled veterans."

"It seems to me there must be others who would share your indignation," I said. "Perhaps you should consider entering politics."

"If you knew what American politics was like, Miss Stark, you wouldn't wish me such a fate. Assuming you wish me well, of course."

"How could I wish you otherwise?" I said.

I ached to tell him that I did know what American politics was like and that was precisely why I thought it needed a man like him. Not for the first time I was troubled by the gap my false identity created between us. But what would he think of Bess Fitzmaurice, the Fenian girl? I avoided answering that question. I trusted—or blindly hoped—in the power of sympathy.

"There it is," Rawdon said, leaning out of the carriage.

The brick house looked no bigger than a toy in the distance. We crossed a broad moor thick with high, waving grass over which sea birds flew, calling shrilly to each other. Jonathan Stapleton said that the marsh had once been farmland, drained by the first settlers, with methods learned from the Dutch. The Stapletons had let the sea and the numerous tidal brooks reclaim it, having no interest in the modest profits of a farm. The marsh now constituted a barrier isolating the house from the mainland.

The road carried us to the coast and a stupendous view of Raritan Bay and the broad Atlantic beyond it. A few hundred yards from the crossroads the road became the entrance to the manor house. There were traces of a road that once ran along the coast beyond that point, but the Stapletons had closed it. The November wind whipped off the water, sharp with the tang of sea salt. The house had Bowood's Georgian style of architecture, but its bricks were a more delicate, rosy red, and it lacked Bowood's imposing bulk.

Inside, there was no attempt at Bowood's splendor. In fact, Jonathan Stapleton said, most of the fine furniture that had once filled these rooms was now in the Northern house. What remained in the sitting rooms was mostly lacquered rattan, filled with old faded cushions. I had expected to find the place cold and musty, but Abner Littlepage had the fireplaces burning briskly, and his mother and young sister had the beds made and everything dusted and bread baking in the oven. The smell of the bread carried me back to Ireland for a painful moment. I thrust the memory aside. The past was *dead*.

In the modest center hall, Jonathan Stapleton gestured to facing portraits. One was of a powerfully built man with an exceptionally strong face. The other was of a petite dark-haired, bright-eyed woman. "My mother's great-grandparents," he said. "He's my namesake. Jonathan Gifford. He was Anglo-Irish, from Dublin. That's his wife, Caroline. He was a British officer before the Revolution. Resigned from the army and settled here and went with the Americans."

"Does this mean the Stapletons have Irish blood?" I asked lightly.

"I suppose so," he said with a brief smile. "We'll have to swear you to secrecy."

Upstairs, Jonathan Stapleton led me to the front bedroom, with its magnificent view of the sea. "This will be yours," he said. "I'll be across the hall. We can enjoy the view together."

His words, his manner, stirred desire in my flesh. He wanted to share more than the view. As did I. Rawdon burst in on us, restoring propriety. "Let's go for a hike on the beach!" he shouted.

"We old folks are too tired from our train trip," I said. "You go and tell us what you find."

"You're a couple of layabouts!" he said, and charged downstairs. From the window, we watched him race boyishly down the drive toward the water. "That's the first time I've seen him in a good humor since I came home," Jonathan Stapleton said.

"There's something hopeful about this house," I said. "With the sea open before us."

"People were happy here," Jonathan Stapleton said. "Perhaps they've left echoes behind them."

"Were you among the happy?" I asked.

"Yes," he said with a sad nostalgic smile.

"Can you not be happy again?"

"I'm afraid I never had the knack. The happiness was created by others. Especially my brother Charlie. He had the gift of laughter. Of seeing the lighter side of things. Unfortunately, he laughed at everything—responsibility, hard work, women, morality."

He paused for a long pregnant moment. "Rawdon has an amazing resemblance to Charlie—"

"All the more reason to love him."

"Charlie was heart and soul on the rebel side of the argument. He died in Cuba hoping to make the island a Southern state. It was to be the first step to a Southern Caribbean empire."

I sensed—no, better, I *knew*—he was confessing a deep dislike of Charlie that was entangled with a demoralizing love. Here was the real source of his antagonism to Rawdon, his fear that the boy was morally contaminated.

"How terrible. But—it's all past. Charlie's dead along with the South's dreams of glory. The sea is like the future—open to you, to all of us."

"Perhaps."

"You should venture out on it—for Rawdon's sake as well as your own."

He gazed intently at me for a moment. I was sure he was going to say, *And for your sake as well.* I sensed his wish to say it. I was certain in that moment he longed for me as I longed for him.

"Will you stay the night?" I asked.

"There's no train back."

"Good," I said. "We can be happy for a few hours, at least."

Those penetrating gray eyes studied me for another long moment. Was he reading my very soul? "We can try," he said.

Amo Amas, I Love a Lass

After a delicious dinner of clams and oysters from Raritan Bay, followed by roast duck, shot only a few weeks ago as he winged south over the marsh, we retired to the south parlor and Jonathan Stapleton announced we were going to play "The Checkered Game of Life." He got down from a cupboard a brightly colored board that had attached to it a teetotum—a spinning arrow, whose point came to rest on a set of numbers from one to six. The board was covered with squares denoting various crises and experiences as well as traits of character. The goal was to get from Infancy in the lower left-hand corner to Serene Old Age in the upper right-hand corner. The teetotum delivered to the player with each spin the number of moves he could make, and in which direction.

It was great fun as well as productive of serious thoughts. The creator of the game had no illusions about America or life itself. If you landed on Influence, you leaped across the board to "Fat Office." The next spin of the teetotum could be fatal for the fat-office holder because it might land him on Ruin, which was very near. This pitched him back to the beginning. Bravery sent you to Honor, Industry sent you to Wealth, but neither advanced you toward the ultimate goal. Cupid sent a player to Marriage, which was also a backward step. There were the disasters of Jail, Disgrace, and Suicide to be avoided as well as the bad habits of Idleness and Intemperance.

I won every game we played. Jonathan Stapleton came close to beating me once, when he reached Success, just below Serene Old Age. But his next spin was a three, which forced him to move diagonally back to Bravery, which in turn sent him back to Honor, very near the beginning. Rawdon was even more unlucky. He had a fatal tendency to land on Disgrace and Intemperance, and he never once landed on Perseverance, which shot you all the way across the board to Success. Eventually he grew disgruntled and quit the game.

"I think you're a couple of cheaters," he said.

"That is no way to talk to Miss Stark—or to me," Jonathan Stapleton growled.

"'Twas the luck of the Irish," I said. "I'll share some of it with you."

I drew him to me for a firm kiss. He stepped back, half smiling. He wiped his hand across his mouth, and for a moment I wondered if he was responding with more than boyish thoughts. "I think it's past your bedtime, young man," I said.

Rawdon confessed he was sleepy and went to bed. The Littlepages, mother, daughter, and Abner, had long since departed. Jonathan Stapleton said he felt the need of some exercise. He asked me if I would join him in a walk along the shore. We found an almost full moon riding high above the bay. The night wind was cool but easily repelled by my gray cloak. The general wore his old army cloak, which he left open to the wind.

We walked for almost an hour, he guiding me over numerous rocks and logs in the path. Each time he took my hand, I felt something flow between us that quickened my heart and pulse. As we walked he told me the story that had come down to them from his maternal great-grandmother, Katherine Rawdon. She had lived through the American Revolution and recalled how her stepfather, Jonathan Gifford, had fallen in love with Caroline Kemble, the mistress of Kemble Manor, even though she was married to the wife of his best friend. The latter had remained loyal to the king and fled to British lines for protection. Caroline chose the American side.

"The old lady made a romance out of it," Jonathan said. "She had Gifford tricked into coming down here one night on the pretext that someone was breaking into the house, and Caroline Kemble, taking the initiative, telling him she loved him—and saw no point in waiting for a clergyman to prove it."

"Do you think it happened that way?"

"I don't know. I haven't thought about it for a long time."

"I don't think it's impossible. Women are not such passive creatures as you men like to think."

"My mother certainly was not passive. My father found that out a hundred times."

"A woman in a revolution—in a great upheaval—may decide love is more important than respectability."

He stopped to search out some landmarks on the moonswept moor. "We'd better turn around," he said. "We'll soon be halfway to Shrewsbury."

Our return journey was not so pleasant. Clouds began to scud before the moon, and the wind developed a cutting edge. "It will storm before morning," he said.

I was trembling violently with the cold by the time we reached the manor house. He flung logs on the dying fire and declared that the only remedy was some brandy from the wine cellar. "This belonged to the original Jonathan," he said as he uncorked it. "He kept a tavern not far from here. That was a respectable business in those days. Before the Irish came over and gave it a bad name."

"What a pity that there's this bad feeling between the Irish and the Americans. They're natural allies, both with such good reasons to oppose the English."

"It's the low types that came over in the late forties and fifties that gave you a bad name," he said as he poured the liquor. "Of course we except Protestants like you. It's the Catholics that we dislike. It's hard to respect people who let priests and popes run their lives."

"Yes," I said.

I spread my cloak before the fire and sat down, holding up the brandy to let the flames glow through it. "Let's drink to ancient Ireland, before there were priests and politics to divide us." I said.

He sat down beside me and raised his glass before the fire in the same way. "To ancient Ireland," he said.

We drank off the strong liquor. Age had soothed its bite and deepened its strength. I felt fire run through my whole body.

"The women of ancient Ireland were like your ancestor, Caroline," I said. "They, too, sought out their men. The old books are full of stories of queens riding on white horses to invite great warriors into their beds."

"Did they find happiness?" Jonathan asked.

"For a while. But Ireland had a way of withering it, alas. I'm thinking of the greatest of them, Dierdre. In the end she became Dierdre of the Sorrows, an image of her sad tormented country."

"Is that why you came to America?" he asked.

"You yourself said it. There's hope here. A future as open as that sea."

A wind that might have risen out of Ireland beat on the windows. The fire blazed, turning our faces and hands golden. Jonathan was on his elbow, staring into the flames as he must have done in a thousand camps in his four years of war. He looked up at me. "I begin to wish I could share that American future with you," he said.

"Let us at least share the happiness in this house."

I pressed my lips against his dry, aching mouth. With a sigh that was almost a groan, he gathered me into his arms. His kiss was harsh, almost angry, full of terrible need. Without another word he picked me up and mounted the stairs to his bedroom. There, with great shafts of moonlight on the floor and the sea wind beating on the windows, he made me—I hoped, I wished, I prayed—his American bride.

His entering me was both a real and a mystical thing. I also entered him, almost crying out with the joy of a blind wish fulfilled. Wrapped within each other's arms we journeyed into the darkness of our opposite selves, all things melting, male and female, age and youth, flesh and spirit, faith and doubt, ancient Ireland and new America. He was a tunnel down which I groped to a world of new hope and fresh promise. I was a bower in the field, a secret cavern in the mountain, where magical refreshment awaited the warrior.

It was violent and brief, that first time, dominated by his need, tormented by the terrible historic voice that haunted him even as he possessed me. I felt the dryness, the harshness, of him—until the great pounding release that lifted me up on a flood of joy, on a river of fire. The youth, the life, that was locked within him cascaded into me, and I returned it to him through my lips, my finger-tips, the nipples of my breasts, the throbbing rise of my belly, the pulse of my thighs. We were one being and my heart was ripped open, defenseless with a love that aban-doned all caution, all rules of survival, that mocked dan-ger and embraced the future. I really believed that we were entering a new country, that together we were find-ing the power to change a world. This indeed was hap-pening, but it was a country of the heart, a world that existed outside time.

I would not, I could not, think about this uneasy truth that night. Perhaps he did. It was harder for him to free himself from the grip of time, responsibility, reality. He wanted to take me to my room almost as soon as it was over, but I would not let him make it a furtive, guilty thing. I refused to leave him. "You're mine as long as the moon is high," I said. "We're equals here, in the house of happiness. That is all I ask or expect."

I pressed my body against him and sealed those words with a long, deep kiss. We begn to make love again, slowly, tenderly, with less of need and more of sweet sensual caring, of seeking and finding and exchanging new pleasure in every touch and turn and caress, in every soft lingering kiss. This time I felt the slow gathering of his desire, I felt him possessing it, controlling it, using it to turn me from queen to servant to woman to queen again, into laughing sighing pleasure into May in De-cember into the sunlit sea on the back of a great white horse springing from wave to wave toward the vast shin-ing horizon.

Yes! My love, my love, yes you are with me and I am with you there is no part of the sea or sky that we cannot reach—

In the darkness—in the sweet trembling moonlit darkness—

O my love, I am there with you again as I write this, so many long years after that night.

At last the moonlight dwindled to a single patch on the ceiling and vanished. I left him with a final kiss and gathered the clothes that lay beside the bed and went naked back to my own room while the house shook in the rising wind. In our separate beds we watched the dawn bring a storm of cold gray rain. It was a kind of omen, a commentary on the summer world we were creating in the face of winter.

At breakfast we met each other as ordinary mortals once more. We discussed train schedules and food supplies and decided to let Rawdon subscribe to New York newspapers to replace the Hamilton ones he read at Bowood. Behind our commonplace words we watched each other with eyes forever changed. I sensed he wondered what I expected from him now. That wary sadness was in charge of his spirit once more, but it had received a challenge from something deeper in him, the youth that early responsibility and a puritanical wife and hovering mother had denied him. He could never go back to that gloomy defeated self, as long as I was here to look him in the face.

He asked me to ride to the station with him, ostensibly to arrange for the delivery of the New York papers. We left Rawdon unpacking his toy soldiers. Abner Littlepage, swathed in oilskins, brought a closed carriage to the door. In its dark interior, with rain beating on the windows, Jonathan took my hand in an almost mournful way, as if we were going to a funeral.

"What shall we do?" he said. "What shall we do now?"

"I told you last night. I ask nothing, I expect nothing."

"Why? Why should you take all the risk and I—"

"Women have been doing that since time began."

He laughed harshly. "When I married, there was a contract, two pages long, specifying who would get what."

"You could still have been happy, if you loved each other."

"I don't believe in it. Not for me, anyway."

"Love."

"Yes. I should. I saw men die because they loved their country. But this kind of love—"

"You think you don't deserve it."

"Perhaps."

The carriage rocked and rumbled. The rain splattered against the sides. "Let me give you an Irish poem to recite," I said.

> *"Amo, amas*
> *I love a lass*
> *As cedar tall and slender*
> *Sweet cowslip's face*
> *Is her nominative case*
> *And she's of the feminine gender."*

He laughed briefly, uncertainly. "I like that," he said.

A moment later he grew serious again. "We must trust each other," he said. "I'm not by nature trusting."

"No, love each other. If we do that, all else will follow. For as long as we want it to follow."

He looked out at the long arms of the marsh grass, thrashing wildly in the rain and wind. "Here in your kingdom of the heart that's possible. But up ahead, the real world begins."

I flung myself against him, pressing my face against his damp cloak. I breathed the battle smoke, the bitter residue of a thousand campfires that was in it. "I've had enough of the real world for a while. So have you. So has Rawdon."

He said nothing. But I felt his hand in my hair. Then he began to whisper:

> "*Amo, amas*
> *I love a lass*
> *As cedar tall and slender . . .*"

In the distance, a railroad engine shrieked a warning. The storm beat maledictions on us, but we were safe within each other's arms. All will be well, I vowed. All will be well.

The Crooked Ways of Love

So we began our reckless love, a compound of our needs and fears, his strength and my wildness, of blind wishes and blinder hopes. He came to us every weekend aboard the train, with its stubby shrieking steam engine, symbol of America's energy and determination. I did not see, I could not see, the confusion into which I was leading us. If he saw it, he thought he had an answer to it. What sustained us, beyond the passionate pleasure we found in our midnights, was the change in Rawdon. Steadily, perceptibly, his antagonism to his father ebbed. We did not completely understand it. We thought it was a spiritual thing, an overflow of our own joy.

There were other reasons. There was a deep vein of poetry in Rawdon's nature, which ill suited the science and mathematics that his father was determined to make part of his mind. With me as his only tutor, he escaped science and plunged deep into poetry—not only the English poetry we read as part of his lessons, but Irish poetry. So much of our verse is speech between lovers—or haters—it was easy to play poetic games with him. One we played over and over again was Lad of the Curly Locks. As I tucked him into bed, I would rumple his dark hair and say:

> *"Lad of the curly locks*
> *Who used to be once my darling,*
> *You passed the house last night*
> *And never bothered calling.*
> *Little enough 'twould harm you*
> *To comfort me and I crying,*
> *When a single kiss from you*
> *Would save me from dying."*

Eyes aglow with the game, Rawdon would reply:

> *"I shall not die because of you*
> *O woman, though you shame the swan.*
> *They were foolish men you killed.*
> *Do not think me a foolish man."*

Then would come two or sometimes three good-night kisses, and he would close his eyes.

Some of this was no doubt an overflowing of the love I felt for his father, but I loved the lad, too, with a mother's delight in his good looks and his ready laugh and his passionate honesty. It was always the truth that he sought, in his endless perusal of the newspapers, in his pondering over the battles of the war, in his searching through books. I could see it derived from the literal, practical directness of his father's mind, but Rawdon wanted more than facts. Young as he was, he sought truths of the heart, of the spirit, insofar as his young understanding could grasp them.

"Do you think people should always tell the truth, Miss Stark?" he asked me one day.

"Yes, of course," I said.

"Father says everybody, even the president, senators, businessmen, lies all the time. I saw it in a letter he wrote to my mother about when the war was going to end."

"It's a shame, but it's probably true."

"Do you ever lie?"

"Sometimes. When you get older, it's hard to tell the whole truth all the time."

"What do you lie about?"

"Nothing important. Come now and read this book that your father brought down, *Moby-Dick*."

"I don't like it. Who cares about hunting a whale?"

"'Tis not the whale that Ahab seeks to destroy but the spirit of evil in the world. He sees it concentrated in this terrible creature. Your father says it's a great book."

Rawdon shook his head. "Stupid."

I found the book hard going myself, but I was not able to blame it completely on the writer. Rawdon's questions had awakened the secret fear that crept within my love for his father and grew stronger with every passing week. What would happen if my deception were discovered, if he found Elizabeth Stark was Bess Fitzmaurice, the Fenian girl? At first I consoled myself with the thought that it would simply be the end of the affair; though we would part with regret, it would be swift and clean, like the stroke of a sword. But as Jonathan's spirit healed, as his nerves grew firm and strong, as his confidence in his manhood deepened, the part that pity and sympathy had played in my love began to diminish, and admiration, delight in his touch, his smile, his conversation, increased to the point where the thought of losing him became pure anguish. In my innermost heart I had opened myself to him, but I still wore deception on my face. I did not know what to do about it.

Doubling the agony was the way he talked frankly to me about his mother, his wife, the family and its complex concerns. He saw his mother clearly enough. He resented the domineering part she had played in selecting his wife for him, though he never said so directly. He was freer in criticizing her pro-Southern politics, which he refused to share. But his mother had a grip on him in other ways, not the least of which was the large amount of stock she owned in the family railroad. Control of this immensely valuable property was now becoming a furious issue within the family. Many wanted to sell it to one or another of the tycoons who had emerged on Wall Street with hundreds of millions of capital at their disposal. The danger in not selling lay in their power to build a competing system, by corrupting the New Jersey legislature into giving them a right of way.

Prudence was probably on the side of selling, but Jonathan Stapleton disliked the idea. "I don't want to become a mere money man, no matter how much we're paid. The railroad was our source of power, not because of what it was worth but because of the men who worked for it. We had spokesmen living in cities and towns around the whole state. Money can't buy that."

"Would you not still have the cotton mills?" I asked.

"Even if we expanded them, they'd still only be a single business in a single city."

I saw the forward thrust of his spirit, the readiness to mount the barricades, and rejoiced in it. The man who came down here in November did not, could not, think this way. He had been exhausted in body and soul. Now, in bleak February, he was ignoring gray skies and ice floes on the bay; he was pulsing with life, vigor, command.

We were on the beach, striding along at his usual pace.

Rawdon was with us but scampering far ahead to investigate pieces of driftwood and dead fish and other flotsam of the winter sea.

"I'm boring you with this business claptrap," Jonathan said.

"On the contrary," I said. "I'm flattered that you take me into your confidence."

"I want a wife who shares not only her love with me but her mind."

"A wife?" I said, my voice dying away with disbelief.

"Do you think I could let you go when we go back to Bowood? Do you think I could turn my back on happiness that way?"

"I—I couldn't preside at Bowood. I'd be an embarrassment to you. There would be scandalous rumors."

"We've had them before and survived. According to my great-grandmother Rawdon, Kemble Stapleton had a love affair with an Irish girl who turned out to be a British spy."

"How would young Rawdon react?"

"I think he may love you more than I do," he said.

We walked in silence between mounds of snow and driftwood, my mind soaring above the wintry wreckage, then plummeting to earth like a stricken bird at the thought of my deception. Would now be the time to tell him? I suddenly remembered William Seward in his secret pleasure house in Washington, fixing me with his cold worldly eyes and saying, *Who are you? A somewhat notorious Irish adventuress.* My courage failed me.

Jonathan broke our silence to reveal he had been practicing a kind of deception on me—not a malicious or intentional one. He had spoken what was in the forefront of his heart first. Now he began telling me why he had to qualify his bold declarations and delay fulfillment of his promise.

"I hope, having told you this, you'll let me choose the

moment. It can't be now, or even this spring. There are two reasons. One is my mother. She wouldn't approve. You aren't on the social level she considers so important for someone who becomes a Stapleton. Her health is failing rapidly. I flinch from bringing further unhappiness into her life—having brought so much."

I wanted to cry out against his thinking that way. I thought he had stopped it. But my protest would have had an ugly note of self-interest in it.

There was also the problem of the family and the railroad. It was very important for him to hold their coalition of shareholders together for the next six or eight months while he showed them that he could withstand the titans of Wall Street. A marriage that some might disapprove could shake their confidence in him when he needed it most.

"Do you understand?" he asked.

"Yes," I said.

There was a falling note in my voice, caused not by his realism but by the impossibility of ending my deception now. Put in the context of what he had just been saying, the truth would have been catastrophic. At least, so it seemed to me then, as I thought of how it might part us and how unbearable that had become.

He thought my sadness was caused by his realism. He stopped dead in the sand and seized my hands. "My God," he said. "I sound like I consider you a block of preferred stock. I'm a monster without a soul. I'll get the local parson down here and marry you tonight."

"No," I said, terrified at the idea of marrying him without removing the deception and even more terrified of telling him on such short notice. "I won't let you do it. Your promise is enough for me, if it takes two years to fulfill."

He started to brush aside my objections. "For your mother's sake," I said. "She received me in the house with courtesy and trust. I understand—I truly understand—her prejudices."

We had lost all track of Rawdon. He came rushing up to us at this moment, a piece of driftwood shaped precisely like the body of a woman in his hand. "Look at this," he cried, then stopped, open mouthed, when he saw that beneath our cloaks we were holding hands. Instantly he began reciting to his wooden woman.

> *"Why should I leave the world behind*
> *For the soft hand, the dreaming eye,*
> *The crimson lips, the breasts of snow—*
> *Is it for these you'd have me die?*
> *O woman, though you shame the swan,*
> *A wise man taught me all he knew.*
> *I know the crooked ways of love.*
> *I shall not die because of you."*

"Where did you learn that?" his father said.

"From Miss Stark."

"It's part of the game of poetry we play when he goes to bed nights," I said. "It's Irish, from the sixteenth century."

"He's too young for that kind of poetry," Jonathan said. "Give me that thing."

He took Rawdon's driftwood woman away from him and flung it far out into the freezing water.

"That's mine," Rawdon said. "You have no right to do that. I wanted it."

"Now, now," I said. "You'll find another piece just as interesting."

He shot me a look of genuine dislike, the first such expression I had seen in months, and ran off toward the house.

"I hope you're teaching him some English poetry, too," Jonathan said as we walked back toward the house.

"Oh, yes," I said. "That's part of his daily lessons. We've done two plays of Shakespeare in the past week. On Monday we'll read some of Dryden. The Irish poetry is just by the by, recited for the fun of it."

"I don't like much poetry," he said, "especially those little tinkling meters that Poe and Longfellow use. Or Shelley, for that matter. But I liked that fellow Walt Whitman. Have you read any of *Leaves of Grass*?"

I had to confess I had not heard of him.

"His poems *march*," Jonathan said. "He marshals words like an infantry general."

"Tell me your favorite," I said.

He considered for a moment and looked past me at the limitless sea.

> *"What we believe in waits latent forever through all*
> *   the continents, and all the islands and archipelagos*
> *   of the sea;*
> *Invites no one, promises nothing, sits in calmness*
> *   and light, is positive and composed, knows no*
> *   discouragement*
> *Waiting patiently, waiting its time."*

"How lovely," I said, the words striking me as almost a paradigm of my own life.

"He wrote that to a failed revolutionary," Jonathan said. "But it's equally true for others, I think."

"My God," I murmured, almost overwhelmed.

I trembled on the brink of telling him everything. By this time we were approaching the house, and Rawdon stood on the steps, glowering. I realized he was jealous. He frankly expressed it a few days later, when his father had returned home for his week of business. We played our usual game of good-night poetry, but after his third kiss he clung to me and asked, "Do you love me?"

"Of course I do," I said.

He released me and fell back on his pillow, glaring. "You really love Father. I can tell."

"I love you both. Each in a different way. I love you as if you were my own son. I love him as—a friend. He's been so good to me. He's given me a home, a welcome in your country. Think of what that means to me, who has no mother or father, nor great fortune."

"I want you to love *me*, not him." he said. "If you love him, he'll hurt you, he'll kill you, like he did my mother."

"He will do no such thing. Your father is done with killing. He wants nothing but peace and happiness for us all, above all for you. Isn't it proof of his love, the way he comes down here to see you each weekend?"

"Not if he comes to see you," he replied.

"He comes to see us both. Does he shun you or show any dislike of you?"

He was silenced but not satisfied. I should have realized his hostility once aroused was liable to awaken his old habits of stealthy observance. I should have warned Jonathan and myself that we were under surveillance. But the flurry of direct protest seemed to subside and be virtually forgotten in the excitement of the next weekend, when his father arrived with a thrilling new toy, which was considerably more than a toy—the Myriopticon. It consisted of a series of brilliantly colored pictures that unrolled off a drum onto a screen, behind which a glowing lamp was positioned. The first series told the history of the Civil War. With each picture was a text, designed to be read by a master of ceremonies.

Rawdon loved it, particularly when I insisted that he be the master of ceremonies. He stood beside the crank, reading the text, while we gazed at the spectacular panorama of Bull Run.

"Next we present you with a very spirited scene in the first Battle of Bull Run, fought on the twenty-first of July, 1861. The Union forces under General McDowell were defeated, and history says they fell back to Centerville, but many of the soldiers, either from the apprehension that the Centerville hotels were full, or in consequence of the impression that Washington was in danger, hastened immediately to the defense of that important strategic point."

This was the general tone of the text, heavily ironic and semihumorous. Jonathan Stapleton laughed heartily at some of the sallies. It was another encouraging sign that the war was loosening its grip on him. He even contributed some humorous stories of his own from the vagaries of camp life between the battles. I was sure it was good for Rawdon, too, hearing his father laugh and joke about an experience that the boy had contorted into a nightmare in his vivid imagination.

When the March wind ceased to howl, and the snow vanished from the beach and the ice from the bay, we began to play another new game, which had less historic significance but was even more enjoyable—croquet. Rawdon was ecstatic. The game, like the Myriopticon, was sweeping the nation. The newspapers were full of stories about it, and he immediately wanted to know if Jonathan was going to let me pin up my skirt to my ankles, so I could use the pendulum stroke. It seems that there was a curmudgeon of a father from Fall River, Massachusetts, who became very upset when his daughter adopted this tactic and trounced him. He said it was unladylike and only permitted her to play again when she promised to let down her skirt and limit herself to the outside stroke—which meant he beat her handily with *his* pendulum stroke.

Jonathan smiled across the room at me. "Miss Stark is an independent American woman. I have no control over her skirt," he said.

With my skirt pinned and the pendulum stroke available to all, we were soon in fierce contention on Kemble

Manor's front lawn. Neither Rawdon nor I could match the fine ruthlessness, the cold-eyed strategy, Jonathan brought to the game. He trounced us again and again. We would be on the brink of victory, in perfect position before a wicket, when he would appear to smash us back a hundred yards without a blink of remorse.

"I'm beginning to sympathize with Stonewall Jackson and Robert E. Lee," I said, when he performed this destruction on me for the tenth or eleventh time.

He finally relented and played with deliberate carelessness to let me beat him. Rawdon cheered for me and cried, "Just like the young lady of Dedham."

"Who is she?"

He proceeded to recite one of the numerous limericks croquet had inspired.

"There was a young lady of Dedham
Who walked all the way to Needham
For a game of croquet
With an aging roué
Who swooned when she bet him and beat him."

Jonathan's good humor vanished. "What do you mean by that?" he said.

"Nothing," Rawdon said, looking honestly puzzled.

"Miss Stark is not the kind of young lady who plays games with aging roués. Do you know what a roué is?"

Rawdon shook his head. He was growing more and more upset and angry. "Surely then there was no insult intended," I said. "I think we're all getting croquet nerves."

This was a popular term of the day. The papers were full of stories about arguments over croquet in which men had bashed each other over the head with their mallets. At that time it was hard to find two people who could agree on the rules.

Later that day, we went for a walk on the beach, leaving Rawdon behind to work the Myriopticon for the Littlepages, who were fascinated by it. "I think we should resume our earlier roles of governess and employer," I said. "Your conscience is troubled by our present arrangement."

"Is yours?"

"I would never have entered it in the first place, if it were."

"My conscience is troubled," he said ruefully. "Not because God disapproves. I've long since decided he has very little interest in our concerns. It's because I disapprove of my own conduct. I want to make you my wife."

He pointed to three or four sailboats scudding across the bay on the brisk April wind. "Our isolation is ending. Soon you'll see fifty or a hundred boats out there. All the country houses around here will be opening up. Friends will be coming to visit. But the situation at home is worse than ever."

He talked of the bitter quarrels he was having with certain members of the family who controlled a large number of shares in the Camden and Amboy.

"My trust in you is absolute," I said. "Tonight will be the last of the full moon. Let it be our last night together until you're free to speak for me."

He shook his head. "I don't know whether I can do it. When I have you in my arms—even when I think of you there—the world has a center. It makes sense. Take that away and it becomes a set of random pictures on a Myriopticon, a ridiculous contemptuous tragicomedy."

"I feel the same way," I said, "but we must make the experiment."

That night was strange and wonderful. We were both filled with an eerie sense of parting, not for a time, but forever. I don't know why. I suppose it was only natural for two people who had come to regard their midnight meetings as the essence of their lives to wonder if even a temporary cessation might produce unexpected results in the deep inaccessible regions of the heart. I had said my trust in him was absolute, and it was, but it was a trust in his word, his promise, which I knew was as true as the steel in the tracks on which his steam engines ran. I did not trust what could happen to alter that promise, especially when I had yet to reveal my deception.

I saw our parting as a step to the revelation. I had no intention of confessing everything I had done, but I also had no intention of apologizing for Bess Fitzmaurice, the Fenian girl. I wanted to make my statement an act of pride, not something whispered in the dark, with eager breasts and thighs offered as consolation for his possible disappointment. If there was disappointment or prejudice or shame, I wanted it faced in daylight.

"Why am I so afraid?" I whispered to him, as the moon dwindled to a last golden patch on the ceiling. "I'll never lose you. No matter what happens, we're part of each other forever."

"Yes," he said. "Forever."

How lovers adore those words. How indifferent the world is to them.

If It Ain't the Fenian Girl

For several weeks, all went well. The spring weather had something to do with keeping our spirits high. Kemble Manor's gardens were a riot of roses—white, red, yellow. Jonathan Gifford, the Revolutionary proprietor, had apparently been a great fancier of them and imported exotic varieties from all over the world. Mingling with them were the wild blaze roses of New Jersey. Rawdon got out his small sailboat from the boathouse and cruised about the bay, meeting several boys about his age, whom he invited back for endless games of croquet on the front lawn. We older folks treasured the garden, with its roses and statues of American presidents and Greek and Roman gods. Beyond it, through a wood, the land broke into a small cove, perfect for swimming and meditating.

We had expected Mrs. Stapleton, Jonathan's mother, to visit us, but she was making her own recovery from grief and announced that she was inclined to visit friends in Newport and wanted to take little George with her. Jonathan agreed, so we remained our triumvirate at Kemble Manor. The world lapped around us like a rising flood. A delegation of New Jersey war veterans came to ask General Stapleton to make the principal address at their Fourth of July picnic. He was inclined to say no, until I talked him out of it. He had a dread of notoriety, a dislike of taking credit for his achievements, which was incomprehensible to me. I suspect it was a fear of ending like his father, a mere politician. He was determined to reserve an interior part of himself free of every sort of compromise. I urged him not to be so literal about it, to wear a mask of the politician, the friend of things as they are. I could see that the deception troubled his proud spirit, but he agreed to try it.

Another delegation came to ask him to be one of the guests of honor at the opening of the new race track at Long Branch. He had no scruples against horse racing. Converted by my philosophy, he said yes. It was to take place on the fifth of July and was, the chairman of the delegation assured him, to be a gala affair. "We expect twenty thousand people from New York," the chairman boasted.

Suddenly the reluctance was all on my side, but I

could say nothing. I had no desire to encounter any New Yorkers, especially when they were almost certain to include well-heeled politicians and public figures like Dick Connolly and Bill Tweed and William Roberts. Long Beach at that time was just emerging as a summer playground of the rich. Hotels were being built at a rapid pace, gambling houses were opening, and the racetrack was supposed to offer the final attraction to round out a resort that would attract millions of New York dollars to New Jersey.

Jonathan spent the last weeks of June laboring over his Fourth of July speech. He delivered it beneath a huge tent at the site of the Revolutionary battle of Monmouth Court House. He was not a great speaker, but it was a strong, manly address, a soldier's speech. It was also a young man's speech, charged with a vision of a hopeful future. He asked his audience to connect in their minds the sacrifices of the men of the Revolution who had fought and had died at Monmouth with the sacrifices of the men who died for the Union. Were these sacrifices in vain? he asked. Sometimes it looked that way. It looked as if they had died for an America dominated by corrupt politicians and get-rich-quick millionaires from Wall Street.

But this was not necessarily the case. Death had long since disbanded the army of the Revolution. Victory in the war had disbanded the army of the Union. But the spirit of that army, its courage and devotion to its dead, must never disband. It must remain a living, united thing, as they marched together into the new America that the war had created. In some ways this new America was a bewildering land, a kind of wilderness. But Americans had fought and won in the wilderness before. They must be prepared to fight now, against new enemies, confident that a nation worthy of the heroic dead would emerge from the confusion.

The applause stormed over our heads for a full five minutes. Rawdon and I were seated in the first row. Behind me I heard a heavy-set man say to a friend, "There's our next governor." Never did I feel more totally American. I had helped to give strength to Jonathan's proud voice. I had rescued his tormented spirit from despair. My pride, my hope, never soared higher.

That night, I waited until the house was silent and dark, then rose and boldly entered his room. He was sitting by the window, looking out over the sea. "I must kiss you again," I said. "I must give vent to the pride and joy that are bursting from me." I sank down beside him and placed my head on his knee. I felt his hand on my neck, in my hair.

"Amo, amas, I love a lass, as cedar tall and slender," he whispered.

"Yes," I said. "Tonight we must break our monastic rule."

I wanted to enter and be entered, to be one with him in the deepest most absolute way that is given to us. I sensed his greatness emerging from the battered, scarred trunk of his spirit, as a great tree in the forest struggles back to life from a lightning stroke.

Other nights, other times, we loved from different reasons, out of need, then out of pleasure of touch and stroke, next out of almost gluttonous delight in each other. That night we went beyond pleasure. We touched joy. A spirit of mutual purpose, mutual admiration, suffused our flesh and made us truly the center of a world. I cried out, I could not help it, when at last I felt his deep pulsing release in me. For the first time I understood why the old poets spoke of love as a kind of death, a holocaust of the spirit, an obliteration of the self. I *was* him, blending lips and thighs, hopes and fears, pasts and futures.

Only when I returned to my own bed did I permit my mind to think about tomorrow. Tomorrow when I would confront those thousands of New York faces, any one of whom might step out of the crowd and ask me if I was Bess Fitzmaurice, the Fenian girl. I planned to deny it smartly and dismiss the interrogater. There was a fair chance, if it happened at all, that I could silence anyone who asked. In the end it might give me the pretext I needed to end my deception when I had Jonathan alone.

How sad, how futile, those thoughts seem now. That night they burned with the purity, the passion, of truth and love. But I was about to discover the blind rapacious power of the past.

The next day we were up early for one of Mrs. Littlepage's ample shore breakfasts. With Abner at the reins, we set out in the open carriage for Long Branch. It was a hot, clear day, good racing weather, and Jonathan, sharing an ancestral love of horseflesh that had come down to him from grandfather and father, spent the ride discussing with Rawdon the pedigrees and speeds of the steeds we were to watch. Knowing not a thing about New Jersey horses, I took his advice, except for the fifth race, in which an Irish horse named Curragh's Choice was competing. I playfully insisted on backing my countryman, and we briskly settled on a private wager of five dollars when I refused to change my mind.

At the handsome new racecourse, Jonathan was one of a half dozen guests of honor, including the governor of the state and the two U.S. senators, who participated in cutting the ribbon. Thereafter we were left to our own devices. It took a half hour for us to walk across the inner grounds to the grandstand, so many people approached to shake Jonathan's hand and tell him how much they admired his speech of yesterday. We had a box reserved in the grandstand, but Rawdon insisted on watching from the rail. I went with him to make sure he did not get lost. The crowd was immense. Jonathan was so busy talking with politicians and businessmen who kept coming into the box that I doubt he missed us.

We had placed our bets with a bookmaker as we approached the grandstand, so we had only to root our favorites home. The first four races proved Jonathan's knowledge of New Jersey horseflesh. All his selections won, and at good odds. The fifth race, the last of the day, was even more sensational from our point of view. Curragh's Choice romped home at 5–1. Rawdon had joined me in betting on him, and he raced ahead of me to collect from our bookmaker. As I followed him, a voice spoke from behind my right shoulder.

"If it ain't the Fenian girl."

I turned to face Dan McCaffrey. I could not believe it. I was sure he was dead. He was dead to me. He even looked dead, or changed in some total way that only death could explain. He was dressed in a flashy suit of white and black checks, with a large fake-looking diamond in his tie. He had grown a blond mustache, but it did not conceal the snide, sneering expression on his lips. His eyes were glass chips without a trace of charm or friendship in them.

"You must be mistaken," I said. "My name is Elizabeth Stark."

"I ain't mistaken. You know I ain't mistaken."

"I have nothing to say to you."

"Not much you don't."

Rawdon came rushing up to us, his hands full of greenbacks. He had collected for us and for his father. "Look at all this money!" he said.

"Who's this?" Dan said.

"I'm Rawdon Stapleton," he said. "Who are you?"

"Stapleton," Dan said. "Is your father the general? Made a speech everyone's talkin' about? Claims he knows how to make politicians honest?"

"Yes," Rawdon said. "Who *are* you?"

"Maybe you seen my name in the papers. I'm Dan McCaffrey. Chief of staff of the Fenian army."

"Wow," Rawdon said. "The dynamite brigade?"

"That's right. You know a lot about the Fenians. She been tellin' you?"

Rawdon shook his head. "I keep a scrapbook. Where did you meet him, Miss Stark?"

"On—on the boat, coming over," I said, looking fearfully around me. The races were finished. The crowd was moving toward the gate. Jonathan was still in the grandstand box, talking earnestly with several men.

"Yeah," Dan said, with a nasty laugh. "We met on the boat comin' over. What you goin' to do with all that money?"

"It's our winnings. I have to give Miss Stark her share."

He counted out almost a hundred dollars. "Now go pay your father like a good lad," I said. "And remind him that he owes us each five dollars for Curragh's Choice."

Dan took the hundred dollars out of my hand and put it in his pocket. "A kind of down payment on what you owe me," he said.

"I owe you nothing. Get out of my sight before I call for a policeman," I said.

"You ain't gonna call for nobody. If you do, the general's gonna want to know why. I don't think you want to tell him, do you, Miss Stark?"

"You are truly despicable," I said.

"Yeah. And you're such a wonderful girl. If I know you, the general's gettin' a lot more than governessin'. After the kid goes to bed, you really start earnin' your money. Ain't I right?"

I turned away from him, too full of loathing even to look him in the face. A moment later, I saw Jonathan and young Rawdon approaching us through the crowd. Jonathan had a perplexed expression on his face. He was obviously in good humor but was puzzled by what Rawdon had just told him about Dan McCaffrey. He spoke from his good humor first.

"I can't believe the way that Irish horse ran. It wasn't even a contest."

"Don't think much of Irish horses, General?" Dan said.

"I take it you're Mr. McCaffrey of the Fenian dynamite brigade?"

"Formerly of, General. And formerly of Jeb Stuart's cavalry. Had a bad habit of pickin' the wrong side, I'm lookin' for work, General. Any chance of a job on your railroad?"

"I'm afraid not. What jobs we have, and they are few in these slow times, will go to Union veterans."

A mindless fury convulsed Dan's face. "Do you think that's fair, General?"

"Yes, I do," Jonathan said. "I think the war was a fair gamble. You lost, and you should take the consequences without whining—or dynamiting innocent people for pay."

"Come, Miss Stark," he said, turning to me. "We have a long ride home."

In the carriage, Jonathan cheerfully settled his bet with me and Rawdon. "Where in the world did you meet that fellow McCaffrey?" he asked.

"On the boat," I said. "I disliked him then and—and detest him now."

"Did you give him money? As Rawdon was pointing him out to me, I thought I saw him take some money from your hand."

"Yes," I said. "I—I felt sorry for him, in spite of all. He told such a pathetic story. He lost his last cent at the races."

"You're too charitable by far," Jonathan said. "The man's a lowlife if I ever saw one. He was an officer in the Fenian army? No wonder the Canadians trounced them." He shook his head. "He makes you think the English may be right about the Irish."

My world was reeling toward collapse. I was dazed with shock and grief. It was almost unbearable to hear him saying such things. By now we were on the coast road, which ran along the magnificent bluffs known as the Atlantic Highlands. I gazed numbly out at the sea glistening in the late afternoon sunlight. How could nature be so at peace while I was at war in my mind and heart?

Behind us we heard the hoofbeats of a lone horseman. I paid no attention to him—my back was to the road— nor did Jonathan, sitting beside me. But Rawdon, facing in the opposite direction, suddenly looked past us and said, "It's McCaffrey! The Fenian!"

Before we could turn he was upon us, glaring down at us from the saddle. His suit was caked with dust. "General," he shouted. "I've been thinkin' about what you said. You're right. No point in whinin', and dynamitin' is no good either, it don't pay. So from now on, me and my girl Bess here are goin' to change our ways. We're goin' to make a lot of people pay—startin' with you."

"What the devil are you talking about?" Jonathan said.

"I'm talking about this," Dan said, and produced his pistol.

Abner Littlepage had been looking over his shoulder at this performance. "Stop them horses," Dan said, "if you don't want to lose your other arm."

Abner promptly obeyed. Jonathan sat there, his arms contemptuously folded. "Mr. McCaffrey," he said. "You're in a desperate state of mind. I'll give you a chance to reconsider this act of folly. All of us combined don't have more than three hundred dollars on our persons. Don't ruin your life for three hundred dollars."

"I'm not thinkin' about three hundred dollars, General. I'm thinkin' about three hundred thousand dollars.

That's what you're goin' to pay, if you want to get young Rawdon here back alive."

Dan laughed exultantly. "You think you're so god-damn smart, General. Hell, we've been plannin' this for a long time. You know who's sittin' beside you there, lookin' like a schoolteacher? That's Bess Fitzmaurice, the Fenian girl. She's the coolest, slickest operator in the Fenian army. She shot that landlord Rodney Gort dead in Ireland. She bedded half the politicians in Washington—Fernando Wood, Bobby Johnson, Bill Seward—to get us across the Canadian border."

Jonathan was looking at me, first astonishment, then hatred suffusing his face. "It's not true," I said. "He's lying. The whole thing is a lie except for the truth about my name."

I was wasting my words, wasting my breath, my tears.

"You—you—Irish scum," Jonathan said.

"Come on, Bess," Dan said. "I told you there was no point in tryin' to soften him up. His kind don't soften. They only understand one thing—this."

He cocked his pistol. "Now get out of that carriage, General. You, One-arm, get down and turn them horses around."

Glaring defiance, Jonathan and Abner Littlepage obeyed. Dan tied his horse to the rear of the carriage and took the reins of the two-horse team. "Don't follow us, General. If you do, the kid gets killed. We'll send you a message about where and when to deliver the money."

He gave a rebel yell, and the team sprang forward. Within minutes Jonathan and Abner Littlepage were small, impotent figures in the distance. Not until we reached a crossroads north of Long Branch did Dan pause to study a map and turn to warn us against calling for help or trying to jump out and escape. I was too demoralized to do or think anything. My ruin was too total for any state of mind but disbelief, numbness.

You Irish scum, Jonathan had said. *Irish* scum. The words came to his lips as naturally as a curse. They were like a nitroglycerin bomb, blasting away all pretensions, facades, the fake stage scenery that I had been building in my naive mind to enhance my self-created drama of love and devotion. My winter world of theatrical make-believe was a heap of sticks, a hole in the ground, in the face of the truth that the summer had brought. I saw the gulf between us, as wide as the ocean. What a fool I was to think my arms could bridge it. What a fool I was to think that I could escape my fate, which was written out for me the moment that Dan McCaffrey strode through my father's door.

Black as a Sloe Is the Heart Inside Me

"Where are we going?" Rawdon asked.

His baffled, frightened young face drew me back to reality. "I don't know," I said.

"Is he going to kill me?"

"No. No hurt will come to you, my darling. I promise you."

"But you really are the Fenian girl?"

"Yes."

A terrible hopelessness overwhelmed me. I saw myself doomed. What judge, what jury, what newspaper, would believe anything but the story Dan had told Jonathan, the story that had drawn those terrible words from his lips? What choice had I now but to join Dan McCaffrey, this man whom I saw as nothing less than a monster, to flee with him as a fugitive and wander the world like Cain's wife? He had come with all the power of the past around

him and claimed me. There was a crude justice in it. That
was the most terrible part of it. I had betrayed the love I
once felt for him, out of pride, out of anger. The reasons
all seemed trivial now. In return he had betrayed me.
Crude justice. Crude, blind justice.

The crossroads enabled Dan to circle Long Branch to
the west and bring us down upon the bank of some tidal
river. There, tied at a dock, a small sloop waited, manned
by a dirty, swarthy fellow about as talkative as a clam.
We cast off and caught the tide, which swiftly carried us
onto the ocean. We stood south before a hard breeze, and
as night fell we bore up off a shore on which white waves
were breaking. The pilot put the helm over and aimed for
a dark mouth in the wave line. In a few minutes we were
gliding up another tidal river. We eased to a stop beside a
sagging dock, and Dan ordered us out of the boat. We
followed him up a steep bank into the deeper darkness of
a stand of pine trees. Within the trees there was a one-
room shack into which our boatman led us. It stank of
fish and was devoid of furniture, except for two small
woodstoves. Roaches and mice scampered for cover as
Dan lit an oil lamp. In one corner was a box of tinned
food.

By now I was beginning, however dimly, to think
about what was happening. It was more and more clear
that Dan had not acted on impulse. Asking for a job, his
anger, had all been sham. He had been waiting for the
moment to execute this plan.

"How long have you been hanging about, watching for
a chance to do this?" I said.

He laughed. "A good month," he said.

"How did you find me?"

"I got Red Mike drunk in England before he blew
himself to hell. He told me. It was pretty easy to get his
brother to tell the rest."

"There's no hope for us, do you know that? You're

dealing with a man who will hunt you down, and me, too, no matter where we run."

"Dead men don't hunt nobody," Dan said.

The words sent a chill of dread through me in spite of the summer heat. I saw what he planned to do. I did not want to believe it.

"I'm hungry," Rawdon said.

"Me, too, kid," Dan said. "Open some of them tins, Bess, and get us some grub."

The box contained tins of meat that tasted vaguely like ham, some salted fish, some pale consommé soup with a chicken flavor, some stale bread, and a bottle of bourbon. I heated the soup in the house's single pot, and we ate a silent nauseating supper. We washed it down with bitter coffee and condensed milk, equally sickening. After letting Rawdon answer a call of nature, Dan bound him hand and foot. Then he sat down with his sinister boatman beside him and composed a letter for Jonathan Stapleton.

The boatman—whose name, I eventually learned, was Pakenham—nodded as Dan explained his part in the plan. At dawn tomorrow he would be off to Kemble Manor. He would by then have placed the letter in a bottle. He was to halloo until he got someone's attention, then fling the letter toward the shore and let the tide carry it to the beach. The letter directed Jonathan Stapleton to board the sloop with three hundred thousand dollars in a bag and return with Pakenham to our hideaway. There, Rawdon would be handed over to him. If Pakenham did not return in thirty-six hours, Rawdon would be killed.

Pakenham departed on his errand. Dan and I faced each other in the yellow lamplight. "So it's come to this," I said. "All the grand hopes and glorious words."

"They were your specialty," he said.

"Let the boy go now. I'll go away with you. I'll do anything you ask."

"Why the hell should I do that?" Dan said. "You got to go away with me anyhow. And you're goin' to do anything I ask, startin' tonight."

"Never," I said. "You'll never touch me again. I'll die first."

"I feel sick," Rawdon said. He began to retch and abruptly vomited. Tied as he was, he could not prevent the mess from spilling on himself as well as the floor. With a curse, Dan strode across the room and kicked the lad in the side.

"Stupid little shit," he snarled. "We gotta sleep in here tonight."

Rawdon writhed in agony. With a scream of pure rage I sprang at Dan and raked my nails across his face. I sank my teeth into his neck, I kicked and smashed at him. I was a mother defending her young. He stopped me with a terrific slap in the face that sent me crashing against the far wall. "You—goddamn—bitch," he said, striding after me.

He whipped a long, gleaming knife from his belt. His other hand rubbed blood from his gashed cheek. "I could kill you now," he said. "And Sonny Boy, too. I don't have to keep you alive. I got a foolproof plan. Twelve hours after I get that money, Pakenham'll have me in Philadelphia. I'll be on a train to Chicago."

"As long as there's life in me, I won't let you hurt that lad. I love him as my own son."

The word "love" was a mistake. It aroused the darkest, vilest rage in Dan's soul. "Love him," he said. "Ain't that sweet. Let's see how much you love him."

He strode back to Rawdon, picked him up by the back of his coat, and held the knife at his throat. "You gonna do what I want tonight?"

"Yes," I said, my head bowed, avoiding Rawdon's eyes.

He flung Rawdon back to the floor. "Okay," he said. "Get outside and take off your clothes."

I obeyed. I was now certain that he was ready to kill me

as well as Rawdon and Jonathan. In a way I almost welcomed it. It was a bitter consolation, to imagine Jonathan seeing my dead body, knowing that I, too, was a victim, that I had not deceived him in our winter months of midnight love. I swayed on the edge of abandoning all hope, of welcoming oblivion.

Dan emerged from the house and stood there, a bulky blur in the darkness. I heard the gurgle of the bourbon bottle. "You bitch, Bess," he said. "Whenever I reach for you, you're always someplace else."

His voice was heavy with anger and another emotion—perhaps regret.

"What do you mean?"

"Can't you see I done this for you? To give you somethin' besides a life drudgin' for them swells? What's the difference between killin' that sour-faced Yankee general and his little rich bastard in there and gunnin' down Lord Gort with his daughter screamin' in our faces?"

I said nothing. I did not know what to say. He drank more bourbon.

"You were fuckin' him, weren't you? I could tell from the way he looked at you."

I love him. The words were alive in my throat, but some deep instinct for survival stopped me from saying them. I sensed that he would kill me within seconds after I spoke them. They would be my last words. That knife would lay my throat open and I would writhe out my life here in this dark pine-scented grove like an ancient sacrifice to a devouring god.

Instead I said their opposite. I played the prostitute he thought I had become. "I didn't know what to do, Dan. I was all alone. He gave me money. I thought you'd forgotten me. I wasn't even sure you were alive."

"Neither was I for a while," he said bitterly. "I was on the run in England for two months. Finally got out as a seaman on a freighter from Glasgow."

"Don't kill the boy. You can do what you want to the general. I really am fond of the boy." I went through the dark and put my arms around him. "I'm still half mad from grief over Michael," I said. "That's why I refused you. But now that I see your regret—"

"I had to do that, Bess," he said.

"He's long dead now. Perhaps well dead," I said. "Touching you now, thinking of what you want to do with me now, is making me melt—making me remember Ireland and the nights on the *Manhattan*—"

He began kissing me with all his old wild hunger. I let him have me on the cold hard bed of dry pine needles, the earth pressing into my back, the way the ancient women of Ireland may have loved their warriors. But I cast off those banshees forever with that last meeting. Somehow the deception I was practicing broke open my mind to an inrush of reality, identity, of present time. I saw myself precisely for what I was, and I faced the past for what it was, a blind procession of false hopes and deceptions that somehow justified this deception because I was able to tell myself that if it succeeded it would be the last deception. I would live the rest of my days, whether they were short or long, without lies.

"O my Donal Ogue," I whispered when he was through. "You haven't changed. You make me love you still."

He began to tell me his dream of what we could do, where we could go with the money. Peru, Mexico. Places where money could buy a kingdom and we could live like royalty. There were gold mines for sale in Peru; there were ranches in Mexico where a man could ride to the far horizon without leaving his property. Mexico, a country where a soldier could become anything—president, emperor.

There was a pathetic, almost childish quality to his

dream. It was heartbreaking because he saw me as a part
of it. I thought of the lines from "Donal Ogue":

You said you'd give me—an airy giver!—
A golden ship with masts of silver
Twelve market towns to be my fortune
And a fine white mansion beside the ocean.

I embraced him as if I shared his greedy rapture. "Ah
Dan, it sounds wonderful," I said, "but you must change
your plan if you hope to win that dream. Take my advice,
go away with the money and me but let the general and the
boy live. The more I think of it, the more sure I am that he
won't pursue us. I'm your insurance, don't you see? He'd
never want me in a courtroom, testifying to what we did
nights. The money means nothing to him. He's worth ten
times that. But his reputation is everything. He talked of
marrying me, you know, but he couldn't bring himself to
take an Irish wife."

That was so close to the truth as I saw it now that my
breath grew short. Before I could continue he was answering me with a growling no. "I want the pleasure of
killing the son of a bitch. Didn't you say he was the sort
of bastard that would never quit chasin' us?"

"That was before I thought this all through. Before I—
I found my love for you again. He's an important man,
Dan. Killing him will arouse the whole nation. Think of
the cry that could be raised against you. Southern officer
kills a Union general."

"Maybe you're right. But I'd still like to kill the son of
a bitch."

We went back into the house and found that Rawdon
had vomited again. He was a sobbing, almost hysterical
mess. I persuaded Dan to undo his ropes and brought up
water from the river to clean him.

"Did he hurt you?" he asked as I fussed over him.

"No," I said.

"I'll never forget what you did for me," he said with tears in his eyes.

I kissed him. "Hush now and try to sleep," I said.

Dan insisted on tying him up again. He turned off the light and propped himself against the only door, where he planned to doze. No one could pass without waking him. It was not exactly a statement of confidence in me. I spent most of the night staring into the darkness, listening to him snore.

Morning dawned hot and clear. Dan flung open the windows and ordered me to make coffee. He ate some more of the nauseating food, which Rawdon and I declined. "It's a lot better'n I ate the last six months of the war," Dan said.

I drank some coffee and gave a little to Rawdon. The hours dribbled slowly away. Dan grew more and more tense. He swigged the bourbon to calm himself. A half dozen times he went down to the dock to look downriver for Pakenham's sloop. Dan had found this fellow in a tavern in Shrewsbury. He lived farther south on the shore and made his living by smuggling and preying on wrecks along the coast. He would do anything for money, but he thought small. I was cautioned to say nothing about the size of the ransom. Dan was paying him only five thousand dollars.

Blackflies swarmed through the open windows after the bits of food in the discarded tins. They assaulted Rawdon, too, and I spent most of my time brushing them from his face and hands. Sitting there, I caught a different rhythm in Dan's stride as he returned from the dock for the sixth time. He burst in the door and said; "He's comin'. And the old boy's on the boat. On the prow, money in hand."

He drew his pistol and checked the cylinder, a sight that

made me grow faint. Five minutes later, we heard the rattle of the sail coming down, the creaking thud of the sloop against the old dock. We waited again in the heat and humming flies until the stamp of Jonathan Stapleton's footsteps sounded dully on the pine needles, more sharply on the steps. Then he was at the door, hatless, wearing a black silk suit and white shirt and black tie. He had a small carpetbag in his hand. He glared at me with concentrated hatred.

Dan pointed the pistol at him, the hammer cocked. "Hello, General," he said. "Have a nice trip?"

"I'm not here as a general any more than you're here as a Southern officer," Jonathan said. "I'm here as a father, and you and your whore are here as pieces of scum."

"General," Dan said, "I would love to put a bullet in you. I sort of agreed with this girl last night that it might be better to let you live. You're startin' to change my mind."

For a split second, Jonathan glared at me. I saw that he did not care whether or not Dan pulled the trigger. He was back in the dungeon of his bitter self. But there was a subtle difference. Where before there had been defeat, confusion, there was now strength, rage. Where death had been a tempting friend, he was now an indifferent companion. He wanted to kill Dan, and possibly me, and was ready to risk anything to do it.

"Don't you want your money first?" Jonathan said, and pulled open the carpetbag. It was crammed to the top with greenbacks. For a split second, Dan's eyes went hungrily to that hoard of power and pleasure. It was the moment for which Jonathan was waiting. He flung the contents of the bag across the room into Dan's face and charged through the shower of money with an infantry roar.

Time stopped, froze. We were like figures in a waxworks

or a painting. The blizzard of greenbacks engulfed us. Down they fluttered, absurd symbolic pieces of paper for which so many sacrificed their happiness, their honor, their pride. The prize for which men betrayed nations and peoples, for which so much blood was spilled, so many hearts broken. Now the two men I had loved met in the middle of this green storm in a grapple that could only end in death.

Dan's gun crashed once, but the whirling money distracted his deadly aim by a fraction. The bullet smashed out a window. Then Jonathan slammed into him, his strong hands lunging for the gun arm, smashing it back against the wall, knocking the pistol loose from Dan's hand. The weapon bounded across the floor like a living creature. I crawled to it and seized it as the two men thrashed wildly in the carpet of money. Jonathan had his fingers on Dan's throat. Dan's breath was coming in hoarse gasps. But Jonathan had no hope of subduing a Tennessee brawler with such a simple hold.

With a tremendous heave Dan broke the grip and flung Jonathan back on his haunches. In the same instant Dan was on his feet to deliver a kick that sent Jonathan hurtling out the door onto the pine needles outside. With a wild rebel yell Dan lunged after him. I stumbled to the door dreading what I knew would ensue. As Jonathan staggered to his feet, Dan feinted a punch and gave him another terrific kick that hurled him back ten feet, crashing off the pine trees. He sprang up and rushed Dan again, trying to close with him. He got another kick in the belly this time and two terrific punches in the face. As he rose dazedly to one knee, another kick all but tore off his head. Barely conscious now, Jonathan still struggled to his feet again and again. But flesh and blood can only bear so much. At last another terrible combination of kicks and punches stretched him moaning on the ground.

Gasping for breath, Dan looked down on him, then slowly drew his knife. Suddenly I knew what I had to do. I raised the big gun and aimed it with both hands.

"Don't, Dan, don't," I said.

He was about ten feet away facing me. Sweat and blood-lust mingled on his glaring face. And contempt. He didn't think I would pull the trigger. He thought that after last night he had me again. He reached down to seize Jonathan Stapleton by the shirt and lift him to cut his throat.

I pulled the trigger. The gun roared and the bullet smashed into Dan's chest just above the heart, flinging him back against the nearest tree. "You—" he cried.

I pulled the trigger again and this bullet spun him around and sent him staggering to another tree. He clung to it for a second in his death agony. Slowly he turned. "Didn't you—hear—what he called—you?" he choked.

He fell. The gun dropped from my numbed hands. Jonathan Stapleton raised his battered body from the ground and struggled to one knee. I walked past him into the shadowed grove. Dan lay with his face to the summer sky. I thought of the soldier in my father's doorway, saying, *Dan McCaffrey*. I remembered the gunman crouched in the road to Bantry fighting it out with a half dozen policemen. I saw the weary soldier in Buffalo, saying, *We've got a good little army*.

Out of me swirled a huge sorrow, black as the Irish night, dark as our thousand years of bloody history, blind as our hopes, ruinous as our defeats. I was Emer keening over Cuchulain, Dierdre lamenting the Red Branch heroes. The tumbling words came out in Irish. What other language could express my grief? I flung myself on him, wailing.

"Black as a sloe is the heart inside me
Black as a coal with the griefs that drove me

Black as a boot print on shining hallways
And 'twas you that blackened it ever and always."

I don't know how long I lay there, keening the Irish words over and over again. How utterly strange, how weirdly foreign, it must have sounded to Jonathan and Rawdon. God knows how long I might have continued it. Jonathan's hand on my shoulder drew me back to the real world.

"We've found a boat in the bushes," he said. "There's a railroad bridge about a mile up the river. We'll go up there and wait for a train."

Pakenham had fled with his sloop. The river was empty. None of us had the strength to row. Luckily the tide was with us, and we drifted to the bridge. An hour later, a train approached. Jonathan flagged it down with his shirt. When the engineer saw his beaten face and torn clothes, he abandoned his regular stops and highballed to our station in Middletown. By six o'clock we were at Kemble Manor again. A doctor, summoned by the station agent, examined Jonathan and taped sticking plaster on two broken ribs. The sheriff was also summoned and told the story. He set out immediately for the Manasquan River to remove Dan McCaffrey's body. He assured Jonathan that they would capture Pakenham in short order. He also promised that the inquest into Dan's death would be conducted with an absolute minimum of publicity.

After a decent meal and a bath, Rawdon pronounced himself healthy. I was also healthy enough in body. After hours of walking the beach alone, I knew what I had to do to bring similar health to my soul.

The next morning after breakfast, I went to Jonathan's room. He was wearing his nightclothes and a light robe, sitting in the chair by the window where I had once come to him with so much love in my heart.

"It's clear that we must part," I said.

"Yes," he said heavily.

"Believe me when I say I never meant to deceive you—except about my name. I would never have married you without telling you the truth."

"Yes," he said heavily again.

"In spite of everything—I'll treasure the memory of our love."

"Yes," he said dully. I saw with sadness that he would be unable to do this.

He stared out the window at the sea for a long time. "Where will you go?" he said.

"Far from here. To a place where the Fenian girl is as unknown as Dierdre of the Sorrows. Or as much of a fable."

He nodded, barely listening now. I was gone from him, that was all he knew. The pain of what he was losing seemed hardly equal to the strength he had regained, the gulf I had helped him cross.

I went back to my room and began packing. I was in the midst of it when Rawdon looked in. "Where are you going?" he said.

"Away, Rawdie," I said.

"No," he said, and ran to me. "Is he sending you away? He can't do that."

Before I could answer him, he raced across the hall to Jonathan's room. "Father, you can't do it," he cried. "You have to marry her. I know what you did to her. I saw her go into your room at night—"

There was the sound of a blow and a cry of pain. I rushed after Rawdon to find Jonathan standing over him, his arm raised in rage, the boy sprawled on the floor, clutching his face. "Don't you ever say that to another living soul. If you do, I'll ruin you. I'll throw you out of the family," Jonathan roared.

The man I had glimpsed so often was dominant on his

face now. I saw him and Rawdon forever opposed, with me as one of the chief causes of their enmity. When Jonathan noticed me in the door he whirled and snarled, "Did you send him in here?"

"Come, Rawdie," I said, drawing him to his feet. We sat and talked in my room. I reiterated my love for him and tried to explain what had been wrong with my dream of loving his father. He would not listen. At last he tore loose and turned on me to cry one last terrible word, "liar!"

I left without trying to say good-bye to him or Jonathan again. At the station I boarded the train and rode through the peaceful fields and prosperous towns to Jersey City. There I took a ferry across the river, then a hack to Archbishop McCloskey's residence on Mulberry Street. I gave my name to a stern-looking monsignor who ordered me to wait in a bare sitting room. I was prepared to sit there for hours, but the archbishop appeared in five minutes. I did not kiss his ring or make any other sign of obedience.

"You remember me?" I asked.

"Of course," he said.

"You told me if I ever needed a friend—"

"Yes."

"I need to confess many sins. But I wonder what good it will do."

"Do you believe that God forgives you?"

"I would like to believe it, but I don't."

"Why do you want to believe it?"

"Because I want to go away and begin again in a place far away from here—and this is a way of saying good-bye to the Fenian girl forever."

He smiled sadly. "You're becoming an American. You want to give your faith to the future, to mingle it with to-morrow rather than yesterday. Perhaps eventually we'll learn to do both things."

From his desk he took a stole, a long ribbon of red silk trimmed with blue, and crossed it on his chest. Priests wore these while hearing confessions. For a half hour I told him everything I had done, from Dan McCaffrey to the murder of Lord Gort to my ruinous love for Jonathan Stapleton. He listened impassively, with no expression on his face or in his eyes. I might have been talking to a statue—or to the God I had ignored for so long.

When I finished, he said in the gentlest imaginable voice, "Kneel down."

I knelt. He drew a cross in the air above my head and recited Latin words of forgiveness. Raising me to my feet, he held my hands for a long moment, gazing at me with a marvelous mixture of sadness and affection.

"Wild Irish," he murmured. "Wild Irish."

He stepped back and became the archbishop again. "Where will you go?"

"I don't know."

"I suggest San Francisco." He scribbled a name on a piece of paper. "Here's a man who's running a newspaper out there. They're starting to hire women. You must make your way alone for a while."

I nodded. The man understood so much.

"Do you need money?"

"General Stapleton gave me a thousand dollars."

The archbishop opened a drawer and pulled out a sheaf of greenbacks. "Here's another five hundred. I refused to give a cent to the Fenians. It almost broke my heart—but I couldn't let them use my name to suck more money from the pockets of our poor. This is my own money—my belated contribution to the cause."

"How can I thank you?"

"Do the same thing for someone else who needs help. If you go to work for a newspaper, you'll see a lot of misery."

An hour later I was on a New York Central train, heading for Chicago, where the Union Pacific would take me to San Francisco. The names of the cities and towns whispered in my soul as the miles slipped by. I was traveling into the immense heart of America with a precarious faith in the pursuit of happiness. Ireland and her sorrows were vanishing over the horizon. Would I find fresh sorrow in this new life? I only knew that there beat within my battered heart a strangely renewed hope.

Afterword

Bess Fitzmaurice worked for several newspapers in California. In her forties she married an editor on the *San Francisco Chronicle.* She wrote this book in the last years of her life and sent it to the Hamilton, New Jersey, Historical Society, where it was recently discovered and prepared for publication under a grant from the Principia Foundation, created by the twentieth century Stapletons to raise America's historical awareness.

Jonathan Stapleton married Cynthia Legrand, his brother Charlie's beautiful, Louisiana-born widow, and spent much of his life trying to heal the breach between the North and South. The rest of his story is told in *The Spoils of War*, which deals with the Stapleton family after the Civil War.

Rawdon Stapleton quarreled continually with his father and refused to participate in the family businesses. He became a newspaperman who mingled revolution with his passion for telling the truth about American society. He was killed covering the fight on San Juan Hill in the Spanish-American War.

Andrew Johnson lost his struggle with the Radical Republicans in Congress, narrowly averted impeachment, and did not seek renomination in 1868. He was reelected to the U.S. Senate in 1875 but died several months later.

Robert Johnson never conquered his alcoholism. He committed suicide in California in 1869.

William Seward never won his nomination for the presidency. In 1867, he bought Alaska from the Russians, hoping it would be the first step to his vision of a United States of North America. Instead, his enemies used the purchase to destroy him. They said the territory was a frozen wasteland and called it "Seward's Folly." He went into political oblivion and died in 1872.

Edwin Stanton became a key figure in the struggle between President Johnson and Congress. He refused to resign when Johnson finally dismissed him as secretary of war, which led to the impeachment crisis of 1868. Stanton was rewarded by the Republicans with an appointment to the Supreme Court in 1869, but he died before he could take office.

Fernando Wood was defeated in his attempt to recapture Tammany in 1867. He spent the rest of his life in Congress and died in 1881.

William Marcy Tweed died in jail in 1878 after conviction for massive frauds.

Richard Connolly fled to Egypt with six million dollars when the Tweed Ring was exposed in 1871. He never returned to the United States.

Peter B. Sweeny fled abroad with many millions. Eventually he gave back a few hundred thousand dollars and was allowed to return. He died in New York in obscurity.

John O'Neil eventually was deposed by the Fenian majority. He tried one more invasion of Canada with a handful of followers in 1870. It was a fiasco. He drank himself to death a few years later.

John O'Mahoney died obscure and forgotten in the

1870s. His body was shipped home to Ireland for a big funeral.

William Roberts quit Fenianism, made his peace with Tammany, and was named minister to Chile by President Grover Cleveland in 1884.